Kit Craig is a former reporter and TV editor as well as a regular reviewer for the *Philadelphia Enquirer* and the *New York Times Book Review*. CLOSER is her fourth psychological thriller and she also writes general fiction under the name of Kit Reed.

Kit Craig lives in Connecticut.

Closer

Kit Craig

First published in 1997
by HEADLINE BOOK PUBLISHING

First published in paperback in 1997
by HEADLINE BOOK PUBLISHING

A HEADLINE FEATURE paperback

10 9 8 7 6 5 4 3 2 1

ISBN 0 7472 4938 5

Typeset by Palimpsest Book Production Limited,
Polmont, Stirlingshire
Printed in Great Britain by
Mackays of Chatham plc, Chatham, Kent

HEADLINE BOOK PUBLISHING
A division of Hodder Headline PLC
338 Euston Road
London NW1 3BH

Acknowledgements

I owe thanks to several people for their generosity and willingness to advise in the preparation of this book. Special aids to accuracy are John E. Levine, MD of the University of Michigan Medical Center, Mack Reed of the *Los Angeles Times* and Garret Condon of the *Hartford Courant*, as well as friends and colleagues at the *St Petersburg Times*, where I did some time. Thanks to Kate Maruyama for notes on story and to Anne Williams of Headline for asking the right questions, to Lori Andiman and Sarah Piel at Arthur Pine Associates for all their help and particularly to Richard Pine for what turned out to be more readings than either of us expected. And before all this, thanks to Joseph Reed for a lifetime of first readings.

This is the last place. It is a place in life that is beyond writing. Writing is just another thing you leave behind, like shit. What you write is not important. It's only what the hand does on its way to doing what you want. Analyze, as taught, so fine. Organize. Plan. Write it down. Then forget what you have written. The body remembers. What the head is beyond thinking, the body knows.

1

'You're what?'

'Ah. Uh. In relationship.' Theo is more surprised than Sally. Funny thing. It must be the boredom. Sit still long enough and you'll say anything. He and Sally Wyler are covering this for the Center City *Star*, but until police divers haul up the drowned car, they are exiled here. They are on the far rim of the granite quarry, where they can see but not hear. On the bank opposite, yellow tape seals the staging area for the grim work. The quarry opens its great mouth at their feet, but the circle of black water at the bottom keeps its secrets. The drop seems stupendous.

Theo leans out, trying to speed-read gestures as divers bob to the surface and signal the winch crews on the far bank. If the *Star*'s source is right, the car at the bottom of their local black hole is a vintage Olds registered to Preston Zax, suspected serial killer, Missing in Action. He vanished the day police went to the house to make the arrest. Is Zax in the car? Too soon to tell. Did he plunge into death like an Egyptian in his chariot, surrounded by victims like some pharaoh and his jeweled concubines? Nobody will say. Sally covers day police. What happens here is her story. It's Theo's job to look into the dead face and confirm that it's Zax. Then he has to snag the killer's mother before police bring her in to identify the body.

Paired winches whir on the far ledge, lowering cables with grappling hooks. The divers are meticulous, fixing hooks to the car at four points so they can balance the antique klunker and bring it up without disturbing whatever waits inside. Theo stares down into the murk. It gives back nothing. Six murders, linked to Preston Zax by the seventh victim, who survived to name her assailant. Six women murdered in this drowned car. What worse things will they find? Is the unspeakable water-soluble? Theo wonders. Does blood leach out and float away when you drown a thing, along with past terrors? He doesn't know. He doesn't know if Zax ran his cherished Olds into the quarry or whether some unknown person killed Zax and deep-sixed the car with him in it. Early today some woman dropped a dime, bringing them all to the abandoned quarry.

Time stalls. This is taking too long. Theo wishes he hadn't told Sally what he just told her. Tell a reporter anything and she's all over you with questions. 'Forget I said that.'

'In relationship,' Sally repeats with one eye on the operation. Yeah, reporters. Drop *one fact* and they follow up – won't quit until they get the whole story. 'Sounds like In Country.'

Theo's head jerks: whiplash. 'What did you just say?'

But Sally mutters, 'Oh shit.' For the fourth time today the surface of the water shudders and the winches cough and bring up empty hooks. Timing! Divers break the surface, gesturing: *no go.* 'We're going to be here for hours.'

This time it's Theo's turn to follow up. 'What, In Country?'

'You know. Vietnam.'

On the far bank the divers confer. Somewhere deep, the drowned car waits. Sally may try to act like just one of the guys, but Theo can't forget that she isn't, not sitting there inside that woman's body with the soft throat and undisciplined hair; if he responds it's like letting her inside his love life so he snaps, 'Don't, OK?'

But she does. 'OK, Slate. Question. Why do you make being in love sound like being in Vietnam?'

'Because it is like Nam.' Not that Theo knows what Nam

was like, but being with Carey Lassiter is like being in a little war both in love and in sex: what Carey wants for him versus what he wants, nonstop fighting and kissing, killing each other and dying and getting up to make love so they can fight some more.

The divers go down again. With her eyes fixed on the spot, Sally says, 'Then you've got a problem.'

'Well it's not your problem, OK?' It's my problem, Theo thinks. A little hell. Trouble is, being without Carey Lassiter is also a little hell, so go figure. He's the one who bailed out of the brokerage to chase the only career he ever really wanted. Carey won't forgive him. 'You're leaving me to move to the boonies *and* taking a cut in pay?' 'People have to do what they want, Care. It's what life is for.' Not her fault that all his life he's wanted to be a reporter, not his fault that in these tough times the best news job he could find was at the Center City *Star*. He doesn't know whether to thank Arch Wills for getting him the interview or hand him an exploding cigar.

Look at this place. Dead center of nowhere in particular. Depressed area, New England in the blasted, rural outpost where the lines between Connecticut and New York and Massachusetts seem to blur. Everything's depressed: the economy, real estate, the *Star*'s circulation, the newspaper business with papers going belly up like parrots in a fish tank. Everybody has to start somewhere. But he won't be here long. He has a plan. All it takes is one big story. He'll use it to move up. And out. *The Post*. Listen, the *Times*. When he goes back to New York it's going to be on his own terms, not Carey's, not his folks'. The MBA was his father's idea. And if his family isn't speaking to him? Fine.

A head breaks the surface. As the diver signals, Sally surprises Theo. Laughing, she elbows him. 'Watch out. Ka-*chinnng*!'

'What?'

'Man, love is war. Incoming!'

4

Make me laugh, will you. He growls, 'I should never tell you anything.' Any other day he'd flop on his face with his hands locked on the back of his neck like a grunt in a Nam movie, yelling, 'Incoming!' He and Sally would giggle and roll. But. Below, motors fire up. The winches groan in unison. Cables go taut and strain. This time all four hooks hold.

Electrified, Sally murmurs, 'Look. The car.'

With a sucking sound the heavy sedan clears the murk and swings high. There is a second in which everything the killer's car contains stays put, sealed tight; then water begins to rush – engine housing emptying, trunk emptying, chassis gushing like a slit beast releasing its soul along with all the blood that's in it. In a miracle of coordination the operators of the two machines swivel to set the car on the bank. In another minute investigators will be swarming over the metal brute, intent on its secrets. Theo gets up. But he is new to the *Star*.

Sally pulls him back. 'Not so fast.'

'I've got to confirm the—'

'They won't let you near it until they're done there,' Sally says. 'You might as well sit down and have another doughnut.'

'But Arch is going to—' Get in there first.

'Chill,' Sally says.

Arch Wills, who showed Theo to his desk with an evil grin. 'Greetings, and welcome to the nutcake newsroom of the Center City *Star*. Make sure your seat belts are securely fastened and your seat backs and tray tables returned to an upright position. You're in for a long, frustrating ride.' Accent on long. Arch is his competition for the prize at the end of the world. He expects to be hired into some national market by fall. In college they interned together at the St Pete *Times*; when they graduated Arch came here while Theo dragged his feet in Indonesia. His family was pressuring him to get an MBA; Dad said, 'If you still want to be a reporter,

5

you can always write about business.' Yeah, Dad. Sure. He did the MBA just to shut them up, got stuck in a brokerage while Arch was piling up clips out here in the world. If life is a race, Arch is running ahead right now. He's a special projects reporter, has his own column, could be syndicated in another year, sorry, Slate.

Arch-rival. Best friend. Theo's belly knots. 'For all we know, he's mugged some paramedic and scored a coverall; that could be him running in with the crew from the meat wagon.'

'No way.' Sally flashes a grin. 'Vera promised. This is ours.'

'Your friend the chief.'

'My friend the chief. Vera knows all about Archie and his little ways. Look,' she says, 'it's going to be a while. Too bad we don't have Delia to send for sandwiches.'

'I could do without Delia.' On the ledge opposite, there seems to be a jurisdictional problem. Forensics and the coroner's people mill and clump, conferring.

Sally laughs. She's interesting. So nearly pretty. So tough. So intent on being one of the guys. 'That's funny. You're her god.'

'Yeah, right.'

'Really. If you don't know it, you'd better know it.'

'Could we not talk about Delia please?' Theo leans forward. Who's going to crack the killer's car? For a while it looks as if nobody's going to crack the car. There is a lot of movement but no action. Theo watches until it becomes obvious that nothing is happening. Fixed on it, he accidentally blurts, 'She's coming.'

'Delia?'

'No. Carey.' For the first time since he left New York for nowhere, Carey is coming. He's rented a house. Maxed out on his plastic to fix it up for her. He has a plan: Amazing Free Offer. He'll do anything to get her to stay.

Probing, Sally says gently, 'You don't sound very happy.'

'I just don't know how it's going to go, is all.' Edgy, Theo watches as somebody tries the doors on the driver's side of the Olds. On the passenger's side. The doors don't yield. Pulling out his notebook, he says to Sally, 'The fucker is locked.'

'And?'

'Who locked it? Zax?'

'Good question. If Zax didn't lock it, who? Look. They're fighting over how to crack it without losing prints. Boy,' Sally says, 'another woman coming to see you. When Delia finds out you're seeing somebody, she's going to freak.'

Theo blinks. 'Say what?'

'Don't you know you're her idol? Look at the woman!'

He corrects her. 'Girl. All I am is nice to her.' Funny kid, DeliaMarie Vent. The *Star*'s bouncy night intern is quick but maybe a little too everywhere, all eager and pink in the face, as if somebody scrubbed her with laundry soap or she got that color running up four flights of stairs to bring you something you'd forgotten you'd asked her for.

'She'd do anything for you,' Sally says, grinning. 'Anything.'

'Not really.' But Sally is right. Delia lingers with that chronic A student grin. Theo tries to pass it off. 'It's nothing.'

'Don't be so sure.'

On the bank opposite, after hours of no happening things are happening. Theo stands up so fast that he doesn't register the warning chill in Sally's tone. He says, 'They've got it open.'

'He's in the car.'

Theo pulls out his flip phone but does not dial. 'You think it's him?'

'Bet. Eight dollars?'

'No takers.' They both know it is Zax. But until he can look into the killer's face and make his own identification, Theo can't move on this story. He has to be sure. OK, there's

7

something more. He needs to note what this is like. He needs to mark it. New to the *Star*, he has looked into plenty of dead faces, but never a killer's. More. He has never looked into the face of a drowned killer. What does he expect to see, the last murder recorded? A snapshot of Zax's own death scene captured in the glazed eyeballs or only the green, luminous horror of decomposition? It is terrifying and seductive. Maybe he just needs to look into the killer's face so he can ride this story out of Center City. He and Carey won't have to have this faceoff after all.

Squinting at the activity around the car, Sally says before Theo knows how she knows, 'Forensics is going first.'

'You're good at this.'

'Yeah. Nobody else in the car.'

'How can you tell?'

'Only one body bag.' His official battle narrator goes on in TV anchor tones. 'OK, here comes the coroner.'

Theo skims the crowd. 'Shit. There's Arch.' Arch, who slouched in late today, claiming he was taking a comp day to detail his car.

'Yeah, shit,' Sally says. 'There's Channel 8 news.'

'He's eating a goddamn sandwich.'

'Let's move.'

Chief Vera Smeel greets them with an abashed grin. 'Wills? I don't know how he got in. I owe you one. I'll keep TV 8 out until you do your thing.'

Channel 8's own Lacey Sparkman tries to attach herself, but Chief Smeel straight-arms her. Theo feels Lacey's light touch; her fingers trail down his arm just as he ducks under the yellow tape.

Inside the perimeter, Arch greets Theo with a jaunty fuck-you grin. Don't ask how he got there, just get something he doesn't already have. Sally blows off Arch's proffered sandwich and she and Theo move into the circle around the car. Forensics has done its thing and they can take their look before the coroner finishes and they remove the body, no, no cameras. Someone has scraped the muck off the windshield of the Olds but smudges remain, like kids' window paintings of fall.

The big car is solid. Sculptured. Impressive, like a bronze sarcophagus. Theo and Sally peer in. It's Zax all right, they found him exactly where the caller said he would be. Dead, but not dead long enough for things that live in the water to go to work on him. The Olds is intact. So is the driver. He looks perfect. In a minute they'll start breaking fingers to pry him off the steering wheel but right now Preston Zax is driving. The missing killer is located for good and all, frozen in the driver's seat with hands clamped on the wheel and cloudy eyeballs exposed because he hit death staring straight ahead. Death finds him driving into hell with his face split and all his teeth showing in an expression Theo does not immediately recognize, a rictus of, oh God . . . Rigored and waiting for the fishes, Preston Zax has his face fixed in an eternal grin.

Nodding, Sally steps back. Theo does not step back. This is a long moment. 'Well,' Sally says, ending the word with an explosive little p, prompting him. 'Slate?'

He does not hear.

'Theo?'

His head snaps back. It's as if somebody's just smashed him in the face with a bat. Or hit the brakes on a runaway train. Everything inside him jars to a full stop. 'Shit!'

Sally jabs him hard. 'Are you OK?'

He coughs. 'Fine. It's just. God!'

'Are you calling the desk, or am I?'

Theo's head fills with something new. Questions buzz like swarming gnats. 'Sal!'

'What?'

When he can breathe again he says, 'He looks like me.'

Sally's brusquely matter-of-fact. 'Don't be an asshole.' Angry for no reason he can see, she repeats, 'Who's calling? You or me?'

9

'I will. I'm leaving anyway. I'm supposed to hit the mother.'

'Statement?'

'Statement. Photo. Anything I can get.'

2

He's on his way out when Lacey calls, 'Hey, gorgeous, tell me what you've got and I'll put you on TV.'

'Give me a break.' Gorgeous he's not. He looks OK, he supposes, maybe a little better in a craggy kind of way. He ducks under the tape. 'Read all about it in the *Star*.'

As his service to a friend and colleague, Arch disables his own car in the road out of the quarry. Arch has already scored on-the-scene interviews with the divers. He can phone it in. Sally has the cops. Theo gets the mother. By the time the TV 8 truck clears the traffic jam around Arch's car, Theo is at the Zax front door.

The house does not look like a killer's house. It's a vinyl-sided box in a development where the only major variations are in color; this one is washed-out yellow instead of washed-out blue or washed-out pink. In this neighborhood homeowners express their individuality with funky mailboxes and the junk they hang on their front doors. The Zax house is distinguished by fading plastic flowers, one of those tokens householders sick of winter tack to the knocker in hopes of spring and then forget to take down.

The woman who comes to the door does not look like a killer's mother, but what does a killer's mother look like anyway? Fresh in the nurse's uniform she wore to work today, Zax's mother has a flat, nice face with mild, bland eyes. Her starched front is still stiff. She looks not so much distraught as faintly surprised at what's happening in her life. It is as if her son and his murders and mutilations exist

11

in another world. She opens the door just wide enough to look out. 'Yes?'

The police have already been. Theo's just as glad. This woman's already had more bad news than he wants to bring. 'Mrs Zax?'

She draws herself up. 'Yes. I am Stella Zax.'

'Mrs Zax, I'm Theo Slate, from the *Star*?' He waits for her to slam the door.

'You're here about Preston.'

'Yes ma'am.'

She plants her feet wide. White legs rise like marble columns out of big white shoes. She is almost as tall as he is, filling the doorway so he can't see inside. 'You can't come in right now.'

'I know.' In a minute she will tell him to go away. 'I just wondered if you could. Um. Ah.' How to put this. 'Uh, your son was accused of . . .'

He doesn't have to finish; she knows. She doesn't deny it. She nods that big head.

'I wondered if you . . .'

She shakes her head.

'I can't.'

He makes a sympathetic noise. 'They haven't proved anything yet,' he tries, thinking maybe the killer's mother will start talking in an attempt to clear her son's name. 'You know, that he did any of the—'

She snaps, 'I know what he did.'

'Then you think he did do those things.'

'I know what he did.' Her sigh is huge and terrible. 'I know.'

'Um. Ah!' Back inside his head Theo is scrambling for his lead even as he frames his next question: '*According to the mother of alleged killer Preston Zax . . .*' No. '*Alleged serial killer Preston Zax's mother admits his guilt exclusive to the* Star. *The killer's mother says . . .*' In fact he can't be sure exactly what she did say. He has to get her to say it. He prompts, 'About the things he did.'

Her face is without expression. 'You know what he did.'

Using the old reporter's trick he repeats her, letting it hang, awaiting completion. 'What he did was . . .'

'Terrible.'

He doesn't want to trick her, he wants her to volunteer it. 'So you're telling me you know he did the . . .'

All she has to do is tell him yes. She is still for too long.

He tries again. 'He did . . .' In a minute he'll be moving his mouth like a daddy trying to make Baby open up for the spoon.

The woman seems to sense that he is dying here. With a skewed, compassionate look she releases him. 'You want me to tell you that he did the murders.'

Bingo! He keeps his voice even. 'If you think he did.'

Stella Zax contemplates him in silence. Nothing she is thinking shows. At last she says, 'Son, if you want me to tell you he did the murders, yes he did the murders. But that isn't the important thing.'

Theo's mind is scurrying after his lead.

'Son, do you hear me?'

'Ma'am?' Drawn taut and stalled at the starting gate, Theo waits for the woman to tell him what he thinks she's trying to tell him.

Stella Zax sighs. 'I guess that's all.' But she is still standing in the doorway. It is not a policy decision. She's not even waiting for anything.

This leaves Theo to feed her the reporter's last straight line. 'Is there anything else you want to tell me?'

'No.' Still she does not dismiss him. What keeps them standing there? Something about her? Something about him? He never gives up. That's one. Stella? He doesn't know.

'I know you don't want to talk to me and I know you

won't do this,' he says, 'but I'm wondering, is there a picture?'

'Picture of my boy?' Her head is at an odd slant; it's as if she is studying him. Theo has no way of knowing what Stella sees but her expression thaws ever so slightly. She is big and sad. 'Not like he is now,' she says.

'No. No ma'am,' he reassures her. 'A good picture. Listen, Mrs Zax, anything you have . . .'

'A picture. I have a picture, yes.' Now she shifts on one foot; should she shut the door on this reporter so she can go and get it or can she trust him to wait here?

'It's OK,' he says. 'You can leave it open. I won't try anything.'

It is so odd; she says, 'I know you won't.'

Without locking the door she pulls it to, leaving Theo to squint through the crack. The only impression he gets of the Zax front room is of beige everything. He steps back on the little front stoop, noting uneasily that the bottom hem of the beige draw drapes shielding the front window is disrupted by a series of little bumps; the tails of china animals marching along the sill.

When Stella Zax comes back to the front door it is with Preston's high school graduation picture, one of those highly colored studio portraits shot against a velvet drop. The killer-in-waiting looks rubbery and unreal, with strobe lights frosting his hair and striking symmetrical glints in the eyes. Riveted, Theo takes it. He starts to thank her and go. Then three things happen at once. The TV 8 truck rounds the corner and heads their way.

The killer's mother gives him a maternal smile. 'Good boy.'

A small muscle in his stomach spasms. *What – does she take me for him?* Theo looks down into the face of early Preston Zax, checking for a resemblance. 'You mean Preston.'

'I have something to tell you,' Stella Zax says. 'My son.'

'Preston?'

'Not now,' she says. On deadline, Theo will not press her. 'Tomorrow,' she says. Even though the TV 8 truck and the police arrive in a photo finish, even though Lacey Sparkman and her two cameras are heading their way, which means the embattled mother has to go inside pronto or turn up on the nightly news looking like a stunned ox. Even with police and TV crews converging, Stella Zax waits in the doorway until Theo tucks the framed photo under his arm and thanks her and goes.

3

GRIEVING MOTHER CONFIRMS DEAD
SERIAL KILLER'S GUILT

*'Terrible things,' says Stella Zax, mother of Preston
Zax, 32, who allegedly murdered and mutilated seven
Center City women before his killing spree ended at
the bottom of Schontz's Quarry, where police divers
found him late yesterday.*

*A surgical nurse at the Center City Hospital, Ms
Zax, 65, confirmed her son's involvement in an interview exclusive to the* Star. *'Yes he did the murders,'
the killer's mother says.*

And on. Front page. Column One under the banner, plus
a jump. Theo thinks his story looks pretty good. Even
though it's carved in stone now, he can't help tinkering in
his head a little: Should he have cast it this way instead
of that?

'Your story is just *great*.' The night intern is standing so
close that he jumps.

Startled, he manages a grin. 'Thanks. Hey, it's morning.
What are you doing here?'

'Couldn't stay away. Look at that banner!' Delia says.
'What a rush!' Because he's waiting for her to go away,
she says, 'You look really busy.'

'I am.'

Her voice is quick with excitement. 'Can I help?'

16

Fob her off, he thinks. Fob her off with some little job. 'Try Sally. Maybe she can use you.'

'Oh, Sally,' the intern says, 'Sally is jealous of me.'

'She what?'

Delia blushes. 'You know. You're always so nice to me.'

'I'm not nice, now go get busy.'

'Got anything for me? Brief to rewrite? Clips you need?'

'No thanks.'

But DeliaMarie Vent hangs over him with that gimme smile while across the way, Sally tilts her head and shoots him a knowing grin. *Delia, eh. Great remora.* To which Theo usually says, 'She means well.' He can hear Sally: *Too well.* Desperate for a toehold at the *Star*, Delia hustles extra work like a Broadway panhandler, hitting him up with that wheedling lilt: 'Anything for me?'

'I don't have anything right now, OK?' Usually he drums up something for the girl, just to get her off his back. It's fun to be good enough at what you do to teach someone, but not today. Wasted from partying last night, with alcohol fumes curling to the roof of his mouth, Theo is shuffling city briefs in a failed attempt to jumpstart his head. He and Sally and Arch were still up at four, hanging out on the edge of the quarry, getting drunk and spinning one-liners off the Zax thing; parts of life are so ugly that you'd better laugh. Carved an X in the buttocks of every one of those women, did he? OK, spin a gag about Zax carving his initials on you or me, so you can laugh. Handle it or go crazy, right? When Theo finishes his backgrounder, he sees Mrs Zax. He has to file and get home in time to clean up for Carey. She comes in at seven tonight. He has to wrap up the Stella Zax backgrounder in ten screens before he meets the plane. Sure he does. It's all he can do to see the damn screen today. Words stall and won't crawl across.

And Delia Vent is lurking with that hopeful, crooked smile, demands, demands. 'You're sure?'

'Really,' he says. Nice kid. At least Theo thinks she's a kid. Vulnerable, unformed. Mysteriously, she makes you want to make it all better for her. 'I'm tied up right now.'

'Besides,' she says forlornly, 'I thought you of all people would know.'

'Know what?'

'You know. The answer.' As if this is a quiz. 'What I asked.'

'Sorry.' Did Delia ask him some question? Probably. It's her way of staying in touch. She blinks those round, no-color eyes so rapidly that he automatically hands her his wetting solution. Resourceful Slate, no problem without its own solution: lenses giving you fits? Try this. Need your life fixed? Take my thumb tacks. Oh, and a roll of duct tape. You'll be fine.

Smiling, Delia takes it, although later, Theo will note that she wears glasses. 'Oh, thanks.' She sighs. 'I guess I should go. I just. It's. You're so nice to me.'

His phone bleats. 'Sorry. Phone.' He clamps on the headphones, grateful for the chance to shut her out. Which he doesn't, at least not completely.

'It's just. The *Star* is my life.' Lingering, she picks up his mint copy of today's paper and pretends to read.

'Theodore?' His full name rattles into his ears in that clotted chronic smoker's voice he knows too well. It's Frederick Slate, who got downsized in some crash or other and pinned all his hopes on his only son.

'Hello, Dad.'

His father sounds up today, in spite of the fact that Theo's just succeeded at something he doesn't approve of. 'This is really good news.'

Front page, all editions, damn straight. 'You heard about my story? That's great.'

'Story? What story? No, I mean about Carey.'

'Oh,' Theo says distractedly, glaring at Delia until she puts the paper down. 'Yes. She's coming.'

18

But his father is on another track. 'Yes. And that's what I called to tell you. She's bringing good news.'

His voice leaps. 'She is?'

'She is,' Dad says. 'I've called in some favors.'

Theo hardly hears. While he's been hung up here, treading air somewhere between his father and the intern, Sally's been to the desk to pick up an assignment from Chick. Now she's madly keyboarding. Arch just breezed past with a secretive, *gotcha* grin and Chick is glaring at him from the slot. 'That's great, Dad. Look, I've gotta go. My boss . . .'

Frederick Slate tries that impressive boardroom tone. 'Then make time.' But he's out of the boardroom now. Benched.

'I'm sorry, Dad. I can't.' Theo clicks off and glares at the intern, willing her to go away.

'I'd do anything to help.'

Think fast. 'OK, go get me everything you can find on Oldsmobiles. OK?'

'Oh thank you.' She makes it sound like *thank God*.

The Zax discovery has brought everybody in today – Arch and Sally are all over it. So is Fred Grable, from the capitol bureau. Al Revenaugh from Editorials is jamming on the in-depth piece and tough Anita Clawson is klunking away on the lone typewriter, a dinosaur with a carriage return that shakes the room. It is the Royal standard office model that she used in the year Twelve, when she hammered out the series that won the paper its Pulitzer Prize. With her bronze hair and her plum fingernails Anita's old enough to be everybody's mother put together. She is also a national treasure. Listens to her own drumbeat, keeps her own hours and writes what she wants. Today it's a heartrending in-depth interview with the parents of the sixth victim, the same couple that after the murder refused to give Theo the time of day, so he's got to admit Old doesn't automatically mean Over With. Anita and Chick Wilbur, the Metro editor, are proof positive. Chick snarls, you jump. In this smoke-free environment he gnaws on a cold cigar.

Surprise, even though Theo scored the killer's picture yesterday and his story took the prime spot, Chick put Arch on today's interview with Stella Zax. It's like being in a cage with a gorilla. He can do anything he wants. Chew you out just to keep you humble. Take you off a story to remind you who's boss. The joke's on Chick. When Arch showed up at the Zax house the killer's mother slammed the door on him. She sent back word. Stella Zax will talk, but only to Theo Slate. Theo and Arch go way back, so he tries to hide his winner's grin. He's scheduled to go at two. Chick dips his head in grudging respect, so that makes up for Anita's score with the sixth victim's parents, at least a little bit.

When Theo gets up to leave, Delia gets up. He dodges into the bathroom to avoid her but she catches him at the elevator anyway. 'Mr Slate?'

'Theo.'

'*Theo.*' She looks so pleased! 'I've got something for you. It's kind of big.'

He says automatically, 'Not now.' The funny thing about Delia Vent is that between times, Theo forgets what she looks like. Every time he sees her it's a little surprise. Partly it's the clothes. You can't tell what's underneath. She wears baggy rayon things in dark colors, string sweaters in muddy shades of raisin, prune and plum, puts them on like a cloak of invisibility. Her cuffs hang to the knuckles; no telling whether the body she's hiding is lithe or awkward; Theo could probably lift her with one hand but somehow she looks leaden, with all her lines slanting down. Delia is not exactly plain. When she's flushed as she is now, the word 'pretty' is feasible, but all that anxiety has left her forever stalled on the border between people you know and people you want to know. Theo can't be sure exactly how old this person is, but since she ranks somewhere between the end tables and the towel racks when he catalogs the furniture

20

in his life, he doesn't spend much time on it. The elevator doesn't come and it doesn't come.

Shifting from foot to foot with a significant scowl, Delia is waiting for him to bite. 'Don't you want to know what I've got?'

'I'm sorry. I can't talk right now.' Thank God, the elevator. He dives in. 'Sorry.'

She lunges after him, too late. 'What I've got, you can use!'

'Later. Gotta go.'

Like syrup, her voice curls after him, slipping through the elevator doors as they close. 'I know them! Listen, I used to go over to their house!'

4

'**O**h Mr Slate, thank God you've come.'

'Yes ma'am.' He studies her. 'Why did you send for me?'

Stella Zax's answer is no answer. 'It had to be you.'

'Me. Is there something special you have to tell me?'

'You'll see.' Where yesterday her face was colorless and smooth, unmarked, like a soapstone carving, today Stella Zax is animated. It's like some physics experiment: heavy water. Everything has fresh significance. 'Come in. Come in!'

Yesterday she stonewalled him on the porch, producing the graduation photo in its brass frame as if she could fend off the future with this icon: studio portrait of her son in full color, highlights in those uplifted eyes like the spots on dice. Lined up against velvet and shot to brighten a mother's heart, Preston Zax looked like somebody you know in the crisp white shirt and black tie he wore for the photo and put on every morning after for his job at the bank. Theo, who has his own set of mug shots, can hear the photog working his subject: 'No, don't look at the camera, look at my hand. There. That's good,' using the old trick that usually surprises a smile out of them: 'Now, say Sexual Intercourse.' Nice smile on Zax that day, preserved forever, or until the color fades. Clear eyes. Nice face the shape of an Easter egg, soft, shiny hair with that wet-comb part a loving mom puts in, that some men forget to change even after they grow up and escape her for good. Preston

22

Zax didn't look dangerous, he looked innocuous. He could have been anyone. 'I said, come *in*.'

Theo is stalled on the porch, fixed in place by his own vision of the killer. It flickered behind his eyes last night no matter how drunk he tried to get; it woke him at dawn and it shimmers between him and the way in. It is nothing like the photo. Rushing into his consciousness like an express train with its headlight glaring is the savage, eternally grinning face of the drowned Preston Zax. He can't bridge the gap between that and this. This nice lady with her face fixed in the banality of welcome. The son. If he has anything here, it's in the disparity. A bigger story, waiting.

'We can't talk out here. Come in.' She stands back to let him in. 'I'm making tea,' the mother says with the smug, narrow smile of a homemaker who has everything perfect, *perfect*. Mother of that smiling graduate with the polished-apple face. The house is freshly vacuumed; she has straightened the plastic sleeves on the arms of the furniture. All her small ornaments are dusted and at attention. To preserve her rug, she has him take off his shoes.

Theo kneels to undo his black Adidas. 'You sent for me?'

The woman fills the room. Where yesterday she met him at the door in the white uniform she had on when she got the news, she has dressed for this event. She has dressed up for him; instead of looking tired in white, she is aggressively heavy in pink. 'I did.'

He should be asking Mrs Zax if she's OK with a tape recorder; he should be starting with the questions he's rehearsed so they won't sound rehearsed, but the mother is in charge today. She crowds him in the tiny living room, backing him into the sofa; he sits down fast and the gold-flecked beige seat scrapes his palms. It's clear from her manner that she has everything just the way she wants it. Today. Oddly, Stella Zax looks unchanged by her ordeal. She is unmarked by last night's struggle

23

to escape Lacey Sparkman's cameras, aired on TV 8 at 6 and 11. She is remarkably composed. Nothing about this woman suggests the horror of the discovery that tore her apart, the pain. The victim who survived Preston Zax's last, botched assault identified the killer. Coming to the house to arrest Zax, police had to tell this nice lady that her son was wanted for multiple murder. Later in the day they had to tell her he had dropped out of sight. How does a mother take that kind of news? What does she do when they come back a day later and tell her that her son the murderer is dead? Did Stella cry when she went down to identify the body? There are no traces in her face. Is she grieving or relieved or is this something different?

Reaching behind her back like a magician, she pulls out another photo. 'You have a good picture of Preston,' she says. 'You'll need mine.'

Puzzled, Theo takes it. 'Thank you very much. I—' He looks down. It's a photographer's contact sheet, stamped yesterday. Combed, groomed, in fresh makeup and her best jewelry, Stella Zax faces the camera with an intent, calm stare. For this picture she has put on her best. 'This is very nice, but I can't promise you anything. I don't know if we're going to need it. I . . .'

'Yes you will.'

'What?'

'You'll need it. You'll see.'

'Mrs Zax, is there something special you want to . . .'

Yesterday Stella Zax was impassive. Monolithic. Today she is agitated but quiet, as if her body is under orders to be still. For this interview, she has chosen pink. 'I'll bring tea.'

'No thanks, I . . .' Theo is trying to see past her into the little hall. The open bedroom door. Zax's room. 'I just ate.'

'You'll like this. I baked.' She pushes him back into his seat. Then she produces a family album, fake leather, gold-stamped. 'While you're waiting, you can look at these.'

'Thank you.'

'If you want to, you can take them. I want people to see.'

Yes. Sunday A section, double truck. Dead killer's life story, in photos, additional material by Theo Slate. Story on Page One. Hey, he thinks, maybe I can beat Arch out of Center City after all.

She says, 'I did my best.'

'I know you did.'

She goes away.

He flips open his notebook. He needs to locate his readers; this is gangbusters. Everything in Mrs Zax's house is beige. Beige drapes, beige carpeting, beige upholstery on the freshly vacuumed L-shaped sectional that overpowers everything else in the room. Bleached blond birch and a beige freeform Formica coffee table polished to extinction. The place is mortifyingly still and clean, like a tomb prepared but not yet occupied. Stella Zax has lined up all her small objects. She has them exactly the way she wants them. Cigarette box. China bird dog. Ashtray. Hummel figurine. Snapshot album. Side by side and all aimed north with such precision that it's hard to believe a human hand put them there. It is stultifyingly neat. There is no sign in this house that the rooms have survived exhaustive police searches, dustings, repeated police visits. Detectives have come and gone without leaving a mark on Stella Zax; they told her the worst and asked even worse questions without making a dent in her.

'I didn't know,' she told police when they came to arrest her son on suspicion of multiple murder. Theo has a copy of the report. 'I didn't know,' she said yesterday, when they told her he was dead.

Now she has Theo here. What did Stella Zax know? What's she going to tell him anyway? There is nothing in this plain, bland house or in her plain, bland face to suggest that she even guessed her son was a killer. Marooned on the sectional, Theo notes that in spite of the fact that the cops have gone over the place from cellar to attic crawlspace, the Zax house looks exactly the way it always did. Stella has seen to it. Never mind that cops have turned the place inside out more than once. Never mind that they questioned the owner for hours. Never mind that they came back with magnifying glasses and tweezers, violating every shelf and every crevice. Stella Zax has righted every wrong.

She calls from the kitchen, 'Make yourself at home.'

How long did it take her to put her house to rights? The almost regimental order leaves Theo hotwired. On the verge of some unforeseen discovery. He hears dishes rattling. Stella comes back in with two cups and lines them up. China sugar bowl. Creamer. One, two. Flowered saucers. Three, four. Spoons. Five, six. The countdown is complete. Then she disappears again. Her voice is remote and clear. 'I'll only be a minute.'

'Yes ma'am.' Perched like a wild bird in a henhouse, Theo looks for at least one outward and physical sign that awful things happened here. If everything in Stella Zax's life marches in order, didn't she *notice* anything? If her only son lived here until he died; if Preston went out and did those murders and signed the corpses with his knife, if he did all that and came back here, weren't there, like, *signs*? Discrepancies? Sheets that wouldn't come clean or knives missing from the kitchen or towels that mysteriously disappeared? No matter how careful he was, the killer must have slipped. He must have come home in the middle of at least one night with his hair smeared and leftover blood drying in his nail beds, blood mixed with the mud caked in the treads of his shoes. He must have come home with blood splashes on his underwear or drying on his cheek. He must have scrubbed it away in his mother's unexceptional bathroom and once, at least once, he must have wiped vestigial blood off the knife he used with one of this careful, attentive mother's kitchen towels. Looked at her with the truth crackling behind that bland face. Too much has happened for it to go by unmarked, and yet on the surface, Stella's world is uncommonly clean. Everything in her house is well-ordered. Still. And yet. Too much has come down. There've got to be traces somewhere – some undiscovered cache of papers or Polaroids that tell the tale, a gruesome wall somewhere in this relentlessly clean little tract house. The kind of wall killers cross-hatch with defaced snapshots and newspaper clippings. It's the way things *are*, or the way Theo's been led to think they are. All those movies. All those deaths. Intricate plans. Revolting secrets of the lair.

'Mrs Zax?'

'Coming,' she sings. 'I'll be right along.'

Nothing can be this ordinary. But ordinary it is, Theo thinks, sticking his pencil behind his ear. Nice house, nice lady, look, she's a nurse. Widow, he guesses, wants everything nice for her son. Brings up her nice little boy the good old American way, Star Wars lunch box, baked Poppin' Fresh and Sesame Street in the ayem, Ring Dings in every lunch. She probably made his sandwiches, popcorn for TV movies on Saturday nights, cocoa and Eggos in front of the TV, you and me, son, we're having a little party. Just us two. Women like her even iron T-shirts, anything for my boy. Parted her Preston's hair with that wet comb and sent him out every day looking clean and nice, and this is what she gets. Not praise for doing her job, just the blown lunch spot on Page One – notoriety because nice as she is, Stella Zax is blood kin to Center City's first serial killer. Spawned him. Hatched him and nurtured him and is therefore responsible. Brought her boy up nice, and now this. The shame! Rubberneckers out there milling around just beyond the shrubbery, cars slowing as they go by, cruising the house. Try and keep everything decent, and now look.

Without her, the room is like a dead thing. 'Can I help?'

She calls from the kitchen, 'I'll only be a minute. You wait.'

The least he can do is look through the Zax family album, proof positive that Stella has done her best. Theo finds snaps of Stella with Preston in a Scout uniform, smiling at a picnic on a long-lost summer day, in white on the Sunday of his First Holy Communion, sweet pictures, every one dappled with light coming through trees in full leaf, so lovely and still that nostalgia almost overwhelms him. Nice mom, nice kid. Nice home. How could this decent woman anticipate what would become of him? How could a mother know?

Coming in as if on cue with a dish of lemon slices, she says, 'That's me with Presty at graduation.'

'Can I see his room?'

'You can see it from here,' she says.

He can. The open door says she has nothing to hide. He can see the maple dresser with ranked ornaments and the tautly made single bed. The braided rag rug washed and stretched to extinction. The white walls. From here he can see a Manet poster – the mother's idea, he's sure. Zax's room. It makes his scalp crawl. 'Nice,' he says.

'Yes,' she says. 'Nice.'

'So what went wrong?' What, exactly, was the matter here? That spawned the killer, or do killers like Zax yield to explanation? It baffles him. He can go with the story about the boyhood and the house but he wants more. He would like this nice lady to produce answers. Some heart-stopping quote that says it all.

Instead of answering she hits him with that mother's smile. 'I'm so glad you came.'

Shit! 'Why did you ask for me?'

The look she turns on Theo is one of complicity – motherly, warm; it's almost as if she knows him and they've already had the conversation. As if they're coming up on some crucial last thing. 'Because you're nice and I like you,' she says.

'Nice!'

'I thought you might as well be the one.'

Bingo. Theo snaps forward. He says in a low voice, 'What do you mean?'

Stella puts down the tray, dead center on the bleached wood coffee table, and heads for the kitchen. 'Cookies. I almost forgot.'

'You were about to tell me something,' he begins as she comes back with the plate; his heart flips. The cookies are beige.

'My son,' she says.

She looks so expectant that he says kindly, 'You look very nice. Would you like me to phone for a photographer?'

'You have your picture.' Her big clip-on earrings have matching pink stones in them. Her hair is newly curled. She's dressed as if today is special. Her pink dress is the one color statement in this serene beige environment; her eyelashes and brows are beige and the careful fringe of curls around her face is freshly dyed beige, that store-bought hair color women use when they want to tell you getting gray does not mean getting old or giving up.

'If you would just let me see his room.'

'It wouldn't make any difference.'

'You keep a very nice house,' Theo says. Yes he is fishing.

'I keep his room clean,' she says. 'Just the way I like it.'

'Yes ma'am.'

'My Preston, he knows that.'

'Yes ma'am.'

'Preston, he's always so considerate,' she says.

'I see.'

She says, 'He knows I want him to keep his room clean. He likes it that way and he knows I like to keep it that way. So he does. A considerate boy. My Preston has always been a considerate boy. It's an important lesson.' She is talking

29

as if her Preston is still among them, here in the present. There is a silence. She tilts her head politely, inviting the next question.

Theo waits. He lets it spin out, that trustworthy reporter's tool, the silence. It just may wring those last, important words out of her. There is more. He is bereft of words.

'He should have known. He had to learn.' She lifts her head.

'Ma'am?' Noises outside magnify until they pervade the room. There are vehicles rolling down her quiet street. No motors. Just the crunch of cars coasting in. If there is something going on out there, Theo notes it only peripherally. He is wacked out on the mystery of what's happening here inside.

'The lesson,' Stella says. 'Everybody has to learn.'

The stir outside intensifies. Theo hears stealthy footsteps: people as yet unidentified, circling the house.

'He did everything in the car,' the killer's mother says. 'That's why I had to get rid of it.'

Theo says dumbly, 'The car.'

'You know.'

Oh holy God. 'You mean you . . .'

'Yes,' she says calmly. It is not a confession. It's a simple statement. 'I did.'

So Theo and the cops approach the truth in stages, but they arrive at exactly the same moment. Did Stella Zax have this planned when she got her hair done this morning, and set the interview for 2 p.m.? If she did, it is an amazing gift she has given him. The story Theo has been waiting for. A way out of his life. As more cruisers pull up out front, as the first officer mounts the steps, he says hurriedly, 'Can I talk to you again?'

They are both aware of cars nosing into the curb. The slamming of doors. The beat of shoes on the front walk. Swelled with importance now, stolid and enormous, Stella

Zax takes Theo's hand hurriedly like a co-conspirator, or a foiled lover. Static electricity shocks them and they jump. She turns fuchsia – something *interruptus* – and at the first knock she whispers, 'If I can. If I can!'

5

Stella Zax doesn't need to tell him who's outside but she does. 'It's the police.'

An officer barks, 'Police.'

'Coming!' She does not immediately go to the door. Like an old star waiting for her closeup, she lifts her head and wets her lips. She touches her throat, settling her pearls inside her pink collar.

Theo notes that the lipstick she has put on for her arrest exactly matches the outfit. Stella Zax has indeed dressed for this event. He understands that she singled him out to do this story as carefully as she selected her clothes. He doesn't know why she chose him, but he knows he has been chosen. *What do you want from me, Mrs Zax?* 'Before they come in. Why did you kill him, really?'

'You already know,' she says in a sad, sad voice. As police knock again she stands. Polite hostess saying, 'Don't get up.'

He's working on his lead. Chick will banner his story in apocalyptic type: *KILLER MOM CONFESSES TO STAR*. But she hasn't, really. Yet. 'Our readers are going to want to know. Your own words.'

She starts putting tea things back on the tray. Her pale, glossy face is empty of expression, as if it's been wiped with a wet sponge. This isn't about me, Theo thinks. I'm just one moving part in a larger plan. Designated writer, put in place to make sure we spell her name right and I get the desk to run her studio portrait instead of a two-column cut of this middle-class mom cuffed and mortified, being frogmarched to jail. My God, the woman has even put on pearls. As police knock again Stella grabs his tea cup and slides the tray under her chair, patting the dust ruffle like a hostess with party flutters. She wants it to look right! She corrals straying objects and straightens a lampshade, smoothing her hair with automatic grace as if time has overlooked her and she's still a girl. Fixing a smile, Stella Zax goes to the door. But she can't quite open it. Instead she turns. 'If you were a mother, you'd understand.'

Theo takes advantage of her momentary distraction, offering, 'Isn't there something you want to tell our readers?'

And she loses it. Her shoulders droop. Stella Zax lets go of the knob and turns, showing him a face stripped naked. It is a face Theo recognizes from bad moments with his own mom, gives you that look and sobs, *I've failed.* Zax's mother is maroon with humiliation, not because she offed her son, listen, she *had* to do it. No, what's breaking her up right now is that she had a job to do and she has failed. She has failed as a mother. This respectable lady battled her environment to a standstill every day of her adult life. All her life she hewed to the straight and narrow and now with this one aberration, she has lost it all. Grief clogs her voice. 'Tell them I tried.'

Bingo. His lead. When the officers come in, Theo manages not to be anywhere. He is lurking creatively behind the half-open door to Zax's room, and if in the course of reading the killer's mother her rights the cops overlook him, fine. He's standing behind the door in his socks with his story prepared – she sent me to check out these books. They don't need to know that he has his Perlcorder running, in hopes. He has the photo. Those sad, sad last words. But if he hangs in here he may get more. What else? he wonders. What else? OK, with cops in her living room, Stella just might explain. If nobody connects the black Adidas at the door to Theo, nobody needs to know he's here. Holding so still that his eyeballs glaze, he fixes on Preston's six-foot shelf – generic kids' books worn to bits, math and English texts from first grade on plus college board test guides, uncracked, testimony to a mom's failed hopes; clusters of bright, banal self-help books, also untouched; an unused Cub Scout manual, uncracked paperback of *A Thousand Years of Solitude* – and, what's this? A diary. One of those big, pretentious jobs with gold stamping that people buy to write big thoughts in. His heart lurches. This could be it.

In the front room somebody coughs and Theo puts it back.

The Mirandizing proceeds as scripted. The cops finish and the front door slams on the departing Stella Zax. So much for her final statement. That window of availability is closed for now.

Theo pads into the front room to watch her go. Through a gap in the irreproachable beige curtains, he watches the team march the freshly minted murderess down the front walk and out of her carefully ordered life. Stella Zax goes along between the arresting officers in her pink dress with the matching spring coat, could be Theo's mother, could be yours, doesn't even notice that these seasoned cops are leaning in like bookends, keeping their legs out of harm's way because a woman may not kill you for trying to arrest her, but she can gouge hell out of your shins with those high heels. This solid, middle-class mother goes along primly, as if kicking and struggling aren't an issue in her orderly universe. These things don't happen. At least not to people you know. Nice lady raises a nice son, gives him life and by God she ends it. Has to. No choice, Theo thinks, but still does not understand it.

Good story. OK, so she did it, but. Why?

Theo ties his shoes and goes back for the fake leather book. It's too fat to slip in his pocket or hide under Stella's photo. Too big to stick inside the back of his jeans. How's he going to get it past the cops posted outside? Juggling the book, he floats in the silent front room.

Artie from forensics comes in. 'What are you doing here?'

Hastily, Theo slips the Zax diary behind him and backs into a chair. 'I already *was* here.'

'Well you'd better clear out. We have to seal the place.'

'I was just leaving.'

Artie's official mask drops an inch. 'Offed her own son?'

'You got it.' Theo tsk-tsks. 'You ever hear of such a thing?' *Good story!*

'Not really.'

He's never going to get this diary out with Artie watching. Carefully, Theo slides it under the seat cushion and makes as if to go. They'll probably find the damn thing, but there's the off-chance that they won't.

'Her own son,' Artie repeats, bemused. 'That'll teach *you* to pick up your toys.'

'And eat your damn cereal.' Theo laughs.

'What kind of mother would do that?'

'This one,' Theo says. Now all he has to do is source the details. His story is guaranteed A-One, all editions: KILLER MOM CONFESSES TO STAR. Listen, she kind of did. This could be the trick that gets him out of Central nowhere. *If I can only get it right.* Problem is, photo's great but what Stella Zax told is all backstory, how hard she tried, what a good mother she was. He needs details to pull this off Page One and into the national consciousness. All he has are his description of the woman in her clean, clean house and the single, amazing quote: 'He did everything in the car. That's why I had to get rid of it.' Plus the last words she gave him, her present. 'Tell them I tried.'

Thin. He really needs ten more minutes with her. OK, five.

At the station they won't let him near Zax until they've

processed her. The chief doesn't know whether they'll have her done by visiting hours, any more than Theo can be sure she'll see him again. TV 8 is everywhere. Arch caught the coroner and moved on to forensics; Sally's in her friend Vera's office, waiting for her exclusive from the chief. So, fine. Theo still has the biggest item in the news budget, but he can't go with it until he interviews Stella Zax's boss, colleagues, neighbors. He has to hit the state hospital and pump his favorite shrink – a little something on obsessive-compulsives would be good. That clean, clean house! As the afternoon dies he doubles back on headquarters but they have Stella stashed in some back room where he can't get to her. It will be tomorrow before Theo sees the prisoner but he has some beautiful stuff from neighbors – blinking lights the night Zax disappeared, small fires in the garage – and best of all, the confession, and if he isn't easy with why she chose him for the honor; if he can't figure out exactly what engine drives her, it's no biggie; he's cool, he thinks, bombing into the newsroom with his mouth going sour. He's got his story. Everything is cool.

6

The notebook stands for his mother now. It's all he has. The first notebook came from her hands before Edward was old enough to write. *Look,* his father said. *Look what you did to her.* After what happened, happened, it was all he had left of her. *Did I really kill her just by being bad?* 'She wanted you to have this.' *Oh thank you.* Alone in the night, he trembled and sobbed. Then his throat opened and he vomited grief. Everything went out of him in an unending cascade of tears and mucus and fire and blood. All the soft parts of himself. Leaving only the book. Mother, but not. He took it into bed with him and loved it and slept with it until he was big enough to understand it was only a book. Then he wrote in it. Write it down and get it right and you will please her, he tells himself, as told. And Father won't hate you for killing her. But what if he fails? *I'm doing this for you!* He would do anything to please her. Anything.

But it keeps going wrong.

He will try again. He always does. Everything according to plan. Unrealized, the schemes in the notebooks are beautiful. Orderly. The future outlined and enclosed. 1, 2, 3. Perfect. A, B, C. *It's all in here.*

Notebook

It's in the book. Procedures. Records. Keeping order is how you keep order. Study the last time. It got away from us e screamed and fought us, e screamed so loud

37

that we had to leave it unfinished. Never again. Step back. Assess. Do as we are taught:

   a. Analyze.

   b. Organize.

   c. Plan.

   And move on.

HOW I KNOW IT IS TIME

1. Signs: *Stirring. The fumes – warm, rich smell of me coming off my skin and out of all our open places, my whole body breathing out, our scent curling up from deep in the bed and layering in the room, you think I am ashamed? No way. There is more to me than what's in jail inside this skin, OK? Inside we are crazy as a mink, gnashing in my belly and chasing its tail, gnawing, can I hold it in? Mother, I must do this right if I am going to do it.*

2. Needs: *Find The One.* NOTE. *Not like last time.*

3. How to begin: *Keep us inside. Tape up our lips. Tighten the sphincter and go out. Go into crowds –* Excuse me did I bump you? *I pretend I don't see you but I am studying. Sort and count, sort and count. Too soft, too hard; too easy, too hard. Fast. Like a broken field runner, shoulder, elbow. Snaking through moving, moist bodies, keep my head low so you won't see me coming or guess that as we collide I check out everything on you, which parts of you cave in, what sticks out, know how the hair grows in your secret places, hear your heart and feel the contours of your butt. I know what's between your legs and what it wants, us checking your goddamn smooth faces, smarmy nothings like so many turds,* not this one, not that one, *running until we give up or give out and then when I am least expecting it all our soft insides run screaming into each other and crash. Then I hear the bell. It's time.*

4. Qualifications: *Male? Female? Who cares?*

Victim he. Victim she. It's all the same to me. To do em I unsex em. E.

FIND AND LOCK ON. E DOES NOT EVEN GUESS.

5. What to do: KNOW EM BEFORE YOU DO EM. Steps:

A. *Follow. Extreme care. Follow em without eir knowing we are following. Study em. Learn. What it's like inside your skin. Sooner or later we will know you, and* then you will know me.

Are you ready, can you wait?

B. *Observe. Know em in all eir places. Workplace. Home. Through the window at night. See em go into the shower, watch em come out toweling eir hair. Note the rags ey choose to go out in. Whether ey stand or sit when ey put on eir underpants. Wait for em to leave. Go in.*

I can get into your house without you knowing it. I can sneak into your room and watch you sleep. Listen, I can pluck the hairs off your goddamn pillow and push my nose into your dirty underwear, we scrape your loose cells out of the bathtub where you scrubbed last night, and suck your old skin from under my fingernails. I chew on the used Kleenex I steal from your trash. This is how well I know you, but it is not as well as I am going to know you.

C. *Encounter. When I learn your paths, I am accidentally there. – Hello. You don't know it is me, but I know you. You are surprised. – Oh, hello again. Go inside. Come out and we are there. Accidentally. Know how hard it is to do anything by accident? Everything is by design. It's all here in the book.*

D. *Second encounter. Again. You blink. – Oh, it's you. You wait for me to go away, but I smile and pretty soon we are talking. I look like nobody to you, nobody at all. Smile so not even The One guesses what we are thinking. I make you smile at me. The rush is tremendous. You don't know it but you have just given up part of your soul. I act all innocent.* – I didn't know you came here.

You smile too. – I work near here so I eat lunch in this park.

– Lunch, *I say,* – I got so busy I forgot to eat. *Oh yes you will get to know me and you will like it. I can get you to give me half your sandwich, if I want. We sit and talk, two ordinary people. Breaking bread, and you can't begin to imagine what it's like inside me. #1. #2. hanging on hooks. Or know I'm scared to undress and see the skin on my belly bulging, as if snakes are fucking underneath; I bang on it with my fists to stop it so I can sleep. Until I do you. Then the snakes can sleep. And we can rest.*

6. Next steps: All in order. A, B, C. This is important. Under One. Two. Three. By the numbers, so there will be no mistakes.

THINGS TO DO

A. Find. B. Follow. C. Encounter. D. Equip. E. Do em.

Later on you will thank me. They always thank me. Oh yes I will leave my mark on you.

7

Theo is rushing in to file when she catches his elbow; it's like snagging your sweater on a nail. You have to tear the sweater or stop long enough to untangle it. He says without looking, 'OK, Delia, what do you want?'

Bright-eyed and jiggling with excitement, the intern advances on him with that raccoon stare that lets him know she hasn't left the newsroom all day. 'I have to talk to you.'

'Sorry. On deadline. Hey, did you remember to eat?'

'It's urgent, OK?'

Distracted by Chick's iguana death-rattle, Theo turns to see his boss glowering from his chair in the slot. Mess up here and you lose your job. Grinning as if she's about to take the trifecta, Anita Clawson's wrapping up her survivors'-reaction thumbsucker; darkhaired Sally flashes that cat-and-canary grin; *this is good, what I'm writing. Really good.* God alone knows what Arch is up to, could have pitched a damn series on the Zax case; the whole world is running ahead and Theo is hung up with the night intern, who can't wait to tell him whatever it is. 'Whatever it is, Delia, I can't do it now, so would you just let go?'

'OK, if you don't want any help . . .'

'Just later, OK?' He sits down and opens a file, typing with such concentration that he loses track of time passing, comings and goings, the fact that clippings, coffee, printouts of Sally's and Arch's stories turn up before he even knows he needs them – Delia's work, he guesses as he queues the

41

finished story to Chick and when he looks up, he sees her receding back. Thank her later. Right. He leans back in the swivel chair and lets the tension drain out.

He finishes. He's feeling good enough to type in his byline and forward it with his idea of a headline. The story begins:

MURDERER MOTHER CONFESSES TO STAR
By THEO SLATE
Star *Staff Writer*

Confounding police, the mother of serial killer Preston Zax today confessed to the murder of her own son, putting a shocking end to the series of murders and mutilations that have rocked Center City in recent months. Before giving herself up, Stella Zax, 65, made her confession in an exclusive interview with the Center City Star.

Preparing for arrest in her devastatingly orderly house at 832 Oakdale, the registered nurse revealed first details of the killer's movements during the last seven months. Although she does not reveal why Zax, 32, abducted the local women, or what drove him to carve his trademark X into each victim, Ms Zax says, 'He did it in the car.'

He queues it to Chick and waits.

'Slate.' Chick clears his throat like a fourth-grader pretending to hock on you. He takes the cold cigar out of his mouth long enough to rumble, 'Good story,' so, cool.

Hang in until they settle the news budget and he'll beat Sally into the prime spot, no way he won't. They're good friends, her nice electric glare says they could be more, but they are rivals first. At Chick's back Delia bobs, his protégée. Jerking his head at her, Theo hits Chick's exact rumble. 'Thanks for your help.'

Delia glows. 'Is there anything else I can do?'

'I don't think so.' Finished as he is, spent and triumphant, Theo focuses for the first time on where he is and when it is. 'Holy shit.' Carey! How could I forget?

'What's the matter?'

'Nothing.' Carey! My God, my girlfriend. Tonight. Did he make the bed? Shit! 'Nothing.' Flipping through his mental Roladex of forgotten jobs, he pulls a card, handing Delia a chore like a diner giving a tip. 'There is one thing. If you could go out to Wal-Mart and get me a couple of things?'

Oh please don't smile like that!

'Sure!' Flushed and delighted, Delia snatches the ATM card Theo absently hands over and heads out to score perfumed soap and candles to show Carey that he cares enough to do things right. He woke up so hungover this morning that he can't remember if he even emptied the sink. Carey's coming. Was it the Zax score, or did he purposely forget? If he forgot, why did he? Did Dad really call him earlier today? What was he on about? Good news?

Listen, he loves Carey Lassiter – pretty, urban, chic, and he's a little bit afraid of this encounter. Can he really make her buy Plan A and keep her in this nowhere town? Amazing Free Offer. Not marriage, that would be cheap. He's going to offer to front for her while she lives out every writer's dream. It's the major business of this weekend, that starts – oh shit, about an hour ago. And Theo is still waiting for his story to clear the copy desk. He doesn't want to do the edit by phone because he needs to see it slotted in. If he blows off this vigil and heads for the airport Chick might bump it and move Sally or Arch into his spot. Ambition keeps him in place. Leave now and Arch could get the arraignment, Chick could give Sally the jailhouse interview with Mrs Zax.

The funny thing is, he needs to be with his own people now. There's no way for him to explain to Carey how a job she classifies with Froot Loops could make his belly tighten and his heart thud. How do you communicate the rush? What words does he know? How can he make Carey see what he saw at the quarry when they cleared the sludge off the windshield and he looked into Preston Zax's face? Sally knows. Everybody in this newsroom knows. These are his people. He has to be with them right now. They understand. So like a guest reluctant to leave a good party, Theo hangs in with Sally and Arch and Chick and Fred and Anita, swapping gross one-liners while at the airport, Carey waits. He gets the idea they're all like characters in that old Buñuel movie, trapped in this existential house where nobody comes and nobody goes. If the sheep dies, you don't push it outside. You cook and eat the sheep. OK, he can't leave. He can't quite leave even after the page proof comes up and he sees his bylined story running down the right-hand column under that banner head that he's beginning to think of as his. Lingering, he runs a last gag by Chick, whose big laugh tells him that for the moment, the master is pleased.

He's heading out when he collides with Delia. 'I'm back.'

'You're back?'

'You know. Back with your stuff?' Beaming, she proffers a plastic shopping bag bulging with soap and candles and rolls of White Cloud; the Zax thing kept Theo so busy he even ran out of that.

'Oh, that. Oh, thanks.' He takes it from her absently. 'That's great! Now what do I owe you?'

'You gave me your ATM card.' When Theo takes it and thanks her, Delia beams. 'My pleasure. But.' Her tone is bright and sweet. 'You didn't tell me what all this is for.'

'Can't talk now.' There isn't time. Got to shed this person and get cracking. 'Um. Ah. Visitor.'

'Your mom?'

'No.' They haven't exactly been in touch.

'Somebody special?'

'I have to go now, Delia, OK?'

'Wait! Remember how you came in and I said I had something to tell you and you said after you finished?'

'I'm sorry, I forgot.'

'No you didn't.'

He sighs. 'What is it, Delia?'

'It's about your story,' she says.

'The paper's closed.'

'It's about the Zaxes. I know you're in a hurry but OK, I know you need to know this and I'm the only one who can . . .' Her grin is secretive and wild. Her voice drops. 'I was in their house.'

'So was I.'

'They had me over,' she says anyway. 'Like, all the time? I was their friend.'

Maybe it's fatigue, Theo doesn't ask. He just waits.

'And there's something else.' Delia whispers as if she is confessing something dirty. 'About the house?'

Wary now, Theo is judging and sorting. What does the night intern know? Would she lie to please him? He's stuck with the girl and the story she stands up in. Eager. Say anything to get ahead. OK Slate, better blow her off. But nicely. Carey's plane is on the ground. 'If it's that good, write it!'

'I can't. It's too big.'

'Look, if it's really important, you'd better tell the cops.'

'It's not that kind of important. I'm just trying to help you, OK?'

Oh, is that all? Theo knows better than to send her to clean up his house for Carey. Not because Delia wouldn't do anything he asks, paint the kitchen, bring in flowers, but he doesn't want her there. He doesn't want her there because – Theo thinks there's a Yiddish word for it – it would cost him more than it's worth.

'You've already done plenty. Go home and get some sleep.'

But Delia is between Theo and the way out, stalling him

with that unremitting sunny smile. 'I'm too excited. Who can sleep? There's got to be *something* I can do.'

It's transactional. Give her a job and she'll let him go. 'OK, Delia, you want to help? OK, listen. There is one thing.'

Her voice dissolves like milk chocolate. 'Anything!'

'OK, then.' The elevator doors open and he backs in. He spreads his arms like Samson as the doors bump his outstretched hands and recede. 'You really know the Zaxes' house?'

'I told you. I went over there all the time. Really. I was their friend.'

She probably wasn't, but Theo asks, 'So you can get inside?'

Delia turns several colors. 'I can get in anywhere.'

'OK,' he says. 'Thing is, I accidentally left something?'

'And you want me to go get it?' She's ready to go.

'In the living room. But, OK. If they stop you, I never told you to get it, and if you get it, nobody knows you've got it, OK?'

'Oh. I get it. OK.'

'If you can get this thing I need, and get it to me?'

'Don't worry, I'll get it.' She looks so pleased! It's as if he's given her a crown and set her up on a Rosebowl float.

If he tells her the place is sealed, Delia is in more trouble than if she doesn't know. Still, he owes her at least one disclaimer. 'There's a problem. The cops have sealed the house.'

She gives him a brash grin. 'No problem, I'm on it.'

'Wait a minute. Maybe this is a bad idea.'

'I said I could do it.'

'I know you can do it, I just don't know.'

'Please?'

Yeah this isn't ethical but he isn't doing it, either. She is. But Theo hesitates as the elevator doors bash his hands one more time in an attempt to close and end this part of the long night. Over Delia Vent's head he sees his best friend tapping away at his terminal – what has Arch got now, is he onto something new? – Sally's conferring with Chick, tomorrow's hounds are already running up his heels. 'OK,' Theo says. 'What I need you to get for me is . . . This item. It belonged to Preston Zax.'

She stiffens like a dog waiting to snatch a Milk Bone.

'It's this brown leather book?'

'A book.'

'I think it's a diary. Under the pillow.' When she blinks, too polite to ask which pillow, he adds, 'In their easy chair.'

Delia says too fast, 'Like, the Barcalounger.' She turns as if to plunge down the fire stairs.

'They don't have a Barcalounger.'

'Whatever. You got it,' she says.

'Wait.' Theo understands that this is going to put him in debt to her. 'This is a bad idea. You can't get in. They've probably posted a cop.'

Delia sees Theo wavering; the rubber lips of the elevator doors gnaw at him in one more attempt to swallow him as she says significantly, 'There's more than one way inside a place.'

'Look, Delia, forget it. Let's not do this tonight, OK?'

But like it or not, Theo has set her in motion. It's too late to stop. Unleashed, the intern changes before his eyes. She sets her jaw. 'No way.' This is how Delia Vent surprises him. Decisively, she ends the standoff. She shoves Theo back into the elevator and pushes the button that will send him straight to the lobby. As the doors close on him she rasps in a new, gutty voice, 'If you don't get it, your so-called friend Sally Wyler will.'

8

Theo drives too fast because he really is excited to have Carey here after this long drought. He thinks about her all the time, hangs on the phone as if that will keep them connected, which they haven't been since he left her behind in the brokerage at the first of the year. In a way, it's ironic, who chose to do what. The woman he loves came out of a goddamn graduate writing program. It's not like going to dental school and coming out a dentist at the end. Carey graduated but that didn't make her a writer. Carey ended up at the brokerage because she had to eat but she still dreams. They bonded over dreams. Now she is in venture capital, while Theo finished an MBA and after six months bailed out of the brokerage to save his life. When he left New York for Middle America, they hugged and promised it wouldn't be for long. They talked about being together, they talked about love. But he wants his terms, she wants hers. When he replays their farewell Theo suppresses the subtext: *no promises*. Carey, trailing her fingers down his arms with that Carey smile: 'We'll see.'

They will, if he can just keep her here. He has a plan.

He rushes into the terminal. He loves her so much but they fight about art and life. How could he make her wait? He sees Carey before she sees him. Beautiful: elegant head with that slash of thick hair, fur vest even though it's spring, stovepipe Levis, three-hundred-dollar boots. There's a glitch in his breathing, like a dragonfly buzzing in his throat. He's been putting it off. Afraid she'll say no. 'Carey!'

'Doctor.' Carey clutches her throat like a plague victim and pretends to fall off the seat. 'Thank heaven you've come.'

It's going to be OK! With a wild laugh, Theo catches her. They hit the industrial carpeting in a jumble. Rolling, they hug and laugh until Carey slips away and sits up with a commanding glare; for a minute she looks like Chick. 'Where the hell were you?'

'Murder. Killer's mother did it. Page One.'

Carey repeats patiently, 'Page One.'

'All editions. I broke the story, Care.'

'You broke the story.'

'The mother handed it to me!' Why can't he make this terrific woman smile and why won't she look at him?

Her mouth is trembling. She's either about to laugh or else she's trying not to lose it. It's hard to know. 'I see.'

He gets up. When she doesn't take his hand he lifts his voice as if to lift her. 'You know what it's like. You're a writer.'

'Not any more.' Not a good sign. He'd forgotten. He and Center City are on trial.

'I thought you'd be glad.'

She says, 'God, this *place*.'

'Oh shit, Carey, I'm so sorry.'

The woman Theo loves may want to hug him and have it over with but she's been stretched too tight. 'I thought you'd never come.'

'Deadline,' he says. 'I'm sorry.'

'And none of this matters.'

'Of course it matters. You matter. It's hard to explain. I love you.'

Her face breaks open. 'I missed you.'

'Me too.' They hug after all and after this terrible long time he smells and feels Carey through the clothes and she feels him through the jacket and the shirt and the damn regulation tie; their bodies remember, so they may be all right. He hopes. When Theo and Carey lie down together, most things are forgotten and the rest seems good; wait till he gets her home! His breath rushes into her ear. 'But now we're here, and tomorrow . . .' He's lying and he knows it. 'Tomorrow is all yours.'

'We have a lot to talk about.'

Her tone is ominous but he says, 'I know.' He doesn't have the heart to tell her that there's no place in town for her to wear the suits and dresses in the Vuitton carryon. Driving in from the airport Theo takes the scenic route. He's so used to Center Street that he likes the granite heaps with their Middle-American charm. Ayuh, there's Beazely's Department Store, third-generation owner, and over there, Welch's Jewelry, where he's priced rings, next to the fourth-generation shoe store; looks like one of his grandmother's *Saturday Evening Post* covers, uh huh. Whatever internal sentries remain on guard keep Theo from saying, 'What do you think?'

She tells him anyway. 'How do you stand it here?'

And the street? It's like seeing a lover morph into a bag lady just as you present her to Mom. Under the yellowish wash of sodium vapor lights, Center Street is *Wisconsin Death Trip* squared. Too many local businesses belly up. Too many plate-glass windows occupied by recycled store dummies dressed by the Future Farmers of America, Junior Achievers, the local Y, anything to make the main drag look less moribund. It's late. Even the bars are shuttered. In the nasty glare the brightest neon pales. Center City's toytown facades look drained of life, as if some cosmic vampire has seized on the town and sucked out the living blood. Theo says, 'It isn't where you are, Carey. It's what you're doing that counts.'

'Don't be so sure.'

'I guess I should have brought you a different way.'

'Is there one?'

'But look. That's the *Star*.' To Theo it looks like home.

50

Even at this hour lights are burning: Sally still there? Arch on a bench with his shoes off, flaked. Chick. His story on the national wire.

Carey's voice drops. 'That? That's it? It's so *small*.'

'It looks better in daylight. You'll see.' Boy it's late, boy he is trashed, she'll come around tomorrow when she sees him at work. After they've had a chance to be alone.

'I'm sorry, Theo. It's late. I'm tired.'

His voice blurs with desire. 'Let's go home.'

Together after all this time. Theo Slate, wrecked in love with Carey Lassiter. But also wired. Filled to the eyes with new material, edgy and tipped off-center because where he's been – no, where this story is taking him – he does not know yet. Meanwhile his beautiful Carey won't talk to him. Unlike the light in the refrigerator, Carey does not turn off when he closes the door. What have you been doing, Care? Who with? In spite of all this compressed *life* they need to share, the silence in the car is intense.

He reaches for her hand.

She rubs his palm with a fingertip and does not speak.

He says into the silence, 'Wait till you see the house.'

And if something stirs in the bushes outside Theo's house as the car rounds the last corner and pulls into the cul de sac where his house sits like a solitary milk crate, he is too wacked out to see. At least Fir Street puts in a better performance than Center Street, with its hundred-year-old maples and sprawling Victorian houses with wide front porches straight out of some sweet, irrelevant past. From here you can almost hear the squeaking of porch swings. They are home free, or almost. They're home free if he can hit the cul de sac and roll into the garage before Carey gets a good look at his place. It's the one-bedroom ranch tacked like a Post-It on the far end of the distinguished old street, where it shrinks behind a stand of trees like an unwanted guest.

Carey says in that tone, 'That's it?'

'It needs work.' He doesn't tell her the landlord says any improvements are Theo's problem, not his. He hasn't even told her he doesn't own the house, although she can probably guess, Carey, who chose security over art. Securities, yeah right, some joke. He coasts into the garage. 'Wait till you see inside.' Ack, he has to get Delia's sacks out of the trunk and rush the White Cloud into the john before Carey finds out. Oh God, he's been away from home so much he can't remember what it's like. In the kitchen his cereal bowl is right where he left it, next to yesterday's. Congealed oatmeal makes the dirty spoons stand straight up. Pizza boxes and his cartons from Ming Gardens overflow the trash; if Carey starts digging she'll probably find the barrel from last week's Colonel chicken, encrusted chopsticks, all the mess he left behind when he stopped living and started chasing Zax.

He lies. 'The cleaning lady didn't come,' he says, kicking a throw rug over the burned place in the linoleum where he forgot that steak and the broiler flared up. 'I was going to have flowers on the table. I was going to do a lot of things, but.'

In this light she looks small and tired. Sighing, she supplies the rest. 'Things came up.'

'A big story. But hey, look. Picture window over the sink. Dishwasher. Dispos-al. I was going to paint for you but at the *Star* you work fourteen-hour days just to keep your place in line.'

'That's another thing,' Carey says, but does not go on. He hears her high-heeled boots making hollow sounds on the bare hardwood as she leaves his explanations behind. Living room. He wonders emptily if she likes the sofa and chrome coffee table, bought with her minimalist taste in mind. Did he clean up in there Wednesday after he ate? Did he throw out the Dunkin' Donuts box? Click click. Hall. Click. She crosses it in one step. Bedroom. At least he made the bed. Click. He wonders if she'll be glad he sprang for the king-sized bed with the built-in shelf, even though it cleaned out his bank account. The Escher print. Bertoia chair. Noguchi shade. Her taste, not his. She'd better like the striped duvet. Click. Bathroom. Too late to run in with the toilet paper. Did he clean the tub? He is waiting for her to go into the bedroom he's fixed up as an office. He's waiting for her to call him: 'Theo, what's this?' Then he'll go into the doorway and put his arm around her waist and say, 'It's for you.' Activate Plan A. He even wrote a speech. *So you can pull together your collection of poems and win a prize. Be a poet after all.* Translated: *Quit your job and let me take care of you.* She clicks into the kitchen where Theo stands, empty-handed, under the harsh fluorescent strip.

'Nice.'

He is painfully aware of smudged cabinets, the naked, harshly reflective window and movement in the night beyond, as if branches of the newly leafed trees are bobbing as some unknown closes on the house. He says sadly, 'You missed the office.'

'Office?'

'I fixed it up for you.'

'Why would I want an office here?'

'You know. Do what you've always, always wanted. Stay with me and write poetry.'

'Oh,' she says with an uncertain laugh. 'Poetry.'

'It isn't how much money you make that makes the difference,' he says. It's the speech he made when he quit the firm. 'It's how you live your life. You have to feel good about yourself.'

'I feel fine about myself.'

He should be warned by her tone but he rushes on. 'You always wanted to write. I'm offering you a chance.'

'You've got to be kidding.'

'Hell no, I'm not kidding. By the time it's done I'll have a job on some big paper. We'll go back to New York on our own terms.'

Carey says without inflection, 'I'm already there.'

She looks so unhappy that he says, 'Care?'

'It's a good thing I came. I just hope I came in time.' For the first time since the airport, she smiles. 'It's. Oh look, I have wonderful news for you.'

He's been afraid to think about it; what his father meant. 'Then it's true.'

For the first time since they came inside, she smiles. Her whole face blazes with it. Then she puts it to him. 'There's a job opening up.'

His heart leaps. '*Newsweek*? The *Times*?'

'No, a job that pays real money,' she says. 'At the firm.'

'I'm done with the firm.'

'You don't understand,' she says too brightly. 'It's writing.' Carey's voice is light; she could be handing him his big present. 'They want to pay you for writing.'

He says warily, 'Writing what?'

'Publicity. Public Relations. Ted Wollinger just quit. I told your dad and he made a couple of calls.' Carey reaches for his hands. 'They were going to phone you with the offer but I said I wanted to hand carry it. Oh, Theo. Your time in securities, now this experience reporting. You're perfect for the job.'

'I thought you came out here to . . .' Warily, he turns, accusing. 'Is this my father's idea?'

'He thinks it's wonderful.'

'Dad. Calling in his markers.' Theo is grateful that his father has any remaining markers but it doesn't take the edge off his anger. 'Don't you think that's kind of cheap?'

'The office is going to want to know where you are with this. I knocked some heads to get it for you,' she says, telling him more than she means to. 'We're counting on you. Don't say no.'

'You'd rather have me there doing something I hate?' It is so odd, Carey and his father in collusion.

She begs the question. 'I'd rather have you there.'

'Well I'd rather have you here.' Take that, Dad. I wish I could relive your life so you win at the end, but I can't. 'This is who I am, Carey. Get used to it. Look,' he says, even though she's pissed and this is not the best time to do it. He knows better than to renew his Amazing Free Offer but it's all he has to put on the table. Prepare the way, then. Make her uncertain. Drive the wedge, drive the wedge. He tries, 'I love you, Care. It's time you got in touch with who you are.'

Vuitton bag Armani suit hair cut in a midtown haute couture line like a gash flip phone laptop modem with fax capabilities she says, 'I know who I am, Theo.' Her look challenges him: *Do you?*

'Does it make any difference to you that I love you?'

'I know you do,' she says. This is the saddest part. 'I know you do.' In spite of which Theo kisses her and makes promises and without believing a word Carey lets him draw her into the bedroom.

She murmurs into his ear, 'Don't say no to this.'

He doesn't. He says, 'I love you so much.'

Her reserve crumples at last and she grins. 'I need a shower.'

He puts out his hands. 'I just want to be with you.'

Yielding, she warns, 'Well you can't be with me here.'

'Oh Carey. Oh.'

She locks herself into the bathroom and, trying to frame the right words for Round Two, Theo pads around like the TV householder, putting out the lights and turning off the cat. He checks the back door. *You can't sell your soul and still have a life.* He closes the Levelors in the big front window and notes the absence of life in his answering machine. *You have to do what you're born to do. You have to take risks!* The mail. Maybe he got mail. He's been so busy that he hasn't looked for days. *Here. With me.* Carefully – when did he become so responsible? – he opens the front door. It's odd; in the remarkably still spring night he

55

is conscious not of movement, but of recent movement; it's as if something big and amorphous has just rushed by. Cut it out, Slate. Get out of this head and close the damn door. For a minute he forgets why he opened it. Oh, right. Mail. His toe hits something soft. It's a Jiffy Bag. Letter bomb? Not in Center City. Pick it up, Theo. Take it inside. Asshole, close the door. Wary, he tries to identify the contents without opening it. If he's tense, it's just sexual tension. Carey in the bathroom, and out here, this. It looks like. He peeks. It is. The Zax book. He weighs it. He ought to open it but he really doesn't want to touch it. He doesn't want to touch anything of Preston Zax's tonight and then touch Carey with the same hands. He can't open the package; he can't put it down.

Then Carey comes out, scrubbed pink with her hair all cloudy, wild curls beaded with the hot bathroom mist. She murmurs, 'Hey?'

'I love you, Carey, but you've got to do what you've got to do, you know?'

She drops the towel. 'Let's don't talk about this now.'

'OK!' Shoving Zax's book back in the mailer uncracked, he drops it, forgetting undelivered speeches, Zax, everything. He's waited so long! 'Oh, Carey.' He walks into her arms. 'Oh, you!'

'Tomorrow we'll . . .'

'Tomorrow,' he mumbles without letting her go. 'Sure.' Theo draws Carey in with him while he showers; even as they stand together under the spray he is aware that she has changed and no matter what they do tonight, whatever is between them is doomed to change but he rushes on, understanding that things have happened in the past week that leave him changed. He is smoked by the flickering image of Preston Zax; it surfaces and bobs like a pagan mask: back, damn you. Down. Back! But then he feels Carey's hand sliding down his slick belly in a subtle, lingering touch so nearly valedictory that Theo knows it is over even before Carey knows, God damn you Mrs

Stella Zax, you and your sacred mission; God damn your son, and then Carey's hand completes its movement and he pulls her into the bedroom. Later they will separate and look at each other straight on. Later they will fight but for the moment *this* is the moment and Theo dives into Carey's sweet, familiar body and for the time being, forgets.

9

Theo is in early. Walking into the newsroom, he straightens with a little *click*. He is a different person here. Not a better person, exactly, but a different one. Love is unsure, but work is certain. He may not know what he's doing with Carey but he knows exactly what he's doing here. It's his job. If he can't keep Carey, his job may turn out to be his life. Never mind what promises she made in love last night. Today is about Preston Zax. His notebook. Gonzo story waiting in these pages; catch the wave and he can ride it out of here. He won't tell Sally and Arch until he breaks the story – serial rights somewhere big, guest shots on network news. Eat your hearts out, friends. He got up at dawn and came here because he doesn't want anybody around when he does this. He's going to saw the top off Preston Zax's skull and look inside. Take a stick and poke around in the killer's naked brain.

But just when he thinks he's alone Delia lunges out of her cubicle, catching her foot on the wheel of her chair and righting herself with such a joyful look that it makes him wince. She's been lying in wait. When he wound his intern up last night and set her ticking, Theo never guessed she'd deliver the goods. When did she get to be his intern anyway? About the time he started owing her. She's his, as in his responsibility.

'Did you get it? Do you have our book?' Freshly scrubbed and wearing a flowered number with the price tag dangling,

Delia waits for praise. Her proud grin makes it clear that he
owes her big.

'Um. Yeah. In here.' He rips the Jiffy Bag getting the
book out and grey fluff flies.

She leans in, craning. 'This is so cool, what's in it? What
does he say in there? I mean, what is it like?'

'Terrific. Absolutely terrific,' he says as if that does it.
She is standing too close. 'So thanks. Really.' Does he really
think she'll say 'You're welcome' and go?

'Better not ask me how I got it.'

Morning light slants in; dust floats in sunshot layers. Sally
and Arch are still in the sack. Even tough old Anita is still
in bed. Except for the yawning night man, marooned in the
slot until Chick gets in, he and Delia are alone. He needs
to dismiss her so he can do this. 'So, thanks again.'

'One A, all editions, two days running.' Beaming, she
hands him a page proof. 'I'm so proud of you. If you'd sign
this for me?'

'Sign it?'

Flash forward to Theo in some bookstore, signing a
thousand copies of – what? Unlike Carey, Delia knows
what he does here matters. He grins. 'I feel dumb doing
it, but sure.' The night police reporter passes on his way
out. Theo hides the notebook; this is too big to let anybody
see before he files.

'Thanks,' Delia can't stop smiling, 'so much!'

'So I guess that's it.' But she lingers. Pile it on, Theo.
'Fantastic, Delia. The book. I never thought you could do
it!'

The sound of her name makes the girl turn colors.
'But I did.'

OK, everybody has a right to tell her story. 'So, how'd
you get it? How'd you get in?'

Morning light washes Delia's fond, blind smile. 'I just
did.' In her excitement, she violates Theo's air space. Call
NATO. Launch the SCUDs.

He steps backward. 'Terrific.'

Like a synchronized swimmer, Delia moves with him. With that sweet, round face she looks like a child today, too young to notice that people don't like it when you stand too close. Yet there is something about her air of resolution; she waits with the concentration of a woman who's older than she looks. 'You haven't told me what's in the book.'

'I – ah . . .' *Haven't looked.* This person broke a police seal to get this notebook for him; she risked arrest and he hasn't even opened it? Churlish, right, but, Carey. Carey last night. Carey this morning, Carey in his eyes and in his mouth. Carey is still in his bed and nothing between them is resolved. And he is here.

'Like, what does it say?'

'Ah . . .' Distracted, Theo waits for the girl to go away. If I'm doing this, he thinks, I'm doing it for the mother. When Stella called him to the house to witness her arrest, she made him an amazing gift. Murderer-mother confesses to the *Star*. To me. He is struck by the strange, sweet weight of the woman's attention. As if she has conferred some responsibility. As if he has a mission here. What does she want in return? Vindication? Just to have her story told? What is her story, anyway? He hefts the Zax notebook. Is the answer in here? Questions woke him while it was still dark. *The book!* Sleeping Carey stirred and threw out an arm as if to keep him. He rolled out anyway, maybe because he knows how all their conversations are going to end. He stumbled into the front room. The book mailer lay on the coffee table like a living thing that you don't want to touch. It makes him feel dirty. It's like having a porno tape. You want to know everything that's in it, but you don't much want to see it. And you don't want anybody you love to catch you looking. No one can know.

When he doesn't answer, Delia cries, 'You haven't opened it!'

OK, this person put herself on the line for him, so he owes her something. He constructs a polite lie. 'I was waiting for you.'

'No you weren't. I know. You got all busy with that Carey and forgot.'

He turns, surprised. 'Carey!'

'You know.'

Did I tell you about Carey? 'Carey is my business, OK?'

'Well, sorry!'

'You did a good job,' he says. 'Sorry I snapped.'

Naturally Delia forgives him with that sweet smile. 'I'm so glad you waited. Can we look at it now?'

'Sorry. I have to do this, OK?' Her face crumples so he says quickly, 'Look, I'll get your name on the bottom of the story. Extra material by. How's that?' It should be enough but it isn't. She hangs in with this avid smile. He won't open the book and she won't back off. He tucks the unopened book under his arm.

Hurt, she says, 'Am I in the way?'

'It's OK.'

Gotcha. Grin. 'You mean I can see the book?'

She's standing so close that he can feel her breath. Sighing, he pulls it out. 'OK.' The shiny binding makes Theo wonder. Was Zax really that neat that he could carve initials in a woman's body and then go and write about it without smearing the book with vestigial blood? When he runs a finger under the gold-stamped cover, it separates from the endpapers with a little snap that tells him what he needs to know before he opens it. *Oh. Oh, right.*

Empty.

Dead empty. Zax hasn't even bothered to put his name in it.

Delia says, 'What's the matter?'

'The book.' Theo catches the thin gold ribbon bookmark. The end is crumpled, as if the book sat on its shelf undisturbed ever since Stella gave it to Preston and he forgot.

Mechanically, he flips pages, checking every opening from beginning to end, front to back, top to bottom. He never wrote in this book. There are no signs that he ever intended to write in it. It's one of those presents a mother gives in hopes that the right present will change his life. Theo takes the book by its spine and shakes it. A carefully printed Christmas gift tag drops out.

FOR PRESTY FROM MOTHER
WRITE AND GROW WISE

That's all. This was never Preston Zax's secret journal. It's just another fucking idea Stella had. One of those presents from Mom that isn't really a present. Designed to improve. Shelved untouched and forgotten until yesterday when Theo picked it up. The girl waits. 'There's nothing you need to see.'

Shifting, Delia tries to see over his shoulder. 'Is something wrong? Did I get the wrong book?'

For a second Theo wonders: what if Delia pulled a switch and this is a duplicate? What if she has a deal with the *National Inquirer*? Not her, not nice, unvarnished DeliaMarie Vent with her no-color curls and her big skirts, not Delia, who seems more upset than he is. 'No,' he says kindly. 'It's the right book.'

'Then what's the matter?'

'It's just empty is all.'

'Empty!' Angry, she smashes her chest. 'It's my fault.'

'It's not your fault.' Without the notebook Theo has to think fast or he'll lose A One. He can't wait until Monday to get the interview with Stella. He has to double back now. He has to see her today. He has to . . . His mind has dropped the book and hung up its coat and gone to work but he and Delia are still suspended here.

She bangs her chest again. 'I'll make it up to you.'

'Hey,' he says. 'Don't cry.' Anything if you just won't

cry. Anything. 'You did good. Hey,' he adds rashly, 'I'm proud of you.'

She brightens. 'Oh, thank you!'

Do you ever see somebody smile at you and know that just now, you have become their idol? That's where Theo is today. After the uneven night with Carey, a little adulation is not so bad. Still, it's embarrassing. The shining eyes. The smile. That he needs at least one person who thinks he's perfect just as he is. 'No prob.'

She says, louder, 'I'll make it up to you!'

'You don't have to make it up to me.' If he doesn't let her, she's going to cry.

'There must be something I can do.'

'OK. OK.' He casts around for some formula to release her. Something to move her out of his personal air space so he can think. 'Tell you what. Why don't you check out the high school? Try and get his records. Yearbook for Zax's year. Find out which classmates are still in town. Call as many as you can. If you get even one good quote, I'll buy you dinner.'

She pounces. 'Tonight?'

'Soon,' he promises.

'Dinner? Really?' All the parts of her face click into place. It's like making Mr Potato Head smile. 'Oh, thank you!' She runs.

He tells Sally over lunch at the Spot. 'Thought I had something, but I came up empty. I've got shit for tomorrow.'

'Bummer,' she says. One thing about Sally that he likes. They are better than colleagues. He can spend the rest of his day explaining what this means to Carey, but Sally already knows.

'Yeah.'

'At least things are good with your girlfriend, right?'

'Could I get back to you on that?'

In this light Sally's eyes are like sea glass. 'Oh shit.'

'I'm OK,' he says quickly. 'Notebook's a wipeout, but I'm going after the mother.'

A voice he doesn't expect breaks in. 'I said I was sorry!'

'Where did you come from?'

Sally says wearily, 'Hello, Delia.'

The intern drops a sheaf of notes on the table in front of Theo with a complicit grin. 'The stuff you wanted? This is it.' Then, without speaking to Sally, she wheels. 'We can talk about it later, right?'

'Yeah. Right.'

'Over dinner?'

'Not tonight.' Oh yes he is in Delia's debt. And for nothing. The killer's book? The book that Theo broke the law and unleashed this girl and got into her debt for and lied, sort of, to get hold of? The book, Theo thinks, standing here with the day's story lying in tatters around his ankles. It was never anything but blank.

10

Angola, Indiana

He has had to put the notebook aside. He is gripping the edges of the Formica table to keep from roaring up like a rocket and crashing to the sky; if he holds completely still he can keep the rage inside. Otherwise the forces inside him will blow the top of his skull like the cap off a volcano and everything will come boiling out in a spray of fire and blood. Hair all over the ceiling. *Look what you did,* he thinks, and his jaw is so tight he can hear his teeth shatter. No one must see what he is thinking. No one.

After everything I did for you!

Sun slants into the mundane midwestern diner with its sleepy patrons and sweet, lone waitress in a soiled peach uniform. Above the cash register, the *Today* show comes in mostly in shades of pink and green on the badly tuned color TV.

All he was doing was waiting for his coffee. He was sitting here with his notebook when he heard, lining up his headings on a fresh page: 1, 2, 3. Then the news came in one of those five-minute capsules at twenty-five minutes after the hour, pretty woman speaking into a nerf ball with TV 8 on the stem: 'And, in area news . . .'

It rocked him. It rocked the table. He got up and bought the local newspaper. Look at it. The table trembles. *Look.*

MOTHER BOOKED IN SERIAL KILLER MURDER

How could you? After everything I did for you?

And underneath the headline, the mother's picture, grave face staring out at him, the woman he has spent his life trying to make reparations to, how could she do a thing like this to him:

This is what you would have looked like if you had lived.

11

The kitchen is a glistening reproach to him. Carey is so pissed and distracted that she has Windexed every surface. She's even mopped. When Theo proffers the box from Capricorn Florists she just looks at him. When he tries to hug her, she backs away.

'Oh, Carey! Didn't you get my note?'

'I got your note.'

'I called.'

'I know you called. You called but you weren't here.'

'I called and I thought you were OK with it.'

'Why would I be OK with it?' Her Filofax is on the counter. 'I came all this way!'

'Oh hell, Carey, I'm sorry. It's this story.'

'I know what it is,' she says. 'I just don't know why you think it's so important. Especially now.' She does not have to say *now that you have a better offer*. Her silence makes him understand that all he has to do now is accept it and everything will change.

'Because it is important.' The silence gets so long that he blurts, 'You haven't even opened the flowers.'

'Oh. The flowers. Thanks for the flowers. You can put them in a vase.'

'A vase. A vase. I don't know if I even have a vase.'

She turns away. 'It's under the sink.'

He pulls out a mayonnaise jar and jams the flowers into it tissue paper and all. He carries the jar into the living room.

'Better leave that in the kitchen. It's wet on the bottom.'

Oh God, she's cleaned up the living room. He retreats to the kitchen to think up his next line. He sticks the jar on the table. The flowers look brave and sad. A dozen tulips and daffodils died, and for this. He goes back to her. 'I was hoping you'd be glad to see me. I was hoping we could talk.'

'I waited so long I don't even know if I remember you. So I guess what I need to know,' she says, 'is where the fuck were you all day? What were you doing that's so much more important than me?'

'It's my job,' he says, even though the woman he loves most is slipping her phone and the Filofax into her shoulder bag. Of course she improved the hour by making calls. Yeah, right, Carey. *Waste no time before its time.*

'So I gathered.' Her expression makes it clear that he has not yet said the right thing. This is an important, busy woman who took off from work just to fly out here and bring him this offer he doesn't want; he made her wait at the airport last night and today he left her alone all day, stuck in the house like something you file and forget. He did it so he could do something she thinks doesn't matter. Now at the end of a long day in drab, featureless Center City, just when Theo's supposed to be attending to the woman he loves for a change, the woman he loves is beyond argument. Carey touches his hand with a loving, dismissive smile. 'I used my phone, so it won't show up on your phone bill.'

'What won't?'

'I had to make some calls.'

Perhaps because he knows what's coming Theo says stiffly, 'Some calls?'

'Something came up. Things happened.' She is mocking him in his own words. She adds some of her own. 'I had to change some plans.'

'But look what I brought you.'

'I don't need anything, OK?' She turns away. Her tone

makes it clear she is hurt. No, angry. No. Angry and hurt.

He says in a low voice, 'Don't you think I'd rather be here with you?'

'But you weren't.'

'I wanted to but I got tied up. Maybe when you see this . . .' Unrolling the *Star* like a blueprint of his central nervous system, Theo offers it to Carey, in hopes. *This is me, Care. Heart and blood and bones.* He turns it so the first thing she'll see is his name. 'This is why I was late meeting your plane last night. I got hung up on the same story today. And when you see tomorrow's . . .'

Carey doesn't even look. She rolls the paper like a woman preparing to swat flies. 'I won't be here tomorrow.'

'Don't do this, Carey, I did this for you.' He is talking fast to divert or forestall her. 'Please?'

'You missed my plane and ditched me here and you were doing it for me?'

He offers with a sweet smile, 'It's hard to explain.'

'Don't even try.'

'It's a tough business,' he says anyway. 'They call the shots. I really do love you and if you would just bear with me until I get established . . .'

Her sigh tells him what she thinks of all his efforts here.

He tries to hand her the paper again. 'It may not look like much to you, but it's a start.'

'I know you're busy, but this is hardly *CNN*.' Carey's tone makes it clear that as far as Ms Lassiter is concerned, not only is Theo a sub-lieutenant stationed in outer hell, the army he's chosen is functionally dead. 'It took a while, but I finally got through to the eight-hundred number.'

And because he really *does* love her, Theo persists in spite of the fact that she's already called the airline and arranged her departure. 'Please just let me do this. Then we can—'

'No we can't. If you know I love you, you know we can't.'

'I thought we could . . .'

'I have to pack. Check-in is at four.'

'Does it make any difference to you that I love you?'

'I know you do,' she says. This is the saddest part. 'I know you do.'

He follows her through the dinky house without speaking. And if there's somebody out there on the perimeter that Theo doesn't know about, checking the mailbox and spooking around on his little front stoop; if she stealthily circles the house as they move toward the bedroom, there's no room in his life for this, no room for the knowledge that she will stand in his yard and stare fixedly at the closed bedroom blinds while his scene with Carey plays itself out. If she retreats to the curb across the street to keep the vigil at a safe distance, Theo is too deep in this with Carey even to imagine it. The place seems particularly drab, as if whoever lived here moved out a long time ago. He can't bear to look at the flowers in their jar. Grieving, he follows Carey past the office he fixed up for her and thinks, yeah, right. *I'd do anything,* he thinks but does not say. He just sits miserably on the corner of the king-sized bed he bought with her in mind and watches her pack.

'Can I help you?'

'No.' It doesn't take long. She zips her Valpack shut with the finality of the coroner sealing a body bag. Turning to Theo with a look he will never forgive, she says, 'We might as well go.'

He reaches out. 'Your plane isn't for hours.'

'Don't. It won't make any difference.'

And the watcher may not be close enough to see or hear this, but she knows. As Theo and Carey move into the ritual of separation, already in mourning for the idea of what they used to be, the silent observer rocks with her fists on her thighs and smiles and smiles.

She has him put her out in the loading zone. Carey departs as neatly as she arrived: Vuitton garment bag. Work stacked and waiting in a Vuitton carryon. Carey Lassiter does not waste time. Useless as it is, he says, 'I still love you.'

'I know.'

'I love you but I can't be that person. I'm sorry.'

Carey looks at him straight on. 'No you're not.' She sets her bags down for the ritual hug. Then she runs her hands down Theo's arms, lingering as if, if she can just make the right connection at the fingertips, she can draw him out of this life and back into hers. When they part he can almost hear the *pop*. He wants to say *I love you.* She says, 'If you ever get a real job instead of a toy job, get back in touch.'

He does what you do in a bludgeoned state. Dazed, he drives in circles until he finds his way home. He doubles back on the *Star*. When Chick spots him he lunges up from his chair as if to grab him by the collar. 'Where the fuck have you been?'

Light. Noise. Like a cryonics client unexpectedly brought back to life, Theo blinks. 'Day off.'

'Your backgrounder just got old. The Zax woman phoned right after you left. One phone call and who does she use it on? You.' He moves the cold cigar to one side so he can finish in that sweet-sour tone that is quintessential Chick, 'But you weren't around. I sent Clawson.'

Anita's plum fingernails, all over his story. 'Clawson!' He tries to let competition take his mind off the hurt. That brassy old Pulitzer retro cliché sob sister is cashing in on his source? 'No way.'

'Relax. The Zax woman sent her back. She also sent word. She wants to talk to you.'

Theo's belly makes a savage leap. 'Cool.'

'Get on it.'

'Right.' OK, he isn't going to die. At least not today. One
phone call from the station and the mother-murderer does
not use it on a lawyer. She spends her dime on Theo Slate.
Accept no substitutes. Take that, Anita. Fuck off, Arch.
Hey, Sally, I pulled the day out after all! What can he do?
What else could he do? He does not write any speeches to
Carey who is as he stands there flying out of his reach but
in the back of Theo's head is the hope that if he can pull
this story out, location will stop being an issue. He won't
have to break up with Carey after all. If he does this right,
he can start looking for jobs back in New York.

12

E ven though she specifically sent for him, Stella Zax sits behind the scratched Plexiglas shield without stirring. It's as if he hasn't come. She doesn't pick up the phone. Instead she waits serenely as if whatever she has to say here, Theo already knows. Slab-faced and monumental, the mother-murderer takes on added significance, like the icon of some religion that has not yet been named. Here's a clean, decent woman who tried to do her best. And became a murderer. What toppled her? It is a mystery. He studies Stella Zax. The woman is no longer simply the linchpin to his story. She stands for something more. *A sign,* he thinks. *Are you going to give me a sign?* Like a fish in a punchbowl, he mouths her name: 'Mrs Zax.'

It's getting late. Other prisoners' friends and sobbing relatives have run out of things to say and are filtering out of the visitors' room, stifling sighs of relief that the thing is done. Soon Theo will have to go. He raps the Plexi with the phone. Like an earnest animal trainer, he puts the receiver to his ear with an encouraging smile. Monkey see . . .

She does not move.

Inspired, he pulls out today's *Star* and plasters A One to the shield. Even without glasses she can read the subhead. It was nothing to Carey but Stella Zax will see he has done right by her. Theo's story runs under the industrial-strength banner: *MOTHER BOOKED IN SERIAL-KILLER MURDER.* His story sits next to the five-column by eight-inch photo of the winch lifting Preston Zax's ruined, dripping car. In 20 pt. Metro bold the two-deck subhead reads:

GRIEVING MOM SAYS
'TELL THEM I TRIED'

Patience has never been one of Theo's strong points. He does the only thing he can think of. Like a new dad visiting the hospital nursery, he waves broadly and mouths *Hello*. Mrs Zax does not exactly respond. Instead she stares at the Plexi as if she sees only her own reflection magnified in its marred surface. Does she recognize him? Does she not? If she really wanted to see Theo Slate today, why wouldn't she see him at two, when he first came? Or when he came back at four? Why did she wait until visiting hours were almost over to pull his chain? Minutes to go and she hasn't acknowledged his presence. It's as if he isn't here. She is like a museum-quality reproduction of some primitive deity – mute, brooding stone.

At last he rips a page out of his notebook and prints: ONE PHONE CALL, AND YOU CALLED ME?

When he presses it to the shield, she nods.

IF WE DON'T TALK IT GOES TO WASTE.

She shakes her head.

Printing furiously, he tries: THEN WHY NOT TALK TO ME?

He hopes she doesn't; he hopes she does. This is so odd. In silence, Stella Zax is filled with promise – it's as if she holds answers to disturbing questions Theo acknowledges but can't yet frame. It's half-past late and if he can pull a story out of this, he has to get moving. He has to tear up the lead to his backgrounder and start with this. He prints: WE'RE OUT OF TIME.

Stella Zax turns her hands to show him they are empty. Her face is slick, featureless and calm. Without the Easter egg pastel coat and coordinated suede shoes she put on for

74

her arrest, stripped of her gold chain and the garish pink suit she selected to meet the arresting officers, Stella Zax is spared the exigencies of demographics. This woman could be anybody. She could be Theo's mom. Still she picks at the collar of her regulation denim shift with the expression of a fastidious, ordinarily stylish woman who has temporarily lost control over her look and will do anything to get it back. It is strange and sad.

Rigid with concentration, Theo waits. It's getting weird in here. So what if he hardly slept? What if he forgot to eat? It doesn't explain what's happening here. Some combination of tension, excitement, the sexual heat of ambition at war with love has bumped him out of the usual and sent him drifting into unknown territory. Some force he can't name has moved Theo into an exaggerated state. If he isn't outside his body, he doesn't have far to go.

A door slams.

And Theo is dislodged. Shaken out of himself. Startled, he sees the room as if from above, he sees the solid part of Theo Slate stuck in on the wrong side of the Plexiglas, my God! What are we, out of body here and if we are, what's next? The long tunnel and the bright light? He grips the counter. Everything is in stasis – Theo, the Zax woman, the air in this dismal room. Then, *wham!* It's as if somebody smacked him in the head. Offguard as he is, wide open and unwitting, Theo is hurled into a new area of vulnerability. Stripped of himself, of all the physical grace and intelligence and faults that make up Theo Slate, and delivered whole into a still, isolated moment in which he perceives himself as either more than Theo Slate – or less. If this woman regarding him through thick Plexiglas could kill her own son, who else can kill? Spinning and disrupted, Theo finds himself shouting even though she can't possibly hear.

'What do you want from me?' He needs to know. Never mind the assignment. This is what drives him. He needs to know. He really needs to know. 'Lady, what do you want from me?'

Stella Zax raises one hand. WAIT.

A few blocks away Chick Wilbur is tinkering with layout, moving Sally's story inside to clear space for Theo's big break which Theo is expected to phone in to Rewrite, to keep Composing from going into overtime. He'll go in to do the polish, but they need to get a start. Visiting hours are almost done and there's nothing in his notebook except grooves where he bore down too hard printing notes to Mrs Zax. Five minutes to go and Stella Zax is mired in that monolithic calm, silent but pleasant, with her smooth, unchanging, affectless smile.

Theo prints: WHAT DO YOU WANT ME TO DO?

Stella blinks. Her head jerks.

Theo either sees or hears the *click*, as if crucial pieces in the intricate machinery of Stella's thinking have finally dropped into place. This is what she's been waiting for. Before his eyes, the woman's surface shifts and begins to change. She is vibrating in her seat like a rocket at lift-off. Theo forgets the Plexi. He forgets the phone. He shouts, 'What? What, lady? *What?*'

On the far side of the shield the killer's mother just gets bigger. Shadows are falling here in the visiting room. Guards are moving in. Soon he will have to go.

Pressed, Theo posts his last note: WHY ME INSTEAD OF A LAWYER?

Here's one she can answer. She picks up the phone. 'I don't need a lawyer.'

Yes! He says carefully, 'Why?' He's got her. He's got her on the line at last and all he can think to ask her is 'Why?' It's bigger than: Why no lawyer? It's even bigger than why she had to kill Preston. Everything hangs on the answer, and Theo doesn't even know what to ask. He jams the phone to his ear as if that will make her speak. He stares until his eyeballs dry out. In another few seconds they'll crack and shatter but he can't stop staring. In this fixed, intense moment, it's as if the boundaries between murderess and reporter are dissolving; Theo is no detached observer. He's in deep here. 'Why me?'

This is how Stella Zax marks him. 'Because I knew you'd understand.' Her passion rattles them both. 'I *loved* him!'

'I know you did. But look.' The weight of her attention is so terrible that Theo backs away. Forgive him, he tries to create a diversion. 'You don't need me, you need a good lawyer.'

'What would I want with a lawyer?' Shrugging, she sums up all she has to say today. 'I killed Preston. Why not die?'

'You shouldn't say that, Mrs Zax.'

'I loved him,' she says. 'So I killed him. That's all.'

He hears that ding: *Good story.* So he prompts her, 'And?'

Her hands fly up to cover her mouth; he can't see her mouth and her voice is muffled, so he can't be sure. He thinks he hears her saying, 'I would do it again.'

Did she say that or did she not say that? Damn the no tape recorder. Damn not being sure. 'Would you repeat that?'

She shakes her head.

'What did you say?'

'Nothing,' she says with a sweet mother's smile. 'That's all, I think. Oh. You asked. Because I like you. I called you because I like you. Besides . . .'

The palms of his hands are itching. 'Ma'am?'

And Stella Zax blindsides Theo and sends him staggering. Murmuring in that low tone that makes him wonder if she actually said it, she puts this into the air in this sealed, congested room; she says, 'You remind me of him.' And this is how she rivets Theo Slate, how she holds his attention and will not let him go until she has given orders; this is how she charges him: 'You tell all this. How I am. How he was, and then . . . You make it stop.'

Nothing in the room has changed but Theo is changed. The clock says the same thing. It's two minutes to six. Guards are removing the other prisoners routinely, as if nothing cosmic has happened here. Time to wrap this up. Ask the last routine question. Fold up your expectations. Get up. Go. Theo can't wait to leave, is casting around desperately for ways to stay. Should he try to disappear in this room, like, hide under the counter or flatten out like a postage stamp so the guards don't notice? Even if he does hide, they're going to move Zax on back to her cell. Should he sock a guard and get busted? What does he think Stella Zax is going to do while he's in the holding cell, tap out messages on the pipes? *You have to explain, Mrs Zax. I need* . . . But he has all he's going to get today. Carefully, Theo suppresses all signs of urgency and asks the routine question. 'Do you have any more to say to our readers?'

'You tell them.'

'Tell them what?'

'You know. Now you make it stop.'

Stormed, he gasps, 'But you haven't told me anything!'

The smooth surface of Stella Zax begins to slide down her face like an avalanche. Everything in her breaks. Even her voice falls to shards. 'I already did.' She is shattered and weeping, shuddering with sobs. The guard touches her arm, signifying that this visit is over. Her farewell astounds him. 'Goodbye, son.'

He says reflexively, 'I'm not your son.'

'Don't be so sure.'

13

Angola, Indiana

NOTES
A. WAYS TO KEEP THIS TIME FROM BEING LIKE LAST TIME.
1. Re: the abort:
A.

Sun crashes into the diner. Morning is best for thought, his scientist father says. Chemistry experiments taught Father there is a method for everything. As he taught us. Analyze. Organize. Plan.

Haik sits at his usual table in the morning sunlight with his head bent. The notebook is open in front of him. It is like a little church. What comes after A.? He can't think.

It's the clipping in his pocket. It is getting huge.

He has to do this and he can't begin. *Get it right this time or you will kill your mother all over again.* Father's voice follows no matter where he runs. 'You have killed your mother!' Father shouted in that bloody dawn, with her lying at the foot of the stairs. Her scream. Child at the top of the stairs clinging to the rails, yes him, but not him now, OK? Father thudding down the hall. Mother crumpled at the foot of the stairs how old was he anyway, three? Four? Sobbing with Mother lying down there broken, *she fell over me*; she was running for the stairs when she tripped and fell over me, Edward was that small, *why was she running? What was she running from?* Still sees her lying all angles at the bottom

79

of the stairs, with her bones sticking out like coat-hanger parts and her neck folded so her head fell sideways and her jaw cracked wide letting the blood roll out slowly, like Hershey's syrup. His world split in half and some big part of him slipped forever into the chasm. Father's big ugly shadow fell on him. His voice was tremendous. The child's belly still trembles with the words: 'Edward Haik, you have killed your mother.'

Well, Edward is gone. When they got back from the hospital they were alone. Turned into a single parent by the accident, that furious precisionist his father brought him up by the book. *Write down your plans, Edward. You must carry them out by the numbers. One, Two, Three. A. B. C.* Made him what he is. Started all this. Too little to run away he tried but it went wrong; it always went wrong! Father would grind his knuckles into Edward's scalp, saying in that harsh, flat loathing: 'You killed your mother once. Isn't that enough for you? You kill her again every time you fail.'

Driven now to do it right. Do it right and he can put an end to it. Close to it, and now this. Botched efforts, #1 and #2, poor planning. He will not fail this time. But there is this, standing in the way. Every time he starts planning #3 the headline rises up in front of him, filling his head until the letters are twenty feet high. Muttering, he takes out the newspaper clipping and unfolds it and smooths it flat.

MOTHER BOOKED IN SERIAL-KILLER MURDER

Has she come back from the grave to get revenge? *After everything I've done for you.* He loved the mother and the only thing he has left of her is sitting on the table here. 'Look what you did to your mother, Edward! Look what you just did!'

No. Look what she has done to you.

He is sitting in the diner in this sweet turn-of-the-century town with the notebook on the table in front of him, trying to begin. His life is in this book, organized under the headings Father burned into him from after they came home from the hospital alone. When you kill your mother you have to make it up to her. A, B, C. I, II, III. a, b, c. According to plan.

But since this thing in the newspaper: subheading *Killer Mother Confesses* he has been distracted. He has not begun to analyze. Can't organize. Nothing's clear. He doesn't have a plan.

The waitress comes with his coffee. 'With or without?'

'With.' He smiles.

She smiles. 'It's on the side.'

He puts on his everyday face for her. He asks, 'You free after work?'

She is standing too close. She is looking at the clipping. 'What's that?'

Not her fault that she is redolent of the kitchen: steamed cheeseburgers, French fries. 'Nothing,' he says, and covers it with his hand. This one is not prepared, e is *not* prepared no e is not prepared and Haik isn't but he . . . 'You never said if you were free after work.'

Do em, yes? And this will shut you up. Both of you.

Warning, Haik. Robot in *Lost in Space* jangling in his head right now clanking: *Warning. Warning.* But Haik will not listen. Warning. It is folly to begin without a plan.

Even from here Haik can see the veins standing out behind her ear where the blonde curls are pulled back: the soft place in her neck wait a minute, the others went wrong because something was missing, was it a signature? *Mark em. Otherwise how will Mother know it's you?*

14

It gets to be summer. With Carey gone, Theo hardly notices that spring's done for. It's just hotter, is all. He can't figure out why these mornings his pillow case is damp and smelly: sweat. He isn't really noticing much these days. It wouldn't surprise him much if he woke up into some dawn to find the whole world leached of color with everything in half-tones, like bad black-and-white TV. Weird, losing somebody like this even when you think you're the one who put the banana peel in the path of the relationship. Who cares who did it? It hurts just as much when you fall.

He takes a job teaching night classes at the community college. Anything to take his mind off his life. Carey. Stella Zax. The killer mother won't see him and he can't let it alone.

Stupid, but yeah. He needs something to do with his nights. Days are tolerable in life after Carey but. He hates the nights, can't call the woman, can't mail the letters he writes. He stays at work as long as he can so he won't have to think about it. If Carey Lassiter blew him off, he thinks in his current miserable state, it's his fault, not hers. Something about him. He stays after work because he'd do anything for company. For whatever reasons, he's begun coaching the night intern. Teaching her the business. OK, it makes him feel big. He's taught her how to write a good lead and helped her get a feature in shape to pitch to Chick. He's tossed her a bone or two, press releases to rewrite, and a couple have actually run, although Chick doesn't know it yet; they went by him, OK, but from Theo's queue. He sprinkles favors like chicken feed just so he'll have somebody to talk to after everybody's gone. Extra little assignment here, some pointers there, instant gratification in her thanks. So what if she doesn't know when to quit thanking him. At least she smiles at him, which is more than Carey did.

When you feel as low as Theo does, you kind of get off on finding somebody to help. Postponing the inevitable moment when you have to go out and eat alone.

Eventually the night man starts Delia phoning funeral homes and Theo drifts out. Usually he eats at the Spot. If he's lucky Arch comes out and eats with him but sooner or later Arch goes home and no matter what he does to string it out Theo runs out of next things to do. Some nights he looks for Sally or goes by WCEN-TV because Lacey Sparkman has started calling him. It's funny. Since he became. What. Available. Since he became available, Sally's been aggressively matter-of-fact, as if knowing it has made her shy. Alone, Theo trawls the deserted main drag looking – for what? Signs of life. Clubhouse where all the other kids are hanging out, talking about their day, but if there is a place out there where everybody else is having fun, they've kept it from him. Instead he finds himself cross-hatching suburban neighborhoods, rolling down tree-lined streets at a crawl, studying houses as if these solid Middle-American families know something he doesn't know. Maybe he'll find a how-to demo in some happy family's lighted front windows, nice well-adjusted people around a table like a department store display, a demo arranged to show lonely guys like him how to live.

Most nights Theo ends up at Schontz's Quarry. He opens the car door on these soft, dense summer nights and takes the path down the stone face to a low ledge. He rolls on his belly and leans out, staring into the water as if he will find secrets buried there. Maybe he can penetrate the black water and look into the grinning face of Preston Zax. *What the fuck were you doing? All those women. What did you think you were doing, man?* Or he'll cruise the deserted Zax house. He parks and sits, as if he can still catch Preston going in or Stella coming out. Grab them and find the truth of this. When she reached out of her misery and chose Theo Slate, it was like a bizarre ordination, or being given a commission in some army whose duty is not yet clear. She has chosen him. But for what? At home, he has begun collecting information. If he can put the pieces together and write about it, he can win prizes. Anatomize killing. Make it stop. But the truth eludes him. Hell yes he'd rather teach. It's got to be easier.

Yes Carey has left him bummed.

At least tonight he has a place to go. Theo is at the front door of the community college building, getting ready to teach his first class. Thank God. Anything to take his mind off it.

After being all alone inside his head most nights, teaching journalism to middle-aged wannabes will be a relief. He's psyched, yes. And scared. Because he's never done it before, he walks into the hulking Richardsonian brownstone overprepared. He's armed himself for this first class with extensive handouts. Clippings. A class exercise. 'Great writers' to read out loud in case one of those silences falls that he's too inexperienced to fill. If he stops talking this class might rise up like Godzilla marching on Tokyo and beat him to death. Or start yawning and fall backwards out of their chairs. Walk out on him. Laugh. Yes he's freaking. At the *Star* Theo knows what he's doing, witness the Zax pieces and the work he's done with poor little Delia. He does it well. Teaching a room full of people he doesn't know is more like animal taming with a broken whip and no chair. Stalled outside his classroom at the heart of the dusty, stifling Center City Community College, he's trying to figure out how to walk inside and face them and begin.

At Theo's back somebody coughs and he jumps. 'Oh. It's you.'

'I told you I'd make it up to you.' It's Delia Vent, looking freshly powdered and in this light somehow insubstantial in a festive little flowered shift. Nothing like the *shmatas* she wears to work. Tonight she has on earrings, sandals. She looks almost pretty for once. Smiling as if meeting a date. In the dimness of the cavernous hallway, her white upper arms gleam. 'I convinced them to give you the job.'

'You what?'

'When Professor Krantz flipped out they asked us if we knew anybody who'd be good for this, so I—'

'Us?'

'Our journalism class. How did you think I got started at the *Star*? All winter I was taking this Saturday journalism class.' She is waiting for him to say something. When he can't, she just goes on. 'And when Professor Krantz flipped out in May they asked us all for, like, recommendations? And I suggested you.'

Not her fault he is studying her; although she's looking right at him her pupils seem to be jittering in the half-light. She is either telling him the truth or she's not telling the truth. Either way, he's here. He studies her. 'That was you?'

She says without blinking, 'Yeah, it was me.'

So it either was or it wasn't. 'That's great.'

You'd think she'd bought him a three-month time share in Florida. 'So, aren't you glad?'

'I don't know whether to thank you or get mad at you,' he says candidly. 'It's going to be hard.'

'You'll be fine,' she says. 'Just tell them some of the good stuff you've been teaching me. I just wanted to do something for you.' She is smiling expectantly. 'You know, to make up for it?'

'Make up for what?'

'That notebook thing. Bringing you an empty notebook, when we'd thought . . . I thought and I thought until I figured

out how to make up for it.' She brushes her hands together –
that's that – as if she's cleared a major debt. 'The notebook,
I mean.'

'That was a long time ago.'

'I never forget. Plus I wanted to thank you for helping me
at the paper, so I got you this class? So, aren't you glad?'

Her smile is so bright that he turns away. 'Look, I have
to go in now, and I . . .'

'I just wanted to do it for you,' she says. 'After everything
you're doing for me.'

'It's no big deal, but thanks.' OK, he has been helping
her, and looking at her now he knows he's been using her
to fill the time without Carey. Anything to fill the time. Do
a favor. Feel a little better. Yeah. 'So thanks again. I really
have to go in now. Aren't you supposed to be at work?'

'So,' Delia says instead of leaving for the *Star* – there's
something else different about her tonight maybe, he never
looks. 'What do you think?'

'I can't talk now, I have to get to class.' Which is probably
just as well. Even though he needed this to get through a hard
patch, working with her has started getting claustrophobic.
He's feeling claustrophobic right now. He looks at his watch.
'Better hurry. Your shift starts at eight.'

'No more. I have a surprise.'

'A surprise?'

'I got switched to days.' Delia lifts one shoulder with
a special, just-us look. She is waiting for him to notice.
But notice what? Exasperated, she says, 'Do you like
my hair?'

You got switched to . . . 'Your what?'

'My hair!'

'My gosh!' It's orange. Where she had bushy, no-color
hair, Delia Vent has superimposed a Bold New Look as they
say in commercials, colored it orange and tortured it over
rollers to make curls. She looks like Little Orphan Annie on
a good day; it's kind of cute.

'You like it?'

'Gee,' he says dutifully, 'you look great.' He reads FINALLY in her thought balloon. So what if it makes him feel a little cheesy? At least he can make one person smile.

'I got it done special,' she says. 'I wanted to look good for your first class.'

15

Scranton, Pennsylvania

H e stands quietly, waiting for somebody to come to the
door. As the owner of the house opens it he blinks and
smiles nicely, as if the door has just opened on sun shining.
'Mr Mallison?'

The homeowner says, 'I'm Frank Mallison.'

'Haik.'

'First name or last?'

'Yes.'

'Nice to meet you.' They shake.

'I came about the room?'

'The room,' the owner says. 'I'm sorry, it's already
taken.'

'I was hoping.'

'Besides, we like to rent to students. You look a little old.'

'I haven't been a student for a while,' Haik says but then
he adds, 'but I have.'

'Have been a student?'

'Have stayed in touch. I like to read up on things.'

'We all do.'

'And write about it.'

'You a writer?'

'Not exactly,' he says pleasantly. 'Analysis.'

'Analysis.' His room's been rented but the householder
stays out here on the front porch talking, have to be an OK

88

guy to keep a man talking like this. Clean-cut, unlike the scruffy undergraduate who took the room. Mallison studies the fair-haired stranger with the smooth, untroubled face and says, 'You in town for long?'

'Indefinite stay,' the stranger says easily. 'Nice town.'

'Then you'll be wanting an apartment.'

'I prefer a room.'

'You don't need . . .'

'I like to keep it simple.'

Haik's smile makes the homeowner smile. 'Looking for a job?'

'I have a job. I'm working at the bank.'

Right. He has that solid look. 'You're a banker?'

'No. Computer programmer. I like everything the way I like it.' Smile. 'Computers are like that.'

The owner shakes his head. 'I don't know, I can't get mine to do anything.'

'It's all logic. Flow charts. Order.' Haik's eyes are so clear that even a careful observer will find nothing in them. The smile is untroubled, bland. 'A. B. C.'

'Order.' The student who took the Mallisons' third-floor room has a beard and a hostile slouch. He looks as if he smells bad. Frank Mallison begins to have regrets. 'You make me sorry I've already let the room,' he says to Haik. 'Tell you what. Get back to me when you get located. If my tenant falls through, I may want to be in touch.'

'Thanks, but I have to see a room before I can make a commitment.'

'My tenant's in right now.'

'I know. Thank you for your time, Mr Mallison. Thank you very much.'

'Thanks for coming by.' When the stranger turns to go, the householder will realize that if he meets Haik again, he won't necessarily know him. He's that ordinary. Nice guy, he thinks, going back inside.

Say goodbye to Haik, Frank Mallison. Say goodbye and

count your blessings. You may think you know him, but you don't.

What he *is* is all set down in writing. Somewhere inaccessible to you. It's in the book. Pages thick with writing in six colors to identify the elements: Schemes. Flaws. Corrections. Needs. Equipment. Procedures. Organized under A. B. C. While inside this unreadable stranger the elements collide in a psychic storm that shakes the world. Internal organs swell and rub each other raw; synapses pop and strain because he is torn apart from the inside by the urge. The only way to end this for good is to find The One and do em. Not him. Not her. Genderless victim, an object. E. Em.

NOTES on #3

Identification. #3 was not The One. MISTAKE: *Misidentification. Know em for sure before I show ourselves. Plan:* MORE ENCOUNTERS BEFORE *Phase II. This is touchy. Not letting us* OUT, *not scare em off before we reach the place where I can do em. Wrong venue.*

CORRECTIVE ACTION

1. Specifications: *The room. Dead square. Ideal location for door and window is: door in the exact center of the wall to the left of the bed. Window in the exact center of the wall to the right of bed. Measure. In these things every dimension matters. Tell them I am measuring for a rug. Make sure the room has only one access. We can't afford to sleep in a room with more than one door.*

a. A room with a sink in it. Sponge baths, teeth, etc. Peeing.

b. Must have a window. For light. Air. Surveillance. To jump.

2. Details: *Door must open in, to show who's in the*

*hall before they come in from the hall. No closet is
best. It isn't safe, any more than it's safe to have a
headboard or a shelf of any kind between us and the
plaster. If you can't hear things moving in the wall
or on the other side of the wall, something you don't
expect will rise up and kill you.*

3. Action: *Survey FOR RENT signs. Newspaper ads.
Avoid realtors. Rent from a man, you know why. If the
door isn't centered in the wall, don't take the room.*

4. Precautions:

   *a. Push our bed hard against the wall every night
no matter how long you live in the room. Do this
nightly, no exceptions. Things slip. Furniture forgets.
Only you remain on guard.*

   *b. Ward off the unexpected. If you don't know
what this means, then you aren't strong enough to
do this.*

   *c. Make your bed tight. Hospital corners. This is
for appearances, plus if anyone sneaks anything into
the bed you will see.*

5. Misc: *Minimum furniture. Nothing enemies can
hide in or find if you have to move.* OK things to get:

   a. Bed. Single. No distractions.

   *b. Dresser. Clothes lying around are a distrac-
tion.*

   *c. Open-backed chair. Put under the door handle
at bedtime.*

   *d. No pictures. Images are a distraction. No
ornaments.*

   *e. Rug, to cut the sound. Washable. Rug pad so
you won't trip.*

B. PHASE TWO
Thursday
1. Hide this book.
2. Tell no one.

16

The class is going OK but that's about all that's OK. It's been weeks and Theo still can't get in to see Stella Zax. His career as a hero ended when his last Zax folo got bumped to the B section; Chick is riding him hard at the moment, chewing him out over every little thing. More: Theo is seeing maybe a little too much of Delia. When he goes to the brownstone college building she's there, straining to be cool in one of her gaudy outfits, as if this is a cruise ship, not a class. Beaming, she lurks until he goes in to teach and before he can get a question out her hand goes up like a cocktail flag: chronic A student, born to please. At work she's in early, stays late. For no reason she's started turning up at the bus stop at Theo's corner. When his car stops for the light she pretends not to see; he could pretend not to see her either, but he can't. She looks pathetic sitting there, so he offers her a ride. When she grins and scrambles in, a *puff* like a sigh rushes out of those dark, full skirts she puts on for work, reminding him that this is a woman sitting next to him, but not one he wants. It's sad. When he comes out of the *Star* at night she pounces, feigning surprise: *Oh, are you still here?* No matter where he goes his intern moves in the same flight pattern, as if she knows where Theo is going before he does.

But he is too preoccupied to deal. These July days he slogs through work and the class and sees Sally when she lets him, but it's like running under water with lead in his shoes. He and Sally are better than friends, maybe halfway to where they may be heading, but only halfway. The *Star*'s police reporter is too smart to let anything slip by unmarked; she knows Theo's concentration is split even at moments when they are close and getting closer, which is what they are. Last week Sally touched his face as if trying to pull him into real life. 'Theo, are you OK?'

'Who, me?' Oh shit, does it show? 'I'm fine.'

'You look like you're not sleeping much.'

'Just busy is all.' He is. He's on a new project. He's collecting data in the office he fixed up for Carey. The problem is, he can't tell where the project is taking him. When Stella Zax called him to the city jail she changed his life. She marked him as surely as if she'd tied her scarf around his arm or tapped him with a sword. Without knowing why, he is amassing clippings. Photos. Grisly news stories going way back. Background, he thinks. I'm collecting background, but for what? Something big, that he can't identify. Whatever it is, it's got him by the throat. If he can't organize and subdue it, it's going to start dragging him around.

Sally nudges him and he jumps. 'I *said*, good busy or bad busy?'

'Awful busy.' He tries to disarm her by making her laugh. 'Like I'm going to tell you about my story I'm writing that's going to kill the world?'

'Like you ever tell me anything.' She is grinning, to take the sting out of it.

'I would if I could, but I don't know myself.' Today he pulled in a clip about a killing in Angola, Indiana, to add to his pile. He can't say why it's murders he's collecting, but it is. Does he actually believe he can do what Stella wants without even knowing what it is? When she chose him to cover her arrest and then called him to the city jail for that last interview, Stella Zax started a chain of thought with no predictable end. God, he needs to see her. He needs to ask: *What do you want me to do?* She waived bail so she's upstate at County now, in the odd, uncommitted period between the arraignment and the trial. She refused a lawyer. She has stone-walled all Theo's attempts to find out why she killed Preston and why she called him to write her story for the world. He's driven up to County three times, gone through the metal detector, waited in the visitors' room with his notebook open and his mouth and his belly drying out but Stella refuses to come down. She doesn't even send word. It's as if she called Theo *Son* and wrenched him out of his life and with that accomplished, forgot him. What does she want? What does she *want*? She sits front and center in his consciousness like a bad carving of a person, lifesized, stony. Immovable. She will stay there until he knows. He shifts uneasily; Sally is studying him. 'Is there something on my chin?'

'I don't know, T. You look. Different.'

Shaken, he says, 'Like, changed?'

'Skinnier.'

He offers her an easy answer. 'Too busy to eat?'

'Yeah, right.' Her blush surprises him. 'Sorry. Not my business.'

'I wish it was.'

Sally turns red. 'Ooops. Gotta go.'

'Not yet!' So Theo stops her with an answer that isn't really an answer. 'What it is, is. It's all these, like. Loose ends.'

'I thought you might be bumming over your girlfriend.'

'Yeah,' he admits. 'That a little bit too.' But he tries anyway. 'I don't suppose we . . .'

She smiles. 'Settle that old one and then get back to me.'

He says in that confident reporter tone, 'I'm on it.'

At least it makes her laugh.

In fact, he's eating fine but he isn't sleeping much. When he gets home after class that Monday night Theo goes back to the cramped office and loses track of time, sifting material and drafting letters to Stella Zax. He's got to see her. Ask. Mrs Zax, what clicked inside you when you killed your son? Did anything change? Did you hear a *snap*? Are you different from Preston, or are you and he the same? Are you different from me? He wants to ask her, how did you feel? When you put the light out in him forever, did it make you feel awful, or were you glad? Opening the Zax file in his computer, he tries:

Dear Mrs Zax.

You keep refusing to see me but if I could just tell you what I'm trying to do here, I know you'd change your mind.

Wrong! For a guy who gets paid for writing, he can't write worth shit.

Dear Mrs Zax.

I didn't start this. You did. So the least you can do . . .

Wrong. He has to bring her around with logic, bing-bang. Delete. Write: *Mrs Zax, you started me working on something important. The least you can damn well do is tell me what it is.*

So listen. If we work together, you and I can locate the point. The moment when something inside a person twists. When everything starts to change. If we can isolate it, put our finger on it, I can tell the world. It's the only way I can think of to make it stop. It's what you want, isn't it? Isn't that what you want?

Listen, Mrs Zax, you've been there. Seen it. Done that. If anybody ever heard the snap *and saw it changing, you did.*

The instant. When the iris snaps shut and you kill.

You saw it in your son. Preston wasn't born a murderer, right? Or was he? He was an ordinary cute baby, right? And later a cute little boy, wouldn't hurt a kitten, right? Mrs Zax, when did he change? In kindergarten? Tenth grade? Last year? Did you see it happen? Did you see him cross the line?

How about you? When did you cross?

He deletes and starts again.

Listen, Mrs Zax, I hope you don't think I mean this in the wrong way, but whatever happened to your son Preston, when it happened, you saw it coming, right? Or were you surprised?

Murder. Is it inevitable or is it an event?

If we're ever going to stop this, I have to know. Listen. Is killing something that just anybody slides into? Like, accidentally? Could it happen to you? Could it happen to me?

Oh shit. He deletes the last sentence and resumes. *Or is it so separate and different that most of us are safe? You can tell me, Mrs Zax. We still have time before the trial. Call and I'll come up any time. Any time, day or night.*

Then – what is he doing! Theo signs it *love.*

Blindsided by exhaustion, he adds:

P.S. Mrs Zax, I hope you aren't sitting there reading this and wondering, why is this guy writing to me? OK, I have this feeling that I'm marked. You want me to write this story. I know you do. The thing is, Mrs Zax, you called me. I didn't call you. So even though you never came out and said it, we have this bond.

OK. About Preston. You must have seen the signs. So what are the signs? You started this, now let's finish it.

Done. He prints without rereading and stuffs it in an envelope. Tomorrow he'll slip it in the mail. It's already tomorrow. Monday has gone downhill into Tuesday. He thought he'd call Sally when he got his head organized, but it's too late. It's almost day. He is feeling unwholesome and weird. In another life he and Sally could just fall in love. They could go out and move in together and get married, but there's too much going on right now. All these unassimilated particles. He isn't fit company. The Project, he thinks, pulling the pillow over his head. It helps to call it The Project. It's just a project, yeah. Hopelessly snarled in sheets twisted like a captive's bonds, felled by need and a complex of other emotions, he finally sleeps.

He is wakened by the phone. It's Carey, back in touch just when he thought she'd never get in touch. The call drives Theo out of bed; cradling the phone he roves from room to room as if retracing Carey's steps the night she told him what she thought of his life. 'So that's it,' she says. 'I've been thinking and I think . . .'

'Did Dad tell you to call me?'

She hesitates. 'Well, we *did* talk.'

Dad, who got pushed out of the driver's seat but can't stop driving; it makes his teeth feel naked. 'I don't play my father's games.'

'This isn't his game, Theo, it's about us.'

He stumbles into the living room did he leave that window open? Not sure. Closes it as Carey talks on. 'Mmm.' He's too sleepy to make sense of it but she seems to think that now that she's told him she still loves him, he's going to take that offer at the firm and come back to Manhattan after all. OK, she says she knows Theo was waiting to hear her say she loves him, if that's what he wants, now she's ready to say she loves him and she wants . . . He mumbles, 'Could we talk about this after it gets light?'

She could be ending a successful meeting. 'So together, we . . .'

Blundering into the kitchen to start coffee and save this phone call, Theo sees fresh flowers in the jar. Somebody brought them in while he was sleeping and put clean water in the jar. 'Who?' He murmurs, 'Sally?'

Carey is on top of it. 'What?'

He hears himself mutter, 'In your dreams.' Yeah, right, Slate.

'Are you awake?'

He is distracted. Later he'll discover that certain items in his house have been moved. 'I'm sorry, I can't talk right now.'

'But,' Carey says as if it's decided. 'We're starting over.'

'What?'

'When would you like me to come?'

'What do you mean?'

'I mean now that it's settled.'

He says, gently, 'I don't think it's settled, Care.' It is confusing. The silence on the other end of the phone signifies Carey waiting and behind her in an odd way, his father waiting and all that comes to mind are TV clichés: *I can't do this right now. I can't be there for you. Let's don't do this, OK?* The last thing Theo says to her comes straight out of daytime soaps. 'Sorry. I need a little space.'

17

O nce again, Haik is in transit. The room looked like the right room but it was not. Scranton, Pennsylvania, was not the right town, any more than Angola, Indiana. Everything went wrong. He will start over here. Do things right and you never think about them again, he tells himself, sitting in a Quality Inn on the fringes of Albany. He has yet to find and rent the room as specified in the design he is making. No. The design that is making him. Do it right and you can rest. Do it wrong and you'll never get shut of it. He will find The One and do em. He will do em good. He has to, so he can complete this. He will find em and bring em to earth in this new place.

E is out there somewhere. *Asking for it.* Then oh yes he will do em and leave his mark and that will show them, the perfectionist father and this mother sitting in jail two states away. She had a son like Haik and murdered him. Do this right and the design writhing inside him will complete itself and he can rest. Intent on completion, he scribbles, doubling back on his notes and crosshatching pages with flowcharts, lines and diagrams. He has to analyze. So we can organize and plan.

NOTES ON #4

Fucked. Fucked and shamed. #4 in Pennsylvania. The

*One, every detail right and it went wrong, MISJOINING!
And e was wrong, OK. Thought e was the right one
but no. Small enough, but. A swimmer. E fought back!
Method, instruments all fine, e died OK but snarling
when I did em. Screams. People running fast I had to
split before he could do all the things and so finish it.
Left our mark, at least and we were out of there. Now
we are here.*

But everything is changed now. Something happened out
there in a city two states away and it changed everything.
When he failed at anything Father used to say: 'You are
killing your mother all over again.'

Now she is killing him. How could she do this to him
when she's the only person he ever loved? She's in the way.
She keeps getting in the way. No matter what he writes, he
doubles back on the same heading:

What went wrong
1. *Fighting back.*
2. *Screaming.*
3. *Dying too soon.*
4.

His pencil stalls. Disturbed, Haik ticks the page until it is
covered with little red flecks like beginning pox. Leafed
into the page is another clipping. He has several versions
now, the same story as it ran in different papers; he assesses
them like a scientist, trying to make data track. What kind
of a mother would do this? What kind of mother would?
MOTHER CONFESSES TO MURDER OF KILLER SON.

His belly twists. He's got to end this. He needs to do #4
and do em right. He says aloud, 'I'm doing it for you!'

Doubt me, will you? Organize. Write it down. *The room.
The One. Do em and do em right.* We will do this and take
it to her. Make her proud. And then we'll see.

And at last he is able to fill in the entry after *4. Split concentration. You know what to do.*

He must see her, he thinks. He has to see her soon.

There is a man in Albany who specializes in these things. No matter where you are, there is always a man who specializes in these things. Haik comes back to the hotel with the necessaries: Polaroid mug shots in various sizes because the size varies depending on the document. Blanks. One for the license, one for the hospital ID; he doesn't know why it amuses him but he has always liked carrying hospital ID; it doesn't matter which hospital, the official taking a cursory look asks, 'Oh, are you a doctor?' 'No,' Haik always tells them, and this is what clinches it. 'I'm a nurse.' He knows he will not be asked to show these things but it is important to him to know that he is carrying these things. Credentials. The son of a scientist, he knows how important it is to establish your location in the universe of dailyness. To keep your place in life, you have to prove you *have* a place in life. Before he leaves Albany there is one more thing he has to do. He can go as soon as he is ready. This will be a quick one no it will not be perfect but he has to take something with him that he can show her so she can look at it and see that he is doing it for her.

Haik is on the bus. Heading for the end point on his calculated pilgrimage, or mission, he broods over #4 and moves on to his notes on #5.

PROJECT: #5

Location? Not sure. Qualifications.
    1. Availability.
        a. Smaller than me.
        b. Alone.
    2. Asking for it.

a. Asking for it. Smell eir pillow and suck eir skin from underneath our fingernails and do this in a dozen places without finding em. How do you know when? Now is when. Who is The One? Find em and you know. You just know.

b. Asking for it.

c. Just asking for it.

Even though he's planning, he can't shut out his father's voice: *Failure. Ask yourself, is there a pattern here?* If Haik does not see the pattern, it's not his fault, it was the distraction. Never mind, he is on his way to take care of that. He is going to show her. And while we're getting there use the time, use the time. Then he will do #5 and be done with this.

He will make his mother proud. He taps the blank page. He has to think before he can write. Unless he has to write so he can think. It is a little like sex. Saliva gathers in his mouth. He can feel it writhing *down there*. It is well for Haik that his outsides in no way match what's going on inside. Looking at him, you'd never know. He hunches over the book.

But as the bus pulls away from its last stop and gathers speed, a shadow falls across the page. Haik's muscles tighten but he does not move and he won't look up.

The woman's voice grates. 'Excuse me, is this seat taken?'

He keeps his head bent over the notebook, covering the still blank page with the flat of his big, clean hand and turning his back to the woman in the aisle to make it clear that he needs to sit alone here. Old lessons came hard but he has them cold: method burned into him by his father the chemist his hands were so goddamn clean. As soon as she is gone he will make the headings.

Analyze. Done.

Organize. Done.

Plan. Four was botched but Haik has business to do before

he moves on to Five. A stop to make on his way to whatever comes next. Plan, yes. It is like foreplay.

'Excuse me?'

Writing *interruptus*. He won't let her see his rage. 'Ma'am?'

The old woman's shadow falls across his book. Until this passenger gives up and goes away he can not continue. It is shocking, like having sex while you are being watched. Haik raises polite, empty eyes to the old lady standing over him with the dyed curls and the weary eyes. Her mouth is trembling. Her smile blurs and slips down her face as the bus rounds a corner and she lurches, banging her hip against the seat with a little gasp. 'Please!'

'I'm sorry,' Haik says with a bland look, could mean anything. They look in your empty face and read whatever they want to. Read my lips. Be glad you don't know what they say. 'You asked is this seat taken?'

'Yes please.' She is old and shaky.

'I'm sorry,' he says, turning away. 'It is.'

'You have a nice face, I . . .'

'I'm sorry, ma'am. Police business.' He waits until the old woman lurches on down the aisle to the last empty seat next to the smelly bathroom in the far back of the bus. Then, hunched over his secrets, Haik curves around the notebook like an oyster around a growing pearl.

18

Delia has a lover, but he doesn't know it yet. His name is Theo Slate. Soon, she thinks, dressing for tonight. When he sees me all dressed up! Love at first sight? No. First noticing.

But oh God, what to wear, what to wear? Every class is like a party, what to wear? Circling the rented room like a trapped mink, she roots through cartons, tripping on the flute case in her haste, throwing bikini underpants and sequined T-shirts and stolen satins over her shoulders – not this top, not that one, which one? For tonight's class she'll put on a whole new person. Gorgeous, different, make him forget the old lady students. He'll ask her out. Yes love is changing her. Her new red hair! Theo is interested, she knows he is. The way he looks at her. Tonight, she thinks, rummaging. Sequined blouse, no. Striped tank, no. Make him fall in love.

Which shoes? Except for the five-inch spike heels, Birkenstocks are the only shoes Delia has left. In the spikes she will be gorgeous but they bite her feet. She feels like the Little Mermaid in Oscar Wilde. Trade your tail for feet so you can dance for the prince. In a tradeoff, you always lose. The mermaid danced like an angel, but they took her voice! She danced until her new feet bled. Then she died and never once told the prince that she was in love with him because they took her voice. You get what you want and it's never what you want. Dance in these spike heels and you may slip in your own blood seeping out through the open toes.

She ought to call home and make them send some of her shoes. Well she is done calling home. She'd rather die. She is through with those people. Expensive stuff in her closet back there, suits she used to fit before she gained all the weight. Nice dresses. Sexy shoes she had, back before she got into the first Trouble and they got so mad at her. Mother. Father. Fuck them anyway. What do those people have to do with me? Maybe she can go downstairs and borrow the landlady's gold sandals, with the lucite heels and the thin gold straps. Like that selfish bitch would loan her anything!

Fine. When the landlady leaves for work Delia will go in and take the damn shoes. Delia gets through the days however, but the fixed point of every night is seeing him. Theo Slate. They are in love. He loves her, he does! Hasn't he started helping her at work? When he points to something on her screen, their heads are *this close*. And in class she sits in the front row, and you know the way you catch a man sneaking looks at you? Well she has caught him.

'*Theo,*' she says aloud now, but not to him. Not yet. '*Theo.*' His name. The secret that you steal from a person and they don't even know. When they're alone she'll say his name and then. They'll make love. And afterwards she will play the flute for him! 'Mrs Theo Slate,' she says aloud, to the empty room.

For now the flute is silent in its case. After what happened the other times – happened, she put it away. You do not play the flute for just anyone. 'Not yet,' she says to the flute. 'Not yet.' Oh God, should she wear the mini with the T-shirt, does it look cheap? But she has these fuzzy legs. She can never get all the hair off no matter how hard she scrapes, so wear something long. This? Or this? Or this? What color? Should she wear green today, to show off her beautiful hair that she spent that whole day getting dyed?

This is so important, God! Be sexy in black? The red wool? No, it's summer and besides, she's saving it for when they . . . And they will, they'll do it soon. If only she can find the right clothes!

19

The summer is getting old. Theo's been so fixed on the way the puzzle in his office keeps flexing and changing that Sally's material comes as a surprise.

'It's about Delia. I know you like her, but I've known her for longer than you have and I thought . . . I think.' Leaning over the Formica table, Sally gives her warning a disarming upflip. 'You need to be careful? Like, you could be backing into a human swamp?'

It's late Friday afternoon. They both finished early and drifted in here. It's sweet sitting here in the light of Sally's intent green gaze. Theo puts out one hand as if to keep her looking at him. 'Hell, I'm just helping her, I'm not going to marry her.'

'She told me you had a date.'

'Well we don't.' He teaches at eight. See her in class, that's all. 'Besides, it's the next-to-last class.'

'She told me.' Except for the counter man, Theo and Sally are alone in the Spot but she keeps her voice down, as if she's afraid of being overheard. 'I hope you'll watch out for her.'

'She's just a kid.'

'What makes you think she's a kid?'

'Would you like to start with the hair?' Theo can't let Sally know that he's secretly tickled by this conversation – close attention after a long dry spell in which he misses Carey in spite of the fact that he's almost over it. With her sharp talk and that great smile, Sally Wyler can take anything

in her two hands and make it better. Tough, sweet Sally with
her dark hair and neat pants and hardboiled reporter act is
a soft, completely different person when she and Theo are
one on one. Her concern suggests that they can be more
than good colleagues. He likes her worrying, even over
something minor, like this idiot girl. 'Listen,' he says, 'loner
like Delia, night-school BA, no family . . .'

'No family?'

'If she isn't an orphan, she might as well be.'

'I'm not so sure.'

'Look, she's all alone here. No family, no money and no
life, anything you can give a person like that, they appreciate
it, you know? Unlike—'

Sally is quick and sharp. 'Unlike Lacey Sparkman?'

He was going to say, *unlike Carey.* 'The Spark!' Embar-
rassed, he laughs. 'Can I get back to you on that?' He's
been seeing darkhaired, glossy Lacey Sparkman but not in
any big way, just a few drinks, dancing, a movie, face it,
minimal laughs; she's a pretty, hollow person, it's a little bit
like dancing with a lovely, ornamental, intricately patterned
snake skin after the snake has moved out. When he and
Lacey Sparkman walk into restaurants, she leans into him in
a flirtatious arc. *Don't go there.* He's sick of being alone.

'Oh, Lacey. You can handle Lacey,' Sally says. 'It's Delia
I'm worried about. She looks at you like . . . I don't know
what she looks at you like, I just.'

Theo shrugs. 'It's not her fault she has us instead of a
life.'

'Remember the story of the tarbaby? I get the idea that
if you let her get too close she'll glom on and get stuck to
you for life.'

'Hey, thanks and all,' Theo says to Sally, who is roaring
along on her own track, 'but be cool. I can take care of
myself.'

Sally crackles with energy. Every hair stands separate.
What Theo likes best about her is now that when she gets

on his case, she's really on his case. She doesn't quit. 'You can give that woman everything you've got and it won't be enough. And you . . .' Her green irises are startlingly pale; that *intelligence*. What she says next takes Theo's breath. 'Right now there isn't enough of you to spread around.'

Abashed, he looks at his hands as if inspecting for spots. Has he caught something that he doesn't know about? 'Who says?'

'Me. You're wearing thin.'

'I weigh the same.'

'That's not what I mean. You're spread thinner than paint on a balloon. You need to take care of yourself, T.' They don't need to cover the ground between them; suddenly Sally is right *there*. Not exactly thinking his thoughts, but caring what he thinks. She says as if she can see inside him, 'You need to get strong.'

'Hey,' Theo says, 'I'm cool. I really am. Hey, listen. You want to know how cool I am?' *Want to know why I'm so hung up on reassuring you?*

'You're so cool you think this song is about you.'

'Very funny, Ms Kermit. No. I'm so cool that I'm teaching people twice my age.'

'Plus Delia.'

'Yeah,' he says uncomfortably, 'don't say it, OK?'

Sally changes the subject. 'J-classes. Cool.' She says what every writer says, adding, 'Maybe you can get a book out of it.'

A book. Theo starts. It's as if somebody's tapped him on the shoulder. 'I could. But that's not the book I'm going to write.'

This puts her on the alert. 'You're writing a book?'

Another cool thing. Sally's just like him. Born in a runner's crouch. He grins. 'Yes. No. Not yet.' It's still so new that he hasn't told anyone. Hey, why not? If nine-tenths of life is trying to make sense of it, maybe reporting isn't enough. Maybe he really is writing a book. When he started this project that's accreting in his home office, Theo thought he was sketching out a major investigative piece. Series, maybe. Start with the Zaxes and fan out into other serial killers' lives. Nail down these killings that mystify and stun. Take them apart. The trouble is he's pulled in so much material that it's mounting out of control. Heaps. Stacks. Folders. Electronic files. And a fresh murder dropped into his collection just last week, Scranton was it. He has to figure out what he's got. When he knows, he'll go to Chick. No, he'll go to the Whartons, who publish the *Star*, get them to take him off GA so he can jam on this. Special Projects. Watch out, Archy baby. Theo is going to ride this project out of what he's beginning to think of as the pits. When he took this job he could handle spending two years paying his dues. Forget it. He wants out of Center City now.

'You didn't say what you're doing.'

He temporizes. 'It's hard to explain.'

'It's OK, T. You don't need to explain to me.'

'Look,' Theo says gratefully, 'want to see my house?'

'Do you need to ask?'

He has a good feeling about it, pulling into the cul de sac with Sally sitting next to him. She does not judge the way Carey did. She says, 'Cool house.'

'Carey says it sucks.'

'Carey.'

They both know that for a guy making what Theo's making, it's terrific. Never mind how much he owes, he's gradually paying it off. Probably because he's never here except to sleep and when he can't sleep he prowls the home office, his house is in perfect order. Kitchen neat, and on top of the fridge, mummified flowers drooping in their jar less like a memorial to the dead relationship than an artful dried arrangement that makes the room look nice.

'Two bedrooms,' he says, leading her into the little hall. 'One for my office.' Carey's office. Well Carey can go to hell.

'Good idea. Wow, is that your living room?'

'Yeah. Yeah, it is.' Theo shows her around like a proud householder, which is what he was before Carey exploded the myth. 'I was going to buy disposable furniture but then I found this sofa and I figured, why not? The rug is a Hariz. It's from my folks' house. The Escher prints, I bought.'

'And your bedroom.' Sally sees Carey's photo on the chest.

Why am I blushing? 'Yeah. And that's my office.'

'Can I go in?'

He says without thinking, 'Sure.'

Theo flips on the light. He isn't even aware of what he's just exposed until he hears Sally; did she really just whisper, 'Holy fuck'?

'Oh,' he says. Shutters. Milk-crate file cases. Laptop dwarfed by the Door Store desk. 'I guess it is a little weird.'

'Not the room. The wall.'

'The wall? Oh. The wall.' Truth? Theo doesn't think about the wall. It's a part of his life. He's never stepped back.

'It's like a shot out of one of those movies.'

'Oh.' For the first time, Theo sees what Sally sees. He winces. 'My project.'

'What kind of project?'

'It's hard to explain.' The wall. About the wall. OK, he has all this stuff pinned, taped, tacked and nailed to the wall above his computer. Clips. Printouts. Glossy 8 x 11 prints. Stand where Sally is standing and the wall in Theo's tiny home office looks like one of those walls the camera finds at the crucial point in every stalker/killer movie. The generic units directors use to show that the perp has been obsessing over some victim for months before the deed. It's as if the world needs to believe that monstrous things are never random, they are always carefully planned. And this is what his wall looks like. So in-your-face obvious that he never saw. 'Yeah. I guess the wall is a little weird.'

'Yeah,' Sally says, 'it's a little weird.'

'It's not what you think!' He hopes Sally can see the difference. The photos and clippings are not of any person Theo has ever known or wants to know or will ever know. This is about people he needs to know *about*. Everybody on the wall is dead or in jail.

'Hey, whatever floats your boat.'

Theo grins. He wants to tell her what he's doing but he hasn't sorted it out; he wants to tell her but he can't for more than one reason. Partly, it's the competitive thing. Partly, it's because he doesn't really know. He tries, 'Background for the Zax story.'

'The Zax story is over.'

'The mother. She's going to see me again.'

Sally picks up on it fast. 'She's really going to see you?'

'Sooner or later. I know she will.'

'I heard she isn't seeing anybody, T. And all this.' Her hands stir the air so all his Xeroxes and clippings lift. 'All this!'

Is he going to have to sit Sally down and prove that he isn't going nuts? OK, in the weeks since Carey left him Theo has logged dozens of nights in this room. He's pulled in everything he can get. Some of the exhibits are posted; more crowd his bulging files. Photos. Crime scenes. Victims before and after. Photos of everybody from Zax and Dahmer back to Berkowitz and on back. For whatever reasons he needs pictures of these guys snapped before anybody even knew they were going to kill. Grinning subjects barbered and scrubbed and posed. Summer snaps of boys-into-men squinting in the sunlight, generic campers smiling at the camera in some prehistoric dawn before society's monsters guessed what they would become. Theo spends hours considering these items and, like a general deploying troops on a map, pulling tacks and moving them in the expectation that sooner or later the parts will fall into place and he'll see what he's looking for. 'I hope you don't think *I'm* getting weird.'

'Not weird,' Sally says, absorbed. 'Wired.'

'I could tell you I'm writing a thriller.' Theo moves to hide an item that just surfaced: grisly new killings, in Angola, Indiana. Scranton. Similarities to killings in DuBuque, Iowa, and Galena, Illinois. Bite marks in the neck. Pattern forming? Please.

'Yeah, but you're not.'

Theo wants to tell her these exhibits are abstract. Like numbers and letters in an equation he's working out. But they aren't. They stand for exactly what they are. Ugly events. Brutish. Beyond reason. Vile. He doesn't know where this is taking him. What he does know is that until the particles fall into place and he divines the pattern, he is, OK: *working something out.* 'I can't tell you what I'm doing, Sally. I'm sorry.'

'Sorry? Don't be sorry.' Sally startles him with a light touch on the arm. 'It's going to be one hell of a book.'

'Book. Right. Book.' *So that's all I'm doing*, he thinks, relieved. *Getting cranked up to write a book.* He draws her out of his office as if freeing her from the sludge in his head. Safe in the hall, he sighs. 'Sally.' He has run out of things to say.

'Look,' she says. 'If there's anything I can do here.'

Touched, Theo says, 'Not really. I have to do this myself.' He makes a half-turn toward her, in hopes. 'But if we could.' It is a sentence he cannot finish.

He doesn't have to tell her what he means. Sally turns too, as if to close the distance and then with a warm smile she puts both hands on his shoulders and fixes him with those steady green eyes. 'It's too soon, T. We aren't ready to do this.'

'I wish.'

'Not until you get yourself sorted out.' She means two things: forget Carey. Lose Lacey Sparkman. Unless she means finish this project and then we'll talk.

'Yeah, right.' He sighs again. He wants this to happen now. 'I'm trying.' He's getting loud. 'I am trying.'

'Shh.' Sally runs her fingertips down his arms and then stands back. 'Be cool.'

'Right,' Theo says, understanding that whatever is about to happen between them will happen, but not today. 'Hey look. Come on in the kitchen. I haven't even offered you a drink.'

'No thanks,' she says with a lovely grin that lets him know she's just as sorry about this as he is. 'It's almost eight. You've got that class.'

'Oh shit,' he says. He had forgotten the class. He lets them both out and on the way to the community college, drops her at her car. 'Take care,' he says because he means so much more and hasn't worked out a way to say it. 'Oh Sally, take care.'

'You,' she says. '*You* take care.'

Yeah Delia is there, dressed as if she's heading out later to pick up sailors: cork wedge shoes and a purple stretch mini up to *here*. She tries to snag him at the lockers, *something to tell you*, but he hurries by. 'Sorry, I'm running late.' In class she can barely hold still, grimacing from her front-row seat. Her smile is shifting with significance like a pot of fudge getting ready to boil over. He knows she wants to talk to him. Afterward she lingers in the hall but as soon as he can get free of the women clustering to ask him one more question, he cuts and runs.

Her voice follows. 'I have something to tell you.'

He says over his shoulder, 'Sorry, I can't stop now.'

She sounds much closer; she's running to catch up. 'But it's important!'

He speeds up. 'Can't stop. I'm late!'

'Can't I walk with you?'

'Sorry. I'm in a rush. My book.'

It's nowhere near a book. It's all this *stuff*. It just keeps piling up. Sordid deaths accrete. He has all these killers tacked up, taped, nailed and stapled to his walls, he should get on with it but where would he start? He ought to bring in a Hefty bag and chuck the whole business, but it's too big to dismiss. Tonight he shouts to the victims, 'What the fuck do you want from me? Who do you think I am?'

Frustration drives him out of the house.

He phones Lacey Sparkman, the slick-faced TV newschick with the perfect hair, and without any preliminaries or discussion of what will happen later, they agree on Saturday night and set a time. He spends Saturday in his office thinking if he can just get things *into the right piles*, but there is a hitch. What he has is nothing without Stella, this is clear. So he pulls out of his garage on Saturday morning without noticing the figure perched on the curb at the end of the cul de sac and makes yet another futile run upstate to the county jail. Yes the prisoner won't see him. Yes he should have known what to expect. So he goes to Lacey's house. She is waiting in that nice summer dress with the spaghetti straps. The dress expects something better than dinner at the Center City Inn or supper at the Spot so he takes her to the nearest big city – dinner and dancing at the top of the Hyatt – and Lacey brushes his cheek with that perfect hair.

By the time they drive back to her house Theo has had too much champagne for a person who's allowed to drive. It takes all his concentration to keep the car on the road and not hurt anybody and so his guard is down when Lacey slips her hand into his lap. It's funny. When she persists Theo thinks but does not say, *You don't understand. I'm saving myself for Sally.*

Maybe, but he's not fit for Sally in his current wacked-out state; in her fond, tough way Sally has made that clear. The unfinished business she needs to see settled is all tied up with Stella Zax. If he can see the Zax, he can get shut of this. As soon as he sorts out the mess in his office he and Sally can . . .

But Lacey has let him take her to her front door and now she's pulling him inside the fairytale witch's house with the leaded glass and in the front window in full view of the world she will pull him close to her for a big, theatrical kiss. Yes. Champagne may not make you forget, but it makes it easier to forgive yourself. So Theo lets her take him into the bedroom and grins while she opens him like a party pack that you pick up off your table at the end of an expensive, messy bash on New Year's Eve. 'Mmm,' Lacey says, after the fact and just before Theo struggles up through layers of temporary blindness and remembers who he's fallen down with. So it's not Sally but glossy, fine-boned Lacey Sparkman lying next to him, humming happily with her face in his neck. She won't let go until he mumbles, 'You're the best.'

When he says he has to go she pulls him back down with her, murmuring into his skin, 'Mmmmm. Not yet you don't.'

Naturally he wakes up feeling terrible because there hasn't been anybody since Carey and the woman he had in mind for this drought-breaking experience has always been Sally, whom he thinks he may love. What if she phones and he's out? But she never calls him at the house. And when he goes skulking home late Sunday morning it is not Sally who knows where he's been and is hurt and angry. Instead he finds a note propped against the door in a handwriting he recognizes on sight. The heavy vellum envelope is lavender; the stationery has a deckled edge and a rosebud embossed at the top. It's perfumed, and Theo understands with a pang that his A student, the night intern who has zilch for a salary, spent too much and bought a purple pen just to write this note to him.

In case you didn't already feel terrible.

Dear (the intern has left his name off the salutation, Theo notes uncomfortably; he hopes to hell it's just because she didn't know whether to write *Theo* or *Mr Slate*, oh God, what if she thinks of him as her *Dear* – naw, no way) . . .

I tried to tell you Friday but you were too busy and then Saturday I waited but you went out. So I came over early. I have wonderful news but you weren't here. I was scared to death when you didn't come home but I forgive you, I understand. So listen, it serves you right. If you want to find out what I have to tell you, you're going to have to beg. OK. I will tell you on Monday. Unless you want to call me up right now, here's the number, or if you want to come in to the office, you'll find me on the copy desk.

Your student,
DeliaMarie Vent

20

Delia feels terrible. She hates feeling like this. It's Theo. She's choking on her big news! Friday she spent hours getting all dressed up to tell him. She even stole a new dress for it, fussing in the bathroom until her landlady stopped banging and went away. She had to smell nice for him, have perfect hair. It's all curly now, this beautiful red color that she spent $50 to get, just to make Theo Slate fall in love with her, which she thinks he almost is. She could hardly wait to get to class and break the news.

The thing is, she just got into Columbia journalism school. Last winter Dave in Personnel helped her to apply. Who knew Theo Slate would come to town and walk into her life? When Columbia wait-listed her, she was glad. She and Theo are in love.

Then she got this letter. They took her in off the wait-list.

Oh God, please don't make me have to go.

She was going to tell him Friday. First he would be proud.

Then, and this is what got her all moist and trembling and leaves her so frustrated now. Then he would beg her not to go. She had it all written in her head.

She'd say, *I'm leaving in two weeks.*

Theo's face would go soft and he would take her hands. *Don't go.*

You want me to stay?

He would hold her hands just a little bit tighter. *Please.*

Then boy, would she make him come out with it. *Oh really, why?* He would have to goddamn fucking say it. *Because I love you.*

Say it again.

I love you.

She would torture him, but only a little bit. *Say my name.*

So he would have to say, *I love you, Delia Vent.*

Yes! And she would say, *Oh, Theo! If you love me that much, I'll just blow it off and stay here with you.*

Well none of that happened, she thinks bitterly. None of it. He just blew me off because he was in a rush.

'Monday,' he said, Friday night. 'I'll catch you Monday, OK?' On the run and running faster, trying to beat her to his car. He jumped in and snapped the locks and scratched off, leaving Delia stalled in the parking lot in her sexy stolen dress and the landlady's gold sandals behind him with her mouth wide open and her hands flying everywhere.

OK, maybe it was wrong to follow him home. But. She couldn't help it. She had to go. She really meant to go home to bed but she couldn't. She walked all the way to his house.

There was a light on in the front window, his car was there. There was a light on in one of the back rooms so she knew he was up but she was too pissed at him to go up there and ring the bell.

She wanted him to sense that she was out there and come out of the house. Call her by name. Ask her in the way true loves do. So she backed off and started circling the house. She walked the edges of his property, excited because she was outside his house in the night and her lover was *this close*, breathing and stirring around inside. Oh God she thought maybe proximity is enough for now, being that close to him.

Of course it wasn't. It never is. After a while the sky turned grey with beginning morning and the light in the back

room went out and she was dying with hunger for him. Theo.
Her Theo. She thought about him in bed, sleeping without
her. She loves him so much!

Why couldn't she get the guts to go up there and ring
the bell? How was he supposed to know she was out here
– telepathy? No. They are not that close. Yet. At first it
was, OK, enough to see the lights go on and off in different
windows and finally see the house go dark. It should have
been enough, just knowing he was in there, sleeping right
next to her spot in his bed.

But she couldn't leave. She couldn't just sit on the curb
across the street watching the house and waiting for him
to get up and come outside so she could tell him about
Columbia. She couldn't just hope he'd come out and say
the things she's planned for him to say. She loves him
so *much*.

If she went inside she could slip into bed next to him;
he'd stir a little when the mattress shifted under her weight
and then he'd roll over into her arms. Then she would touch
his cheek. And then. And then.

Afterward, everything she'd planned for them to say
would be easy to say.

If she could only get in.

It was easier than she thought.

Every time is the first time. First like a spy behind enemy
lines she went out of the cul de sac and into the neighbors'
gardens, gathering roses and daisies and marigolds out of
the flower beds around those elegant houses to give to him.
Once a dog barked; once she dropped to her belly when some
ancient early riser stumbled on his front porch looking for
the morning *Star*. She braided ferns around the flower stems.
Then she went into the house. Never mind how. Delia knows
how to get into houses, never mind how.

She put down the flowers. Oh God, she was so close.

All this, coming up to the last minute, and when she
cracked the door to his bedroom and peeked in at him

sprawled with his head under all the pillows he looked so helpless. *Oh, my love.*

She was that close. *That close.*

And after what happened with her lover last time. God! Never mind what it was, made her parents so mad and ended so badly never mind. Just. The memory made her scared to go in.

Then Theo rolled over in the bed and coughed.

And in a panic, she backed out. Held her breath in the kitchen for what seemed like hours and then like smoke caught up in an exhaust fan, drifted out of the house. It was hard to leave him and harder to go home. But a light went on inside the house and she ran, going over the grass in her bare feet like Cinderella and back at her place she fell like a tree in a storm and slept and slept.

When she got up it was late. Saturday. Her big night! She fixed her hair and went to Theo's house in her red T-shirt and the landlady's leather mini hot for August no problem it's so short, she'd shaved her legs, only bled in two places, she looked so cool. He had to ask her out. She did not take the flute. Too soon.

He wasn't there. He wasn't there! She thought OK, I'll wait.

She would wait forever, if only he'd come back.

Why, Delia, he'd say with that smile. *What are you doing here?*

And it would begin.

The trouble is, Delia sat on his steps for hours. He didn't come and he *didn't* come. She waited through dinnertime, past time for a movie, past the midnight show. She walked up to the corner and back a dozen times and he still didn't come. She practiced her speeches: 'Guess what,' sitting on his steps with her hair fluffed and her best expression on her face, springing up every time she thought she heard the car.

It just got darker and quieter and her best face started

to slip and her stupid orange hair started dying in tendrils like a squid but never mind, she did stay cheerful. Working on the speeches. She even kept the smile! She jumped up smiling every time she saw the headlights of a car coming but it was never Theo's car.

Delia waited until waiting got tired. Then she went back to the boarding house and phoned. She called and called, it was so fucking sad. Sunday she was up with the dry swallows by 4 a.m. She was worried about him. She had to go back to the house and check. She had to know if he was all right!

What if he got mugged somewhere, what if he was lying out in an alley bleeding? What if he got in a wreck? She couldn't rest until she was sure he was all right. The garage door was down so she couldn't tell if he'd come back and put the car away and gone inside. Was he in there? Was he not in there? She had to know.

She had to go inside because she was so scared for him. Look, if he was in there sleeping, maybe she could make breakfast for them and wake him up with a kiss.

A good way to start the conversation. Either that or they'd fuck and they wouldn't have to talk about it at all. It was so quiet inside; the bedroom door was closed. *Good,* she thought. *He's in there sleeping.* And parts of her went all squashy over what was going to happen next.

It was way early, everything was quiet, so fine. She took off all her clothes and folded them neatly and went into the bathroom and made herself nice for him. Then she took his toothbrush and brushed her teeth and touched herself *there* with his best cologne. Then she stood outside his closed bedroom door and waited. She was so excited. She wanted to just go in but she loves him so much that it made her scared.

After a long time, she knocked. She waited and waited but he didn't come. Then she opened the door a crack and whispered through the opening, 'It's me.' With her butt chilling and goose bumps walking across her flanks she pushed it open a little wider. 'It's me and I'm freezing,' she said, louder. 'Can I come in and get warm?'

Then she opened the fucking door and saw what she had already suspected. The bed was as smooth as a beach after a hard rain.

He wasn't there.

She'd stripped and come naked and gorgeous to her lover and she knew he loved her but her lover wasn't there! Naked and alone in his house, ready and waiting, and he wasn't even there. So the bastard had slept over somewhere. Where? She put her damn clothes back on and played the fucking messages on his fucking machine.

That Sally Wyler: 'It's Saturday, T. What's happening? What's new?'

And then this TV bitch's bitching TV voice: 'I was going to tell you to bring champagne but I guess you've already left.'

So Lacey Sparkman got him instead of the one who loves him most. It isn't fair. It isn't fair! Sunday morning and his bed not slept in plus nobody else had been in it either, Delia put her face to his sheets just to make sure and believe me she would know. All this time she was afraid of Sally Wyler, and now this bitch! Lacey Sparkman with the smooth hair and expensive clothes, good shoes, tiny waist.

What can I do against that! Me with my shit clothes and no money, well fuck you. Lacey Sparkman, God damn her guts. Her with her shiny mouth, probably not the only part of her that snaps open and shut like a red lacquer box. Well, I'll get you.

So the thing rising up to get you is never the thing you're afraid of. It never is. And all she could do was leave him a note.

Monday. Something awful has happened and Delia had to move into a new place. It's sad, the things you lose because of love.

She is jammed in the corner of this basement furnace room. She's been sitting on the floor in this dank corner with her arms clamped around her knees replaying her tapes – for how long? God, since late yesterday, when she got back to the boarding house and they had the fight. Her landlady threw her out, the bitch!

Never mind what this place looks like, it's not important. No place is important right now, she is moving to a nicer place. Inside her head. She's furnished it with Theo, after all, they are in love. All she has to do is get up and change her clothes so she will look nice when she goes in to the newspaper.

All she has to do now is find Theo and tell him her big news. They can play the scene she wrote for them. They'll announce their engagement and all this will go away. She can move into his house and the landlady can go to hell. Except there's one thing in the way.

She's here because Theo didn't come home Saturday night and she knows exactly whose fault that is. If he'd been home he would have begged her to move her stuff in there. Instead she's here because Theo was out and that stupid bitch her landlady caught her coming in Sunday and blew her stack over the leather miniskirt. One thing too many, one extra black mark in the book and the bitch kicked her out. Out on her ear, OK, she was pissed because she'd finally figured out what happened to her missing clothes, all her best things torn at the seams because the bitch is too skinny for a normal person to fit her clothes. Plus since the class started Delia's bought so many new clothes to make herself look nice for Theo that she kind of got behind on the rent.

Right, Delia is pissed at the landlady, but that isn't the real reason she's pissed.

It's that candy TV woman. Lacey Sparkman, Delia thinks, rocking, rocking in the middle of her cluttered, murky space. The bitch. This is all her fault. Lacey Sparkman. She knew

Theo was in love with me and she didn't care. She knew it and she used her fucking body like a candy cane to grab him by the neck and take him away from me. Well she is going to pay for it. Take him away will you, Delia thinks, insofar as she is thinking.

Well, watch your back, TV lady. I am going to make you pay.

21

Theo goes in at dawn on Monday because he's promised Lacey Sparkman to meet for coffee at eight. He's trying to figure out how to break the news to Lacey that Saturday night was a mistake because he can't get Sally off his mind. It's still dark out; it's even dark inside but Delia is here ahead of him, setting up a little display on his computer. Model intern, you bet. 'What's this?'

The smile Delia turns to him is voracious; she is drawn taut. There are shadows under her eyes, as if she stayed up all night preparing this. 'Big news!'

He's already pissed at her for making him feel so guilty and pissed at himself for feeling guilty, so he has to be extra nice to her. 'Sorry I missed you yesterday. I was—' Uh.

Breathless with excitement, she rushes over his unfinished sentence. 'I thought you'd never come.'

'I got your note.'

A bubble glazes over her wounded smile. 'I waited and waited.'

'I'm sorry,' he says again. *I should have known.* Wait a minute. What should he have known? Something about this encounter is eluding him. Why, when his business is his own business, the girl's reproaches make him feel so bad.

'Look at this!' Delia has propped a letter on his keyboard along with forms in three colors, each bearing an academic seal. She looks up at him like a small animal protecting something it's afraid you'll want to eat. 'I was wait-listed. Now I'm in.'

'In what?' Theo notes peripherally that Delia is oddly dressed today. Nothing matches. The clothes look as if they came out of different Dumpsters. Everything clashes, even the smile.

'In what? In what! Just look at the letter!'

He says, without looking down, 'These forms. College admissions forms?'

'College, hell. I just got into Columbia. Journalism school!'

'Congratulations. Hey, New York!' If it was anybody else, Theo would hug her, he's that relieved. He can see the window opening, and he can hardly wait to help her get up on the windowsill so she can jump out of his life. The girl has a place in the journalism school at Columbia this September. *There is a God.* He's already a half-ton lighter and he can feel the rest of the weight lifting. Free. 'This is great!'

But Delia says carefully, 'That was before. Now you're here and everything's changed. So. I'm in, but . . . Ah . . .' She falters. 'I have to be there in two weeks.' She creates a weighted pause. She is waiting for him to say something.

He can't think of anything more to say.

'I. Ah . . . Isn't there anything you want to say to me?'

'Congratulations.' He can already hear the buzzer: *wrong.*

'I just don't think I ought to go. Now that I'm in good at the *Star.*'

'Columbia's a lot bigger than the *Star.*'

'I just thought. I'd hate to let it break up . . .' She is waiting for him to finish the sentence for her.

What does she want from him? Studying the intern with her varnished black sweep of eyelashes and her trembling mouth, Theo realizes that it's been a long, hard summer. He understands how tired he is. Too many damn particles. This. He can't wait to get her out of his life. 'Listen.' Hopeful, he presses on. 'Seriously, Delia, this is terrific.'

She blushes at the sound of her own name. 'Thank you.' She can't quite say his.

'So. When do you go?'

'Go?' Delia's head snaps back on her neck but she recovers quickly and cobbles a smile. Like a pet looking over its shoulder and willing you to follow, she leads him to the next thing. 'Why would I want to go? I mean, I don't think I should go, do you? You don't think I should go either, right?'

It makes him uneasy. 'Of course you should go. Columbia!'

'I'm learning so much right here! You know. Your class.'

'Oh, the class. That's over. It ends next week.'

Somewhere out of sight a complex mechanism *clicks*; she looks so pleased! 'No way. They came around with the forms again? And since I got you to teach for the summer, they paid special attention to what I said?' She grins. 'They think you're teaching it again this fall.'

He is backpedaling furiously. 'That's fine for me.' It is. He can pay off the furniture. 'But you. Community college isn't a real journalism school, OK? The staff. Networking. The city.'

'Yeah, well, that's another thing.' She regards him with pale, reflective eyes. 'The money.'

'You can take loans.'

'No credit rating.' Smug grin. 'I can't possibly go.'

'We'll find a way. The paper will help. Hell, I could help.' He's talking too fast and he knows it, anything to make this happen. 'Or you could ask your folks.'

Anger transforms her. The flash of rage is frightening. 'My folks. Fuck my folks.' Unaccountably huge with it, full-breasted and furious, the intern ages ten years. She was never a girl. The woman says bitterly, 'My folks are dead.'

'I'm sorry.'

'Don't be. They don't give a shit.'

128

Better not ask about that one, Slate. Think fast. 'Listen, Delia. Don't give up on this, at least not until I try a couple of things.' Accidentally he gives her a valedictory pat – unless it's a push – and jumps as the woman turns in blind gratitude at his touch and flows against him.

'Oh,' she says, gasping. 'Oh, you!'

Backing away hastily, he barks, 'Funding. I'll get on it.' Like Chick. If I can only sound like Chick. 'I think—'

'No, don't!' Delia cuts him off. 'I love the *Star*. It's so late in the year anyway and besides I can take your class this fall and besides Chick's started using my stuff and I just don't think I should go, do you really think I should go away right when everything is going so well?' She is changing right here in front of him, but the modulations are so swift and so subtle that there's no sorting them out. 'Just tell me! Don't you want me to stay?'

'The Whartons,' Theo says. 'That's it!' The *Star*'s publishers will pay. 'Don't sweat it. I'll find you the money, OK? So be cool, Delia, OK? Look, I can't talk any more,' he says. 'I can't.' He turns her bodily and moves her out of his cubicle. He has got to end this. 'I was just leaving. I have to meet somebody for coffee now.'

'I thought you would be excited.'

'I am excited,' Theo says. 'It's good news.' He repeats unnecessarily, 'Really good.' Then he speeds her out the best way he knows how, fobbing her off with a promise. 'If it works, I'll take you out to dinner to celebrate.'

'Dinner.' She melts into syrup before his eyes, flowing away from him with a gooshy look over her shoulder. 'Dinner. Oh!'

So he is free. At least for now.

Funny, how the next thing happens. Saturday night's encounter with Lacey Sparkman clicked one part of his life into perspective. *That's not what I want. A quick hit and run.*

He goes to his séance with Lacey choked with apologies

that she doesn't seem to need. He says, 'This is crazy but I thought I ought to level with you.'

She taps bright fingernails on the pistol-handled table knife. 'I only have a minute. Do you want the cruller or the Danish?'

'About us.'

Even at this hour her face is as perfect as a Kabuki mask. 'What us?'

'I like you, Lace, but I have to tell you up front. I like you but I can't do this.'

To which Lacey responds so quickly that it stings, 'Who asked you to do anything?'

He tries, 'I don't usually. Ah.' How do you tell a woman you don't usually hit on them and run? He tries, 'I'm coming down off a bad relationship.' He tries, 'You were nice to me and I thought.'

'Well, don't,' she says with that glossy for-the-camera smile. 'My real guy is at ABC-TV in New York.'

'You should have told me.'

'No explanations, no apologies, Slate. Really.' She is cool with it. She really is. And this is how Lacey supplies him with the vocabulary. 'You were just a quick bang on my way to making a buck.'

'You're a good person, Lace.'

She gives him a wicked grin. 'Oh no I'm not.'

Absolved, he is too focused on this to see who watches them going into the Spot that morning or who stands there waiting to see them coming out.

He takes Sally to dinner that night. Nice place in the next big city, expensive, to signal that he means everything he says to her and everything he'd like to say. She lets down that one-of-the-guys facade for him and he tells her stuff about himself that he doesn't tell most people. Everything. Well, almost everything. He tells her Carey called and that he blew Carey off, that he's over it and he'd like to start seeing her. And Sally?

Sally grins and comes back with a gag line, 'OK, my people will get with your people and we'll get back to you on this.'

Theo takes both her hands and sets them on the table to hold her in place. He won't let go until she meets his eyes, linking them. 'No. Let's us talk, one on one.'

22

It's hard to know what's happening to me, Stella thinks, pacing her shoebox cell in the heavy coverall – humiliating to a woman who cares about what she wears. But after what I did, it's as good as I deserve. God, she thinks. I thought I would be dead by now.

Whatever Stella Zax was before she fell out of her careful, nice life and landed here, whoever she thought she was, it is all being leached out of her. Pride. Emotion. Thought and self. When they brought her up here to the county jail she thought it was all settled. She did what she had to. The state would make her pay. God knows she is ready to pay. She wants to be punished for what she did so she can put her heart to rest.

What she did was so terrible that when she stepped back from the car that night and it roared over the edge and plunged into the quarry, Stella was blind. Deaf and dumb. Waiting to be struck dead. *Now. You can do it now.* Nothing happened to her. She walked out of the jaws unscathed. Sobbing, she staggered away from the pit while the drowned car was still belching air. Then she had to walk to the road and wait for the bus.

When she was arraigned and sent to County she thought something blinding would happen. Then she could die. They would try her at once. See she was guilty and hang her or gas her or whatever it is that the state does to end the lives of murderers. But there is no electric chair where Stella is being held and no gas chamber. County, she is only in the county jail. She is in Holding, awaiting trial. On her good days Stella knows this, but the monstrous shapes lurching through her head are rearranging knowledge and memory so profoundly that she's losing track.

Live in silence long enough and your own thoughts will rise up and scream until they deafen you.

Wait long enough for anything and you will go out of your mind. This is Stella Zax, who killed her best and only son because she loved him, reflecting on who she is and what she is.

What she is, is waiting for the sound of something she can't identify.

Something that will eventually happen?

Some truth about to be revealed?

She does not know. But in the weeks since they showered her and deloused her and searched her privates for things she would never think of hiding, since they handed her the uniform and she put it on and let them march her out of the single cell they reserve for defendants in capital crimes, Stella Zax has been in stasis. The meals come on time and she eats them. The lights go on and off on time. Visiting hours come and go as scheduled. The reporter comes on time and because she has nothing new to tell him she sends him away every time. The mail comes on time, but except for these sad letters from the reporter, nothing comes for her.

Or nothing did. Every night Stella would pad in circles on the cement praying, *Oh God, if You won't strike me dead, please send me a sign.*

Now it has come.

It is a letter. *Mother, I miss you so much.*

'Presty!' Grief makes her howl.

But this is not his handwriting.

A manila envelope. A gift box slides out. It's a flowered pocket handkerchief. This is something Presty would never buy, but there is a gift tag with *Mother* embossed above her name.

Another letter, with a photograph.

It is the photograph that unseats Stella Zax and overturns the reasonable part of her and leaves it flailing inside her skull, because she's seen it before but she's never seen it like this. It is her own likeness. Hers and . . . Somebody has sent Stella the studio portrait she had taken for the arrest, a little blurry yes, but definitely her. But now there's somebody else in the picture. His handsome head is lined up right next to hers, as if they had posed together on the same day. He looks nice enough, dress shirt with a tie and a half-smile, good-looking young man, head shaped a little like Presty's, never saw him before so what does it mean? What could it possibly mean?

And the letter that comes with? One line. *I can't wait to see you after all this time.*

It is strange, disturbing and either beautiful or monstrous. What's happening, and how have these things come to her? Gnawing her knuckles, Stella paces and goes on pacing through exhaustion until she is beyond reason. She does not know. She doesn't know!

23

Sally slides into the booth next to him. 'As Jeffrey Dahmer said to Lorena Bobbitt, are you gonna eat that?'

'Stop that!' Theo defends his French fries with a blind, loving smile. 'I just did this amazing thing.'

Laughing, Sally kisses him. Yes they're that far along, even though it's only been two weeks; she comes to his house now, but will not sleep over. Yet. 'Like what?'

'I got Delia's tuition out of the company.'

'You squeezed blood out of the Whartons?'

'I convinced them that they're supporting the next Anna Quindlen, Ellen Goodman crossed with Edna Buchanan rolled into Kathy Lee. They even threw in walking-around money. A check for her.'

She grins. 'Better get her out of town before they see her up close.'

'She's going tomorrow.' *Not soon enough*, Theo thinks. No more letters on lavender paper. Phone calls at odd hours. Little presents. Fresh flowers in the kitchen. He's changed the locks. No more flyovers, just when you thought you were alone.

'Not a minute too soon.'

He winces. 'I'm taking her out to dinner to celebrate.'

'Lucky you.' Then Sally takes him by surprise. 'At least it isn't Sparkman.'

His head jerks. 'What?'

'You know.' She is not exactly smiling. 'I know about

your thing with Lacey, T. Your friend Delia likes to dump your phone slips on my desk by accident. Then she mentions it, in case I didn't get the point.'

'I'm sorry. I asked her to stop calling.'

But Sally goes on. 'Then she tells me about how you went to Lacey's and slept over.'

'That was before we ever.' *How did she know?* 'Oh Sally, I'm sorry.'

'You should have told me. No. Maybe you shouldn't have told me.' In a way, Sally's distress is encouraging. Theo's brought her this far hoping she cares. Now her tone tells him that she really does care. 'Oh, T.'

So he puts two fingers in her palm and looks at her straight on. 'I'm sorry, Sally. I should have told you. Delia shouldn't . . .'

'She doesn't like Lacey much either,' Sally says.

'Thank God she's leaving town.'

'Remember I tried to warn you. I did.'

'I got so hung up on this project I—'

'You mean all your mass murderers and serial guys?'

'I really am sorry. You're the only thing that matters here.'

Sally curls her hand around his fingers. 'It's OK, T. Things will clear up when we lose Delia. She's crazy about you. How did you get her to go?'

'I told her it was the only way we could stay friends. She registers Monday. New York.' Without even a pang for Carey he grins. 'Wish it was Mars.' About time, Theo thinks, he's sick of being wakened by Delia's phone calls; the woman has a seventh sense. She's all over him. 'At least she'll quit calling. There aren't enough quarters in the world.'

'She's still calling you?'

'Yeah.'

The intern always starts with that 'UM . . .' she uses instead of his name. 'UM . . . Have you got a minute?'

Then she lets this pointed silence fall. It's as if Delia is waiting for Theo to follow a script she's written but will not divulge. He's supposed to guess. What does she want from him? He's afraid to ask.

He hates to see her coming. For somebody he hardly thinks about, she's too much in his life. She calls the house when Sally's there and right after Sally has kissed him and gone and he's alone. Monday he and Sally heard rustling outside: hedge crunching and soft footsteps under his bedroom window. Theo threw on a T-shirt and blundered out: 'Who's there?' He leaned into the dark. 'Who's there?' He half expected to find his greatest fan on his doorstep swelling with good intentions, but the night seemed empty and like Delia in broad daylight on a work day, innocent enough. Listen, it was nothing, but the woman makes him feel not exactly haunted, but uneasy. It's like having poltergeists. You get up in the morning and everything in your house is still the same but it seems different, as if something you didn't notice has been moved somewhere you didn't know about. You bet he had the locks changed.

You bet it's time for her to go.

'Tonight,' Sally says.

'Dinner.' He folds her hand under his chin. 'Then it's over.'

'It's way past time.'

Funny. Delia won't let him pick her up at the boarding house. Instead she arranges to meet him at the *Star*. She's wearing a raincoat in spite of the late summer heat and in spite of the heat she keeps it on when she gets into the car with her face overflowing with rehearsed speeches and a blush that starts somewhere inside her coat collar and boils up to the roots of her hair.

'Gee,' she says. 'This is *so great*.'

'Listen,' he says dutifully, *count your blessings, Slate, it's almost over*, 'you deserve it. You worked hard.' He notes the case Delia is carrying, black leatherette with a monogram – not hers. 'What have you got in there?'

If she would only stop *beaming*. 'You'll see.'

'It's ninety degrees. Aren't you going to take off the coat?'

'After we get there,' she says.

'Aren't you hot?'

'Not really.'

Yes it makes him uneasy. All those short stories about people naked under raincoats. Movies. Bad TV. 'You're not. Uh.' Don't even think it. 'We're going someplace kind of crowded,' he warns.

'That's OK.'

'It's kind of dressy.'

'Oh, don't worry about me.'

He does not add: and well-lighted. 'Top of the Hyatt. A lot of people there.'

'Great!' For the first time since he's known her, Delia giggles. 'Dancing?'

'Not really.'

'I love dancing.'

'I don't think they have dancing.' Theo is lying; they do.

She will not stop beaming. Her voice softens. 'Top of the Hyatt. This is so wonderful! You're taking me to the top of the Hyatt.'

'Just this once,' Theo says.

'Oh, once is enough for us,' she says.

There is no right response. He turns up the radio so he can pretend not to hear. When they get to their table in the revolving restaurant he offers to take the slim black case. Delia jerks it away – what's she got in there, assault weapon? Forty-five? At the waiter's insistence she first clutches the coat defensively and then unbuttons it and lets it go. The minute she unveils Theo is sorry. It is no relief to find that the girl is in fact wearing something underneath. With naked, he could just cover her up fast and dial 911. Naked would be better than what she is wearing. For this casual supper in honor of her leaving Center City, the woman's put on an elaborately constructed, expensive dress of red wool that exposes her arms and her throat and the curvature of her plump, freckled breasts. She grins up at him with lipstick on her teeth and blue mascara fringing her eyes. 'Oh,' she says. 'Oh, Theo.'

'Here,' he says. 'You sit here. Are you comfortable?' Theo is extremely uncomfortable. Shrouded in one of those rayon Jiffy Bags or the hooker outfits she contrived for class, Delia was easy to dismiss. Unveiled, she is only slightly overweight and alarmingly feminine, with everything not already showing easily revealed. It's embarrassing, seeing her dead white upper arms, rounded and without muscle, as if they have come to her unused. She's done heavy makeup and her orange curls are sculpted and sprayed in place. Her eyes are pale blue, it turns out, pale blue and swimming. In a way, this is scarier than naked. It's like coming too close to the real person, with her lips parted and her fixed, moist stare.

'Oh yes,' she says. 'This is so *great*.'

'Ah.' He coughs. 'Ahm! I bet you can't wait to get away.'

'Oh Theo,' she says mournfully. 'I don't know!'

'So, what looks good to you? Lobster? Steak? Sky's the limit.'

She murmurs, 'After dinner I have a surprise for you.'

'Lobster,' he says. Lobster will focus her on the mechanics of getting the thing open and getting it eaten without sending shells and juice squirting all over the place. 'Lobster, I think.'

'I just hate that I'm leaving.'

'Don't say that.' He says falsely, 'We're here to celebrate.'

Food helps. She thanks Theo for everything he's done

for her – coaching at the *Star*, the class, he's the best teacher she's ever had and this is all thanks to him. He gets all bashful and grins. Then she promises she'll make him proud of her and Theo says generously, 'Yeah, you will. You can be the best.'

And, wham! She comes back with, 'Better than Lacey Sparkman.'

'Lacey?' Wary, he squints. 'What is your problem with Lacey?'

Delia looks down; her lashes have smudged her round cheeks. 'She. Uh. I didn't want to tell you but, she's been sneaking into your.' But she doesn't finish. Instead like a magician she conjures up something completely different. 'Oh look, the dessert cart!'

Then Delia falls silent, as if she's waiting for Theo to say something he still hasn't said. By the time he tells her a fourth cup of coffee is definitely one too many, he is crazy to end this. He overtips the hatcheck person and hurries her into the raincoat – cover her *up*! She picks up the black case and hugs it to her breasts so he has to give up and drape the raincoat on her shoulders. Then he bundles her into the car and drives back to her boarding house with retro rock blaring out of all four speakers so when they don't talk she won't notice, and if she blurts whatever's on her mind, he can pretend not to hear. He'd like to open the door and shove her out without slowing down and speed away like a Mafioso delivering a corpse, but he can't. He parks and manages the patience to wait while Delia collects her belongings and sits for entirely too long before getting out. When she leans back in as if to speak he cuts her off politely. 'So, congratulations.'

'Oh Theo,' she reproaches him. 'Don't go. This is so wonderful.'

'I'm sorry, I have to . . .' What? Anything else but this. As he slams the door her voice rises. 'Please wait.'

'Sorry, I can't.'

'Wait.'

'I can't.'

'But I have a surprise for you.'

'Sorry!' *No more surprises!* He starts the motor, only peripherally aware that Delia has dropped the coat. She's standing in the street in front of the darkened boarding house in her sad, sexy dress with her arms spread and her mouth open in beginning speech.

So when Theo ends this and scratches off her words will follow him, rattling behind the car like a string of tin cans tied to the back axle: Delia's Amazing Free Offer. 'Wait,' she cries. 'Please wait.'

He leans out. 'I can't, I'm late.'

'Late for what?'

He is going to Sally's but something makes him keep this from her. God, he's afraid to tell her. He calls, 'It's about Lacey.'

As Theo steps on the gas DeliaMarie Vent gives him this to take away with him. Standing with her arms spread and those orange curls bobbing, the woman cries in that wounded, musical voice of hers, 'I only wanted to play the flute for you!'

24

You can get in to see anyone you want in the county jail. Anyone. As long as they agree to see you. Stella Zax's visitor is familiar enough with prison procedure to know this. Present yourself at the desk. Go through the metal detector and surrender anything that might be construed as a weapon. At this particular county jail, take a number. Send your name upstairs and wait. He also knows what to say to bring Stella Zax down to the visitors' room.

The guard comes to her cell. 'Your son is here.'

Stella grunts. It's as if a fist has slammed her in the chest. Her heart jumps and begins to thunder. Her mouth dries out. *My God. He's here.* But who? 'My son?' *My son is dead.* He is dead but it is confusing. Letters lately. Presents. Picture he sent.

'He's sitting right down there in the visitors' room.'

'No he isn't.' Even as she speaks Stella is studying the photograph taped to the cement-block wall of her cell. She looks at it all the time now, trying to find the blurred outline or the infinitesimal flaw that will tell her this is a composite. They look so sweet together, Stella and this person she thinks she doesn't know. But he sends presents. On her open shelf the handkerchief sits in its box next to a pretty carved wooden rose. It's nicer than any present Presty bought for her. Nice, she can see that in the young man's face in the picture. Now he's down in the visitors' room. She doesn't know what to do. So very like Presty and not like Presty oh God she misses him so much.

'I know you aren't seeing anybody but . . .' A mother herself, the guard is glistening with good intentions. 'Come on,' she says. 'Whatever has come between you two, he's all you have left now.'

'I can't,' Stella says, but she misses her son how could she not, she would give anything to erase it and start over again.

The guard cajoles. 'Of course you can. That's a good girl.'

'I don't know,' Stella says.

'Come on,' the guard says kindly. 'It'll do you good.'

I'm not so sure. 'You can't know that.'

'Here, put on your lipstick. You want to look nice for him.'

Following the guard down to the visiting room, Stella runs her hands over her hair with a sigh of regret for all the pretty things she had to leave behind her when they dragged her out of the house. Soft blouses, earrings. She laments the unbecoming prison coverall with its ugly connotations. So sad! Here he is at long last. Whoever he is. A second chance, Stella thinks, maybe God is giving me a second chance. Whoever he is, he'll take me out of here and we can go home together. By the time they reach the visitors' room she is unsettled and jittering. God, she is excited. She hurries into the long room with its Plexiglas partitions and little stalls, where other prisoners lean in to talk to their visitors. From behind they look like so many horses feeding. The guard shows her to her own stall. On the other side, her visitor is waiting. My God! Seen in outline like that, he looks a little like Presty. Sitting down in a giddy, hopeful rush she leans in to take a close look at him through the aging Plexiglas. 'Who?'

Then with a smile that makes Stella wonder how long it's been since anybody smiled at her like that – if anybody has; smiling, he picks up the phone and waits for her to pick up the phone. When he speaks the sound rushes into her head and judgment takes flight. There is an arresting pitch to his voice, smokey and seductive. It fills her head and drives reason out. Lifting everything they say out of the physical world, he casts it on some alternative plane where nothing is certain and anything is possible. The stranger says, – Aren't you glad to see me?

– Who are you?

– Don't you know me, Mother?

– You're not any son of mine.

– Don't be too sure. Do you know me? He leans in so close that his breath fogs the shield. – Don't you know me now?

– Whoever you are, I can't see you. I can't see anybody.

– I'm not just anybody.

– So you might as well go now. She ought to signal the guard to take her away but she can't bring herself to leave just yet. Not with his voice filling her head, not with him smiling like that. Instead of putting down the phone she says, – You told the guard you were my son. I only have one son.

– Had, he says. – Preston.

– And now he's dead.

– And I'm here, he says with an expression so warm that she can't bear to turn away.

– But you're not my son.

– What makes you so sure?

– I only had one son, she says. She does not have to say, *and I murdered him.* She doesn't know how he knows, but he knows.

– And now you have me to do things for you. You have me to be proud of. He holds up a copy of the picture. – We look nice together, don't we?

– That isn't us.

– Of course it is. Here we are together, Mother. You and me.

– We were never together for a picture, Stella says.

– Oh yes we were. Don't you remember, Mother?

His smile is so nice that she says, – I wish I did.

– Don't you remember that day? We had such a sweet time together that we decided we should have our pictures taken. And the photographer said, do you want to know what he said to me?

The voice is so hypnotic that she says yes just so he will keep talking.

– He looked at us and he said, 'What a nice family.' And we are. Sorrow darkens his voice. – You were so proud of me.

Stella's vision clouds. With tears? She doesn't know. – We . . .

The stranger who is beginning to look sweet and familiar smiles engagingly and after a pause in which Stella absorbs what he is trying to tell her he says, – Aren't we? Mother.

– I have to go.

– Don't go. Mother.

– Don't call me that, Stella says with her heart breaking. *My own son, and I . . . I can't kill him twice!* She can't bear to do it, not even accidentally. Grieving, she says, – I'm not your mother.

– But I'm your son. Look at me, Mother. I'm your son, he says, and what he says next shakes Stella Zax to the deep place where reason sits, unsettling some crucial part of her before she understands what's happening. He says, – We all are.

She was about to get up. Now she can't. She sits down hard, staring intently through the crazed Plexiglas. When she can speak she says in a low voice, – What do you want from me?

He does not answer. – That was a terrible thing you did.

– I know it is. Not *was*. That's the hell of it. It still is.

– A terrible thing.

Her eyes widen and her pupils snap open like black holes bored through to the back of her skull. She ought to leave and she can't leave. She has to stay here and listen. – Who are you?

– I came to set things straight, he says.

Wild to understand, she blurts, – Like that reporter.

– Reporter? What reporter?

His glare is so sudden and intense that she says protectively, – Never mind. I think you'd better go away. She can still escape from this, she thinks, but inside her, crucial parts are dropping off the walls and smashing like the first stones in an avalanche.

– Yes, he says. – If you want me to go, of course I'll go. A mother like you. Her grimace of pain tells him he has selected the right weapon. He drives it home. – You never loved me anyway.

I did love you! – What do you mean?

– All I'm trying to do is make you proud, he says in an altered tone. – How could you do it, Mother? After everything I did?

After everything I did. She gasps. – I'm not your mother!

– And am doing. And you. Then, unaccountably wronged, this stranger so like her son reproaches Stella Zax in words that make her surge to her feet. They'll follow her out of the room no matter how fast she runs; they will follow her upstairs into her cell; they will overflow and fill her life, reverberating until they hit a frequency that sends her rocketing into her own chasm of despair. Speaking in her dead son's voice, the stranger *so like him* says this, overturning certainty. In time it will bring her down. – Look what you did. You'll be sorry, Mother. I'm going to make you proud.

25

Delia is on the bus now, with most of the things she cares about – flute in its leather case, the book Theo accidentally gave her, the best of her clothes. She is riding away from Center City with a sense of grief.

She loves him so much! But, she tells herself, I'm doing this for him. Columbia! He wants me to be as good as he is so we can get jobs on the best newspaper in some big town. God how is it that I have to go when all I was trying to do was make him beg me to stay? The trouble is she isn't exactly crying except she is, tears making her so angry she wants to smash something. She wants to smash something and she can hardly see her way to the empty seat at the back of the bus.

Never mind, you have to do this because he loves you. This is the little song she sings to herself. When we're married and we both get good jobs in big places you'll be glad.

It makes her want to vomit, thinking about it.

Unless I am having his baby, she thinks wildly. Look at me, ready to throw up. She's bigger in the middle; she is. Her belly twists and something inside her lurches and begins to kick. Strange things happen for no reason. Maybe I am pregnant with his baby. I wish I was having it *now*.

Then the bus pitches and all her possessions slide out of her control. Then one way or another somebody has put her into a seat and somebody is jamming things on the shelf above her head – *don't be so rough*. The flute case skitters out of her reach and goes crashing into the aisle and all her grief is bubbling up and if it gets away from her the flute oh God; she bangs her head and teeth cut into her lip. *What if he forgets me?* It's as if parts of Delia's insides are still tied to the post in front of Theo Slate's house in Center City and the bus is pulling her out of herself like thread off a spool, heart and soul, body and substance. She grunts in pain and frustration. 'Oh!'

'Are you all right?' There is a man leaning over her in the dim light from the tinted bus windows.

Startled, she jumps up so fast that she bumps her head. 'What do you mean?' Her flute case pitches off the overhead shelf and as she saves it the shopping bag riding on the seat next to her topples and she lunges to right it.

'I heard you groaning.' The man puts everything back in place for her.

'No you didn't.'

In this light, it's hard to make out his face. 'I know I heard something.'

'Well it wasn't me.'

He waits until she sits back down. Then he says, 'Are you sure you're all right?'

'I'm fine.'

The stranger is swaying in the aisle as the bus goes; he has a nice enough face even in this light; he says, 'Is it OK if I sit with you?'

There are plenty of places on the bus. She needs to be alone with this so she can figure out what to do next. 'Not really.'

But he has such a nice way, this guy, saying to her nicely, 'You look like you could use a friend.'

'I'm fine,' she says. 'I'm wonderful.'

'Can I sit down?'

The stranger with the fresh haircut really is OK-looking; if she and Theo weren't in love, if they weren't about to,

Delia might even. His eyes are warming her. 'Oh,' she says finally. 'OK.'

They ride along without talking for a long time.

'So. Where are you heading?'

'New York.' The rest comes out. 'But I don't want to.'

'Why not?'

She can't tell him the truth so she says, 'I hate big cities.'

'I know just how you feel,' he says. 'I hate them too.'

'All those people you don't know.'

They seem to be hitting it off so she says, 'All those people.'

'But that isn't the real problem,' he says.

'No,' she says. 'No, it isn't.'

'Do you want to tell me what it is?'

'I can't talk about this right now, OK?'

'You have to tell somebody.'

They ride along and they ride along. He sits quietly next to her. She can feel him waiting. 'OK,' she says. 'It's my boyfriend.' She wants to tell him everything, she doesn't want to tell him anything. It's like the place between your legs. Too private. To divert him, she asks, 'What about you?'

'Me? I'm looking for a new town. Not just any town. The right town for me. Not too big.'

'Then you don't want New York.' She is shaking her head like a paperweight and in her current disrupted state it is filled with old, familiar images. The tower. The Green with its three churches; she's never been in even one of them but it gives her a glow. The warmth of the familiar. The heavy tires of the bus are making a regular bobbidy-bobbidy sound that is like his voice, easy and reassuring.

He considers. 'You're right. New York is too big for me.'

Bobbidy-bobbidy. 'It's probably too big for me,' she says.

'But you're going to . . .'

'New York. Yes. But you. You might like New Haven.'

'New Haven?'

'It's on the way.' Then, lulled by the roar of the bus and the presence of this nice stranger, she tells him more about herself than she's ever told anybody; DeliaMarie Vent, who may be traveling under a name that is not her own for reasons she doesn't talk about, Delia says, 'I wouldn't mind living there.'

'New Haven? Are you from there?'

'Yes. No. I used to be.'

'But you're going to New York.'

'Yeah, and it's too far away.' If he is watching her, she isn't aware that he is watching her. She isn't exactly paying attention here. Her mind is traveling out Whitney Avenue like a Steadicam, onto a side street so pretty and familiar that she has to pull back before she runs up, sobbing, and starts pounding on the front door.

He is studying her smeared face. 'Maybe you need a smaller town too,' he says.

He will barely be able to make out her muttered: 'I can't go back there.'

'If you want to, you can.' They ride along. The nice thing is he doesn't ask her any questions.

In New Haven, he gets off. 'Thanks for the tip.'

'You're welcome.' Delia sits in her seat for a moment. Sweat glazes her face and trickles down her belly; everything about her is trembling. She ought to ride on and she should, but she can't. She's just looked out the window. She's here. She can't do New York right now, but she can handle this. Fresh passengers get on and find seats. The driver comes back. As the motor starts up she lurches to her feet. 'Wait,' she cries. The driver opens the door and lets her step down.

He is still in the station. 'You decided to stay.'

She doesn't answer. She and her seat partner hesitate on

the curb out front. He asks if she knows any good places to stay. She recommends the Y.

– And you? he says in a voice that's new to her but confident of an answer. It is as if they've traveled somewhere else to have this conversation. – You'll be going home?

– I'll never go home. The truth. – I'd rather die.

– Where will you stay?

– I'll find a place. And she will. The Whartons gave her enough walking-around money to float her until Theo comes to his senses and comes for her. And when he does, why, the trip will be that much shorter. The stranger is still standing there. She tells him goodbye. They shake hands and he turns to go. They promise to stay in touch. She says, – Where will you be? Where should I look for you?

He turns with a smile. – Don't worry, he says. – I'll find you.

26

Theo thought with Delia gone life would be simpler. In a way it is. No more evasive maneuvers, no more looking over his shoulder. The woman is in New York. Out of reach. He can breathe again. He and Sally can just be together without the complications and pressure of nightly flyovers and eerily timed gifts. He didn't realize exactly how much psychic space she occupied. It's like having an elephant lifted out of your living room. Suddenly it's light again. There's plenty of air. You can sit anywhere you want. You are free to expand.

But relief is clouded by the death of Lacey Sparkman – nice woman, they were together exactly once and now she's dead. Discovered in her own garage, days after the accident. Car slipped out of PARK and into DRIVE and mashed poor Lacey against the back wall. So here's a different kind of death to add to his collection. His daily explorations into death are overflowing into his life. New killing outside Albany like the ones in Scranton and Angola, signature bitemarks, savage and without reason but oddly repetitive, like the epic killings tacked to his office wall. Atrocities mount until the numbers overwhelm him. He needs to find the pattern! Troubled, he tries to see Stella Zax and she still won't talk to him.

The phone calls have started again. Delia. *Did I do something to bring this on?* She hangs on the line and won't quit. It's gotten so he jumps every time he hears the phone.

'I'm sorry, I can't talk right now.'

'Oh, Theo,' Delia says anyway, 'I'm so sorry about Lacey.'

'We're all sorry . . . How did you know?'

'My old landlady,' she says with a forced laugh. 'My best friend. Oh Theo, I miss you so much!'

'I can't talk right now, OK?' Why does this make him feel soiled? He hates the phone. After a while he quits answering.

This brings Sally to his door, looking sweet and grave. 'Chick wants you. It's Stella Zax. She just tried to rip the ears off a guard.'

The warden at County has assigned a private room for this encounter. Stella Zax comes down in shackles. She is leached of color, as if drained by her own violence. If Theo is profoundly altered by his material, so is the prisoner. The gates to her face are thrown wide; the army has departed, leaving her undefended. It's like looking into the heart of a ruined city. Bleak. Sad. For this interview, the woman who wants to be remembered for her nice jewelry and matching pastels is swaddled in canvas. Hair cropped to the bone. She looks at Theo over the guard's head as the matron works on the restraints. She sits patiently while they undo the buckles on her canvas sleeves, freeing her arms so she can sit without toppling. Then both women withdraw to bracket the door.

On the far side of the one-way glass, the warden is watching. The county sheriff is watching. The prosecution and the public defender are watching. Although she sees nothing but her own reflection, Stella looks straight into the occluded eye of the window with a complicit nod. 'You wanted a statement.'

He sets his tape recorder on the steel table. 'Do you mind?'

'Of course not.' Stella Zax lays her palms flat on the soapy grey surface; blunt instruments shrouded in canvas.

153

She leans forward. It is unclear what has brought them to this moment. 'Isn't this what you wanted?'

'You could have just called me,' Theo says. It troubles him that Stella Zax attacked a guard just to get him here. What does she think, that she can confess to Theo and he'll give her absolution and she can walk free?

'It wasn't time. Now it is.' After a long pause, she says from somewhere deep, 'Something is happening to me.'

'I'm not a priest.'

She sits across from him like a huge canvas package that will destruct if he tugs the wrong strap. Fixed in an uncanny calm place where nothing can touch her, the prisoner will not release his eyes. She smiles as if she has made a different mistake in her head. 'I know that, son,' she says.

Should he be afraid? He doesn't know. Can guards restrain her if she lunges? Did they sock her full of Thorazine to render her harmless? *What am I doing here?* 'You know I'm not your son.'

The silence that follows is awful.

In the medical Stations of the Cross that stand between what doctors call 'alert and oriented times three' and somnolence and coma, there is a grey zone called 'aware.' Stroke victims go there; they know *that* they are, but not *who*. Stella Zax is none of these places. Today she is in a zone as yet uncharted, from which she sends back this dispatch, forged in pain and delivered whole. 'And you know I am a mother.'

'Yes ma'am.'

She lets out a prodigious sigh. 'I am a mother before anything. That's all I am.'

And a murderer. 'Is it OK if I start the tape?'

'When you become a mother you're a mother all your life. It's what you are. You don't stop being a mother just because he dies. You don't stop because they do disgusting things and you don't stop being a mother when you find out what they are doing. It isn't what they do. It's who they

are to you. Mother. Son. I love him. Do you understand
me, son?'

'I'm trying.'

'Then listen. Just listen to me, son.' And so her story
spills out whole, falling into the room like a gross, unwieldy
infant that got too big inside her, tearing flesh to escape
her body.

'You think I am ashamed, but I am proud. I did my best!
When you make a person, you have no way of knowing the
future. If you could, it would kill you. The grief! So sweet
and little. So cute. You think, *Look what I did. Oh God, look
at what I did. I made him breathe!* Your miracle. You started
this life! And no matter who you thought you were before,
no matter how homely you are or how bad people treat you,
you have changed history.'

She smiles a blind mother's smile. 'Now, that's power.'

The woman's irises shudder and start to spin. What yoo
hoo pills have the prison doctors given her? 'I couldn't
afford your fancy college. I am a nurse. People know
you well enough when they are sick, they do. Oh help,
nurse. Please, nurse. You are their god. They get well and
forget. Doctors, they use you but they don't see you. You
are furniture. *The nurse.* Never mind that you know their
jobs better than them. They take the scalpel from you and
the sponge; they give orders and they never see your face.
Fuck you, Doctor. That should be me making the cut. If
I had your money that would be me in the OR. Not you.
If I had your physical strength that would be me cracking
your chest open with the ribspreader, and me sawing off
the top of your skull. Me staring into your miserable brain!'
She scowls. 'Women are born screwed. Fucked. Behind in
everything. But we get it back. We do! Men can't create
people. We can. Sons, we make, to go places women can't
get into. Do things we could never do.'

'I'm sorry,' Theo says.

'For my baby's father, I chose an MD. Thank God we

only had to do it once. He never knew. He was only the instrument. Blind prick. I made a son. I thought, *Now you will get it all for me. Together, we will get it back. Fucking doctors*. Preston, that's a doctor's name. *And in my name you will get back at them*. I had it all planned. Chief of Surgery. Big house. Expensive car, pretty wife size six, perfect kids, one of each. We would spit in the eye of every doctor that thought the only name I had was *nurse*.'

Her eyes blaze. 'Preston. My future. Talk about power.'

This is so weird; in the space between Stella's last word and the next one Theo hears Delia's plaintive reproaches: 'I know you're there, pick up. Why won't you talk to me?' He never touched the damn girl but his heart lurches. *What if she's pregnant?*

Stella's moan shakes the room. 'We should have both died. But who knows, when they put your baby in your arms? You are so proud! Your eyes. The father's mouth. Toes! You have made this, and it will go on forever. This *perfect little thing*.'

With a bright face, she lifts her shrouded hands. '*Look what I did!* You get it baptized and take it home. But the baby cries and you feed him and he cries and you change him because when you are one woman alone, no man will help. Flowered nighties that you iron. Everything boiled. Beautiful tiny clothes. Soft things to make him happy, warm ones to keep him safe. You do all this but the baby cries anyway. Oh Preston, please don't. Hug him and he cries and walk him and he cries, can't get him to stop, you think if I hug him closer, if I hug him tight between *these here*.'

She turns a bludgeoned face to him. 'See how easy it is?

'Everything is within your power. The son you made out of yourself and some doctor is completely in your power. So power is what you have, power and control. *My life has not been so good but when this is done he will be perfect. Perfect!*'

Theo needs her to go on. He wishes she would stop.

'But you have guilt. Guilt over shaking him when he cried and you couldn't make him stop, guilt over worse things you didn't do. Guilt because you made this life and *at any time* you can end it. So you have to make it up to him. Give him the world so he won't guess. You spend your life on it. The life you create for him. How he will be. As soon as he can sit you prop him in his little chair. Sit him in the kitchen, where we have all our talks. You bake cookies. You give him milk with tea in it, very grown up for him.'

She forgets the sleeves and, bewildered, tries to comb her hair with her fingers. 'You keep it perfect. The house, even though it's killing you, the rent. No problem, second job. Best chair. Finest sofa. Top-quality carpet, wall-to-wall. Keep your windows covered so your nice things won't fade. Where you don't have plastic, run a damp cloth over the upholstery to pick up lint. A dishwasher is essential. So are the Hoover and your Dust Buster and the Dirt Devil, but when you finish with those you want to go over everything with the mop and the rag. Make him keep his toys in their places on shelves. You are training him for life. "You don't want to own anything you'd ever need to hide."

'Everything has to shine. Clothes. Iron everything. Underwear. Shoes, you make him wax the shoes. When you go out together the world will see how fine he is. You are goddamn good at what you do. Buy him the best. Exactly the right lunch box. The expensive coat so the principal will look at him and *know*. Clothes and pants the best quality. Make him sit in the front row at school and never lean back in the chair, you have ways of knowing if he forgets. Make him be first to raise his hand. And always give the right answer. He has to get A's. Proof positive that we are superior.

'If there's trouble, do his homework. If the other boys are mean, complain to the principal. If there's trouble in class, blame the teacher, but do not let anything slip. If he brings home a D you make him cookies. Our tea. Then sit

157

him in that chair for one of our talks. Talk. Keep talking until D turns into an A. If he does well, you bake for him, *a little party, just us two.*' The smile is sweet and sad: too many teeth showing.

'This is only the beginning. In the end he will park his big car in the Chief of Surgery's slot. And whatever happens, take good care of your son, your treasure, keep him clean as your house. My son the doctor. From the first day he knows. Toy doctor bags you buy for him. Candy pills. And later, things you bring from the hospital. Certain instruments. Syringes without needles, until he is old enough. Things you buy. Melons – honeydews, so he can give injections and learn how to make the first clean cut. Your boy turns the scalpel over in his hands with his mouth working. You say, "Some day." But you and he have a lot to do. Brandy and fudge when it's going well. When it's not, the basement. The chair. Reward and punish in equal measure, but always finish the day with a reward.

'Cookies you cut out with a wine glass. I always dip the rim in sugar to be nice. Our talks. The chair. Trouble at school is never his fault. It's the teacher's fault or the psychologist's; if they say bad things about him, it's because he's so bright that they don't understand him. And they're jealous. After all, look what you have! But you think ahead. If there is trouble, you act. Sit him down in your kitchen. "Now I'm going away, but I'll know if you move from this spot. Do not move until you know in your heart you are going to do better. Promise." You leave him. You know it will take hours. Call from the other room: "Now sit up straight."

'It gets dark. You hear him crying. You hear him stop. You hear him call, "Can I get down now?"

'It's late. "Promise to be good?"

'Liar. He sobs, "I didn't do it."

'Too easy. This is important. Persist. From your easy chair call to him, "I need to hear you promise."

'You will sit all night to get this done. In the end, he will promise anything. "Anything, Mom, I will do anything," he says at last and you go in. That dear face – the doctor's, *yours* – is red and streaked from sobbing. *I hate to see us this way.*'

She has bitten through her lip without knowing it.

'So you hug him and forgive him and you take him in your arms. You love him so *much*. You wish he was still small enough to take on your lap. He sobs. You tell him, "Good, that's good. Now go wash your hands and face and I'll make us something nice."'

'Love, yes, but first things first. Remember, you will lose him when he leaves for Harvard. While you still have him to work with, everything counts. Gear all your efforts to success. And keep it clean for him, house so nice, his clothes, like costumes for the big show. Keep reminding him:

'"This is all for you. Everything I do is for you."'

'He turns eighteen; the future is *close*. But then. Then! He doesn't graduate. All those A's he brought home were forgeries. You are the last to know. You thought he was headed for Harvard. Now this is my fault for being ignorant. I gave Preston cash for college applications, I didn't know he threw it away on cameras. Knives. Disgusting magazines. And whatever he did when he sneaked out at night. Oh well, I thought. Next year. How was I to know?

'I sat him down in the kitchen and I talked to him. You bet I talked to him. I went to the school. They said, "Those grades."'

'I said, "I thought they were . . ." They showed me. "But, Harvard!"'

'They said, "Not with these scores." He never told me there were tests you had to take. They said, "We've been meaning to talk to you, Mrs Zax, but you never answered our notes."'

'I said, "What notes?"'

'They said, "Mrs Zax, we think you may have a problem."'

'You said, "Our only problem is you goddamn jealous people! He can go to Harvard next year. He'll graduate next year."

'They said, "Not from this school." But education is their business. They cover their tracks. "At least, not without help," they said. They do not mean help like I give him, they mean psychiatric help. A hospital. They want me to put him in a place.'

She sobs. 'I'd rather die. I take him away. We have our pride.

'And when I get him home – I talk to him.'

Theo can feel his testicles shrinking. He raises a hand to stop her while he turns the tape. She shifts in her chair. He can't bear to look her in the face.

'Mr Slate! Look at me!'

'I am.'

'No you're not.' Her tone is forbidding. Enormous. '*Look at me when I talk to you.* After all, you wrote to me. You write to me and you ask me, "What are the signs?" Like I'm supposed to tell you just because you ask.'

'Yes.'

Her voice is heavy with disapproval. Thunderous. 'Don't you know you have to earn these things?'

Shivering, he understands this is the tone Preston heard. 'Yes ma'am.' Right now she is so fierce that he would tell her anything.

'You want me to tell you, *What are the signs?* Now I am a mother and I can tell you what are the signs. The signs?' Stella Zax stops. She won't go on until Theo capitulates and meets her glare. Their eyes connect and lock.

She wants me to stare into this without blinking. 'OK.'

'About the signs.' Stella lowers her head, releasing his eyes. 'You can forget about signs. There are no signs. You see?'

Theo slumps. She makes it sound so random. Stella Zax

is turned in on herself, absorbed. He stops the tape. After too long she clears her throat. He starts the tape.

'Yes!' She has arrived at the dark center of her story. She tells it as if to the world outside this room. 'He had to get a job. I bought his clothes. Haircut. The best job I could think of was the bank. My son the doctor, and he was going to work in a bank. "OK," I told him. We were in the kitchen. "It's the best we can do." Fine, at least he could end up bank president. Not a surgeon, but OK. We decided after one of our talks. An executive gets the same big house, expensive car, the kids. He can't cut people open, but that's OK. He can still get in all the best places. Fine.

'And it went all right,' she says. 'For a while. He worked at the bank. I held the ladder so my boy could climb. Then I looked up and he wasn't climbing. I went to the bank president. "Other people get promoted. Is it something with my boy?" He wouldn't say. Preston's life went on. Up early, gone all day, out nights. It seemed OK. Then. I don't know.' Pain thins her voice. 'I just don't know.'

She says, 'He started going places I didn't know about.'

She says, 'He started doing things.'

She says, 'He started staying out all night. I thought, oh fine, a girlfriend, I was only a little jealous – after all, I loved him but she could love him in a different way. I thought, oh fine, when he's ready he'll bring her home. Then I thought, oh God maybe he's ashamed of me, so I bought all new clothes. I changed my hair. But something else was changing. And it wasn't quite. Whatever it was, it wasn't quite right. There was trouble.'

Her sigh rocks them. 'The trouble was this. Mess. Dirt in his clothes that I couldn't get rid of, strange kinds of dirt that you can't tell what it is, things that sink into the fiber and stain. Hair and mud on his Nikes. Out all night. I could hear him sneaking in. Ugly stuff in the grout around the bathtub. "Come here," I said, and Presty held his hands out for me the way he did when he was little. Clean, all the way down to the soft skin underneath the fingernails. His face was sweet as milk. "Oh, son," I said, "why can't you keep your room as nice as your beautiful hands?"

'He gave me the sweetest smile. "I have you to do that for me, Mm." Not Mommy. Mom. Mother. He could never get the word out; he never called me Ma or Mummy; my very own personal son that I made out of nothing and he never called me anything.

'Just, "I have you to do that for me, Mm." It's true. He did. I always did it for him. Made the bed, mopped, scrubbed, straightened his shelves, hand-washed and ironed the clothes and fixed up anything that went wrong. I did everything for him and he . . .'

Pain corrugates her face. 'I did my part. Why couldn't he? It broke us in two. Too much, I couldn't keep up! All that mess and disorder, Preston out God knows where and bringing home God knows what and never telling me. Dirt in the clothes, and on the sheets . . . "Son, I didn't bring you up to . . ." "Preston, I didn't work my fingers to the bone for this." "Son, why is this happening?" Too much to say to him and I couldn't talk to him. I had such hopes. *The dirt!* He had lost all . . . I did not know what he had lost, I just. But his room! Trash in his dresser, dirt and rags, stuff that I didn't know *what* it was, and the poor surgical tools I'd brought him from the hospital, bright from the autoclave, expensive instruments jammed in every whichway, rust on some of them, it was terrible.

'So I confronted him. "Son. About the mess."'

Theo flinches. *Son.*

She doesn't see. She says, 'Preston. His *face*. You should have heard him. Shrill. High, the way it was when I sat him in the kitchen for our talks. He said, "I can't help it, Mom."

'I grabbed him hard. I tried to shake him but he was too big. I looked him in the eye. Inside I was dying but I spoke to him in the old, strong voice. "Oh yes you can."

'So he promised. But it was a lie.'

She sighs. 'But I'll say one thing for him. To the end he was considerate. He did it in the car. I didn't know! You ask me how I didn't know? He did it in the car because he thought he could do that and I would never know. So maybe we're done here.' She puts her hands on the table and makes as if to stand.

Threatened, Theo holds his breath. He waits. The woman looks down at her canvas-shrouded hands for too long. Finally he says, 'You killed him.'

'Yes.'

He imagines he hears all the clocks in the world ticking. Attached to unexploded bombs. 'And you're his mother.'

'Yes.'

They sit with this until Theo starts to turn off the tape recorder.

She waves him off and resumes. 'You wouldn't know this because you were never a mother, but when you are a mother you love your child. You try to make him a perfect world and the world . . . It just gets away from you. Vile things in the paper. Murders in our town. On top of wars and starvation and riots, all the horrors you try to spare him, these awful killings. People you know! I wanted to protect him. The world splits open, if you aren't careful it's going to spill us all into hell and my son, *my* perfect son that I kept everything nice for.' Stella waits until she can stop her head from shaking. '*I couldn't even get him to clean out his dresser!*' Her sigh sweeps the room. Behind the occluded eye of the window, figures stir. Theo is afraid she won't go on. He's afraid she will go on. Then she goes on and he is even more afraid.

'But it was his closet in the end. If you want to know the truth it was the condition of his closet. Cartons, other people's mail that I don't know where he got it, scraps of paper with notes you couldn't read, newspapers that had been left out in the rain all mulching together. And it didn't matter what I threw away or how hard I tried, it just kept piling up. It didn't matter what I scrubbed or burned, there were smells in the clothes that would not go away no matter what, things he wouldn't let you send to the cleaners, but he kept those hands of his so clean and beautiful, I still had hopes. He gouged that skin under the fingernails to keep it white, his hands were clean as a surgeon's, and God forgive me, I couldn't let it rest.

'So I called him into the kitchen. I had to straighten him out. I said to him, "This has got to stop."

'He just smiled at me.

'I showed him what I'd found in his things. It was an ear.

'And all that came out of him was, "I can't help it, Mm." I thought we would talk the way we used to, I would make him cry and promise to stop. Then I'd forgive him and we could hug just the way we used to hug, but we were nothing like we used to be. The chair where I used to sit him? He picked it up. He *picked it up.* Like a lion tamer. Jabbing me. "Stay back!" We were both breathing hard. We stood that way until his arms got tired. He put it down.

'Now I was the tamer. Whipping him with my glare. Until I cracked him. "Son," I said. "Don't apologize. Don't promise. Don't say anything."

But he gave me the same old look. *I can't help it, Mm.*

'I didn't argue. I said, "Sit. I'll make tea."

'I made it with milk. I made it with milk and the stuff from the hospital. Who knows what I had in mind, maybe I thought anti-psychotic drugs would solve our lives. Or maybe I knew from the beginning what I had to do. So after we'd had our tea we went out to his car. I said, "Son, we're going for a little ride."

'And he saw how I looked at him. He knew. But he started around to the driver's side of that Oldsmobile. He loved it better than me. I took his shoulders. "No." I pushed him into the passenger's seat. He didn't argue; he didn't fight. Maybe it was the pills. Or maybe he wanted it. So I buckled him in. Then I said the next to last thing I ever said to him. I said, "I'll drive."

'On the way out there, we didn't talk. He couldn't. Not any more. We got to the quarry and I put on the brake and got out of the car. I had us at the top of the ramp. I unbuckled his seat belt and shoved him over behind the wheel. Listen. My son Preston? His eyes were wide open when I did it. He looked right at me when I put the car in DRIVE and slammed the door on him.'

Theo hears a deep sigh. He won't know until he plays the tape that it is his own.

'I know what you want, son. I know what you're expecting me to tell you. That you see something in a killer's eyes. Some sign. Some sign that you can look for in people so you can stop them. Well forget it. Now look into mine.'

Mesmerized, Theo looks into her center. He sees nothing.

'My only son!' Her grief displaces all the air in the room. 'So I did what I had to. Now he is dead. And I am nothing. Everything about me is gone. Don't worry. I don't cry. If I started to cry I'd cry into eternity. Beyond.'

There is movement behind the one-way glass. The woman has stopped talking. Is this over?

The great head swivels. 'But you.'

Everything stops. Theo is conscious of his own breath struggling to get out.

'You came all the way up here, son.'

Don't call me . . . He says in a low voice, 'You brought me.'

'You. You think you can write about me and everybody will know what are the signs. You think there are
signs? Well I'll tell you. There are no signs. There were
never any signs. There was only Preston and what he
wanted. There was me. There was what I saw at the
end and there are signs in the one who came to see
me.'

This goes by so fast that Theo won't mark it, much less
pick up on it. 'You just said there weren't any—'

She cuts him off. 'Shut up and listen to me, son.'

He snaps, 'I'm not your son!'

She is gentle, relentless. 'There are good sons and bad
ones, son. You could be the good one. And that's why
I brought you here to tell you what I have to tell you.'
So this is how Stella Zax hands Theo the sum of her life
and with it, the obligation. She begins by explaining, 'The
signs? Signs are things people make up afterward, because
they can't stop what's happening and they can't explain
it. Signs are something they invent because they've got
to have something to blame. No. Somebody to blame.
Neglect. Abuse. The father. The mother. Me. Well there
are things in the world that nobody can explain. Nobody.
Not you.'

'I just . . .' Theo doesn't know what he just. It doesn't
matter what he says. What he says is nothing here.

'Not me. Now listen.' She reaches across the table and
seizes his forearm. 'When I killed Preston? When I slammed
the door on him and he knew he was going to die? His
eyes? They were wide open. He knew it was ending. We
both knew.'

At the door, the matron's head lifts. The change in
the prisoner's tone has alerted her. We are approaching
a conclusion here.

'Then I said the last thing I ever said to him. I said,
"The Lord giveth and the Lord taketh away."' Her face is
crumbling. 'I did my best!'

166

Theo says gently, 'I know you did.'

'Now. This is what I brought you here to say to you and this is what I want you to take to the people. This is the message I want you to put out there so he won't . . . So nobody else will . . .' With her floppy sleeves, she reaches for Theo's hand. 'You have to tell them. You have to tell them.'

Theo holds his breath. The people behind the one-way glass are holding their breath.

'When I stopped him?' Stella creates a space to make room for her next words. 'He was glad.'

Theo gasps. It's like being whacked from behind.

'Now. Your story.' They're almost there. At last Stella Zax reaches the point that brought Theo all this way. She lets the silence fall like the shadow between the intention and the act. It falls and magnifies. Then at the exact moment when it gets too big for the room she finishes. 'Forget signs. Forget excuses. Think. People like Preston? All those . . .' She cannot find the noun. 'All those . . .' Her voice breaks. There is no word for it. 'They want to stop. They would give anything if you would make it stop.'

'Thank you.' He is shaking. 'Oh Mrs Zax. Thank you.'

She stands. It is finished. Theo stands.

At their stations by the door, the matron and the guard shift uneasily. Is this confession over? Is it not? But mother and son confront each other without speaking and without moving. Silence lulls them and they lean back. Then Stella Zax moves. By the door, the women jump. On his side of the table, Theo holds her eyes, moving until they meet at the end of the table, face to face with nothing between them. Unexpectedly, the prisoner closes the distance. She and Theo are uncomfortably close. The guard and the matron make as if to step forward and protect him. With new dignity, Theo waves them off. Then he waits with his head bowed as this peculiarly distilled, unvarnished object of her own creation raises those canvas-shrouded arms and before the women in charge can remove her, clamps him to her in a brief hug.

Then just as she releases him she binds him forever, saying, 'You know what to do.' When you stop them, they are glad.

27

New Haven

'The room's all right?'

'Yes, thank you.' Bed over here. Window there. Alignment wrong. He will have to rearrange it. 'It's fine.'

'The bathroom's down the hall.'

'I know. I know it is.' He waits for the landlord to go. He's been in town for three days, found a used car, walked into a temp agency and picked up a job; getting work is never a problem for him. Things are going much better now that he has warned the mother. He confronted her. You bet she's ashamed of what she did. To keep her unsettled, he has been sending her little things. The next time he goes to see her, she'll be proud. Better. He thinks he's found The One. He will do em and ey will stay done. *Male, female, it makes no difference. Objectify so we can do this. Em. Prepare em. Kill em. Do em right this time and we're all done.* Anticipation makes his mouth flood. This will go smoothly. Once it's planned.

The landlord lingers. 'Anything else?'

He controls his voice. 'I'd like to be alone now.'

But the landlord looms in Haik's private space. He is a bald, round muffin of a man with a shapeless nose; the Ben Franklin wire-frames keep sliding down the bridge. 'Everything to your taste?' Haik does not answer but he keeps talking. 'We're all decent working people here, scrub the tub, wipe whiskers out of the basin.'

169

'I understand.'

'Now, there are some girls operating out of the garage apartment, I hope that won't bother you.'

'No.' Haik smiles complaisantly. 'That won't bother me.'

'And I'll expect two weeks' rent in advance. Is that a problem for you?'

'No problem.' – *I could kill you right here. I could kill you in a minute.* Haik's mind rehearses the phrases even as he smiles and hands over the money. – *But there would be nothing in it for me.*

The landlord has a rubber finger protector. He takes a long time counting the money. As if waiting for Haik to give him something more he says, 'Well, if that's all.'

'That's all,' Haik says. He is like a congregation of sex-starved lovers itching to be left alone with this; prurience locks his jaw and writhes in his belly and when the landlord finally goes he takes out the notebook and opens it with a passionate intake of breath. Anticipation. Realization. Who's to say which is better?

I. IMPROVED PLAN: STEPS

1. Selection: as before.

a. Under way. E will be the one we spotted at the library. Followed. Available. Lives alone. Dark hair. Skinny, except up top so, good. Small: minimum fight. Maximum pleading. Asking for it. *Soon.*

b. URGENT. *Before proceeding: Get em used to you.*

c. Things to do:

i. Get em familiar. Important, so ey don't get afraid and scream or fight. Encounter. Done. Smile. Done. Talk. Done. E thinks we have a whole life outside of what I am thinking.

ii. Our looks: Fresh shirt. Haircut. Teeth squeaky clean.

d. Next meeting. Accidentally, outside the library. Again.

– Oh, what are you doing here?

Our smile. – I love books.

See em trusting: – I can tell. *We go for coffee. Talk.*

2. Preparation:

a. Place.

b. What comes next. Details t.k.

Haik reviews his notes on the last two: *what went wrong.* You go into a town and set yourself up and line em up and something goes wrong at the last minute. Ey are stronger than you thought. Father rises up out of your childhood, scolding: *your mother hates disorder.* Plan. Plan! A strip of skin catches in his teeth; absently he flicks it away with a fingernail. He ticks the page until one of the missing parts drops into place. 'Yes!' It is inspired. Absorbed, gnawing his wrist until it bleeds, he prints:

3. BACKUP: in event of failure, target backup. Two is better than one.

a. Possible backup: Girl from the bus. Already knows me, no prep needed. Run into her again **accidentally** – Is that your flute? Would you play it for me?

i. Advantages:

A. Availability: Smaller than me. Alone. Never be missed.

B. Looks: Unpeeled face. Body parts jiggling. A present begging to be unwrapped and ruined.

C. Asking for it.

ii. Disadvantages:

A. Orange hair. Too conspicuous?

B. Asking for it. Too easy to be any use?

UNANSWERED QUESTIONS

a.
b. The rest of the questions

Pacing, balancing the book in one hand, Haik writes in growing haste. He is getting low on pages and he wants to finish in this. Organization demands outline, which outgrows the page. A warning bell rings: WE ARE RUNNING OUT OF SPACE but what to do? As taught: Itemize or you will never do this. Which he does, scribbling furiously until spit flies and his fingers spasm.

II. Things to do:

1. ANALYZE. TOPICS.
2. ORGANIZE. SUBTOPICS.
3. Problem: how to organize. so we can do #5. DECIDE

III. Precautions. To be decided.

* * * PROBLEM * * *

WHO. I myself. Here. Now.
See details under One (1.)
Must for now: *Solve the problem.*

* * * PROBLEM: WHAT IS THE PROBLEM? * * *

If you don't know, you're not ready for this.

The problem is . . . Haik thinks he knows what the problem is. Completion. All this and he still can't get it right. You spend your whole life under your father's thumb, doing things by the numbers because the father says *fail and you kill your mother* and you believe this even though you saw her dead, Father came thundering down on you as she landed all broken and he blamed you and made you cry. You would do anything to make up for it. Father: 'Edward, look what you did!' Well, there is no more Edward now. *Analyze*. Haik. Diagrams. Haik. Growing inside of you. *Organize*. Headings and sub-headings. *Plan*. The notebooks. *Write it down.* And fail.

Sobbing with frustration, he starts a new diagram in the notebook. Death laid out under topics and subtopics, a, b, c. *I will show you, Mother,* he thinks, scrawling. And he will not know which mother he is talking to, only that he has to do this right so he can end it. *I will do em and show you.*

He has written through dusk and into sunset but the details won't fall into place. Gnawing his wrists, Haik paces, maddened by the gaps. Did he lose something when #4 started screaming? Did some part of his brain go soft when e wheeled with a rock and tried to bash us and we had to smash their brains out and make a mess instead of doing it right? This is the measure of his disruption. He can't get this organized. Thoughts keep sliding away.

Establish contact

a. *contact, indirect*
   i. *phone call: if e answers, hang up*
   ii. *message through friends.*

* * * PROBLEM, WHAT FRIENDS * * *

   iii. *observe*
   iv. *track*
   v. *surveill*
   vi. *Question: is observe the same as surveill?*
b. *contact, direct. Locate em*
   i. *approach on street*

Scrawling, he has run out of headings and sub-headings for contingencies: he is down to:

ii. problems under D *PROBLEM*

name categories for subtopic category under I, etc./1., etc./a., etc. /i., etc./A/subtopic name subtopic. 1? No. Taken. i.? Taken. a.? taken all taken. What?

* * * PROBLEM: DESIGNATIONS, SUBTOPIC * * *

* * * ORGANIZE * * *

There is no place left to go! Writing, he won't hear his own scream. He is running out of numbers and letters! The diagram keeps thrashing inside him like a spiked monster intent on getting born. Pain drives him to try to let it out. Again. Again. When the notebook will no longer contain his skeletal trials and errors he starts on the walls.

He hears knocking. Snarling like a wolf, he goes to answer.

It is the landlord. 'Everything all right in here?'

'Fine. Just fine.' Haik fills the doorway so the landlord can't see into the room. He smiles that workable smile. *Keep standing there and I will kill you. Then we'll see what's all right.*

'Just checking. Good night now.'

'Good night to you too,' Haik says.

'Take care.'

'I will. And you take care.' To look at him, you'd never know.

When he goes out to work tomorrow he will do two things. He will buy two hasps and a lock so he can secure the room. And to accommodate the complexity of the plan, he will buy a new set of ballpoints and a rainbow armory of magic markers.

28

It's been three weeks. Theo is jamming on a piece for *Newsweek*, thanks to Stella Zax. The prison interview was her gift to him. She didn't confess to the warden or the national press, she called the *Star* and asked for Slate. The Sunday his story ran Sally wakened him with bagels and the papers: his exclusive made Page One in New York, Washington, Boston. Los Angeles. She handed the papers over in such a mixture of love and envy that Theo almost forgot Stella Zax. That morning Sally touched his face and for the moment he forgot all the ways in which Stella's gift has left him obligated; he and Sally were both laughing. 'Yes!'

'Yes.' Sally pressed her hand to his face as if she could stamp her palm print on his cheek. 'Theo,' she said, and her face shone. 'Theo Slate.'

Morning, he thought, is us beaming at each other. 'You,' he said. 'Sally.'

Later they went through the papers, one by one.

MOTHER EXPLAINS WHY SHE MURDERED KILLER SON

Stella's best quote made it into the drop on front pages all over the country.

MURDERING MOTHER:
'WHEN YOU STOP THEM
THEY ARE GLAD'

OK metro papers, news magazines, take note. OK networks,

175

CNN, this is me. OK, Dad. It may not be what you wanted for me but it's what I want. *I went out there and I did that and the feeling is* not *what I expected. But I did that. I did it. Me.* Even Arch treats him with grudging respect and yet Theo feels suspended somehow, oddly unfinished. The sharp breath you take in. And hold.

'You know what to do,' Stella Zax said to him, but he doesn't.

It is confusing. One immediate byproduct is the *Newsweek* piece. He pitched it on the basis of Stella's story: firsthand account, and they bit. His big break, if he doesn't blow it. Timing's right; they're planning an issue on killers, deadline next Wednesday, no problem. His working title is *Mothers Who Kill*. The piece will be short, but it's dense. If it runs, they banner it on the cover. Could help him get an agent. Contract for this book that he can't quite begin. Vile details spawn in a dizzying geometric progression. Bundys and Dahmers and Gacys fight for space with the blind, dead faces of the victims and survivors, drenched and bludgeoned by grief. It's overflowed into his life.

He's pinned a lot on this *Newsweek* piece. If he can make it fly, maybe some part of this will be exorcised and he can move on.

But just as he's about to wrap it up Theo is bushwhacked. A stringy little woman in flowered flares leans over him with a belligerent glare. 'You know Delia Vent, right?'

He has to pull himself hand over hand out of Stella Zax's head. 'Who?'

Like an outsider shouldering into a family snapshot, the little woman leans in, smiling for the camera. The Sophia Loren glasses make her eyes look like magnified bugs. 'Don't try and tell me you don't. She knows you. She stiffed me for three months' rent. Delia. You know who I mean. DeliafuckingMarie. Your girlfriend.'

'She's not my girlfriend.' He never gave Delia one sign of encouragement. What did he do to bring this on? Calls he's afraid to pick up. Letters he throws away. Something in his mailbox every day and it doesn't stop. 'Look, I'm on deadline. Could this wait?'

'This has fucking waited long enough. I need the money. She's owed me since she moved out in July.'

He corrects automatically. 'August. She left for Columbia.'

'July. I had to kick her out.'

'She's in New York.'

'New York! Yeah, sure.'

'She is. Our publishers are paying for graduate school,' he explains, as if this will get her off his back.

'Yeah, right, graduate school. She's got debts here. Big debts. Utilities. Back rent. Plus there were damages,' the landlady says darkly. 'Damages that have to be paid.'

'Ma'am, I have to get to work.'

'The mattress. Other things. Certain of my clothes. I even went to the family.'

'She doesn't have a family.'

'That may be what she told you. You should have heard the father! They don't want anything to do with her.' Her voice sinks to a hoarse, suggestive rasp. 'Especially after what she did.'

'After what she did?'

'You know, last time. They had no choice!' She shakes her frizzy head. 'So that's why I'm coming to you.'

'I can't help you.'

'She said you were engaged.'

'She what? We're not engaged!'

'Then all I can say is, you'd better watch out.'

'Look, lady, I can't help you,' Theo says, but there are questions drumming in his ears. *Last time?* He can't stop to ask. Stella's story is coming to a boil. *What do you mean, last time? What last time? Last time what?* No time for that now, lady. Theo says what you say. 'If there's a problem, you should probably take it up with my boss. That would be Mr Wilbur, over at the metro desk.'

'He said you would know what to do.'

'No ma'am.'

'He said if anybody would know, you would, because you and she were close.'

You bastard. Chick. 'We were never . . .'

'Yeah, right,' she says wisely. 'That's what they all say. Guys! OK, OK, don't get pissed at me. When you talk to your girlfriend, tell her send the goddam money or I'm taking her to court.'

He taps the earphones and opens the *Newsweek* file without looking up to see whether the landlady has gotten the message and left. He starts the tape. Stella Zax's story unwinds. Again. For the first time since he started reporting, he's got everything he wants. The tape is dense with drama and the skewed pathology that makes readers pant faster over their Wheaties, writhing in their chairs, excited and ashamed because they're so ravenous. He has quotes to die for, a winner with that sick, mythic flip that daily accounts of shootings and bashings with blunt instruments can't touch. Stella's compulsion lifts her out of the ordinary. Unfurling, Stella's story takes on the eerie sheen of Dayglo plastic in a garbage dump; bodies decay, but this is forever. This killing didn't die with that day's paper. It won't die with the magazine. It will live in the world. In the litany of past killings and killings to come, people will have to number this. And it's all his.

All he has to do is get it right. The truth. Problem: Which is the truth? These are living people you have cracked open like fucking Shelley's chest; you have stared into their entrails. You plunged in your bare hands but you can't tell what you've got hold of. What's this you're pulling out? Is this the truth? Is this? The responsibility is brilliant and terrifying.

He does what he can. He reads it from the top and clicks on SEND.

At his back a woman murmurs, 'Terrific.'

'Sally!' How long has she been reading over his shoulder? When did he look up and find the world had taken a weird turn and everything was changing in the light? He thinks he's saying thanks but instead he mumbles this bizarre little admission. 'All I want is to get shut of it.'

'What?' Sally bends to peer into his face. 'I thought you loved this story.'

'It isn't that. It's.' He can't explain it.

'What are you talking about?'

'Nothing. OK, the Zax woman left me a little bummed. Yes. No. Maybe. Maybe it's all this – *stuff*.'

He doesn't have to tell her about the material piling up in his home office; she's seen. She says, 'Your wall.'

'How did I end up with all this stuff?'

'It didn't find you, T. You went looking for it.'

This is not a question. It's a statement. 'I did.'

'You were the one who wanted to know everything there is to know about serial killers.'

'And now I know too much.'

Sally makes as if to touch his face but does not. 'Or not enough.'

'That's the whole trouble.'

'That's showbiz,' Sally says unevenly.

'Maybe we should go get drunk.'

The woman he loves is looking into him like a one-woman triage unit, deciding if he's going to live or die or what. 'Are you all right?'

Drunk is not such a bad idea. 'Could we please not talk about this please?'

She laughs. 'Let's don't get drunk, let's go shopping.'

It seems like an even better idea to go out to Brands Mart to score Theo a laptop it will take months to pay off if *Newsweek* bails on him and he's left with a kill fee; Sally thinks it's his present for doing this story, but it's really his present to himself for surviving Stella Zax. Now that he's done this, maybe it's over. He can batch his clips with the *Newsweek* piece on top. Write letters to all the major markets. When he follows with phone calls, by God he won't have to explain who he is so, cool. He is cool, OK?

'This is cool,' he says as he lets her out at her house.

'Take care of yourself,' she says. Sally is on night police so they kiss goodbye and he goes home. He has so nearly forgotten all his existential worries that when he pulls up in front of the house he thinks he's walked into a Pixar cartoon.

His front door looks like a space platform at liftoff, buoyed by masses of what look like floating ETs waiting to lift him off the planet and perform rectal probes. Mylar balloons joined by ribbon curls bob on a stick thrust in the brass-veneered middle-American knocker. He approaches cautiously. He sighs. Yeah. Right. The balloons are stamped CONGRATULATIONS and BEST WISHES and GOOD LUCK. There is a card with the logo of the local florist, who also does balloon arrangements. He doesn't have to read it to know. It gives him a certain grim satisfaction to go into his pocket and give each balloon its freedom with his Swiss Army knife. He does it without looking up to watch them bobbing away. On a better day, he'd break the stick over his knee. Instead he throws it in the bushes.

'OK Delia. Enough!' Inside, he notes that the answering machine is blinking in a staccato pattern. He gropes for a pen but before he can push PLAY the phone rings. The *Newsweek* desk? Without thinking, he picks it up with a snappy 'Theo Slate.'

'You didn't like them!'

'What?'

'My balloons. You didn't like them!'

'Who is this?' His throat closes. 'Oh. Delia. I was just going out.'

'No you weren't. You just came in. It's about the *Newsweek* piece. I was so excited I just had to call.'

'But I just filed it. How did you know?'

'Just tell me where you are with the flowers.'

'Flowers?' He paces from the hall into the living room; there are flowers lined up like massed Barbies. Delivery people in here, who let them . . . Better change the locks again. 'How did you know?'

'I miss you so much.' She's waiting for him to say, *Me too*.

'I can't talk right now.'

29

New Haven

In the main he is a quiet tenant. Locks the room with the Yale lock and the hasp. Comes down in the morning, makes nice to the other boarders looking up at him over their Wheaties like raccoons lined up over the garbage, 'Nice day, isn't it?'

Haik says nicely, 'Nice day,' pours coffee into his Thermos and goes out.

'Nice day,' the landlord says, passing him in the hall. If he minds the extra lock the new tenant's put on the door he hasn't mentioned it. The rent comes regular.

Haik smiles. 'Sure is. You take care now.'

'You too. Have a good one.'

'Thanks, I will.' Pleasantries. Keep the surface as it is. If they could see his walls . . .

After some weeks the temp job has extended into perma-temp; he can work there for as long as he wants. Schooled by his father in all respects he is meticulous. Dress shirt fresh from the laundry every morning, light starch, black tie; clean shave with a straight razor, sandy hair combed wet over his well-shaped head so the marks of the plastic teeth are still in it when he sits down at his computer. Goes through the days sorting data; he is so good at programming that they have moved him up from entering data to sorting it. Order, the surface is beautifully ordered, nothing remarkable, nothing to worry any landlord or employer.

It's what's inside.

See it expressed in the notebooks and growing like a living thing on the walls of the spare rented room. The unrealized diagram writhing inside him. If he can't get it right, it's going to tear him apart. When night comes he rolls in the bed gnawing on his wrists until the pain drives him out of bed and he starts. Racing like a graffiti artist on roller blades, he draws flow charts on the walls. And in the notebook, the single empty page, waiting to be filled. *PRECAUTIONS*. To make this work, he has to perfect the ritual. This time he has to get it *right*.

The room is right; the city seems right, not too small, not too big, lots of secret places where you can go. The woman from the library seems exactly right, lonely, *ASKING FOR IT*, sure. Follow her every afternoon, speak to her twice a week not too often not too seldom.

– Oh, it's you.

Smile at her. – Funny how we keep running into each other, isn't it?

His backup in place, she doesn't know it but he followed her home one night; she's found a room in a brick warren way out State Street, every once in a while he checks. If he needs her he'll walk in on her. She will look up at him and he will smile. She will say as if it is the most natural thing in the world:

– Oh, it's you.

Everything ready. But he can't begin. He is in touch with the mother, sends her a card every week, some little thing tucked in the envelope, never mind where he gets some of these little things. He went and saw her and she knows now that she made a mistake when she killed the son.

Now that she's seen Haik she will think twice before she tries anything like that again.

Even so, he can't begin. There is still something missing. Some last piece that will perfect the design. It is driving him crazy. It's like a new computer problem; until he works it out he cannot rest. One thing more he ought to be doing. One thing more. Six colors of Magic Marker differentiate the elements in his schemes and he still hasn't hit on it. The design is growing like a jungle vine along the walls. A jungle vine with a missing piece.

It is in the notebook. One blank page. A heading, waiting to be filled in. *PRECAUTIONS.*

'What?' he shouts, so loud that he wakes the landlord in his bedroom downstairs. *'What?'*

How can everything go wrong when everything is so nearly right? He is coping with a reversal. The designated next, the woman from the library, is leaving the city. All this preparation and she is going out of town! He found out when he cruised her room last night when she was out. *New York.* It's on her calendar. Today he followed #5 to the train station.

Day trip? Long weekend? What? What if she never comes back?

But there are only three sets of bikini underpants and an extra bra in that shoulder bag she carried through the station this afternoon. He knows. So she'll be back. She will be back. He followed her through the station. He considered getting on the train with her, *do em in New York*, but this is outside the scheme. He turned to leave and then. Then! She was staring out at him from the magazine rack, *face I know.* Big and square. Fake pearls. Pearl earrings. Photo tinted by the studio photographer.

'Mother!' Not the real one. The mother from jail.

Snarling, he snatched it out of the rack. 'Mother, you bitch!' The face of Stella Zax. And this, written in the strip across her breast: *A MOTHER'S DUTY.* He walked out of that place in a fury put on his shades so nobody would see red rage boiling in his eyes; if he'd wept today his eyes would have dripped blood. He ripped open the magazine, never mind that people were running out of the station shouting after him, walked through the traffic without caring what hit him because he was in deep, tearing the magazine open like a human belly. Like a wolf he pulled out the contents so he could see what was written about him. What she said.

— *WHEN YOU STOP THEM THEY ARE GLAD*

'Glad!' His voice rocked the street. People stared. He was standing across from police headquarters with the magazine open to the centerfold, and it was an obscenity. Not naked women showing themselves *asking for it* that is nothing next to this. This, written about him.

About him! *WHEN YOU STOP THEM THEY ARE GLAD*.

The staples pricked his fingers. Blood dotted the page and he folded it yes *how could you,* trembling with rage.

'This is a lie. A lie!'

GLAD. Too angry to remember that he came in a car, Haik walked through back streets and across busy roadways, folding the centerfold smaller and smaller as he went and as he rounded the last corner before the boarding house, unzipping his fly and slipping the obscenity into the naked bulges and folds of his crotch, yes let it sit next to me, rubbing him *there* where he will keep it, a constant reminder. Of what, he does not yet know. *Show her,* he thinks; *show her we have a plan.* And if that plan fails, the backup. He knows where she is, he can just walk in.

— How will I know where to look for you?

— Don't worry. *Look at her. Smile.* — I'll find you.

Lie waiting to be untold: *GLAD*. 'Glad!'

He can't unclench his belly so he won't be able to eat and he can't stop gnawing the raw skin of his wrists. Furious, he hurtles into night, pacing and planning, dabbing like an action painter at the unfinished diagrams and schemes spreading like a staph infection on the walls of his room. 'Glad,' he says aloud. Growling. 'Glad!' He throws himself on the bed with a tremendous groan, rocking through the night while down below the landlord will wake gasping and reflect that the tenant's money's good but not good enough to make it worth losing sleep. This racket. Shouting in the night!

'Glad!'

Eventually Haik stops rocking and plummets into sleep; at last the landlord sleeps.

When Haik gets up in the morning, he shaves with great care, rub the matter out of your eyes, bandage your wrists. In the bathroom, study the magazine centerfold. It is rubbed white where you folded it and it is still warm from your crotch. Button the starched cuffs to hide your bandages and go down to the dining room and start all over, 'Nice day, isn't it? Nice day. Nice day.' Tell them you are going away for the weekend, yes. Racket in the night? It will be so quiet on the weekend that they will forget.

GLAD. Get this out of the way so you can do that, he thinks. The mother. He could kill her but he won't. She'll beg to die.

30

It's two in the afternoon. Theo wakes in a sweat. 'Who?'
He comes to consciousness thinking in old movie logos.
Just when you thought it was safe to go back in the water,
he thinks fuzzily, groping for the phone. *Be afraid. Be
very afraid.*

'Is that you?'

'What?' Muttering, he clings to the fragments of sleep
he's had. He hung in through Friday's *Newsweek* edit,
which makes brain surgery look easier than flossing; he
worked through the weekend on the series he's doing for
Chick. It's his payback for liberties granted while he was
jamming on his piece. Chick's already chewed him out for
an error in a city brief so his moment in the sun has passed.
It's part of the deal in the news business: yeah, but what
did you bring me *today*? It's cool. Theo was cool until he
picked up the magazine. He saw Stella's face looking out
at him from the cover and for absolutely no reason asked
for a comp day and crashed. Yeah he's been asleep. He
would like to stay asleep but some stranger is in his face
all hearty, acts like he knows me, who . . .

'I said, congratulations!'

'Who is this?' He knows, but he doesn't. Sleep is blurring
the obvious to protect him. Psychic white sound, but at
bottom, he knows. A chronic victim of telemarketing, he
positions his thumb over the *reset* button and braces for
the pitch.

'Why aren't you at work?'

187

Oh. Oh, right. Sigh. 'What is it, Dad?'

'I just called to congratulate—'

'Well, thanks.'

'Your mother and I are very proud.'

Not Dad's fault that Theo hears a mouse click. Buy low, sell high, doesn't the market ever close? He sighs again. 'I'm glad.'

'Now that you've proved yourself, you can—'

'Finish the job.' Somewhere between the last sentence and this one Theo has rejected whatever Amazing Free Offer his father is poised to make. Oh wow, oh Stella, I don't know what this is, but I've got to figure it out. 'Yeah. Do it!'

'What?'

'I guess you hadda be there. Sorry, Dad. Gotta . . .'

'Have you been drinking?'

'. . . prove myself.'

His father's voice follows him. Some occult power drives him to make a startling admission that Theo won't want to hear right now. 'I'm not trying to push you, son, I just want you to have better than I did.'

Oh God. 'I love you but I can't talk right now. Bye, Dad.'

His father is not the only intrusion the *Newsweek* cover brings. In the days after Stella Zax made her first confession to him, the usual covey of bottom-feeders came into the state; national reporters were turned away from the county jail, Stella isn't seeing anyone. Frustrated, they tried to piggyback on Theo's material, garner quotes he is not minded to give, get him to intervene with Stella; honest working press plus infotainment scouts aiming to bleed him white for video cuts that will run without any reference to him. With the appearance of the *Newsweek* piece, he's in for a second round. Last spring when they busted Stella, Theo was like a randy teenager, would have boogied with any partner who asked him, but in an odd way Stella's charge has focused him. No matter where he is, it draws him back to the display in his office.

You know what to do.

If only he did.

Beached at the Door Store desk, thumbing through a fresh batch of Xeroxes, Theo reflects. Somehow it gets to be night. He is held in place by Stella's charge and the specific gravity of the material collecting here. Compounded by the pressure of Stella's expectations, it's hit critical mass. These nights he paces and sorts, sorts and paces, falls into bed but can't much sleep. He won't sleep, really, until he's arrived at the end point of all this psychic disruption. The disturbance began when he first looked into Preston Zax's face, but since he accepted Stella's confession in exchange for duties not yet named, it has become acute. It is turning him into a different person. The growing display in his cramped home office seems more like a symptom than a solution. Old stories. New ones. There is the matter of the bitemark killer, recent stories from Indiana, upper New York State, suspected killings in three Western states, signature markings on the victim's cheek and yes the bitemarks match. Not enough victims to put this one in the serial-killer class. Yet. OK, Stella, is he supposed to write about this or prevent it? Absorbed, he won't hear the snick of a credit card sliding down the cheap lock on his kitchen door. Nor will he wonder how someone could get into his garage. He doesn't even hear himself saying to the absent Stella, 'What do you want from me?'

His Zax material has joined the grisly collection of clippings and photos that grows, spreading like fungus until it obscures the walls.

If there is someone moving through the house he does not hear her moving through the house.

'What, Stella. What!' Yes he is getting a little weird. Then someone speaks.

'Aren't you glad to see me?'

Blindsided, he leaps away, gouging his leg on an open file drawer. The woman is just standing there. Beaming. It is the Vent. He won't know when she stopped being a person and started becoming an alien force. The Vent. 'I changed the locks!'

Delia's words rush out to him. 'Theo, I missed you *so much.*'

He yells, 'Get out of here!' The horror is that he's shouting and she doesn't even blink.

'And I know you missed me.' Delia Vent looks the same and she looks subtly changed, hair maybe a little more tightly crimped and aggressively garish, as if she's drenched it with extra color especially for him. Her getup is straight out of college issues of *Vogue* or *Mademoiselle*. The lipstick is a bronze frost and she's layered some cheap brand of bronze makeup on her face along with brown eye shadow and brown mascara that plasters her eyelashes to the skin every time she widens her eyes. Except for the yellow silk scarf Delia is dressed in rust, everything new and carefully assembled so that all the pieces match: new sweater and big plaid skirt in the same shades, matching jacket with a price tag still hanging from the sleeve, gold tights. Only the canvas hightops look as if they came off the city dump.

He keeps his voice level. 'You can't stay here.'

She pours her heart out to him. 'It's been so long!'

This so shakes Theo that he is harsher than he means to be. It may be the only way to make his point. 'I said, you have to go.' He shouts. 'Do you hear me!'

The Vent doesn't hear; she's playing some alternative scenario in her head. Her eyes are glistening with love. 'Oh, Theo. I love you too!'

'I'm sorry,' Theo says firmly. 'Out.'

'You've been working too hard,' she says absent-mindedly, touching the massed clippings on his desk.

There are strange, unpleasant things about having the

Vent standing this close to him. She smells bad. It's as if the air around her is moving, stirred by her progress from the ordinary person Theo thought he knew into this strange night visitor. For this encounter DeliaMarie Vent has curled and dyed her hair and done makeup and dressed carefully, but it's clear she hasn't washed below the neck for longer than is healthy. The condition of the hands is shocking. Blackened fingernails. Flakes of dried blood on gnawed cuticles. He steps away. 'I'll take you to the bus.'

She moves with him, closing the distance. Her lips part.

He is afraid to see her teeth. 'No. I'm putting you on a plane. You can't afford to miss any classes.'

'Class. Oh, class. I'm doing so well that they gave me the week off.' Her smile spreads like jam on a plate. 'Thanks to you.'

He propels her into the living room.

'Where are we going?'

'We're leaving now.' It's interesting, talking to somebody you thought you knew in the fresh knowledge that she's crazy. The question, then, is: when did Delia cross the line? She's not who you thought she was, Slate. Take care. What you took for an ordinary mentor-student relationship is something completely different.

'Oh,' she says girlishly. 'You mean until after we're . . .'

Yes the woman has crossed the line. She has crossed the line and yet she is still somebody Theo used to know and tried to help, nice enough even though she's going nuts and she's standing here in his living room with this mad, meaningful smile and he doesn't know what to do. If they hadn't been friends back there before this happened, he'd just step to the phone and dial 911. Cautiously, he repeats, 'After . . .'

'After we're married, of course.'

'That does it!' Mad. The woman is crazy mad. Stick it to her, he thinks. Stick it to her straight. Hurt her feelings so bad that she'll never come back. 'We're not getting married, I'd rather go swimming in vomit. We're not even friends. So you're going back to Columbia, and you're going tonight.'

But the woman's blind excitement at seeing him has obliterated reason. 'I'm so glad we're together again.'

Theo grips her by the elbows and starts her out the door. 'So I'm putting you on the next plane back.'

'What are you doing?'

But Theo opens the front door and propels her onto the stoop. 'You're going now.'

At his touch she flows against him like a passive resister. Another half-turn and the woman will have him locked in a romance-novel embrace. 'Not now! Not when we've both waited so long.'

Theo is moving her across the little front porch when his toe collides with something soft. He looks down. It is a sleeping bag. Two shopping bags and a canvas tote are lined up on his stoop. 'What's this?'

'My things,' she says.

'Your things?'

'Not all of them. We'll have to go back for the rest.'

'Get in the car.'

'Where are we going?'

'Airport.'

'The airport!' She is like a little lighthouse making an irrational sweep to light up a patch of the recent past. 'If that Carey woman is coming back to bother you, I'll get her off your back. Don't worry, she'll never bother you again.'

Somebody you thought you knew turns into something you don't recognize and you understand they've crossed the line. It is a life-threatening event. 'We're nothing,' he says. They are at the car. He opens the door. With his fingers biting the soft inner arm just above the elbow, he turns her. 'It's over. You're leaving. Now get in.'

31

'Mrs Zax.'

Stella Zax is on the floor of her cell when the matron comes in; she is hunched in the corner behind the sink with her knees drawn up, turned inward. She has been turned in on herself ever since the wrong son came; he said terrible things to her, terrible things. Guilt pooled inside her like tainted fish and she is sick with it. Guilt and fear. She is foul enough without the meds they added to keep her quiet, she's a nurse, she knows what these things do to you. She did what she could. She put the whole thing in that young reporter's lap and thought: *There.* 'Here, you carry it. You know what to do.' She told because she wanted to feel better. All she feels is worse. Exposing Preston. *I have killed him twice.* And all she hears now is that handsome boy, reproaching her. *Mother, how could you?* She's afraid of him. He was so angry, he said he was going to . . . Said he was going to . . . It is this question that rattles her inside the cage of her body. What is he going to do?

'Stella, do you hear me?' So Stella is turned on herself *only place I am safe* and then all of a sudden she isn't. She opens up and a part of her comes out to see. Something's changed. Instead of slapping her mail down and leaving, the matron stands over her, smiling like the hospital visitor bringing chocolates to a patient who is too sick to eat.

'Who?' Presents began to come. Strange things. Things she doesn't understand. Objects have come, wrapped in Mother's Day cards. A pressed flower. Bits of fabric that

193

make no sense to her. A pretty black curl. What does it mean? *We are all your sons.* A new son, how wonderful. A new son. She is excited and afraid. The only safe thing to do is draw her knees up and hide in here.

'Stella, look at me.'

Yet when he came he left her changed; all her inner parts are quivering with loss, it's like having her son ripped out of her heart all over again.

'Aren't you excited?' The matron is trying to bring her back in stages. 'Your picture on *Newsweek*, he was so pleased. Don't you want to see him?'

A second chance? This is so awful. *I don't know.*

'Come on, it'll be good for you.' The matron's fingernails dig into Stella's armpits as she hauls her to her feet. 'Let's go.' It is a good thing they are both big women. The matron is lifting her and something inside Stella begins to lift too, as if she is in the hands of angels; it is so strange! *A second chance. Is this my second chance?*

'First let's fix you up a little bit.'

It's not the matron's fault that Stella doesn't want to see her face in the mirror. A lot has happened to her since she lost control of her looks.

'We can't have him seeing you like this.' Deftly, the matron dabs with pink lipstick. 'There. That's much better.' She turns Stella like an inert object and moves her out.

Presty. Stella lumbers faster. In her confusion she thinks, *Maybe I didn't kill him after all. When they see he's alive they'll let me out and he can take me home.* But when she gets to the visitors' room it isn't Preston at all, it is the other. Smiling, he gets up from the little table. Everything in her sags. She mouths. *You aren't my son.*

The matron beams, handing Stella over to him like a problem patient to a specialist. 'Family visits are always good for them.'

This isn't . . . She ought to tell the matron but she can't. *If only he was!*

'She's been having a hard time,' the matron says gently. 'I thought it would be nice if you had some privacy.'

Stella trembles. Alone with him in a room without the shield?

'If you need anything, I'll be right outside.'

He is smiling. He has shaved for this, he has put on a fresh shirt and dress pants and in this light he really does look like her flesh and blood, but sweeter than the one she knows. He is not stony the way Preston was so often in the last months; if there is hate in his eyes it is hidden so deep that what shows looks more like love. Maybe this truly is her second chance. God has brought her a whole new person. This nice-looking new son will get her released from County and take her home. No. They'll start over somewhere nice, get a little house.

He holds out his arms. – Hello, Mother.

And without knowing exactly what they are doing here Stella moves forward and they hug, mother to son or something like it, and with a benign smile the matron heads for the door.

'Wait.' Stella makes a half-turn, gesturing as if to stop her. *I ought to tell her the truth.*

The matron turns and when Stella can't or won't speak she says maternally, 'Have fun. I'll be watching through the glass.' She leaves. After all, the prisoner's confessed. After all, this is family. Stella's lips are moving but if sound comes out only this new son is close enough to hear.

What she says won't touch him. Helplessly, she murmurs, – I don't have a son. *Strange son, smoke in his voice so I can't tell what is and what isn't. Why do all our words to each other fall into a dream?* – I don't have anybody. `

As if in a dream he steadies her. – You have me.

She finds herself fearful but drawn; if she can find the right things to say he will absolve her. It will be as if none of this ever was but he looks strange, he smells strange to her, nice but not like her flesh and blood. Her face crinkles in confusion. – But I don't know you.

– It doesn't matter. I know *you*, he says. Mother. I am your son. We are all your sons.

WHUSH. Stella is weak in her loins and in her heart. – Yes.

– So we understand each other now. Mother. Yes?

To her surprise she is still standing; the new son is supporting her. They are so close that she can count the pulse beating in his throat. Stella's breathing slows to match his; it's like having a respirator set several notches below normal. There is almost no air left in the room. – Don't, she says, with everything bubbling up in her throat, pain she's felt and pain she may have caused him, and she says miserably, – Don't hug me, I don't deserve it.

– I know you don't.

She shakes her great head. – Then let go.

His fingers tighten on her elbows. – But you're the mother.

– You're not my son. *Why won't he let me go?* She wants him to she doesn't want him to it feels so *good* touching another human person after so long. Presty never hugged her after he got big. It still hurts when she thinks about it, and God knows there are no men for her never any men and here she is surrounded by strong, clean arms Stella with his sweet breath in her ear . . . – I don't deserve to have a son now please let go of me.

– But you have me. Now sit down.

Her heart rushes out to him. – Oh, son.

– So I am your son.

Joyful. – Son!

But now that he has her, the new son withdraws like a lover stretching out the moment before climax. He says in a low voice, – And look what you've done to me.

– What? Her mouth opens and shuts. – O. – O. – O.
O. O.

– Look what you said! He turns his back to the door
and produces a creased magazine page so worn that she
can barely make it out, it is softened by age, rubbed white
at the folds.

– What's this?

– First you murder me and now. Now you humiliate
me. Look!

She looks at the large print. It is so strange, you tell
your story and someone writes it up and it never looks
like what you said.

WHEN YOU STOP THEM THEY ARE GLAD.

– Look what you did.

These are words she does not remember coming out of
her mouth. – I could never say that. She did!

The face he turns to her is suffused with blood. His
voice makes her tremble. – How could you?

Blinded by tears Stella says irrationally, – Let the dead
bury their dead.

He taps the page. – Mother, look at this! What are we
going to do about this?

– Whatever you want. Deep in grief, Stella bows her
head. – Go ahead then. Do it. Do it to me, she says in the
same tone she used with the doctor that one time. When
she had to get pregnant, and did. – Do what you came to
do. Go ahead and kill me.

– Why would I want to kill you?

– Hurry up, she says with her head bowed. – I deserve
to die. She wants to rush into his arms like a queen into the
arms of death. Will he pull out a knife? Bludgeon her with
the metal chair? Strangle her? Anything to be done here
and have this over with, she thinks, anything. Breathing,
as to a lover, – Please.

But her son steps away; is he trying to punish her?
– That isn't what I want.

– It's what *I* want. The truth comes out of her in a rush. Grieving, Stella cries, – I'd do anything to keep from feeling this way.

– But you're my mother.

– That's the whole thing.

– No it isn't, he says.

She offers, – And I killed you.

Gravely, he taps the page. – You have killed me twice. Look what you did here. Look what you said!

– What did I say, son? What did I really say? She can't remember she can't *remember*. Everything is within her grasp, a son, a second chance, and it's all slipping away. Stella cries, – Whatever I said about you, I'm sorry, I am!

He lowers his voice even further. From the door they will look like loving family in close conversation. He puts one hand on the back of Stella's neck and draws her closer. His fingers grind tight. – Terrible things.

A part of Stella that she has lost touch with quickens and begins to shudder. – Oh, God. She is weeping now; she can feel the tears coming but she doesn't hear them. – What do you want from me?

Smiling, her son grips her wrists; to the matron looking through the glass square in the door it will look as though he is loving and fond. – Unsay it.

– What? she cries. She does not remember, she does not *remember*. – Unsay what?

In a low, stern voice the stranger son repeats: – *WHEN YOU STOP THEM THEY ARE GLAD*.

Stella's face collapses in on itself. She tries to pull away but she doesn't know where she is going no she has no place to go. She loves him and she is so afraid! He's here after all this guilt and loneliness, his touch is warm and all she wants is to be forgiven. She killed him and she wants him to forgive her and oh, God forgive her, she lies.

Oh my God this is so craven. Yet in her grief and

confusion, Stella Zax gives up the reporter. – I didn't say that. I didn't!

– You didn't? His grip turns into a caress, fingers sliding down hers as if to draw the story out of her. – Who did?

And in her love and hunger Stella Zax betrays that nice young man who took her story, saying in a low voice, – That reporter.

Then he whirls on her so swiftly that all his teeth flash. – What? What is his name?

– It's on the story. It's on the story! Stella is already afraid for him but in her terror and her greed she points. – See it? Theo Slate.

There is a terrifying pause. Something in him clicks shut like the camera's iris freezing tissue on a slide. – Theo Slate.

In that moment Stella falters. – No. Son, I made a mistake! She says hastily, – It wasn't him!

But he is fixed on something else. He stiffens and his head lifts. There is a thunderous silence. Before Stella's eyes the son who may not be her son turns into something else. – *GLAD*.

She needs to stop or turn this, but she can't. – Don't.

– *GLAD*.

– It was a mistake. I made a mistake.

His voice grates. – Well, I am going to show you glad.

This catches her where you die. Stella does not so much groan as empty all of the air out of all her pouches and cavities in a long lament. – *Oh, God.*

– No. Not God.

– What are you?

And this new son looks at her out of Preston's eyes. – You made me, Mother. You know what I am.

– Oh, son. Son! So Stella sees what he is, and she sees what images flicker in the depths of his dreadful eyes and she is afraid to read the text or look any closer at the rushing pictures. And worse yet, she loves him! Shuddering, she pushes him away. – No!

– I'll show you, Mother.

– Please no!

– I'll do what I have to. And I will make you proud.

'Nooooooo.' Stella has been weeping without sound but in this moment of push and shove her voice comes out, and as the shriek spirals up the matron comes running into the room.

'Poor Mother,' the new son says to her with that nice, even smile. 'She got overexcited. You may need to give her something.'

The matron tsks. 'I'm afraid you'll have to go now.'

He gives her a complicit smile. *Just between us who are OK here*. 'Of course. And thank you for the time.'

'Poor Stella, I guess the excitement was too much for you.'

But Stella is screaming now.

In spite of the racket she is making Stella hears the new son murmuring just to her, – Goodbye Mother. Wait for the news.

– Nnnn

– Watch the papers. Watch TV.

Stella staggers into comprehension. 'No!' There is nothing she a murderer can say or do to warn them, or prevent this. *Even though he is not my son* this new man *is* her son in a way. In one sweep he has conferred on her the blame and the terror like a mantle: *We are all your sons*. And her punishment for betraying all these new sons of hers is knowing ahead. Loving them and knowing what they're going to do. 'Help,' she cries. She cries, 'Oh God oh God,' as the matron drags her past her waiting cell and into the infirmary; the prayer or lament just keeps coming out of her, 'Oh God oh God oh God!' It will keep coming out of her until the tranquilizing shot paralyzes her and she finally falls still; hours later Stella will wake into grief and she will keep waking into grief every morning of her life because he is gone, her son, and she is transfixed by the pain of loss repeated endlessly.

Because the minute they are torn apart she misses him. She misses him terribly.

32

'Who's there?' Theo stiffens.

It's late. The house is too still.

'Sal?'

Sally would answer. Nobody answers and nothing moves.

'What is it?' Theo isn't jumpy exactly, but the Delia Vent thing has changed him. The final violation was having her turn up inside a house he thought was locked. It's nothing he can explain to anybody, exactly. He doesn't understand it himself. Why he twitches every time the phone rings, why he hates checking the mail, why night noises have turned him into a neurotic. What it's most like is being little and having somebody you trust smash you in the face. Before it happened, you weren't afraid of anything. Now every little movement makes you flinch.

The only time he forgets is when he's deep in work. Lost in the white hum of concentration, he can lose track. But while he's been fixed tonight, trying to work through his material, something has happened. Creaky from sitting too long, he stands. 'What?' He moves into the narrow hall. Nothing. But there is something. No one's here, but he's certain someone has been here.

It is as if the house has just breathed out.

It is an eerie violation. It's like not knowing whether you've been raped or not. Uncertainty resolves as anger. Theo is gnawing his knuckles, shaking with it. *The Vent is turning me into a deranged paranoid.* He shouts to no one, 'Why don't you leave me alone?'

202

Somebody else would have handled this better. How could he be so stupid? Should he have known the signs? All he was trying to do was help the damn woman. How did it turn into this? At the airport he gave her the lecture from hell and shoveled her on the plane and in spite of everything he said she's still calling. The letters come. He throws them out. Now this. Movement in the house when there is nothing in the house. He needs to wake up in a place where nothing weird ever comes. Even though it's three in the morning, he goes to Sally's. He lets himself in and slips into bed next to her. He strokes her hair, murmuring, 'Hey, it's me.'

She mumbles and rolls into his arms.

They are wakened by the phone. Groaning, Sally rolls over and picks it up. 'No, goddammit, and stop calling.' She disconnects and throws it across the room.

Theo says, 'Hey.'

'I don't want to talk about it,' Sally says.

The phone rings again while she's in the shower. Theo lunges for the corner where Sally threw it and taps it on. 'Hello?'

There is that long pause at the other end that lets you know the caller has just reached somebody they never intended to talk to. The quick intake of breath right before whoever it is hangs up.

'Delia?' Theo shakes the phone like a wino trying to shake off a rat. Angrily, he shouts into dead air, 'If that's you, Delia, you're going to be . . .'

Sally comes out of the bathroom, murmuring, 'Shh.'

'Has she been calling you?'

'I didn't want to tell you.' In this light her skin looks transparent. Vulnerable.

'The Vent has been calling and you didn't tell me?'

Sally grimaces. 'I figured you had enough on your plate.'

'I wanted to keep you out of this.'

203

She shrugs. 'It's no big deal.'

'She ought to be in jail!'

'What are you going to do, go to New York and get her arrested? Fat chance.'

'I'd like to kill her.'

She's cool. Everything about her says, *I'm cool*. 'I've dealt with worse. All she wants to do is cry on the phone.'

'The police.'

'I told you, all she does is cry on the phone.'

'If she's threatening you, we can tape it. Get the cops.'

'Forget it, T.'

'What if I moved in? At least you wouldn't . . .' What? Keep getting these calls? Be alone when Delia comes for you? God, he wants to do something but he doesn't know what to do here. 'Sally? What if I moved in? What do you think?'

Sally sticks her head in the closet and keeps it there as if her wardrobe choice is a matter of life and death, but they both know she is composing her face. When she turns, she is sweet and grave. 'I don't think that's a very good idea right now.'

'Something I did?'

She shakes her head. 'We just need to let the particles settle, OK?'

'Then it is something I did.'

'Not really. You're spread in too many directions, T. You've got a lot of stuff to work through.'

'I know.' He sags. It's true. Somehow the Vent and his project on killers are linked in his mind. Get rid of one and he can lose the other. Until he does, he's not fit to be with her. He says regretfully, 'I know, but I thought if I was here with you, the Vent . . .'

'Would bother you instead. I don't think that's how it works.'

He is boiling with frustration. 'I've got to do something.'

'Chill, T. I'm not going to let the intern from hell or anybody else stampede me. And neither should you.'

'I love you.'

'About moving in.'

'If only.'

Sally's trying for a tough look that doesn't quite come off; her voice gives her away. 'I just want us to be sure.'

He gets back to the house late that day. Automatically moving into his home office, he sits down with a reflexive sigh and brings his computer to life. But something is different here.

'What.' Is he ever going to live a life without surprises? Can he get up some morning and not hear himself barking, 'What!'

There is a new item slipped into the sheaf of Zax clips on top of the Bundy pile. The clipping is old, torn out of some rinkydink daily. He skims until he skids into the string *mark of a human bite*.

'OK, Delia,' he says, 'you might as well come out.'

But he is alone.

33

New Haven

He comes into the office smiling.

Although the trip back has been hard, Haik arrives looking fresh. Picked up a new shirt last night at a Marshall's in was it Quincy, Mass? Scrubbed in the station, bought a disposable razor and shaved. Now he is here. Say good morning. 'Morning.' Smile.

The nameless person at the terminal next to his smiles. 'Have a nice trip?'

'Very nice.' Nice. The trip was nice. Everything is so ordinary here under the fluorescent strip lights.

'Business or pleasure?'

'A family matter,' he says, pulling the day's work up on the screen. It is the truth. Poor mother. She gave up the reporter person. The one who really told the lie. It sticks in Haik's quivering flank like an elephant goad. GLAD. Well he will obliterate glad.

'I hope it went well.'

'Mmm.' He clicks to open a window. He clicks again. The order of the figures is beautiful.

'I said, I hope it went well.'

'It went well,' Haik says, although it was a close thing. If he had found the reporter at home when he went in he would have garroted him and ruined everything. No, he would have bludgeoned him to death out of passion and wrecked the plan. You don't kill anything you can use;

Theo Slate fits in the design. Design is everything and if this one is unfulfilled and tearing him up from the inside in its struggle to emerge, it won't be long. The pain is intense. It is exciting and strange.

A woman speaks. 'I said, Mr Simmons?'

He does not always remember which name he is going by so he does not immediately look up. He is considering. He can't ruin this one by moving too fast or by killing on impulse – the botched thing last night in Quincy; too hasty to deserve a number miscarried *let my cock lead me my mistake.* Hastily contrived event, self-contained. Outside the design, Haik carelessly tearing the fat face instead of . . . Badly botched, had to throw em in the water to get rid of it *yes Father I am ashamed. Ashamed. Analyze. Organize. Plan.* Never operate outside the plan; there is that blank page in his notebook waiting for completion. Design! 'Write it down.'

'Or do you want it black?'

This time I will do em right. When he kills em, ey will be The One as planned. Ey and no other. He is working it out on the walls of his room. Yes he is working it out on the inside walls of his skull even as here in the office he pushes numbers around the screen with a neutral smile because this is his day job while the other is his life. Haik is in so deep that for the moment he doesn't hear the receptionist. Then he does hear her and he blinks. 'Did you say something?'

'I asked if you wanted your coffee black.'

Standing there in that wildly patterned sweater dress darkhaired big boobs built not unlike #5, he thinks not a bad prospect but you never shit where you eat.

'Sir?'

He remembers to smile. 'Who, me? Oh no. Thanks.'

She lingers. She may be flirting. 'I asked if.'

'No coffee today, thanks.' His prospects! Haik is on his feet. A break in your concentration can cost you. He's been away. He has to check on #5. And the backup. #6. What if they slid out of place while he was gone? Anxiety burns inside, itching in his belly and in his sinus cavities and so deep in his esophagus that no finger can reach; he gives an inadvertent cough. 'As a matter of fact, I was just going out.' He is running even before he reaches the street.

At the library his mark is right where he wants her to be, sitting behind the desk in the reading room. Fine. She looks up with a faint half-smile that means she is beginning to accept him as part of the picture here and so, assessing, he lingers at the desk even though the plan is incomplete and it is far from time. The white pocks in the skin where too much sun has leached the color. The black, moist down on the wrists. She's ready. He knows because when he flirts she flirts back it is only a matter of time before we hear the click and we can forget she. Forget he. *E is just a thing to us.* Forget black hair that hangs long and swinging boobs rubbing each other under the wool now we will have done with you. Objectify.

She lifts her head. 'Did you say something?'

Haik becomes aware that his insides are roiling dangerously close to his outsides; he has to leave before what's inside begins to show. 'Who, me? I'm sorry, no. Have a nice day.' He gives her his careful smile and goes.

The other one is harder. His backup is still in the room on State Street; to make certain, he lets himself in the locked building and roves until he finds the room. It isn't hard. She has the door open as if she doesn't care who or what comes in. She sits crosslegged on the floor like a little icon in a shrine. Her paper sacks and canvas bags are open as if she's living out of them, but they lie next to the door as if she is getting cranked up to move out. #6 orange hair squashy face *ASKING FOR IT* why is she packing a puzzle *ASKING FOR IT* and what we say when we are in close like this is fluid, when we are done talking everything that is said between us diffuses like smoke so if anybody asks her later what happened here she will not know; safe in this so he asks because we cannot have our backup flying out of our design:

– Are you running from me?

She blinks up at him. In the world she lives in now, nothing comes as a surprise. – No, I've been on a trip.

– That's funny, so have I.

She says gravely, – But I'm back. For now.

Librarian so static and this one shifting on her plump haunches as if she could bounce up at any moment and fly out of his reach, but she likes him. He can tell. He says, – Then you are moving.

– Not now, but I hope soon. I kind of have to.

– Move?

She nods and the dirty curls bounce. – Running out of money. I can't afford the rent.

– I can help you find a place.

– Really?

– Won't cost you anything, he says. *A good idea this. Put you on ice where I can find you.*

– Like where?

– Tell me when you want to move and I'll show you. I could give you a ride.

He has moved too fast. Wall-eyed with suspicion, the backup says, – Oh, I'm not moving yet.

Used to me. Get her used to me. This is only his backup. He hasn't given her enough thought. Say carefully, – But you look like you're going soon.

– Not really. I just want to be ready when he calls.

– Who?

– My boyfriend.

– Oh right, you were visiting your boyfriend.

She whirls. – How did you know where I was?

No need to tell her how carefully he keeps track of things. – I just knew.

– You didn't, like, follow me or anything.

– No, a friend told me you lived nearby.

– You live near here?

– No, not exactly. He lives in central New Haven. The ungentrified brick Federal where he finds her is halfway to the dump. He says reassuringly, – Somewhere not too far.

She keeps shifting on her haunches, rocking like a little rubber Buddha. She says, – Well I can't talk any more right now, I'm kind of busy. I have to practice.

– Practice?

– My flute.

It is sitting in her lap. He repeats, – Your flute.

Her smile is sweet and shy. – Yes, I. Don't you have to go?

But Haik is in the presence of somebody whose will is weaker than his so he stays in place. – Practice because it isn't perfect?

– How do you know that?

Remember to smile. – I know a lot of things.

– Yeah. Perfect. For my boyfriend.

No way. No departures. – So you're playing for him soon?

– I hope so.

– When?

– I'm waiting to hear.

– Where would you be going if you were going?

– No place you need to know. Pretty soon I'll go there and I won't have to be here *any more*. This place. Look at it.

– It's good enough for winter.

– My boyfriend has a really nice house, plenty of room. He just painted the living room for me. Her hands sweep the room. – It's nothing like this.

The breathy little hesitations tell Haik that #6 is by no means fixed in place to be done at his leisure. She is sliding around, her story is sliding around. She could be anywhere tomorrow. She could be anything. He repeats as if to ground them both and bring her back to the starting point: reality check. – So you really did have a good time?

But #6 is wandering somewhere else. She comes back with a little shudder. – Where?

– On your trip.

– My trip? Oh sure.

– You were with . . .

– My boyfriend. Her smile swells up like a cheap balloon. – It was wonderful. He was surprised.

– And did you have a good time?

– I already told you. I did.

– You look so . . . He does not say *unhappy*. He says, – You look so sort of. I wasn't sure.

– I told you, it was wonderful. In fact, we went dancing every night. He took me out to dinner in one of those revolving restaurants. And he bought me a beautiful ring.

– Oh, he did? Can I see it?

– Not right now. I can't wear it yet. We have to wait until he tells his folks.

– Unless he never gave you a ring.

– He did!

– Can I see it?

– It's at the jeweler, OK? He's having my initials engraved.

He could do this one right now and get it over with but time has taught him hard lessons. – If you're so much in love, why are you here and not there?

She is pink and squinting. – We're going to be together soon!

– But you wouldn't go anywhere without telling me.

– Soon, she cries.

Haik is studying her. ASKING FOR IT. Could do it and she'd be glad. That shaky, sick smile, the round white hands with no bones in them. This one is not like the librarian. This one is borderline but he needs to determine where the border is. He probes, testing the limits of her delusion. – Tickets don't grow on trees.

– Oh, that. My boyfriend is taking care of it. She just smiles. She smiles and smiles.

So she is lying. If she is crazy this is too much like shooting pigs in a poke. That's why this one is only my backup. Too much like shooting pigs in a poke. Pigs.

Pigs can't run. PROCEDURES.

Can't tell. PROCEDURES.

An unformed idea torments him, buzzing close. Testing, Haik asks, – You mean he's sending money?

– Oh, he gave me a first-class ticket.

Yes! She is one of life's prisoners. Paralyzed here. He grins.

– Now, don't go 'way.

– Where are you going?

– Have a nice day. He roars downstairs, fixed on it, and even though it is nowhere near night he goes back to the boarding house and locks himself into his room, muttering as he darts at the walls with his Magic Markers in an orgy of planning, come clear, come *clear*, yes he is making too much noise but that is of no concern to Haik because he is closing on it, yes. Oblivious, he stabs at the walls with his jaws cracked wide, filling in the infernal diagram. Do it, do it by the numbers; do it *right*! When he gets it right he can put it in the book. Burning, he scrawls PROCEDURES, plowing through the thicket of black lines and color that rages like exploding blood: moaning, he scrawls, blinded by unremitting pain, slashing at it until two words present themselves. He writes without knowing what he is writing: PREPARE EM.

It is like a light going on. 'Yes!'

34

Theo is sick, maybe something he ate but he won't take a comp day. He'd rather go to work than sift through his stuff. His head is littered with ugly details: instruments, orifices, blood and prurience. Screams that will not be silenced. He'd rather be out on the interstate covering a five-car crash. But when he broaches the front door he finds Delia Vent camped on his stoop. 'I told you to go away!'

'You know you love me.' She half-sits in the sleeping bag and the rising air is rank with that unwashed smell. 'You don't have to pretend with me.'

What he hates most is the fact that this leaves him so shaken. How did this happen to her? How did she get this way? 'You can't keep coming back like this.'

'Oh, Theo!'

Somewhere deep, a nerve twitches when he hears his name. It's if she's dragged a thumbnail across his groin. 'Stand up.'

'You'll make me leave.'

'You heard me.' He wants to drag her to her feet and straightarm her off the porch and frogmarch her off the block and out of his life but the woman is an emotional tarbaby. Punch her in that soft body and his fist will sink in so deep that he'll never get free. 'Do you want me to call the police?'

Without transition, the smile takes a sick, toxic turn. 'Why would you want to do that?' Then in a swift, mad reversal, it turns sweet. Where this woman who loves him is now, there is no reaching her. 'It's OK, I know you're in a hurry, but when you get back . . .'

'You won't be here.' He starts moving her aside with his toe. He knows better than to kick; as it is her eyes widen at the touch. She smiles blindly as he says, 'I've changed the locks. Understand?'

If Delia does understand, the knowledge doesn't touch her. As he strides to the car her reproach curls after him and clings, pervasive and cloying as spilled honey. 'Why are you hurting me?'

Locked in the car, he phones the cops. He's tempted to stay to watch the bust but he doesn't want to give too much importance to this. No. He doesn't want to give any importance to this. He calls the station later to be sure the police have done the deed. His contact on the desk says, 'I don't know what kind of poltergeists you think you've got, Slate. I sent a car out to the house but there was nobody around.'

'Pete, the woman was glued to my front porch.' He flashes on the sordid little pile she made: grocery sack, flute case, canvas bag. 'She had a lot of stuff.'

'We didn't find anything.'

'She didn't just disappear. Did you check the house?'

'No sign of illegal entry. No sign of anything.'

Yeah, he thinks dully, groping for a packet on his desk. Yeah, right. 'I was hoping you'd get her off my back.'

'Dream on, Slate. If we can't find her, we can't do anything. You know we can't touch her even if we do.'

'But she's.'

'Your word against hers.'

His jaws are working. Something tastes bad. 'Breach of peace?'

'Not on hearsay, Slate. You know the law.'

'Loitering?'

'Read my lips.'

'OK. Public nuisance?' He swallows hard but he can't get rid of the taste.

'You have to prove it. Get some neighbor to corroborate.'

'I don't know any of the neighbors.' He does not add that his plain little rented property is more or less ostracized, stuck in its own Coventry in the cul de sac at the mean far end of the otherwise gracious street. The Vent could scrub her panties on his stoop and hang her bras on the porch rail to dry and nobody would see but Theo.

'Maybe if we catch her in the act. Look, if she turns up again, keep her there until our people come.'

To his surprise, Theo finds he's chewing two Maalox tabs at once. 'If she comes back.'

'Even then I'm not sure you'll have grounds. Why don't you just take a nice trip until this blows over?'

'And lose my job? I don't see why you guys can't—'

'Sorry, call coming in on the other line.'

'I'll hold.' Yeah the phone is dead. He's been shunted into oblivion.

Arch drifts by the desk. 'You got a problem?'

'Who, me? No, no problem. Why?'

For the first time since Theo's known him Arch hesitates, as if he needs to hunt up the right words before he speaks. 'You just look like you've got a problem, is all.'

'No, I'm cool.'

Also for the first time since Theo got here his old friend says kindly, no, protectively, 'So, OK. So, Slate. Let me know if anything happens where you are not cool.'

In his tender state Theo barks, 'Why would I not be cool?'

It seems important not to tell Sally. What's driving him nuts is the suspicion that he brought this on himself. *Is it something I did?* Did he inadvertently turn this woman from a reasonably acceptable human being into a frowzy, insistent nightmare? He doesn't know. He doesn't know why he feels guilty but he does. He would like to go to Sally's for the night but he isn't easy with it. Not with Delia in town. It's not that she's done anything that he knows of. He's afraid because he can't predict what she'll do.

He's troubled by the calls she was making to Sally, that Sally tried to keep from him. Is Sally protecting him? If the Vent is still calling her, does Sally think he's in too crazed a state to be told? It seems important not to let the Vent find out that he and Sally are still an item. He hasn't looked at the reasons for this decision. It's just something he knows he has to do. Therefore when they meet at the elevators after work, Theo lets one elevator go by so he and Sally can ride down together alone. When the doors close he runs his hand under her hair and she turns her head to meet his hand and lays her cheek against his palm. He says, 'I can't see you for a couple of days. I've got extra work.'

Sally grins that bashful grin that says she's sitting on something she's proud of. 'It's OK, I'm tied up with the Whartons.'

'The Whartons!'

'Women staffers' caucus. We're going to stick it to them on policy.' She adds quickly, 'Take care, Protestant white male. You wouldn't know.'

Theo forgets and blows his cover. 'How about tomorrow?'

'I hate this just as much as you do. It's a two-day retreat. I don't get back until Sunday.'

'Love you.'

Her smile gets wider. 'Yeah.'

He coasts into his driveway with his flip phone open, prepared to speed dial. In a way he's disappointed that the Vent isn't camped on his front steps, just asking for it. Showdown. Arrest. He could press charges and have done with this. He pulls into the garage. He raises the blinds in his office and sits down to work. Let her show her damn self. Just let her try. If she does, should he get the encounter on tape? He isn't sure. The ugliness is of a piece with the ugly detail littering his desk.

The night passes quietly, no incursions, but even before he wakes the next morning Theo knows. He doesn't have to open the front door to know. She's there. He calls the cops and then dresses. To make this work, he has to keep her here until the cops arrive. Better yet: spur her into some bookable offense. Revulsion is in a footrace with expedience. It's a crapshoot. Will he hit her with something or can he wait for the cops? He shoves the door open hard, so that it hits one of her soft places. 'I warned you.'

'Oh, Theo.' Any attention, even raging, reads like love to her. Looking up from the sleeping bag, she pleads, 'Don't be mad.'

If he doesn't hit the woman, it's partly because this is Theo Slate, who doesn't solve problems by hitting, would never hit a woman in any case. But there is another reason. She is so clearly begging to be hurt. 'You get off on this, don't you?'

'No, I just . . .'

'You want me to kick the shit out of you.'

'. . . just want you to let me in.' Her tone makes a sudden swing from plaintive to threatening. 'Is there somebody else?'

'No!' Theo shouts. 'Now leave me alone!'

'I thought we were in love.'

'Well you were wrong.' Timing: he hears an approaching car – nobody comes to the cul de sac except Sally, so he knows it is the police. It's time to wind this up and move on. 'Are we clear?'

DeliaMarie Vent does not argue; she only looks up at Theo and in that musical voice of hers sets the parameters of coming encounters. 'Why are you hurting me?'

'OK. The cops.'

Once he's taken the particulars the fat officer says to Theo, 'Do you want to file a complaint?' Theo doesn't know this team so he is starting from scratch. There are no favors owed.

He looks at Delia. Certain things are left over when somebody you thought of as a casual friend turns into an object that you hate. Weak spots start to show. This poor woman used to be my friend. 'Depends.'

Delia mourns, 'I don't know why he's hurting me.'

The woman officer quickens like a hunting dog. She helps Delia to her feet and asks solicitously, 'Did he . . .'

Delia just sniffles and won't speak.

Before Theo can protest the woman officer says, 'Unless you have something substantive, Mr Slate, you'd better be careful.'

The fat officer is apologetic. 'Without a complaint, there's not much we can do.'

'Wrongful arrest,' his partner says brusquely. She has established eye contact with Delia. 'Without grounds, you're in for . . .'

He shrugs. 'So I'm sorry, Mr Slate, we can't . . .'

'Why don't you see if she's carrying a concealed . . .'

Delia wheels on him with a furious glare.

'Come along, ma'am. I'll help you carry your stuff.'

'She could have anything in those bags,' Theo says desperately. 'Anything.' But they are leaving. 'You mean you're not going to . . .'

'We can't. Unless you want to get a restraining order.'

Moving into a close grouping with the woman officer, Delia stirs; he can't bear to look at her. 'If I have to I'll have to.'

'It'll have to wait until Monday,' the fat officer says. He adds, generously, 'Tell you what. We'll give her a ride out of here. Come on, Adele.'

His partner says, 'Wait a minute, Harry, maybe you and I should find out exactly what's happened here.'

Ignoring her, the fat officer shoots Theo a look: *Women.* 'Come on, ma'am. Let's go.'

While soberly, like a wronged lover rejected by her beloved, DeliaMarie Vent gathers her collection of sacks and small objects and shambles down the steps. 'I wasn't bothering anyone.'

'Enough.' Groaning, Theo slams the front door. He won't see Delia sidle closer to the woman cop as they approach the cruiser and he won't know that as they get into the car she leans close to the grill, whispering to the woman officer, who turns her head so she can hear better.

By the time the cruiser heads off, Theo is aching all over. Muscles burn and he can't get his jaws unclamped. Somewhere just under his ribcage and in his belly and his flanks fresh bruises are throbbing, soft spots filling with blood as if he's been pushed down six flights of stairs or kicked to death by forty gorillas. He would like to go bury his head in Sally but he's just as glad she's out of town. He'd feel better if she stayed away until he could make sure the Vent is gone for good. It just isn't safe. If he was on better terms with the weekend staff he would follow up on this. He calls Sally's house and leaves a message on the machine. 'It's me. I don't care what time it is when you get back, call me.'

At this point the corruption in his office looks better to him than his life, but when he sits down he can't work. He sits for hours, strung taut and listening. No sound comes from outside. Nobody rings the bell. The woman's gone, he tells himself. She'd better the hell be gone. He can't stand this. He has to check. 'No!'

She is sitting on the step. She's unzipped her sleeping bag and wrapped it around her against the evening chill. The tip sticks up like a monk's hood. 'Oh please don't hurt me any more.'

It is the repetition that's killing him. The sheer, brute repetition of the act. It's like scraping dogshit off your shoe over and over and coming inside to discover the smell. He does not speak. He slams the door on her and makes his third call of the day to the police. *Harassment,* he thinks. *Maybe I can nail her on harassment.* The night desk Sergeant says, 'I'm sorry, Mr Slate, we can't keep sending people out there.'

At least Sally is safely out of the way. Sally. All his soft parts collide and begin to shrivel. He's got to get rid of her before Sally . . . 'She could be dangerous.'

'Yeah right,' the woman says. 'I heard about you from Adele. Adele talked to her today, so be careful. As a matter of fact, she told Adele all about you.'

'I'm not kidding, the woman is—'

'Yeah, dangerous. Yeah, right. Sure she is.'

35

re: #5

2. PREPARE EM

a. Do em fast. No screaming.

b. Eir tongue shall be cut off and shoved inside the mouth so e won't tell. The mouth will be sealed. Needle and thread too crude. Try duct tape: If duct tape wrong here, try needle and thread for #6.

c. The head shall be cut off and buried separately so e will not tell on us.

d. The hands shall be removed and buried with the head so e can't point to us.

e. The feet shall be cut off and buried so e can't run away.

f. Burn the rest.

g. Call it done.

He will get it this time, and he will get it right. Then he can show it to that damn reporter and that damn reporter can write it up. Then he will be done.

36

When a person you thought you knew turns into something else, the territory is ambiguous. Do you have
an obligation because you knew her once? Did you push
her across the line? Don't dwell on it or the ambiguities will
destroy you. Watch out. She has the power to turn you into
something you never intended to be. To you, she is nothing
but an object. One you can't move out of your life.

She's out there again. Theo can hear her through the door.
'I can't wait for us to be together.'

Fine. He'll wait her out. He has work to do. Best-case
scenario, she'll freeze to death. No. She'll give up and go.
Meanwhile, use the time. Preston Zax. The only murderer
who ever begged to be stopped? He doesn't think so. There's
this guy Heirens, went into his victims' bathrooms after he
wasted them and wrote messages in lipstick, unless it was
blood. His outcry riveted the country. Then it passed into
the culture. Repeat anything often enough, no matter how
shocking, and you get used to it. Eventually it turns into a
catchword for a deteriorating culture. A grisly gag line:

STOP ME BEFORE I KILL AGAIN.

Nice folo, Theo thinks. Nice story. I can wrap it up
tonight. Although he has them by heart he replays Stella
Zax's tapes from the top, pausing at the crucial point.
'They want to stop. They would give anything if you
would make it stop.' Stella fills his head. It is as if her
consciousness becomes his consciousness. *'When you stop
them, they are glad.'*

Fine. Evil at war with the vestigial humanity that recognizes what it is doing and begs to be stopped. Personal essay, try *Newsweek* first. Zax at the moment of death, his relief. Heirens. Others, who cut wider and wider paths, just asking for discovery. STOP ME. Just asking for it. Absorbed, he loses track. He won't look up again until he takes off the earphones and discovers that his telephone is ringing. Sally's voice crackles into the room. 'Where the fuck have you been?'

'Oh, Sal, I tried to reach you.' He laughs in relief. 'The Vent is back.'

'I know.'

'How did you find out?'

'How do you think I found out? I was there!'

'You were here? You can't be here. You're at that retreat thing.' His voice explodes in exasperation. 'All weekend!'

She says patiently, 'T., I came to your house.'

'You were here and you didn't come in?'

'I couldn't,' Sally says.

'How could you not come in?'

'She was all over your front porch. Said you went away, said you told her to wait. I thought. Oh hell, Theo, I don't know what I thought.'

'And *I* thought you were at that damn . . . God, I tried to reach you!'

'It ended early.'

'You were here?'

'Yeah. I got back early and I thought you and I could . . .'

A little part of his life has been lost forever. He mourns, 'Oh, Sal.'

She is grieving too. 'I thought she was lying but I couldn't be sure. I should have rung the bell.'

'I wish you had.' Theo is aware of background noise filtering in from wherever Sally is making this call – police station, probably. Checking her machine in the police press room.

223

Her voice drops. 'She isn't letting anybody on the porch.'

'She what?'

'I'll explain when I see you.'

'Are you OK?'

Her tone tells him she isn't. 'I thought you'd hear us and come out.'

'Hear you?'

'There was yelling.'

'Sorry. Headphones. The Zax tapes.'

'She said you weren't seeing anybody.'

'She *what*?'

'If I'd known you were home I would have pushed.' There is an odd catch in her voice. 'It's just as well I didn't.'

'Where are you?!' Cradling the phone, Theo gets to his feet.

'I've gotta go.'

'The station, right? Hang on, I'm coming.'

'No! Don't go out.'

'What's the matter?'

'She really is crazy.' Sally's voice is shaking with rage. 'I came home to see if you had come over here? I don't know how she got into my house or when she did it, T. I can't even prove she did do it, but the woman was there. She slashed a couple of paintings and ripped the hell out of my bed.'

'Shit no.' Theo punches the wall; the punky sheetrock gives under his fist. 'Shit!'

'I guess I'm lucky she didn't rip the hell out of *me*.'

He says through his teeth, 'I'll take care of it.'

'No.' She is sharp and quick.

But Theo is groping in the kitchen tool drawer for a chisel, the hammer, anything. 'I'll handle it.'

'She has a knife.'

'I don't care!'

'Wait for the police.'

'The police. The police have already blown me off.'

She says firmly, 'Not this time. Not after what I told them. They're on the way.'

'Dammit, Sally.' Theo is too wild to be able to tell whether the sirens he hears are in the background wherever Sally is calling or outside his house. He shouts as if he is talking to her over thousands of miles, 'How do you know they're on the way?'

'I'm at the station, filing a complaint.'

The police shake Delia down. If that was her knife that she used to score Sally's paintings and savage the bed where Sally and Theo make love, the Vent has lost it, along with any other weapons she might have had under her corduroy skirt or in that mangy duffle coat. To Theo, she still looks dangerous. He's angry now, less at Delia for this relentless courtship than at himself, for giving it room to fester and grow. He was a damn fool for being nice to her in the first place and being too civil to drive her away before she could turn him into a prisoner in his own house. Yes civilization hampers as much as it controls. People put too much faith in rational solutions. In observing the forms. Beaming blindly now that they are face to face and she can see him up close, the Vent waits for the formalities to be over so they can resume. Her moist mouth works, preparing speeches he doesn't want to hear. He only wants the cops to Mirandize her and take her out of his life.

The officer is somebody Theo knows, usually works dayside. He listens. He nods. 'OK, we're going to take her in, but I don't know if we have enough to hold her.'

'You *what*?'

'At least we can keep her overnight.' He turns to Delia, who flashes her teeth in an odd, wild look. 'OK, Ms Vent. Officer Hatcher will help you with your stuff. This is going to work better if you tell Mr Slate that you won't be back.'

The Vent says dutifully, 'I won't be back.' She looks

leaden standing there, less like a danger to him than to herself, bedraggled in the beige duffle coat, matted and flecked with broken leaves, with her sleeping bag hanging from her arm like an extra skin and those orange curls of hers hanging in matted loops. There is nothing threatening about her now. She stands between the officers in the odd composure of somebody who knows she is being wronged. It is as if the perpetrator or perpetrators have vaporized and DeliaMarie Vent is the injured party here. If she had a knife, it is nowhere on her. In no way does she look like a perp. What does she look like, then? Theo is not sure. She looks oddly neutral, but he gets the idea that she is resting for the next bout. She is like a hibernating animal, gathering strength. When it wakes, it may kill. He wants to ram her in the midsection and have this over with. He'd like to kick the shit out of her and keep kicking until she stops moving for good. He keeps his clenched fists at his sides, where nobody will see. *Born victim*, he thinks angrily. Wherever he moves her gaze follows, loving. Sweet. *And you get off on it.*

For the first time since the cops came Theo speaks to her directly. 'It's over.'

Expanding in the light of his attention, Delia takes on an odd sheen. 'Whatever you want.'

'I just want you gone.'

'But I.' She does not have to say, *love you.*

37

B eautiful, so close, Haik has the librarian in place.
Got em used to us. E may even want to start
something with us, e blushes just like a woman and e
tilts eir head but this is no longer a woman. This is only a
thing that we must do. Male. Female. It doesn't matter. E is
the object now. No need to ask er if e lives alone. He already
knows. We have rested his dick on the pillowcase where e
puts eir head down and e doesn't even know. Yeah we know
how to do er we have done em before, it is almost time.

Sitting on the bed, he consults the notebook: the page
marked *PROCEDURES*. Filled. Everything is planned now,
everything. In her bed halfway across town #5 is sleeping.
All that is left to do now is to be sure that #6 is in place. Shall
he do em too, regardless? He is not sure. He will decide that
later. Now he is deep in the design. He moves from one wall
to another, muttering and making last-minute adjustments:
this line flows from this branch. And becomes *this*. When
he is done he will go out to check on #6. Then he will come
back here and sleep. In the scheme of things he wants this to
come down tomorrow. Tomorrow looks like a good day.

Rapt, he is too caught in the beauty of the design to hear
the cough in the hall or the low voices, people conferring
outside his locked door and people going away; gnawing
his wrist, he writes on as the thoughts flow out of him in
pure sound even as they set themselves down on the wall:

227

You will know us when he comes because we will do what I have to do and then we will silence your mouth and still your hands forever.

'Perfect.' Who said that? *Did you call?*

He is becoming something else.

He is the factor. 'Now.' Haik snaps to attention like a surgical patient waking in the recovery room. Cold air knifes into his lungs. It's a beautiful night. He will go once past the librarian's ground-floor apartment. He doesn't even have to look into the window. Then he will drive out State Street to check on #6.

He comes back raging. The bitch is gone!

It is a mortal rage, but to see him nobody would guess what is going on inside. Haik shows a bland face to the landlord, who is going downstairs as he comes up, and if the man has been watching for his restless tenant from an upstairs window and if he is headed for a phone where Haik can't hear, the factor will not know.

Rage grips him but it is a controlled rage. *The factor.* He is no longer the worthless son who could never get it right. *Analyze. Organize. Plan. Write it down.* He is the factor now.

Re: #6 Reasons not to do #6

1. If preparation w. #5 is correct #6 will not be needed.
2. #6 is out of town. For good?
Reasons to do #6.
1. To make sure.
2. E is part of the plan.
3. Do em extra, to make the mother proud.
Procedures:
Wait.

Frustration fills him. The compression is intense. He is

gnawing at his wrists again. Strips of skin catch in his teeth and blood drips down his upraised arm as he darts at the design on the wall with the marker gripped in his fist like an ice pick, driving it at the plaster as if he is sticking it into eir belly; Haik transformed by compression that surfaces in long, savage strokes in red. *Wait. We have to wait!* And as he writes, flames curl up his thighs into our belly because when we are designing it is like the seconds before we explode in sex, which signals the end to passion, for now. Which is better, anticipation or realization? The act, or the scheme for the act? Everything in his life would be different if he stayed in the world of design but he is driven to action by the harsh old voice from his childhood: *What did I teach you I want results. Results.* This charge is what drives him, it will drive him until – *I want you to get this done and do it right* – so close to completion and now . . . Haik boils over, scrawling until without knowing it he is not writing on the wall but hammering so the marker splays and he begins to shout.

'Bitch!'

He hurls himself on the bed, gnawing until his wrists are raw and the pain concentrates him, propeling him out of bed and back to the wall where he prints carefully, assuaged by the order printing imposes:

What to do about #6

Possibilities
1. Designate new #6.
2. Find em, question:
   a. How?

Writing, we won't know how much time passes and we don't hear comings and goings in the hall, he hears only his own voice bubbling in his throat 'How. *How?*' desperately listing next steps:

i. search her place.
ii. find somebody who knows her.
iii. go ask the.

'What? Ask what?'

iii. go ask the . . .

He does not hear the police knocking because he is almost on top of it, what steps to take to locate her, how to bring her back. With the reporter out there to write his story he has to get everything extra right *WHEN YOU STOP THEM THEY ARE GLAD I will get this and I will get this right and then I will get YOU*, Haik no the factor is Haik is the factor is scribbling so fast that he does not hear the rattle of the door knob and he won't hear the rap of the night stick on the panels or the shouting. He is alerted only by the blunted *thud* of bodies crashing against the door. Wild, he springs away from the wall at the last minute and skates the pack of markers across the floor as if that alone will stop them and, panting, leaps out the window seconds before police hurtle into the room.

The room crashes into light.

Somebody says, 'My God.'

It is brilliant. Encrusted, the walls and ceiling are like the interior of a living organism, crosshatched with ganglia and heavily veined, colorful and dense as the walls of a distended stomach or the interior of some sexual organ whose purpose has not yet been discovered or is too terrible to name. Sheets hang from the bed in a dizzying tangle and these too are covered with drawing and writing in colored ballpoint that makes them look like a spy's silken map of the most dangerous country in the world; there is writing on the mirror and there are aborted attempts at writing smeared on the floor, and buried in the lodger's sheets they will find the notebook and police will impound it even as the landlord and the tenants on this floor turn to each other in bewilderment saying, 'But he seemed like such an ordinary guy.'

38

It's Sunday night. Even though the police have taken the Vent in, Theo can't shake her. He has a sense of his personal stalker perched like a raptor at the head of Sally's ruined bed, watching them. Like the stunned victims of some natural disaster, they spent Sunday repairing the damage to Sally's apartment; they aired the room and changed the bed. They have turned the mattress but Theo sees the slashmarks even in his sleep. In a half-dream he sees Sally slashed. Electrified, he wakes: *Who called!*

Sally rolls against him. 'Shh, T., it's OK. It's me.'

'I'm so sorry.'

'It's only stuff, T. It's just stuff.'

'It could have been you.'

'No it couldn't.' She turns the digital clock on its face.

'What is it with these people?' Theo is posing more than one question here. With this violent act, the Vent moved into a new territory. In some way he hasn't figured out, she is one with his serial killers. 'What winds them up and starts them ticking?'

'Could we not talk about this?'

'Is it something in them?' He sighs. 'Or something about us?'

She turns on the light. 'Can't leave it alone, can you?'

'Like, something I should have done.' He blinks as the shadows recede. It's just him and Sally. Really. 'I feel so – *responsible*.'

'Well, don't. You've got bigger problems. While you

weren't looking, Arch got himself a new job. He was bragging at the caucus.'

Theo snaps to. 'Arch was at the women's caucus?'

'Whartons invited him, don't ask. He's going to New Haven. *The Register*. He said since you're kind of wrecked . . .'

'I'm not wrecked!'

'. . . would I break the news.'

'It's a shitty paper.' Small consolation. 'Shit!'

Sally moves into the curve of his body and Theo locks his arms around her. 'If you're not wrecked, prove it. Drop the Vent.'

'After what she did to you?' His chin digs into her scalp so his voice makes her skull buzz. 'It's not like I ever led her on. Look, I think you should ask for comp time and go see your folks.'

'And lose my place in line? I'm a reporter, T.'

Twenty-four hours away from the slashing and they are sparring. What Theo loves about Sally is that she never gives an inch. 'You'll do anything to win an argument. Look. It isn't safe.'

'Forget it, T. I don't run away.'

'Just until this thing is settled.'

'I said, no.'

'If you love me, you'll do it.' For Theo there will always be movement outside the bedroom window. Shapes plying back and forth in the darkness. The shadow you don't expect rushing down on you.

'I love you and I'm not going anywhere.' Sally turns the clock up and then slaps it back on its face. 'It's four. Now, sleep.'

He can't. He lies rigid, waiting for it to get light. Then he goes to the station. He wants this over with. He wants to see Delia charged and arraigned; he needs to know she can't make bail and nobody will make bail for her. He wants to see them lead her away.

Ted Dane, who's handling the case, shakes his head when

he sees Theo. 'I tried to do you a favor, Slate, but it didn't work out the way I thought it would.'

'What time's the arraignment?'

'Forget it. We don't have enough to make the charges stick.'

'After what she did?'

'No cloud without its silver lining, Slate. She's gone.'

Incoming. Ka-chinnng. Theo wheels like a bushwhacked Rambo. 'You mean you fucking let her go?'

'Not exactly.' Dane's face is rumpled and dingy, as if he's been up all night. 'Silver lining, Slate. Until this came up, we didn't have enough to hold her.'

Theo keeps his tone even. 'Until what came up?'

'You could call it a psychiatric crisis. We were going to evaluate her, release her, do you a big favor and front for her ticket out of here, but—'

'OK, where is she?'

Dane says, 'She was evaluated,' as if he's handing Theo a present. 'Wake up and smell the end of the tunnel. She flunked. Bigtime,' he says. 'We got Dr Drash in and the woman blew up, hair all over the walls. He socked enough Valium into her to bliss her out for a month. Yeah, right it did, by three a.m. she's running at the walls like a gorilla with an Excedrin headache.'

'So she's—'

'In the state hospital. Danger to herself, you don't want to know. We had to wake up Judge Bolt to sign the order.'

'How long is the commitment?'

'The usual. Three days.'

'And then she's back on the streets. My street.'

'Cross your fingers. It could spin out to thirty if they can't stabilize her meds.'

'Thirty years isn't long enough.'

'It's as good as it gets.'

Theo prompts. 'And then she goes before the judge?'

'Told you. We don't have enough to hold her on. Count

your blessings.' Clichés are Ted Dane's stepping stones out of every crisis. 'If she hadn't gone wacko on us, she would have been out of here yesterday. Look, if you want to know the truth, I don't think a hearing would have gone so good for you.'

There is something so inevitable about this that Theo asks heavily, 'OK Ted, what are you trying to tell me?'

'She claims it wasn't her. Says it's jealousy. You were boffing her and Ms Wyler found out and trashed her own place. She did it to implicate Ms Vent.'

'That's a lie.'

'It's her word against yours,' Dane says.

'Let me see the chief.'

'The chief is in a meeting right now. She's already got the paper on this. It's this way. She claims she never left your property. Says she was there while the Wyler place was being trashed.'

'And you believe her?'

The detective says patiently, 'It doesn't matter what I believe, Slate. It's what's entered in the record.'

'Fuck the record.' Theo is getting loud.

His shout brings the chief out of her office. Theo thinks she spends more time dressing for this job than she does preparing for it. Still she is a good-looking woman with a strong jaw intersected by steely, blunt-cut hair. 'Is there a problem here?'

Dane is offering, 'Look, you might want to get a restraining order.'

'What good is that going to do?'

'It might give us a little leverage.'

The chief repeats evenly, 'I said, is there a problem?' She has an AIDS ribbon on her lapel.

Theo's voice grates. 'No. No problem. Hello, Vera.'

'Hello, Theo. If you want me to go over this with you.'

He looks from the chief to his friend Dane to the chief.

235

Acknowledging favors already done him. 'No. Ted's done
that. I'm clear on it. I'm probably too clear on it.'

'The *Star* isn't going to . . .'

'Conflict of interest,' Theo says.

'Fine.' Because she knows Theo and Sally are together
now, the chief does him another favor. 'Look, since you're
already here, you might want to talk to the parents.'

'The parents!'

'When we brought her in we ran her name through the
computers. Some other stuff turned up.'

'Other stuff?'

'Later,' the chief says.

'The parents.'

'We were hoping they would . . .'

People like the Vent don't have parents. They spring out
at you from shadows, where they've hatched. Parents. Like
a jerk he hopes. 'They've come to get her, right?'

The chief does not answer. 'I think you'd better talk to
them. In there.'

The couple who get to their feet as he comes into the little
room look entirely too well-assembled to belong to the Vent.
These two upper-middle-class people are north of middle
age. Steady, borderline chic in clothes out of J. Tweed.
Too composed to be any kin to the disheveled prisoner
with her kaleidoscopic expressions and fixed, doleful stare.
Everything about them is well-kept. The father is taller than
Theo. 'Martin Vernon.'

Vent. Vernon. How many names does she have? The
father's expression is so stark that Theo says, 'I'm sorry,
Mr Vent.'

'Vernon. After last time she changed her name.'

'Last time?'

'You're not the first. We know about you, Mr Slate.'

Theo pushes on. 'I'm sorry we have to meet on this here.'

'I don't know why they called us in the first place,' the
mother says angrily.

'But you came.'

'We only came to settle this.' They speak in tandem. The father: 'To make sure there's no liability.' The mother: 'To make it clear she's not our responsibility.'

He has to pretend he doesn't understand. 'She needs help.'

'I'm Cordelia. You are . . .'

'Theo, ma'am.'

'And she . . .' The mother does not need to complete this sentence. They both know.

Theo admits, 'I'm afraid she did.' *Why do I feel guilty?*

'So you're the man.'

This sounds so like accusation that he hurries on. 'Look, this isn't really a police matter. She needs a hospital. A private hospital. Somewhere near you, so you can—'

Vernon snaps, 'And who's going to pay for a private hospital?'

'Near us!' His wife shrinks as if warding something off.

'Before she hurts herself.' Theo is waiting for their faces to soften. He's waiting for them to beg to see their daughter. After all, they're the parents. He's waiting for them to tell him they're taking her away.

These are well-educated people. Canny. Well-informed. The father says, 'Surely there's a state agency.'

'Where there's a family . . .' Theo hesitates, waiting for somebody, anybody to rush in.

Vernon says, 'Unless you want to assume liability.'

'The state expects the family . . .'

'We're not her family,' Martin Vernon says.

His wife says, 'Not any more.'

Oh shit. He gropes for formula: anything to make it sound impersonal. 'The state always hopes the family will. Uh.'

Vernon shakes his head. 'No.' The mother: 'Oh, no.' The father's words snap into the air. 'No way. We've washed our hands of her.' The mother rakes a nail across the corner of her mouth and is surprised by blood. 'After last time.'

This pulls him up so short that his jaws click. 'Ma'am?'

Her voice clots. Blood mottles her skin. 'After what she did.'

'It was bad.' Martin Vernon says, 'This professor at her college. She wouldn't quit. It was the first time and we thought—'

'But we found out. It's all in her records,' the mother says.

'We tried everything, but when Delia . . .' Vernon has trouble going on. Instead he cuts to the bottom line. 'It's in her records. We paid damages. We made what restitution we could, we—'

'It took everything we had. It almost killed us. She almost killed—'

'She *what*?'

'Nothing.' The mother pitches to the father, who covers quickly. 'Herself,' he says. 'We can't go through that again.'

But the mother can't stop. 'And when they found her! It was humiliating. And when we came to help . . .'

'She's beyond help.' It's as if this is some stranger's case. 'We did everything we could.'

'The therapy alone. But she blamed us. What she did to Martin.' The mother says, 'Show him.'

Stiffening, the father retreats to a safer place. 'No. You haven't seen what she's like when she's. The anger.'

'Yes,' Theo says thoughtfully. The passive love that is closer to hate. 'I've seen it.'

'And what comes after.'

Theo's lungs collapse. He can barely speak. 'What comes next?'

'You'll know it when you see it,' the mother says.

'You're talking like this about her and you're her mother?'

She freezes. Theo can see all her doors slamming. 'That has nothing to do with us.'

238

'But she's your daughter!'

Vernon says firmly, 'Not any more.'

She offers, 'But all that. That was a while ago. Ten years.'

'Ten years!'

'Besides, she's too old now. She's not our responsibility.'

The father completes the transaction. 'So it's the state's problem. Not our state, yours.'

'What Martin's trying to tell you is that whatever she is, DeliaMarie is an adult. She's the responsible party here. Why did they have to send for us at all?'

'She's legally of age.'

'Well beyond legal age.'

Theo jerks to attention. 'How old is she anyway?'

'Thirty-five on her next birthday,' the mother says sadly, as if admitting some ugly truth about herself. With automatic vanity, she covers. 'I was nineteen.'

Shit, Theo thinks. This girl I thought I was helping. She's older than me. 'She plays so *young*.'

'In a way she is. Unformed.' Now that she's signed off on this, Cordelia Vernon can afford to be generous. 'She never . . . Some people have children who are retarded. Retarded I could live with, but this. Some other part that never grew. The rages!' Her face is sliding out of control. 'Those and the way she never. She never. Not even when she was little.'

'Never what?'

They don't answer. 'No, she never did,' the father says.

'So she's not ours, not really. She was never really ours.'

They both look a hundred years old. 'The law says you can't divorce your children. But when it comes right down to the minute, you do whatever you can. We have our lives. We have our *lives*. So we'll be going now.'

'Don't walk out on this.' How did Theo get to be *in loco parentis*? 'Please. Something has to be done.'

239

Their smooth, bland expressions tell him that it's his problem now. These two are leaving. Turning in the doorway, the Vernons make a solid front. They are leaving Theo alone with this. He is alone with this and everything that follows. 'But not by us.'

39

*W*hen you fail. Order is everything. Design. Haik's father taught him. He taught hard. For experiments to succeed, each element must be aligned. Exact. Once his outline spells itself out as designed and executed – 1, 2, 3; once he has the items lined up, a, b, c – the rest will snap into place. Perfect. He becomes the machine and it is done. Until then, the factor is in stasis. The hand stayed, just when it is about to strike. Suspended.

This means that before anything, Haik has to settle the matter of the missing #6. But he has more immediate problems. He needs to find a new place. This may be complicated. When they broke in on him Haik went out the boarding-house window with nothing but what was on his back and in his pockets. IDs from a dozen different sources. Cash. He can't go back to the room. He ran out barefoot. He needs a jacket. Shoes. That's easy enough. Just wait in the station parking garage. The commuter who is just his size won't recover from the head injury any time soon. When he does, he won't remember what happened to him. He never saw.

The clothes are fine but credit cards are useless. They draw attention. Owners always reports losses; ey quit crying and call the 800 number. You can only use them once. Haik only deals in cash. After a visit to the commuter's ATM he destroys the card and pitches the wallet. He calls in sick:

emergency root canal. He takes the morning to buy what he needs. Topcoat. Razor. Fresh shirts. Canvas shoulder bag so that when he presents himself at the front door of the next rental, he will be himself. Smile.

But renters in downtown New Haven are wary. There is too much crime in this city. Nobody wants to be next. References? Haik won't call the office to have them vouch for him. He can't afford to forge any links. Instead, lie. Smile. Offer fake names. Sterling citizens of other cities who would be happy to vouch for Randolph Mantooth or – what name will he use with them – yes he is playing a game with fate when he offers this one, who reads newspapers anyway, who that watches TV remembers what they are seeing – Theo Zax. 'If you don't mind paying for the call.' Deposit? He does not write checks and he doesn't have the cash. The smile? At the third rental he tries, the smile works. For now. So he has a place to sleep. At least tonight. Haik goes back to the office that afternoon but he is too tired to concentrate on what comes next. The gap in the flowchart he has made for this final enterprise. In Father's scheme of things there is no room for accidents or surprises. In his time Haik has had both. It has made him patient. Methodical. If #6 is missing, the rest will have to wait. Yes this is a problem. It is a problem he should be solving but the circumstances are wrong. It will take time and thought to fill the gap and he is too spent to recover solutions. Today. This is Haik: factor immobilized. It's all he can do to push numbers around the screen.

Late afternoon. Haik goes rigid in his chair. The building pressure is tremendous. He can do one of two things. Destruct: fire and blood, shrapnel all over the walls. Or settle in. Inside him, the factor waits. And this is what informs him. And keeps him in place. Smiling. Silent. Still.

Nothing. This is nothing. Just a mechanical problem I have to solve.

242

40

Three days. He's got three days. One down. Two to go and unless something goes terribly right, the Vent is turned loose. Nobody wants to warehouse a marginal person. It isn't cost-effective. Put them on Haldol or sock them full of Thorazine, hope they don't hurt themselves and put them back on the street. He goes to the prison psychiatrist.

'I think we've got the basis for a longer commitment.' Ed Drash looks so much like a Rotarian that it steadies Theo. The police psychiatrist is calm, square and a little too white, like something that's been kept out of the sun too long.

'How much longer?'

'Depends. When I first saw her I would have told you she was pretty stable. Then I hit a sore spot and she blew up.' Congealed blood seals long scratches on the doctor's cheek. 'Her grip on reality is pretty tenuous.'

Theo notes the marks. 'That looks like the least of it.'

'She thinks she's an orphan. She thinks you and she are getting married. That you begged her to come back so you could have the wedding at the *Star* because that's where you fell in love.'

'Bullshit.'

'I'm only telling you what she says. Of course that was before she started tearing up the place.' Ed Drash doesn't seem to realize he is dragging his knuckles over the damaged cheek. 'You're having a traditional wedding in the foyer at the *Star*. So she's delusional.' Drawing back, the doctor nails

243

Theo with a professional squint. He snaps forward. 'Unless she's telling the truth.'

Anger flashes like heat lightning behind Theo's eyes. 'What do you think?'

'I only have what she tells me.' Accidentally, Ed dislodges a beginning scab. 'She says she's at the top of her class. She claims you're quitting your job and moving to New York to teach journalism. Incidentally, we checked.'

'You're bleeding.'

'Columbia really did have a place for her in September, tuition and fees prepaid.'

'Our publishers picked up the tab.' Something about the doctor's scrutiny makes Theo start laying out his credentials. If somebody's crazy, it isn't him. 'The Whartons. As a favor to me.'

'But she never showed up. She never checked in at housing.'

A cold wind blows through Theo. 'Then where in hell has she been living? Where's she been all this time?'

'I told you reality is not part of the picture here. She says she has an apartment on the East River. Job at *Time Magazine*.'

'What else?'

'She says you start teaching at Columbia in January. She's best friends with the dean. She made him give you the job.'

'Is there anything else I need to know?'

'It's all in her jacket.' The psychiatrist taps the folder.

Theo reaches for it. 'Fine.'

The doctor slides it away. 'Sorry. Confidentiality.'

'Look, she's been living on my goddamn doorstep. She trashed my friend's apartment. Is she dangerous or is she not dangerous?'

'I can't answer that.' Pause. 'You know you're not the first.'

Parts of Theo rattle in the wind. 'I heard. Who was he?'

'Her professor. She fixated. Wouldn't leave him alone. Told the police he was in love with her. The family had her committed.'

'But she got out.'

'They always get out.'

'And you can't tell me what she did. OK. The least you can do is put me in touch with the professor.'

Ed Drash turns that bland, Rotarian expression on Theo as if to defuse the information, rendering it somehow safe. 'Nobody can. He's dead.'

'She didn't . . .'

'Suicide. But I need to ask you a few questions, so we can figure out how to proceed.'

Bemused, Theo lets the shrink lead him gently through a Q. and A. session designed to flush out the truth of this situation. 'I had a lot of time on my hands when I started helping her,' he admits. 'The woman I thought I was going to marry dumped me. Training your patient was, like. Occupational therapy.'

The doctor tries, 'You fell in love on the rebound?'

'No!' Theo fixes Drash with his eyes as if in earnest of the truth. Then in a kind of sweet resignation, he thinks it through. 'What it is, is. OK. You feel low so you get off on helping people, OK, cheap thrill. So I helped her. I taught her everything I knew.'

'So you were in a mentor relationship.'

'No. I wanted to be a fucking hero,' Theo admits. 'I thought, OK my love-life sucks, but. At least I'm good at this. So I guess you could say I brought this on myself.'

The doctor fixes him with a keen look. 'What do you think?'

'Helping somebody is so cheap! Nice is cheaper than brave or tough. It's kind of low risk.' He considers. 'Right, I made a mistake. Look. I'll tell you and then you tell me.' He takes the Vent story from the top. Step by step. 'When does helping somebody start being a mistake?'

Drash shrugs. 'It's a risk you take.'

'This is like some fucking monster movie. How long?'

'No promises. I'll take all this into the hearing. Second prize, they keep her until the meds stabilize. First prize, we get her committed for thirty days.'

'Thirty days!'

'That's all we can do under the law.'

'But you said she was delusional.'

'Delusional isn't dangerous.'

'But you said her psychiatric record—'

'Her record is sealed. I'm sorry. It's the law.'

'She ought to be in longterm storage.'

'We can only do what we can do. You're going to have to get comfortable with this.' Drash taps the folder. 'If it makes you feel any better, there are no assaults in here.'

'Yet.'

'Look, Slate, I know you've been straight with me and I know this is hard for you, but it's the best we can do. The state system's jammed. They've got patients hanging from the rafters. Look at it this way. It's thirty days.' The doctor sees Theo's face changing and adds reassuringly, 'A lot can happen in thirty days.'

Theo's mouth is filling with sand. Sand clogs his throat and rises in his skull; mounting to overflow his eyes. 'And she ended the night bashing her head against the walls. You said she was fine until you pushed the wrong button. What did you say to her?'

'Oh, that.' The psychiatrist turns mild, bemused eyes on him. 'She said she was having your baby. And what I said to her, that torched her fuse.'

Theo says savagely, 'Listen, if it worked for you it could work for me.'

'What I said, that set her off and blew her up in little bitty pieces that scattered all over my office? Pregnant. Really. I had to make her see she is delusional. I said, "Does everyone agree with you?"'

246

41

The phone wakes Theo. He's alone in his own bed for once. It's 1 a.m. With Delia stashed on a thirty-day order it's OK to be here. It's even safe to answer the phone. 'Hello?'

'Yes. This is . . .' Mumblemumble. It's one of those calls that comes in the night, some detoxed 12-stepper in the confession phase, wrong number, random drunk, friend out of gas come get me, news that your mother has died. But this is not any of those things. The voice is bland, professional. Is he from *Hard Copy*? *AJ*?

'Who?'

The caller repeats the name, as if Theo ought to know.

The name has a lot of Bs and Rs in it, could be Braemar Bruden, could be anything. 'I'm sorry, I was asleep.'

'Oh, I woke you. That's too bad.' The caller is easy and assured, confident that Theo is pleased to hear from him. 'This was the first free minute on my calendar and I forgot. Time zones.'

'You're in Los Angeles?' Theo wishes he had Sally here to shake him awake. 'Right, three hours. LA, right?'

The caller repeats, 'Time zones.'

'Time zones. And you were calling me about . . .' What did he say? *Hard Copy*? *Current Affair*? Probably not, but Theo's friend Arch is headed for New Haven and if he wants to catch up he'd better go wherever this conversation takes him. 'About . . .'

'Your *Newsweek* piece. Very interesting.'

'Thank you.'

'We discussed it at the meeting.'

'The meeting.' This might make sense if he could only wake up. 'You're a producer?'

The caller rolls right over the question. '*Stop me before I kill again.* The way you get inside people's heads.'

'Just one head, really.'

'At least you *think* you're inside people's heads. But. That isn't the whole story. The whole story is waiting to be told.' The modulation is bizarre. Like a prelude to an obscene phone call. Up close and personal. Very close.

'Who is this?'

The silence is devoid of background sound.

'OK,' Theo says harshly. 'What do you want?'

Everything changes. The air crackles. 'What I want, you don't know yet. But you will.'

42

Arch's departure rubs Theo raw. His friend is a good reporter but Theo knows he's a better writer. And he's busted ass on this job. Now he's spinning his wheels in Center City while Arch, who got him here in the first place, packs up his floppies and goes.

'Have fun.' Arch is trying to be cool about it but his grin reminds Theo that life's a game and Arch is the winner here. 'I'll send you a dirty T-shirt from Times Square.'

'Don't you mean downtown New Haven?'

'Naw. That's the last pit stop on the road to where I'm heading. Bigville.'

'Yeah, right.'

'I'll let you know if anything opens up.'

'Don't do me any favors.'

'It's the least I can do,' Arch says, but that grin he can't stop says, *Gotcha.*

'See you in jail.'

'Keep those cards and letters coming, T.'

'Right, I got tied up with *Newsweek* and forgot.' *Back atcha.*

OK, getting a job is a full-time job and Theo has slacked off here. He got out the first round of clips and letters but then his life filled up. The Vent. The chasm she's opened in his life makes his project on serial killers seem like dessert. He's been living with his murderers for so long that he can match names, dates and body counts with the obsessive accuracy of a baseball fan; he sees a web linking Gein and

Speck to Heirens to DeSalvo to Gacy, Bundy, Dahmer and Zax, invisible skeins connecting all the unnamed who shake civilization with brutal acts and then slouch off into endless night; there's a truth festering that he cannot yet penetrate.

'OK,' Sally says, 'so he beat you out of town.'

'Arch. I didn't even know he was looking for a goddamn job.' He says, gravely, 'Look. We should all leave town.'

'But I like my job.'

The Vent's slashmarks bother him no matter how many times they turn the mattress. The paintings can never be restored. Sally plays tough but her skin is so thin it's almost transparent. The blood pulses too close to the surface. You bet he's worried, but he's not allowed to say so. 'This isn't a very good place to be.'

'I love it here.'

They're going to have to talk about the Vent part later. Along with the fact that since Delia, it isn't safe here. Instead he says, 'Center City. Central nothing. This place died while we weren't looking.' He sees the end of the world with the survivors staggering across a blasted landscape. 'We should move on.'

'Look, they've put her away and by the time she gets out she'll be so zonked that she won't be able to bother anyone.'

'I didn't say anything about Delia.'

'I know what you're thinking,' Sally says.

'You do!' This makes him grin. 'If you know what I'm thinking, what am I thinking now?'

'We can't do that. It's noon on a Thursday, but tonight . . .'

Seeing the advantage, he presses her again. 'I know she's locked up, Sally, but she knows where to find you. Ted Dane told me she blames you for this whole thing.'

Sally stiffens. 'I can take care of myself, T.'

'If she comes after me, I can deal with it, but . . .'

'Leave it alone.'

'. . . what if she comes after you?'

Sheer tension makes her snap, 'Leave it alone!'

He says in a low voice, 'Not until I know it's going to leave me alone.' He is not allowed to say *I'm worried about you.* He can't let Sally know that even when they're standing close he's looking over her head, plumbing shadows for whatever may be hiding there: eyes glinting like twin reflectors, Vent watching. She may be off the scene; she may be in a locked ward but the Vent sits dead center in Theo's psychic landscape like a cement garden troll, too heavy to lift and too ugly to ignore. Once a thing like this gets in your life it's always there. It's part of his history now. Beyond revision. An object that can neither be created nor destroyed.

It changes the way he lives. He can't go to bed without checking every lock and poking at closets to be sure she's not hiding behind the coats. When he's not with Sally he keeps calling to check on her. Yes this thing is changing him. When he comes out his front door the Vent springs up in a dozen places; she's lurking behind partitions in the newsroom, *I've been waiting for you.* Going to Sally's, he skims the rearview mirror; is he being followed? In parking lots he sees the Vent scuttling like a roach between cars or hunched behind the wheel of an eighteen-wheeler, poised to roar down on him. He carries his head at a tilt, listening: for footsteps, for the soprano rattle of a woman clearing her throat. It defies reason but wherever Theo goes, day or night, hospitalized or not, the Vent is lurking somewhere just ahead.

Things start coming to the house. He doesn't know who delivers them or how the offerings get inside. He's found a laminated tear-sheet of his big story. The unexplained bottle of wine. The bikini underpants, twice worn; it gives him the creeps. The woman is locked up, for God's sake. Where is this stuff coming from?

He calls the state hospital. 'I need to check on the status of one of your patients. A DeliaMarie Vent?'

The operator runs the name on her computer. 'Yes, she's registered. You're a member of the family?'

'She doesn't have a family. I'm.' He breaks off. 'She hasn't, ah. Like. Been released?'

'Not according to our records.'

'Been out on leave, maybe. Town visit?'

'That wouldn't be in our records.'

'Would it be on your records if she'd signed herself out for an hour?'

'I'll connect you to the ward.'

'I'm only trying to find out if she's been off the grounds.'

'I'll connect you to the ward.'

The charge nurse says, 'Ms Vent? She's here. Do you want to speak to her?'

'No!'

'Who shall I say called?'

'I'm from the *Star*. You're positively sure she's there?'

'She's here and she's been here, Mr . . .'

'You're positive?'

'I'm looking at her chart right now.'

'Her chart! Have you checked her room?'

'I think this is a matter for the attending physician.'

So without wanting it, Theo finds himself on the line with Delia's psychiatrist. He tries to explain to the woman without explaining himself. 'I. Ah. Have an interest in the case?'

She says coolly, 'And you are . . .'

'I told the nurse. I'm calling from the *Star*. We're just wondering what her status was.'

'Her status? Mr. If this is an interview, Mr.'

'Off the record. We need to know whether she's still in a security facility.' From where he's standing Theo can see the last foreign object that turned up inside his house, defying all his efforts to secure the place. It is a purple satin bra.

252

'Until the medication takes hold, yes. Then we'll re-evaluate.'

'So she couldn't possibly . . .' He is looking at the bra. The doctor overrides him. 'But Mr Slate.'

'How did you know it was me?'

'My patient told me about you.'

'I bet she did.'

The woman says wisely, 'She warned us that you'd call.'

'She *what*?'

'And now that I have you on the phone. We might as well clear up a few things.'

'Details in her story?'

The doctor says after a pause, 'In yours.'

'I answered all those questions for the police psychiatrist.'

'Questions beget questions, Mr Slate.'

'You have her records. You have my statement.'

'I do.'

'What I say stands. So we're through, right?'

'Not quite.' The doctor says the last thing Theo wants to hear. 'I need your cooperation on this case. Ms Vent has asked to see you.'

'See me!' This is so ugly and inevitable that Theo shouts, 'It's out of the question.'

'From a clinical point of view we think it might be useful for you two to sit down in the same room.' Her tone changes. 'We have some things to work through here.'

'I'd rather die.'

'Or you do.'

He says in a low voice, 'Tell me what you mean.'

'If what you say is true . . .'

'You have me on record. Interview with the police psychiatrist. My deposition.'

She says coldly, 'That doesn't mean it's true.'

'Testimony at the hearing.'

'Just to verify.'

'Under oath.'

'We still need . . .'

'Right. A reality check,' he snaps. 'You think I led this woman on?'

'I don't think anything, Mr Slate.'

He says bitterly, 'You think these things don't just happen to people.'

'These things don't come out of nowhere, Mr Slate. I'm only trying to be fair to my patient.'

'You mean give her the benefit of the doubt. The woman is nuts. She has a history!'

'She's been through a lot,' the doctor says. 'If we're going to make any progress we need to put her in direct confrontation with reality.' There is an irritating pause before she finishes, 'Whatever that is.'

'What are you trying to say to me, lady?'

'Mr Slate, are you afraid of this?'

'Look, lady, I didn't stalk the woman, she stalked me.'

'I'm not coming to any conclusions, Mr Slate.'

'The hell you're not!'

'These cases always take some sorting out. It isn't always clear cut. Who is the victim.'

'Get another turkey,' Theo says, and flips her out of existence.

It's become so automatic to look to the left and to the right – up – *down* as he comes outside that Theo sees the object on the doormat before he steps on it. It's one of those hard-cover notebooks college students take to classes, with a place on the front for the user's name and a neat margin in red drawn down every one of the lined pages inside. It is apparently unused. Theo considers for a moment before going inside for his kitchen gloves and a Ziploc baggie. He is so intent on getting Art in forensics to examine this thing that he doesn't notice that there is a slight change in his arrangements. The oatmeal bowl he dropped in the sink at dawn is smeared as if some hungry intruder has run a wet finger around the inside, voraciously cleaning it out.

43

'You said on the phone that you were a reporter.' Glen Singleton's widow is neatly assembled in a tweed suit with a sweater and pearls, the uniform of Theo's mother's generation. Mary Singleton looks too young for this place by twenty-some years but she's made her peace with it. She has that fading beauty that makes you homesick for the person she used to be.

'Don't worry, we'll make this confidential. I'm not here to tell your story, Mrs Singleton.'

She surprises him. 'I wish you would.'

'I'm sorry.'

'I wish somebody would.'

'I'm here on a personal matter,' Theo says.

'I just want it on the record. To set people straight.' She sighs. 'All these years and even our friends think Glen did something to set her off. Like he was asking for it, you know? She was a woman, she was only nineteen, it had to be his fault. Nobody can believe this kind of thing comes out of nowhere.'

'I do.' They are in the sunshot lobby of a highrise 400 miles west of Center City. Theo took a comp day and drove through the night to get here. He had no choice. He needs to talk to somebody who's seen Delia Vent in the grips of this. Fixation. Theo gulps. Uncontrollable love. A living witness. The scary thing is that this woman's husband was a suicide. Delia's obsession pulled her professor into the spin cycle. He died; she survived. When they let her out of the hospital, she

changed Vernon to Vent. And now she's Theo's problem.
He needs to know what to expect.

Mary Singleton goes on as if he hasn't spoken. 'It's so
out of nowhere that you don't see it coming.'

'I know.'

This stops her. 'You do? Wait a minute. You do! I'm so
glad you came. I've needed to . . .'

They meet like exiles in a foreign city. Without any transition, they are speaking the same language. Theo admits,
'Me too.'

Her sympathy is immediate. 'You poor kid.'

'Man, Mrs Singleton. I'm no kid.'

'Mary. You know what I mean.' They are sitting in a
glassed-in alcove. The beige carpeting is laced with sunlight.
It seems like an ordinary day. She says, 'I'm sorry I can't
ask you up to my apartment. I just.'

'It's OK.'

The widow hugs her ribs as if she's squeezing the words
out with her elbows. 'I just need to keep it out of my
house!' She gives him an apologetic smile. 'I hope you
understand.'

'Yeah. That's the problem.'

'But you. You look like you could use some coffee.'

'I'm fine.'

'Coffee, and I'll buy you a croissant. They're through
serving breakfast but they keep the dining room open for
us . . . residents.'

'It's nice of you but I'm not hungry right now.' Theo says
apologetically, 'I should have explained on the phone.'

'You don't have to explain. I'm just glad to meet somebody who knows where I'm coming from.' Mary waits.

Theo doesn't know how much to tell her. He doesn't
want to direct or change what she's about to say to him.
He needs her story straight up. *How does she choose us?
Is it, like, random?* 'I guess I came to find out if you know
anything I need to know.'

257

'You look as if you already know a lot.'

'That's the trouble. I don't know anything. I guess what I'm asking you is . . .'

'What happened?'

He opens his hands. 'How come it happened to us.'

'That's the puzzle and the mystery. Look,' she says. 'It's nothing we *did*. It's . . .' Mary studies her own hands as if trying to read the truth between the lines. She shrugs. 'Not clear. To be explained later. I don't know how these things happen to people. It's like walking along under a clear sky and being hit in the head with a rock.'

'That fast.'

'You know, I've thought about it and thought about it, could we have done anything to stop it, could Glen have done anything, could I.' She turns her hands. Theo notes that her rings have gotten too big for her fingers. 'I've spent my life ever since then thinking about it and you know what I think? I think there's nothing we could have done. There's nothing anybody could have done.'

'How did it start?'

'We felt sorry for her.'

Oh, shit! 'She asked for your help.'

'Not exactly. She was too shy to ask. She just kind of *happened* to us. You look up one day and she's there.'

'Yes.'

'What it was, was, we found her on the terrace? That last week in May when everybody on a campus goes crazy. We always gave a year-end party for Glen's senior survey course. The class is so big that he marked A's on her papers without knowing which one she was. She was the only freshman – advanced placement.' The widow touches Theo's arm. 'You know she's not stupid.'

Startled, he jumps. Then he understands she's like a sickroom visitor gently waking the patient. 'That's the problem,' he says.

'That's part of the problem. And the rest? You know, I

have the feeling we could sit here talking forever and still not know.'

'I just need to know what happened,' Theo says.

'It was a big class. It was a big party. Nice people, juniors and seniors, students I knew, all those nice faces, all that energy; she was there but I guess I didn't notice her.'

Theo notes that not once has Mary used Delia's name. If you're trying to get something out of your life you'll do anything to get it out of your life. Responding, he finds that he doesn't want to use the name either. Like this nice lady, he wants her not to exist. 'She's the kind of person that nobody notices. At first. That's one of the problems.'

'That's only one of the problems,' Mary says. 'I liked Glen's students. It was such a good party that we had to kick them out at two. Glen made a last sweep to make sure there were no leftovers making out on the terrace. He found her in one of our lawn chairs. It was such a cold spring that I hadn't put the cushions out. She was sitting on bare metal with her arms wrapped around herself and she'd been there a while. Glen spoke to her but she didn't look up. For a minute he thought she was catatonic. Should he dial 911? University Health? She was just sitting there, shaking with the cold. Then she looked up at him. What could he do but ask her in?'

Theo sees his own instant replay. 'She gives you no choice.'

'That's one of the things. I don't know why, but we both got the idea that she was an orphan.'

'That's what she wanted you to think.' Oh shit, he thinks. If only I'd listened to Sally. 'Did anybody try to warn you?'

'Nobody knew.'

'Somebody warned me. She used the words "human swamp." Look. If you'd known . . .'

'Nobody knows those things! I'm sorry, I didn't mean to bark. But you *did* ask. So Glen brought her inside. We felt sorry for the girl.'

259

'Been there. Done that.'

'Of course. She wasn't exactly crying but she wasn't all right, either. We couldn't just leave her that way and go to bed. She was only a freshman after all. She kept shivering. We tried to find out what was the matter and after I gave her one of my sweaters and we warmed her up with some port she finally cried. She was just so happy, she said. Do you know what she said to us? She said, "You're so nice. It's so perfect. I'm so happy I just can't go back to the dorm." There she was, overweight and shy and sitting there in our living room in this hideous dress and something about it. We both felt guilty just for not being miserable.'

Theo says, 'Like the stray you start feeding because you think you can keep it outside and it won't eat much.'

'She makes you feel so *bad*. Glen and I, we thought with a little there-there we could make her smile and with some of my old clothes she'd look better and she'd thank us and go get a life.'

'Like, she wouldn't need you any more.'

'As if we could wind her up and set her down and she'd go off on her own.'

'As if you could get shut of her.' Instead of killing her.

'I don't know.' Mary sounds hollow, like an actor on an empty stage. Perpetual mourning: a life draped in black. 'I don't know what we thought. So Glen gave her a summer tutorial in Dickinson to prepare her for his advanced poetry class, a favor he would do anyone, run of the mill. We weren't paying attention, we weren't paying *attention*, do you understand? You stop watching a thing and it . . . It was so logical; when you help a student she gets better and better at your subject so she signs up for more of your classes and you admit her because you're building on what you've already taught. The next thing you know, she's in every class you teach.'

'And she sits in the front row.'

'How did you know?'

'Fucking A student. Excuse me.'

'Fucking A student,' Mary says so easily that Theo is shocked. 'I probably don't need to tell you the rest. Phone calls at all hours. Notes. Tiny presents for Glen. I started getting calls too, but not from her. Friends in the department. Other faculty wives. Warning me. Gloating. "Did you know Glen was having an affair?"'

Theo accepts this without surprise. 'She told everybody your husband was going to marry her.'

'She told everybody he was leaving me as soon as she graduated. I knew they weren't having an affair because I know Glen. Correction. Knew Glen. Do you know I wanted to kill her? Still do. Is that terrible?'

'No. It's the way you feel.'

'You really *have* been there,' she says.

'Am there.' Yes. He is. And it is not good.

'I know. Have you tried the police? Of course you have. It should have been the first thing we did but it was the last thing we did. First Glen had her into his office and sat her down. He told her she had to drop his classes and go to University Health. She said what about her scholarship and he promised her credit for the term. She promised to get psychiatric help but of course she never did. Then she told Glen she loved him and she knew he loved her and she left. He came home and told me it was over but I knew. None of it stopped. Nothing stopped. It just kept on going. Do you know what I mean when I say it kept on going all over again?'

Theo nods. It's all he can manage.

'The more he tried to avoid her the more she stepped up the letters and the calls. Flowers. Presents he was too upset to touch, I had to throw them out. Flute music, under our bedroom window.'

Theo's teeth clamp so hard that an abscess at the root of one of his molars comes to life. The tooth begins to ping.

'When we called the police she moved off the property

but she didn't go away. She camped on the curb across the street. By that time she'd quit going to classes altogether. Glen was trying to get her suspended, but the dean gave him a lecture about liability. Remember, she was only nineteen. A child, the dean said. He thought she was a child.'

'She still comes on like one.'

'Liability! As if Glen was at fault in the thing. And our friends . . . You don't know who your friends are until something like this comes up. Then they think the worst of you. And you understand that you never had any friends. So be careful. Whoever you are, be careful.' She falls silent.

Theo's tooth won't stop pinging. Outside the little alcove, there is activity. Spunky old guys and blue-haired women go back and forth but he and his companion are marooned here. This calm, empty voice. All this sunlight. It makes Theo feel like an old, old person trapped in his wheelchair in some remote solarium. 'I'm OK,' Theo says to no one. 'She's in the state hospital.' *For now.*

'So the police did something for you.' She mourns. 'We should have called them right away. But what do you tell them? People like us don't do things like that. We think we can settle things like grownups. Among ourselves. And these calls from my so-called friends, warning me to watch my husband. I think I was the only one who believed Glen. The administration would say sexual harassment. We knew what our friends would say. Colleges are hotbeds. So we were stupid.' Mary breaks off. 'Did you know she was in one of these things before Glen? Her high-school French teacher?'

'I think there have been a couple since.' He is thinking of Dr Drash's folder. 'Maybe more than a couple.'

'If we had known what she was! We still thought it could be finished rationally. We thought she was a rational person.'

'No.' The tooth is driving spikes of pain into the space under Theo's left eye. It makes him say too much. 'Irrational force.'

Mary's voice is light and sad. 'We thought we could confront her, get her suspended, she'd go back to wherever, and we could start trying to forget. We did manage one intervention. At her dorm. But she . . . It's hard to explain. By the time we left the room Glen was convinced he had to let the girl back into his classes or something would happen to me.'

Sally. Theo knuckles his jaw.

It's as if he's spoken. The widow says, 'What?'

'Nothing. It's OK.'

'No,' she says. 'It is not OK. I don't need to tell you this story. You know this story. Her and her only, her in every room and around every corner, she was everywhere. In his class, on the lawn, in our face. I don't know when she got in the house but I know she got in the house. Did she watch us sleep? Could she hear us making love? After a while it didn't matter who heard us because Glen couldn't. He was too strung out. So that stopped, and he stopped sleeping. He jumped every time the phone rang. He was afraid to go out. Things started happening to us. Little accidents.'

Thudding into Theo's head along with the pain comes the knowledge that Lacey Sparkman's death was no accident. 'Accidents!'

'Or not. And all Glen's colleagues. The administration. Our so-called friends lining up with the girl. On top of these accidents. And the whole time, poor Glen. Poor Glen!'

'I'm sorry.'

'You know, he did it for me.'

Theo goes rigid. 'Ma'am?'

'He thought if he died she would give up and go away and I would be safe. I wish she'd killed us both.'

It's getting hard to see.

'Do you know she was at the goddamn funeral? Do you know what they said? Do you want to know what everybody said?' Mary looks up. Her right hand is fluttering out of control. 'They said it was because Glen abused her and he was ashamed. Somebody comes into your life and takes your life and . . . I can't!' Everything about her fades. She's told him all she is going to tell him today.

Theo takes it to steady her. 'I'm sorry.'

'Thank you.' She withdraws. 'It's all right. I'm OK now. If you want to write this up,' she says hopefully. 'If you want to put this in the papers . . .'

'I didn't mean to mislead you. This is for me.'

'I just wish I could get somebody to write it up. Then people would know.' Mary is trying to sound calm but she's just about to crumple. 'All those people who thought it was Glen's fault would know . . .'

'If I can find a way to do it, I'll try.' Theo stands. He needs to get out of here and find a walk-in dental clinic and he has to do it without making this woman feel any worse than she already does.

'I hope that's enough . . .'

'You've been terrific.'

'So you'll write it up . . .'

'Oh, ma'am.' No promises. He has to keep his dignity and get out of here. 'I don't know. I just want to thank you for taking the time to talk to me.' He likes this woman. He would like to give her something but he doesn't have anything to give her. Yet. He doesn't know what, exactly, he is going to take away from this but he thanks her anyway. 'I just want to thank you. And. Look. You take care, OK?'

When she doesn't say anything Theo thanks her again and turns to leave the alcove. Her voice follows him out of the alcove. 'At least now two of us know.'

44

In Transit

Haik is without a place now, but you would never know it to look at him. Nice shirts, shaving kit, spare trousers, good jacket, he can start over again anywhere. He does not need *things* to reinforce him. Until this week he has been sleeping in a new space every night. At this stage he is reluctant to rent another room. Credit check, references, too many questions. Better to keep it simple. Stay well-groomed, shave in the washroom off the lobby before he goes into work, buy a day's membership at the health club whenever you need to shower. Do not stint on dry cleaning and always have your shirts laundered. When Haik comes into the office these mornings he looks the same, he is as even and pleasant as ever but it is an effort.

Things have gone wrong. Whatever he left in that room is in the hands of the police. So although he looks the same to the people he works with, he is running ahead of that possibility. But what can they hold him for? He hasn't done anything. Besides, the name Haik gives at the office is not the name he gives elsewhere, so they won't find him. He has long since stopped giving his real name. He keeps no checking accounts for exactly this reason. The office manager vouched for him so he cashes his paychecks at the branch bank in the lobby. He has money but no place to spin out his plans. Instead the design etches itself in his head and inside his body, driving him even though he keeps the outsides calm.

He has to do this and do it right. And soon.

But his backup is nowhere in the city. His #6 has taken her flute case and gone. Her things are here, he has been in her room in that brick fleabag and he has put his face in them, but she is gone. This should be a small enough thing to fix but unfortunately, in these designs the units are not interchangeable. Designated ones are designated precisely because they are unique. No substitutes. *Every time you fail* . . . He cannot afford to fail again. Too many people are waiting. Father, from hell. The mother, in prison. The reporter who will write it up. For now, he has to wait. His backup will be back, her things are here.

He is sitting in her room. Saturday he doubled back on the State Street rooming house again, and found his #6 still gone. He settled in to wait. The landlord came. 'What are you doing?'

'Waiting.'

'How did you get in?'

He lied. 'She left it unlocked for me.'

'You know this tenant?'

He nodded. Standard smile, always works. 'Have you seen her?'

'You're a customer?'

Haik in his clean shirt and new coat looking nothing but decent, decent. 'She doesn't have customers.' He acted offended.

'She had to be doing something.'

'I don't think so. She had a little money,' Haik said. He did not say, I think she was running out. 'I'm her brother.'

'Oh, that's different.'

'Different meaning you know where she went?'

'Different meaning you have two choices. You can move her stuff out or you can pay her back rent.'

'The rent,' Haik said. He paid a month ahead.

It has worked out well for him. Since ey are not in the room he can pay up eir rent and sleep on eir blankets in the corner until ey come back and he can get on with this. It will do for now, he thinks, even though the bedroll smells of em, frizzy carrot hairs in it, disgusting. When e comes back he will move em out of here. He has a place in mind where he will put em until #5 has been done and he knows if e is needed. He won't do em here. You don't eat where you shit. This he knows, even though it is not written.

Analyze. Organize. Plan. *Write it down.* A ripple of pain cuts into his soft places. Mother. What bothers him most, then, is losing the notebook. It is like losing her all over again. Haik's first memory, he's four. Some old woman – grandmother? someone else's? – gushing, *Oh you poor child you've lost your mother.*

Father's voice comes thudding into Haik's skull. He can feel Father's sharp knuckles in the soft part of his throat: *You are killing your mother all over again.*

There is a noise in the hall. Haik starts to his feet. Blood flecks his cuffs. He has been gnawing his wrists again. He can't do #5 until his #6 comes back but he can't be here either. The mother in jail. The one who tried to murder him. He promised he would make her proud. She is waiting and he hasn't done anything to prove himself. All right, that has to wait, but while he is waiting he can make his mark. Make his mark on some*body* so that when #6 comes back and he does #5 as planned, there will be no question as to who has done em.

He will put his mark on the body of some person. He will do that and he will leave this city just long enough to make sure that the lying reporter knows that he has done it.

Things have gone wrong but this is not necessarily bad. Exigencies. Haik has been thrown back on himself by exigencies. He discovers that there are parts of the notebook that he has by heart, the crucial points, under *PROCEDURES*: From *a. Do er fast. No screaming*, it is filled in: what to do with the tongue, the head, the hands, down to *g*. *Call it done*. And under that, the unfinished heading, that sent him from wall to wall, diagramming and screaming. That drove him out into the streets in the first place:

h.

Unfinished *h*. The design, the mother, the reporter, the missing notebook and in that book the missing element. It comes to him. What he must do. Yes! Under *h*., then, put: *Get it in the papers*. Get it in all the papers. Then the world will know. It is the end point of everything, the proof he needs. He won't hear his joyful shout. 'I will show you glad.'

Haik stands. Rigid with purpose, he moves out. He will do someone, he will do her tonight. And he will put his mark on her. Anyone will do. Anyone. Who she is won't matter because this is not one of the designated murders. This is outside of the plan. It is not any kind of end product. It is only the calling card you leave to get their attention.

45

S ally says, 'This proves you're more anxious than
depressed.'

'Gee,' Theo says, grateful for the warmth of her. 'And
I thought I was more depressed than anxious. How do you
know?'

'I read it in the papers. Depressed guys just roll over
and go to sleep,' she says. 'But *anxious* guys . . .' In
another minute they will get up and start dressing. Her
sunny bedroom seems bright and safe now that the Vent
is safely locked up.

Theo meets her grin. 'Did you ever notice how depressed
and desperate have most of the same letters in them?'
He got back late and came here at first light. Blundered
through her thrift-shop furniture and funky pillows and
small objects marshaled like familiar pets. His house stopped
being anything but a bed in a box after Carey dumped him.
Somewhere deep he is homesick for something he's never
had. He wishes he and Sally could wake up together every
morning, as in be together for the rest of their lives.

'How was your meeting?'

'Singleton's widow. I found out more than I wanted to.'

Sally kisses his hand and slides out of bed, looking maybe
a little too translucent. Like a porcelain that could break.
'You looked kind of wrecked when you got here.'

'Poor lady! Her husband killed himself. The Vent. She
doesn't let go and she doesn't quit.' Theo would like to rivet
Sally into a Teflon suit until this Vent thing is over.

269

When Sally comes out of the shower she has stopped looking fragile; she has put on her office self. Heavy sweater. Khaki slacks. 'You mean if you don't kill her, she kills you?'

'Like that. At least we've got some time.'

In that neat tweed jacket and the tough boots she looks bulletproof. 'Time?'

'As long as the woman is locked up . . .'

Then Sally does that take that lets you know things are not as you thought. The feigned clearing of the throat that signals a reversal of fortune.

'What.' Yes Theo is shouting. 'What!'

She sighs. 'Yeah. Yesterday. She tested fine after two weeks on the meds and they couldn't keep her.'

'Where is she?'

'They got her a room at the Y. She.' Sally is trying to decide how to tell him the rest. 'We know because she called. She wants her old job back. Don't freak. Chick said no way.'

'I wish to hell . . .'

'Do you want to move in here?' She has misread him.

'No! Worst thing.' He can never prove the thing about Lacey, but he won't do anything that would bring the Vent into Sally's bedroom ever again.

'Thanks a lot.'

'I don't want you paying for something stupid I did.'

'Quit beating yourself up. Go for that restraining order.'

'You think that would do any good? Single woman? Guy twice her size? She almost got the professor jailed for harassment.'

'Right, it's a who-to-believe situation. Who does anybody believe?'

'Even if the court did believe me. Even if we got an order . . .'

'She'd keep coming back.' Sally is getting ready to leave.

Theo takes her by the wrists and tries to make her look into his eyes. 'How about you promise to be careful?'

But this is Sally; she doesn't mess. She tries to pull away. 'We can't just stop living our lives!'

'I'll handle it. I just have to figure out how.'

'Face her? Tell her to go away?' She's been through this with him and she still doesn't understand. Not really.

He pulls her closer and this time she lets him. 'You don't explain to that. That's the whole thing.'

'Fine. Have her kneecapped.'

'Yeah, right. She'd be thrilled. The only thing she'd like better would be if I did it.'

'Cheer up, maybe she's over it.' Gently, Sally frees herself. She reaches for her shoulder bag. Her coat. 'Maybe they've socked her so full of stuff that she's forgotten you.'

'That kind never forgets. It doesn't forget and it never gives up,' Theo says. He is considering. When he speaks again his voice is tight and sharp. 'OK. We have to do a couple of things.'

'Raise the drawbridge?'

'Don't, Sal.'

She is trying to be funny and it isn't working. 'Arm the peasants?'

'Bear with me. Look. This is important. I can't come here any more.'

'For God's *sake*, T.'

'I can't come here for a while, anyway. And you shouldn't come to my place. I want her to think we broke up.'

'Did we, Theo? Is there something I don't know about?'

'You know better. It's just. If she thinks we aren't together she'll leave you alone,' he says.

'Don't you think that's pretty elaborate?'

'It's the best I can do right now.'

'Like, I love you go away?'

He nods. 'You got it.'

271

'Look, T. I knew you'd freak so I phoned the hospital. The woman's shrink swears eight ways to Sunday that with this new medication, she's fine.'

'You think a few pills are going to make any difference?'

'They wouldn't let her go if she was still dangerous.'

'They'd let her go just to get rid of her.'

'It isn't fair.' Sally stalks to the window. 'Why do we have to sneak around when she's the one who's fucking crazy?'

'Because they never believe people like us. They believe people like her because she *is* crazy. The world is crazy.' He says in a low voice, 'I'm scared of what she may do, OK? Look, I love you.'

Turning, Sally beams. 'I'm so glad.'

The more he sees her shining the more he knows he has to protect her. 'Take care,' he says. 'We'll find ways to meet.' Hearing what they're saying to each other, Theo is amazed by the matter-of-fact way in which they've adapted to an intolerable situation. This thing with Delia has become part of their lives and right now he can't imagine any life without it. 'We'll be together. We will. Just not right now. And not here. Can you bear with me?'

'Did you really say you loved me?'

'Right here. And in broad daylight.'

'OK.' Sally won't stop smiling. 'OK, I can handle it.'

Something about this makes Theo say, 'Take care, take care!'

Delia is waiting in front of the *Star*, grinning like a mendicant.

'Forget about Sally. We broke up,' he barks and slams inside.

It is a week later. They are sitting in the back of a suburban coffee shop when Sally remembers. They have come in separate cars, which is how they travel these days. It's crazy, but without discussing it Theo and Sally have concluded that they can't spend a lot of time together at work. It is understood that they don't meet at each other's houses. They proceed as though Delia is watching. Even if she isn't, she could walk in that door at any minute. They aren't ready to deal. Their precautions are elaborate. They have driven miles out of their way today and circled before meeting in this strip mall. They go inside separately and take a booth in the back, where Theo can keep an eye on the front window. He puts Sally in the corner beside him so nobody looking in will see her.

For a while all they do is hold hands. Then Sally says, 'Did you check your voicemail at work?'

'Forgot my phone.'

'While you were gone Arch called.'

'Arch?'

'Something in New Haven, he's all over it. He wanted me to ask you if you're still interested in the bitemark killer.'

'Shit,' Theo says. 'He gets the job in New Haven and he also gets the bitemark killer?'

'They think he's in New Haven. They aren't sure it's him.'

'What do you mean?'

'I don't know, ask Arch.' Sally's voice drops. 'Where've you been, T? It seems like you're gone all the time now.'

'I'm just trying to look gone,' he says. 'The Vent,' he says. He does not tell her stuff has started turning up in the house. Not presents exactly, just signs somebody's been there.

She sighs. 'Delia.'

'The Vent. I'm so sorry. Why did we have to get stuck with this?'

Sally won't answer. 'You didn't say where you'd been.'

'Making myself scarce. If she can't find me maybe she'll give up. Do you believe motels?' He picks a different one every night, only goes home for clean clothes. He's doing his job, but his project on killers is gathering dust. It seems more important not to be anywhere the Vent knows.

Sally is grinning. 'Motels?'

He laughs. 'It's not what you think! Look, if she can't find me, she can't lean on me.' He means, *she can't hurt you,* but he knows better than to say so.

'Motels,' she says silkily. 'I can handle motels.'

'Cool,' Theo says, and gives her the name of the place where he's perching tonight. 'That's one way.'

'Room service. Dip in the pool. Color me there.'

'Tonight's is kind of a dump. No pool.'

Sally laughs. 'Do you think I really want to go swimming?'

'They're all dumps,' he says.

'But you were gone all day yesterday too. Chick was freaking.'

'I went up to County.' He makes an accordion of his straw wrapper and pops it at her. 'I tried to get in to see Stella Zax.'

'Stella Zax.'

'They said no way. They said since the last time her family came she's been too zonked to see anyone.'

'Family? You said she didn't have any family.'

'She doesn't. Weird, isn't it? I thought OK, this started with Stella, so maybe she could help make sense of it.'

'Sense of the Vent?'

'Yes. No. I don't think so.' It is disturbing; all the elements have begun massing in Theo's head; in some odd way he can't define they are intermingled. He tries to sort it out for her. For himself. 'What she did to her son. What her son did. The Vent. Serial killers through the ages. All I have is that they're all *crazy*.' He pauses for a few seconds too long and repeats, 'Crazy.'

'But you're not crazy.'

'No. *It's* crazy. If I can only pull a thread through it.'

'We're not crazy,' Sally says, 'but we're going to get crazy if we have to go on living like this.'

'If I can figure it out.' He opens his hands as if to show her all the pieces, but even he can't see them. It is disturbing. 'If I can just . . .'

'What if you can't?'

'Then it's no good.' He doesn't know exactly what that means.

'If you can't, I will.' Sally starts to get up. She looks ready to wrestle Stella Zax to a standstill and take on the Vent. 'I'll do whatever I have to, T.'

'No.' Theo pulls her back down. In a funny way he thinks it's the Zax story that brought this all down on him. The empty notebook, that he unleashed Delia to get. One favor. All he accepted from the intern was one favor. He's been paying for it ever since. He puts his hands on Sally's, bearing down to make her understand how heavy this is. 'Don't go there.'

'Theo.'

'Don't.'

It will come as no surprise to either of them that as they come out to their cars, not touching and not exactly speaking, just in case, DeliaMarie Vent is getting off a city bus at the crosswalk leading to the strip mall. It's no particular relief that she pretends not to see them.

46

Should she call her lover or should she not call him? Should she just drop by or is it better to run into him, like, accidentally, be in those places that he always goes. Act surprised. 'Oh Theo, I'm so glad!' He'll smile! 'Oh, it's you.' It's all a matter of timing. Bad timing made it go wrong. *I was dressed all wrong.* If she hadn't messed up they'd be together now, happy in his big bed. It's one great big misunderstanding, but if he won't talk to her, how can they kiss and make up? You've got to make your own luck. All she has to do is orchestrate and he will see her all dressed up and smiling and he'll fall in love with her all over again. They will hug and she'll say, 'Theo, I've missed you so much!'

In our house we'll have all antique furniture. Oriental rugs. His print over the fireplace. Of all his things, I like it best.

Please don't let me make him mad again please don't let me scare him off, everything is so right, why did it come out wrong?

Cordelia's hair is dyed again, clean curly red for him and she is clean down to the beds of her fingernails; at the Y she can go into the pool and stay until her fingers prune up, and shower whenever she wants. Clean feels good after weeks with only a basin to wash in. It would have worked out better if she'd showered before, no wonder he . . . They are in love but Delia's hair was all greasy, nails like funeral notes and only my traveling things no wonder he didn't hug, not clean, no wonder he didn't make love to me . . .

The stuff they are giving Delia is like having an operation that you don't feel but you are awake for; things are happening to you all the time. You just can't feel them while they're going on.

If she could just get double the stuff she would feel better. Not enough to do any good. She might as well stop taking it.

47

Theo is at the Center City Y. He rolled out of bed in the Holiday Inn in Dravitz to take this assignment. He sleeps in a different town every night, don't ask. Chick beeped him at dawn. Now he is here. The staff found one of their regulars dead in his bed today, bullet wound. Theo's on it in the unlikely hope that it's murder. Something suspicious here or nothing suspicious here? Good story or no story? He is waiting for the coroner to finish. Then the desk will buzz him up. Even with DeliaMarie Vent registered in the women's wing of this very Y, Theo is easy right now. Waiting under the artificial ficus, he is almost comfortable. For the first time in days he isn't being followed. He just saw the Vent go out. The Vent. An object he has to deal with. Swaddled in layered coats and jackets, she hurried through the lobby without even seeing him. *Purloined letter,* he thinks, sick of hard beds in cheap motels. Hide in plain sight. Right. Maybe I should move in here.

The place is a little like purgatory, if there is one. Theo is stalled in the vestibule of changing lives. One stop on the road from what you thought you were to something else. In spite of the Mylar banner and glass brick planters with plastic bromeliads, the Spanish stucco lobby is strictly a Depression item. So right for depressed Center City now. The half-timbered ceiling is tired. The tiled lobby floor is tired and the spongy astroturf runner is dense and clotted, as if somebody's been scrubbing frying pans with it. Everybody is in transit. Residents paddle in front of the cork board with purposeful squints while buffed yuppies trot past on their way to the pool or the weight room. Scrubbed and combed and dressed for the big meeting, the town's business leaders finish and sprint out, leaving the regulars bobbing in their wake. The dense air around the unemployed seems to shift and whir because they too are in transition, on the sliding scale between viable and homeless. The light shifts and they become nothing in a cosmic act of sleight of hand. The disturbing part is that many of them are still young. They catch Theo looking and it makes him ashamed. It's like accidentally walking in on somebody naked in the bathroom, finding them with everything exposed. Flash forward and see them sleeping in cartons or frozen to the bank under the Interstate. Me too?

The rooms in the men's wing are uniform and aggressively clean. Open doors show single beds with regulation spreads. Each room has a metal desk. A chair. He sees few personal belongings on the regulation dressers. No photos. Walls of no particular color. Anonymous, like the motels. Easy in, easy out. The director is waiting in the dead man's room. The coroner gives Theo a brief statement and leaves. He and the director have a few minutes here before the undertakers come and volunteers empty the drawers and roll the mattress, leaving the room as neat and barren as if nobody has ever lived and died here. He says to the director, 'I'm sorry.'

'I don't know whether sorry is it.'

'Nobody wants to die.'

'Don't be so sure.'

'Then it is a suicide.'

'Couldn't you just report it as a natural death?'

'Why would I do that?'

'We're raising funds right now.' Standing as if to protect the privacy of the dead man, the director seems more tired than upset. He says to Theo, 'You may not want to look.'

'I'm used to this.' Part of him flies up to the ceiling and

looks down at the figure on the bed. It sees the Vent with its eyes closed and blood all over the pillow, that worry over. Finished. OK. He wishes her dead. But this is only a dried-up old wino, light as the shell of a cicada after the cicada has moved out. Discovered in death with his eyes popped and his teeth on the dresser. Theo flips open his notebook and takes the particulars. 'Has the family been notified?'

'There isn't any family. There's never any family.'

Theo says uncomfortably, 'Transient or regular?'

'Regular. Twelve years. Worked at Waldbaum's.' The director says, 'I don't know where he got the gun.'

'The police bagged it and took it?'

The director nods. 'We haven't had one of these in years.'

For a head wound, the opening is surprisingly neat. That part of Theo that he can't control is banging around somewhere near the ceiling. What if Delia did this? What if he could prove it and get her booked? He tries, 'The coroner is sure it's suicide?'

'I suppose you have to report it.'

'We can't exactly say he got hurt cleaning his gun.'

'You know how this makes us look. It makes us look as if we aren't doing our jobs. Our residents don't have weapons.'

Theo looks at the corpse and shrugs.

'We haven't had one of these in years.'

'These things happen. It's not like you failed.'

'If you could just.'

'Look,' Theo says. 'The best I can do is report it and come back later and do a story about your program here.'

The director is shaking his head. 'We had him in our chapter of AA. We thought he was doing pretty well.'

Theo is looking at the dead man. Neatly arranged and eternally still. He frowns. 'There's no access from the women's wing?'

'This is going to hurt us.' The director looks up, surprised. 'The women's wing?'

'You've got a new resident. She has this weird history.'

'The women. The women are a different story. There's a quicker turnover. They're more focused on changing their lives.' Like a magician who's finally captured his audience, the director brightens. Yes he is pitching to Theo. A flattering feature would do some good right now. 'A lot of our women residents come out of terrible situations. We make a real difference in their lives. Prostitutes and junkies. We help them get straight. Battered women, and they are our saddest cases. We do everything we can to restore their self-respect. We get them back on their feet.' In spite of the director's enthusiasm, Theo's question lurks in the back of his mind, approaching its destination as if on foot. 'New resident?'

'She's been violent. She could be violent now. A Ms Vent?'

Everything changes. The director. His tone. He says in a new, hard voice, 'Oh. You mean Cordelia.'

'Whatever she's calling herself.'

'You're not . . . Oh.' Discovery writes a new message on the director's face. His voice hardens. 'Oh. You. She's told us all about you. You're the one.'

'I'm sorry?'

'The one who.' He breaks off. Then he says sternly, 'We know all about you.'

Theo is still in the room but outside himself. He sees the outraged director facing him over the corpse as if it is Theo who has done the killing here. Then in a quick reverse he sees himself lying dead on the bed. He says carefully, 'The one what?'

'If I'd known I would never have agreed to see you.'

'The one what?'

'I'm surprised your editors haven't fired you. I'm shocked they would send you here.'

'You haven't answered me.'

'After what she told us, I shouldn't even be talking to you.'

'What did she tell you?'

'After what you did.'

'Wait a minute.' Anger makes him harsh. 'What does she say I did?'

'That's closed to you. Our social service records are kept confidential.' Brisk and officious, the director moves Theo toward the door. He will go out through the avenue of deadbeats and come blinking into the street. 'You have everything you need. We're finished here.'

Theo is disturbed by echoes. *Me too?*

Theo himself is in transition. Information he can't act on. Stuff piling up in his office that he's quit trying to sort, so he is disturbed and guilty about that, too. Is he ever going to start the book? Can he write a book? If he can't, has he failed Stella? Is this what Stella really wants from him? It is not clear. Nothing is clear and she is inaccessible. Uncertainty gnaws at him.

Arch phones him at the office. He thinks the bitemark killer may be in New Haven. He lays it out tersely. 'Woman's dead here. Looks like it could have been your guy.'

At Arch's back, sirens go. He says, 'Somebody bit her on the face, but that's the only similarity.'

'What do you mean, the only similarity?'

'I guess you hadda be here. You wanna come check it out?'

Theo looks moodily into the phone. 'Can't. Troubles here.'

So there's that. His stomach is soured by bad meals in so-so restaurants. There are other signs of disruption. The loss of small objects. A different bed every night. The Vent just around every corner of his life. Trouble in his house. Last week he found a fresh clipping, woman murdered, no details. The Vent left it, he's sure, but what does it mean?

How did she get in? He thinks Sally would be safer if he left town. He can't afford motels much longer. It isn't just the money, it's the time. Hours lost on the road because the Vent has turned him into a fucking refugee. She's snug at the Y, where she can roll out of bed late and take her post in front of the *Star*, while Theo struggles out before dawn and drives miles to work. OK, her job is easier than his. All she has to do is be where he is before he even thinks of going there: the Spot, his house when he goes back for clean clothes, the *Star*. Security has orders to keep her out, but last week she turned up at his desk with that hopeful, gooshy look. When she's thwarted, she can always lie. So the Vent does her job, which is resident stalker, while Theo has to play elaborate games just to get to work.

Chick's staff live within ten minutes of the newsroom, ready to roll out day or night. Except for Theo. For the moment, Chick is indulging him. 'Right, Slate, we should have seen this coming, so I'm cutting you a little slack.' He gets the needle in. 'Cheer up. When you get shut of her you can write a series.'

'Fuck you,' Theo says. 'Ten more minutes of this and I do you a series on the locked ward at the state hospital. Inmate's view.'

'Chill, Slate.' Chick pulls the cold cigar out of his face long enough to flash a snide grin. 'The glamour. The attention. You love it.'

'Yeah, right. Or I will. Right after the lobotomy.' He's not sure how much longer he can manage flip punchlines. His cheer is wearing thin. OK, he is wearing thin. He hates going home, hates sneaking to see Sally; even night school isn't safe. He never knows when he's going to go into the brownstone heap and find the Vent in his front row with her wet eyes and a glistening bubble sealing her dreamy smile. She'll sit and bubble until the campus cops drag her out. Or God strikes her dead. It's not the continuing presence that's the problem, it's the mystery. What does she really want from him? If he proposed marriage would the Vent be pleased or disappointed? Would she be happier if he beat her to death?

Chick says, not unkindly, 'What's the hangup, Slate? Tough guy like you. Letting her jerk you around.'

Confused and angry at himself, Theo snaps, 'Give me a break!' He's angry because it's true. She has worn him down over time, like acid on a stone.

'If I were you . . .'

'You'd know how to handle it.' Theo grimaces. 'Yeah, right you would. Until you've been there, you can't *know* what you'd do.'

'Take ten and go eat.'

'Not hungry.' The Vent's out there. 'It's safer here.'

Their encounters are as brief as they are terrible. They don't exchange words. He doesn't tell the Vent to go away and she's stopped reproaching him. They are at a standoff. Two entities occupying the same space; sooner or later one of them has to go. For now they are deadlocked. The Vent approaches with that beggar's slouch, pilgrim to Dalai Lama. Theo carries his shoulders high and his head at an angle because he never knows which direction she's coming from, only that she's coming and he is strung so taut that he can hear his tendons squeak. The woman is everywhere: outside every restaurant, outside City Hall and even the police station, loitering in alleys, lurking in the post office when he checks his box. She's there no matter where his assignments take him. It doesn't matter where he goes. She's there. Sometimes she's carrying the flute and sometimes she isn't. Theo isn't sure which is more terrible, knowing she wants to play for him or wondering what else she wants to do. He hates being anxious all the time.

OK, Chick. You're right. This thing is changing me.

48

H er son came to see her again and Stella thinks it's not something she did that makes him mean, it's who she is; she was dumped out on this earth to suffer and her new son is here to ensure it. The drugs make it worse. She came down to the visitors' room with all her secret, inside parts going soft in their privacy because she made him angry and he still came back. He must love her after all! Preston is gone and this is all the son she has right now, thank God he came back. Coming into the little room she tried to smile but the shots, the pills, it's been too long and her face doesn't remember the trick of smiling. She did the best she could. She held out her hands but he just let her stand there with her arms sticking out. When he wouldn't speak she spoke because his being here is in itself some kind of testimony and a marvel.

– You came back.

He didn't even say hello. He said, – Where is he?

And she struggled out of the fog to ask him, – Who?

Yes he was furious. – You know. That lying reporter.

– I don't, she said and her breath shook. Guilty yes she lied about that poor boy now she has to protect him. – I don't know who—

– Yes you do. He hasn't slept in his bed. Where is he?

– I don't know! I even know what you want . . . Oh! She cried, because she couldn't help it she was so glad to see him! Her heart just went rushing out. – Oh, son.

And he did not deny it. But he wouldn't look at her he

285

would not look at her. He just forged past her into some new place she didn't recognize. – I saw him and now I don't see him. I knew where he was. Now I don't. *But I was in his house. And when I find him* . . .

So befuddled, crying: – Whatever you're saying, please don't.

His mouth was a furnace rimmed with teeth. – *I will make him pay.* Odd. He stopped cold. – He's not anywhere. Not in town.

A part of Stella flowed out in relief. – He isn't hurt? She knew not to cry; she vowed not to cry. It only makes them mad.

– If you loved me you would tell me where he sleeps.

– But I do love you, she said. Oh God she doesn't even know who he is, this new son of hers, but as soon as she said it, it was true. She loves this boy heart and soul, blood and bone. Who else does she have left to love now that Preston is demolished? *We are all your sons.* – Son.

– You won't tell me where he is? After everything I did for you?

Got to tell him, got to warn him; she says, – I can't.

OK he made her cry after all. He showed her a picture torn out of a newspaper. – Look at this, Mother. Look what I did for you!

– Oh God, don't. I can't! Stella doesn't even know why she can't, or what she can't and it is this that most troubles her, this sliding into *can't* after so much *doing.* She did what she had to because she is strong. But she has gone from doing to *can't* and there is no reversing it. The drugs. She can't do anything.

The new son fell silent, just to punish her. It went on too long, her sweet boy *this close* she should have been so happy and all she felt was grief. She looked at him. He looked at nothing.

Got to do something, got to – Aren't you going to talk to me?

– If you won't help me find him, I'm leaving. He got up to go. – But I will find him.

She can't do anything because she forgets. – Oh, don't!

– And when I do . . . That's the last thing Stella truly remembers; she thinks the son said some other things but she can't bring them back and she can't make them make sense. He named and numbered exactly what he was going to do, ugly things so many and so awful that she moaned and stopped her ears. She knows but she doesn't know. If she did know she couldn't bear it so she forgets.

At the end Stella uncovered her head and cried, – Oh, son.

But he was gone.

So worry sits on top of her other miseries. It makes her want to die. She wants to die all the time now, terrible. Urgency stirs under the skin and in all her soft places; she has some obligation that she's beyond knowing. Somebody she's supposed to tell. Something. That nice boy she thinks, the one from the paper. That gentled her and let her lay down the weight of her story, just lay it down. He put it in the paper, and he understood! And she betrayed him. She gave him up to the new son. She has to warn him but how? The drugs. Where. How. What if he's lost? It is more than Stella can handle; everything is slipping away from her, God! Needs to warn him, but what? She has stopped knowing, and what she should do about it is not clear and, God, even if she had him here she couldn't talk. She has lost the language. If she could only get it back!

A bizarre thought skims her brain like a bat flying across the face of a silver moon. Have I been raped in jail?

Son. Things Stella should know and things the reporter ought to watch out for are entwined with this other thing that softens her heart and belly, legs and fundament: her new son was here he came back and she loves him so much oh, God! The other one! Where is he anyway? I have to warn him, he needs to know!

287

49

C oming home for clean clothes, Theo finds a note. It is
dead center on the pillow on Sally's side of the bed.
Block letters on brown paper: I WAITED FOR YOU. His hands
are shaking but he does not throw up.

'OK, you bitch. OK.' He never used to yell in empty
rooms.

He moves fast. Two phone calls. One meeting. Fine. It is
settled. He finds Sally in the press room at the station. The
Vent may know he's here but she'll be afraid to come in. One
place they can be together and not be seen. He says urgently,
'I want you to take time off and go to your folks.'

Alarmed, she turns. 'What's happened?'

'Nothing I can't handle. I just.'

She is smiling. 'Then stop trying to get rid of me.'

'This is serious.' He takes her face in his hands and looks
into it. 'You're not going to do it, are you?'

'No.'

'Not even for me?'

This is who she is. It's what he loves about her. Sally pulls
his hands down, holding them tight. 'Nobody chases me out
of my life.'

'OK.' Theo takes a deep breath. It's a big decision but
he makes it on the spot. 'If you won't go, I will.'

He is gratified to see how quickly distress flashes across
Sally's face. Hey, you *care*. She says, 'Oh, no!'

'Shh,' he says. 'It's OK.'

'What happened?'

It seems important to beg the question. 'Nothing. The Whartons are giving me time off is all. Special project.'

'Your book on killers.'

He nods. This is happening too fast. If he goes, he'll have to write the damn thing. But if he can, maybe he can wrap up a few things. Put an end to this weird passage in his life.

'I don't think that's such a bad idea, T.'

This catches him offguard. 'I thought you would be pissed.'

'I am, but I'm not.' She shakes her head. 'It's eating you up, T. Your killer guys, the body count. How they did it and what they were thinking about. And all for no reason.'

'I'm trying to find out the reason.'

'No, that's what you *think* you're trying to do.'

Troubled, he asks, 'What do you think I'm trying to do?'

Sally answers with a sweet, level look. 'I think you're trying to work it through for your own reasons. And that's the trouble. You don't know.'

'God,' Theo says, 'God.' And I thought it didn't show.

Sally can't quite smile, but she is trying. 'So, look. I think this is not such a bad thing. I'm sorry I can't leave town for you, but it wouldn't solve the Vent.'

'Then this had better solve it.'

'You know something? Maybe nothing will.'

'I've got to try.'

The rhetoric Theo puts in place for leaving is the project on serial killers. Unpaid leave. Research trip. He isn't running away, he's writing a book. He's taking a loan from the Whartons to get a six-month leave to write this book. New Haven is the logical place. Major psychiatric community. Research libraries. Medical school. Maybe there's a big lab somewhere at Yale with the brains of known serial killers floating in jars. And lurking in this thicket of reasons, the possibility that the bitemark killer really is in New Haven and that in some arcane way yet to be realized, the killer and Theo are linked. And Arch is there, no they don't want to share a place but at least one person he already knows, and if when he's done with this book he can put the arm on Arch's bosses and get a job at the *Register*, and if that means he never has to come back to Center City in central New England, fine. He will close the book on Stella and make his mark. Then he can come back for Sally and they will be everything they've ever wanted to each other.

If he can figure out what Stella wants.

If he can really lose the Vent.

50

New Haven

Haik is almost ready. Everything else is where it should be. After this long, hard time. The next to the last piece has been set down in the design. The reporter Haik needs and hates is in the city, did we bring him here with our . . . He does not know. But the reporter is here; we have seen him on the green. We have passed *this close* and the lying bastard never guessed. *Stop me before I* . . . Lie about us, will you. We will show them. One more piece. *One more piece.*

When the missing element drops into place we can begin.

In the rundown brick Federal far out State Street, Haik is waiting in eir room. It's where he comes at the end of every day, keeps up the rent, avoids being seen coming or going, no one will trace him here. He leaves nothing on the walls; it's all in his head. We are the slate on which our plan. We wait for the last piece to fall into place. Haik has to wait because *when you fail you kill your mother* and we will not fail in this one.

He is sitting in eir rank bedroll same as every night when ey walk in. After all these weeks. Our backup opens the door. Stumbling into eir room with eir flute case and eir bobbing orange hair, zoned out on pills, tongue lolling, already halfway out of eir life.

The last piece drops into place. *Clink.*

– You. Our belly twitches and our prick lifts, smiling.

E says to us, – You. Eir eyes are blurred and eir mouth

smudged with dirt. E is exhausted but e scrambles away from us. E is drooling the way we remember from the one time they drilled Haik full of that stuff because they thought it would quiet us.

– Don't be afraid. I am here to help you.

– Nobody can help me. Eir whole face is running down eir face, sweat and snot, spit and drool. – He's gone!

Backup. A necessary thing. Useful, like the rail or windowsill you steady your rifle on. Play em like a fish. – You can't stay here. It isn't safe.

Blasted and dazed. Coming to earth here for no real reason. Ey are dazed and crying. Empty pockets. Empty of everything. – I know.

– I know a place.

Helpless. – No money.

– It's free. I found it for you.

Asking for it. – For me? Oh yes e is ours.

We lead em there. We choose a spot near the entrance where we can find em. Put em and eir junk in place. – You'll be safe here.

And in the dead part of the city, down by the unfinished Oak Street connector, Haik goes back to his own place, nobody can trace us here. Found on one of the night passages. Big. Empty. Perfect.

Everything is ready now. Librarian. In place. Our backup. In place. Our plan. Complete. Do em. Prepare em. Right! End this. Have it over with and get it in the papers. Make her proud.

Who, we know who it is

What, is waiting to be discovered

When? When came in under sub-subheading *h. Get it in all the papers.* Our notebook is out of our hands now but the design is etched deep in us, pain burning in its lust to be delivered.

The when

Is now

51

By the time the story of the killing breaks Theo will have been in place for more than a month. He is in downtown New Haven, close to the libraries and the Yale psych unit for interviews he has yet to set up. He's taken a studio apartment in the shadow of Crown Towers where Arch lives. He's in one room with bed, table, tin cabinets and a sink, where Arch is in a real apartment, like working people have. Theo is living off his loan. Except for one round of drinks in which the haves battled the have-nots to a standstill, they haven't exactly been in touch. Arch has a place to go in the mornings. He has a desk. Arch has colleagues and a job to go to. What Theo has is Stella's nonspecific but pressing charge to him compounded by cartons of material that makes no sense to him. Instead of structure he has time. It yawns like a bottomless pit waiting for him to fill it with whatever he thinks he is.

Stop time.

'Fuck time.'

He hasn't figured out how to divide it up. The job used to decide for him. He has trouble getting started these mornings because there are no imperatives. Just Slate and his supposed-to-be-a book. He and Sally talk every night but except for that fixed point, the days just spin out. He nukes TV dinners and eats when he thinks of it and goes out when he feels like it and sleeps when he can't think of anything else. Mostly, he's holed up in here. Mail doesn't come. Except for Sally, nobody phones. He is alone. He spends hours sifting the debris in the cartons that moved with him. They sit like faithful animals, ready to rise when he rises and go wherever he goes. If he can't figure out what he's doing here, they're going to follow him for the rest of his life.

Every clipping he turns over has a photo of a dead face embedded in it. Every photograph carries its tragic freight. He feels like a ghoul at a crematorium, sitting crosslegged in the cold furnace, letting bits of ashes and bone flow through his fingers in hopes of finding gold.

There are too many books. Every serial killer spawns a biographer to hear his confessions for the specific purpose of bringing the mixed message to the people. More often than not, this biographer is also a shrink. In some odd alchemy, shrink and subject seek each other out. Do they come to celebrate atrocity or explain it or just make a mint on it? This isn't always clear. What Theo decides, taking notes on history and conjecture and jeremiads and lipsmacking confessions, is that at rock bottom, even the best shrinks don't know. He's trying to draw a straight line through all the life stories, but they slide around. He would like to find that in the end it is all one story. That there's some thread that you can pull. A central truth you can divine. Something you can change. Instead he finds multiple murderers fixed in place by writers who circle the subject and poke and question and quote and then plunge their hands into the guts of the unknown and come up with an uneducated guess. There are no answers, only worlds of effort by researchers trying to quantify what can never be understood.

This is where Theo is in his study of obsession. And it is this circularity that fixes him in place so he can't get into his book and he can't get out of it. That it can't be understood. In spite of *or because of* the fact that in one of these books some shrink lays it all out for him. The trail to murder in five easy pieces. Neat stages that Theo just doesn't buy:

a. Initial thinking disorder
b. Crystallization of a plan
c. Extreme tension culminating in crisis
d. Superficial normality
e. Insight and recovery

It shakes him. Like, if I do some poor person it makes me feel better? Yeah, right. It makes no sense. What makes this particular psychiatrist's scheme perfect? *Is* there a perfect scheme? Do killings come down in exactly this order? How are we supposed to know? In the end all these encounters are one on one. Killer. Victim. No one can guess what is in either party's mind.

Can any of us know what's in some other person's head?

The more he thinks about it, the worse it gets.

When Arch phones, he catches Theo on the floor surrounded by slithering glossies that shine like roach wings and piles of clippings weighted down by books laid on their faces so their spines crack. Thank God it's the phone. At the first ring Theo lunges with his voice bright with gratitude. Relief. 'Arch!'

52

The Last Place

This is the last place. It is a place in life that is beyond
writing. Writing is just another thing you leave behind,
like shit. What you write is not important. It's only what the
hand does on its way to doing what you want. Analyze, as
taught, so fine. Organize. Plan. Write it down. Then forget
what you have written. The body remembers. What the head
is beyond thinking, the body knows.

It's time to go and do. Haik rolls out of the sleeping
bag where he has kept certain pieces of em, The One he
followed into eir life. To take em out of it and *do*. He
owns em now. He has taken the most secret parts of the
librarian without em knowing – scuzz scraped out of eir
bathtub with crumpled toilet paper, his collection of eir
pubic hairs gathered over time and laid in neat lines on
the place where he puts his head, toenail cuttings from
eir bathroom floors. He has other parts of em saved
up that he will refer to later but that is for later. It
is nothing to him now. Now it's time to leave these
parts behind. He will go out and do, and if he does
it right this time it will be done for good. Then that
mother will know what is and what is not. Everyone
will know.

It's today. What he feels now insofar as he feels anything?
Release: this is better than the gasp at the first cut of the
surgeon's knife, the spurt of poison out of an abscessed

gum. Beginning! It's better than orgasm. Almost as good as . . . Yes. It's time.

The water in the building where he came to earth has been shut off for decades. He takes bottled water and a flashlight into one of the bathrooms. Shaves and bathes himself in the sink. Cold as it is in this echoing place, he strips and washes every morning. Meticulously. Armpits and neck. Down there. Jockey briefs fresh from the laundry. Clean shirt, light starch. Neat chinos. Tweed coat he was wearing when he fled the police. Down jacket only slightly faded by age; he found it in one of the cartons in the basement here. Spit shine on the shoes although he will have to take them off later. When he goes out he will look fine. To the world he looks as clean and plain as you. As me. Walking out today, Haik will keep checking his reflection in the plate-glass windows, to make sure. Anybody running into Haik heading along Chapel Street with his new attaché case will take him for a businessman or a city employee heading for work. Smooth head, wet-combed hair steaming slightly in the early spring chill. Bland face composed in a near smile. Nobody will guess that he dressed in this ruined, cavernous place. Nobody will even suspect what obscenities hang dripping in his interior caverns. So, fine.

Leaving the building, he takes great care. He goes through avenues of cartons and upended counters without bumping into anything that would stain his chinos or snag the coat. If the fixtures are in ruins at his feet and his shoes crunch broken glass; if unknown sleepers scratch and stir in the dark nearby, if rats run among the cartons in far corners it is no problem for him. For the first time in Haik's life his surroundings and his inner landscape match. He would like to live here forever. This place is so right. What he does best, he will not do it here. He walks down the frozen escalator and goes out through a back room far from the boarded-up display windows. In the back of a storeroom, he lifts a hatch and squirms through the opening. He comes out in a deserted parking garage where he stands for a minute taking in the fresh air. Then he picks up his equipment and heads out.

It is amazing. Perfect. Nobody sees him come. Nobody sees him go. The only source of confusion is the time. The sun is high. It is almost noon. A surprise to Haik, but a good enough surprise. He will begin by day but he always finishes by night so whatever he had planned for morning needs to be put aside. Follow em on certain errands. Well, he has done that on other days. The timing is: go direct to the encounter. Accidental. Encounters have to be, or e will be wary and not let us talk to em. The world is a dangerous place for em. Full of perverts and creeps. But e is used to him now, he has gotten em used to us, and this is at the heart of everything that follows.

Coming down the library steps e will be pleasantly surprised. E will smile. – *Oh, it's you.*

He will smile the smile he has taught himself. – Yes. It's me.

Haik crosses the green and waits in front of the library. Other people looking past him as the main door opens would see a woman coming out. Dark hair. Sloped shoulders suggesting a rounded body under the plaid tweed coat; the woman is leaning toward middle age, a little hurried, makeup smeared. Her expression is sweet, but blurred. What Haik sees is something else. He sees what he needs to see. An object. That he will do. And do the prescribed things to. He hurries up the steps and they collide.

– Oh, e says. Exactly as scheduled. Backs up. Brushes emself off. Not quite smiling. – It's you.

– Yes. It's me.

He can see a bird inside of em flutter. E says, – I can't talk now, I'm going out to lunch.

– Lunch? Haik has been on this job for so long that he knows the right smile by rote. – Yes. It's about that time, isn't it? Calm. Bland.

If e knew what was in his head e would run from us. E says pleasantly enough, – Yes, it's about that time.

– Would you like company?

Eir dark hair has changed color at the roots since we started watching em. *You think I don't know what brand dye you use?* E says, – I'm meeting a friend.

– Do you mind if I walk along?

– If you want. E is wary but slightly flattered. E shrugs. – I told you, I'm meeting a friend.

– A friend? He knows it is a lie.

– Is that a problem for you?

– No. No problem. He is studying the profile; the sagging flesh around the jaw, as if the skin is tired. He allows a flicker of contempt; age won't be a problem for this one much longer. – I won't bother you if it's a bother.

– No no. It's fine.

So Haik walks em up Church Street to the little Chinese restaurant and opens the door. He stands back so e can go in.

If e looks anxious, he does not know anxious. E says, – My friend's not here yet.

– Maybe you and I . . . He knows what e will say before e does; he is already turning away.

E says it. – It would be OK except my friend is really shy.

– Well, goodbye.

So he stands outside for long enough to confirm that there is no friend coming; there was never any friend. But by this time he is in possession of the lint and crumpled paper that collected over time in eir coat pocket. He puts it into his mouth and waits. At the end he sees em get up to pay. Seconds before e comes out of the restaurant, he slips around a corner so e won't see that he is there.

Then he follows em back to the library without em knowing and after taking the bus out to perform certain errands of his own in the place where he's going to take em, he comes back. If he used to have a car, he doesn't have the car. He follows em to eir doctor's appointment without em knowing and ey don't know he is in the pharmacy when ey get eir prescription filled and ey do not see him following em as ey go back to the library. He follows em inside. It gives him pleasure to be in eir own place without em noticing. Outside eir ladies' room when ey come out. On the other side of a metal book stack following em title by title; if e looked over the tops of the books e is shelving, e would see his eyes. He follows em to the bathroom and waits for the sounds. Enough for now. Then he goes back outside. He posts himself on the rail fence across the street and waits like a dog.

When e comes out it is getting dark. So, dark. So, fine. E walks to the bus stop and he follows. He takes the next bus and walks the familiar way from the bus stop to eir house. Then he makes his way into the bushes underneath eir bedroom window. A place he knows as well as he knows the smile. Ground-floor window, as per original plan. He is too late to watch em change and he can't watch em bathe but he does watch em come out of the bathroom in eir grey sweatsuit with the University of Connecticut seal on the shirt. Then as e goes into the other room to get eir supper he opens the bedroom window and lets himself inside.

E is in the kitchen with eir spatula, scraping corned beef hash into little heaps in a frying pan when he comes up behind em and slips his arms around eir waist.

– I've waited so long.

– My God. The pressure of the knife in eir ribs warns em not to scream but e cannot stop breathing words. My God. My God. My God.

– I'm not going to cut you.

– My God.

– Stop that. I only want to talk to you.

– Let go! My God.

He shakes eir arm until e drops the spatula. – Put that down and come along.

– No!

– I'm not going to hurt you. Now come on.

E tugs against him with all eir weight. – Where are you taking me?

– Place I know. Somehow he has worked em around so e is facing away from the stove. Deftly he reaches behind em and turns off the burner. Then he says, – Get a coat. I don't want you to be cold.

E is trembling and breathing in little gusts that pull air in and don't seem to let any out. When the air does start coming out of em the sound will be tremendous. Unless. He thinks to cover eir mouth so e won't scream: the tape. He can hear sound trying to come out from under the tape in huffling little sobs. Later he will have to use nail-polish remover to get rid of the adhesive scars. He thinks to take eir pantyhose off the floor and tie eir hands, but only after e gets the coat out of eir bedroom closet and forces it on the way you have to force clothes on a dog. E is struggling so hard that he can't tell whether e is trying to keep the coat off so ey will have to stay here or get it on so we can go. Does e think e can throw emself against a passerby when we get outside, or fall down and get attention from somebody on the street? There isn't anybody on the street. He marches em out through the empty front hall and down the steps and into the bushes so he can retrieve his attaché case with the equipment. Now he will march em to the place. When he chose this one he did it with extreme care. Never choose an object before you find out where ey live in relationship to the place you choose. You want it to be near. If the object happens into you and you know e is The One, then you will scope the landscape in increasing concentric circles until you have located The Place. Location may not be everything but it is important. Isolated. Sheltered. Still.

It is near enough. Another factor in his choice. A block

from eir house. Overgrown, some kind of park in the shadow of the big rock that holds down this side of the town map. Some day when we are famous Haik will get a car and take one to the top of this rock and do em at the monument, maybe for the TV cameras, but not this time. It passes without notice that he is already thinking of past this one to the next. There is not the liberty to notice because this is getting harder than it should be. For one thing, e will not stop struggling. He marches em along but e kicks and snuffles and hurls emself this way and that way, hurling emself this way and that lunging to break his hold so finally he has to smash em up against a tree in the park and smash her and smash her until her knees give a little and he can take her the rest of the way in peace. Her. She!

Goddamn it. Not an object like she is supposed to be. A woman. Here. He has dragged a Goddamned woman here.

But they are near the end. He peels the tape off the mouth. He needs to hear her gasp for help. He needs to hear her beg.

Only one word comes out of her. – You.

All the weeks of targeting, following and collecting, all the weeks of *accidental*, all that smiling and hello to her and hello to me, and of getting this one exactly how he wants so he can show the mother and the one that wrote about the mother. He is going to show them all. But after all the steps he put in place and followed out you would expect more than what comes next. He has brought the two of them to the end point of all this planning and the moment of discovery is summed up in two words.

Hers. – *You.*

And ours. – Yes.

So she recognizes him. Recognition is the center of the moment for him. But then it is not. It is not enough. Nothing is ever enough. He wants her to want to fuck him. He wants her to NOT. He wants her to beg. More than anything he wants her to try reasoning with him. He would like her to get it on tape to leave so the police will know and the newspapers will know. Clamping her wrists, he holds her in place. He fixes his eyes on her eyes. And he waits for what comes next.

Get them used to you and when you do them they will know you. They will look into your eyes and they will know what you did to them. You want to see their face when they understand what is happening. When you do it they have to know what you are doing but that is not the most important part. This is the most important part. They have to acknowledge that it is you. Acknowledge you.

He takes a long, cold look into her. – Is that all?

She does not speak. Unless she can't speak. She swallows her tongue he thinks, swallows her tongue or something worse happens in her throat as she begins to change. The body that seemed round and weak is tough and wiry in desperation and she will not speak and she will not stop fighting him. So, Haik thinks sourly. *Every time you fail you kill your mother . . .* Might as well have been a man. The One, he thought. What you want is never what you get. The One you think is the one is never the one. At least not this time. Just as well get it over with and finish this. *Procedures.* Do em right and it may still be OK.

The trouble in the end is that it is not easy to kill a person. No matter how carefully you plan. Of course she screams and he has to smack her on the side of the head so that she slumps against the tree but he wants her conscious so he has to make sure she is aware but she is sagging so he has to hold her in place while he takes the cord out of his case *memo* next time tie the cord around our waist so it is right at hand and she is flopping so he has to hold her in position so he can put the cord around her neck and the whole time she is fighting him. Fighting! They grapple and he loses his loop. Again. Terrible struggle getting worse because the loop escapes him, slippery nylon cord escapes him and then she does, scrambling almost out of his reach before he grabs with his long arm and yanks her back by the coat and the next thing he knows she is writhing out of the hairy plaid coat and Haik shouts he doesn't mean to, God damn it. God *damn* it because nothing is going right.

Then he makes his loop and turns her so that he is behind her, drawing it tighter, tighter, tight and he knows how this will end; first cessation of motion and then twitching but he will keep holding the woman because he knows this death, it comes in waves and what you do is never truly done until it is forever and truly done. He hears the final wheeze and jerks hard but then he has to hold her through another round of twitching and he holds her a little longer until the sound and the smells let him know that all the substances and fluids in her body have let go.

Then he lets her down. He opens his case and sets up the light. But the preparation is going to be harder than he thought. First he has to compose the body but she has died in such contortions that it takes longer than it should. Parts of her are rigid and other parts flop, lie still. Lie still. Then the nail polish remover from his equipment case to clean the black lines the duct tape left around her mouth, skin all red where he ripped it off. And then the moment in which he squats in contemplation. And thinks. Strip her naked and leave her here while he does the rest? It seems too cruel. She would be cold. But the preparation. He must complete the preparation. He has to complete the preparation before he can call this done and walk away. He puts on tight, unlined kid gloves like a beautiful woman drawing on a pair of hose. Then he begins. It's all in the case. Everything he needs except the two items he left here in the park this afternoon when he dug the hole.

With the knife, Haik cuts off the woman's tongue and stuffs it in her mouth so she can't tell. The woman. That's all she is. His mistake. She was never The One. Having cleaned the face, he hesitates before taping it shut again, as planned. Then with the hack-saw, he takes off the head and puts it in the plastic bag he has pulled out of the case for just this purpose. He adds the hands. Even with the light he has to circle twice before he finds the place he picked out this afternoon and prepared so he could bury these things. He kicks the heap of twigs off the hole he made for the head and pulls out the can of gasoline he left hidden in the hole this afternoon after he finished digging. He opens the plastic bag and pulls the head out of the bag by the hair. He contemplates the dead face without expression for a moment before he holds it over the hole and drops it in. He will cover it with earth so she can't tell on us. Then he takes out the hands and almost as an afterthought, removes the index fingers so she can't point to us. Left one. Right one. He drops them in. Then with the shovel he kicked under a pile of leaves after he finished digging, he covers the spot and moves the twigs back over it. It occurs to him to put more twigs over the shovel. He wants it found, but not too soon.

He goes for the can of gasoline. He takes it back to the place where he left the woman's body. If she has moved. If she has moved! No. It is exactly as it was before. Why did he imagine she would have moved? To break this. No. To make it different. Final is never what you think. Final is something you can never leave behind. You can only hope for it. What he thought he was doing when he completed the notes on preparation, that would make this one the one he did for keeps. There are two more steps left in the preparation but he already knows this is not the final preparation. Wrong one, for one thing. Wrong one instead of The One. And the rush. He doesn't feel the rush. Why not? The rush got lost in the difficulty. Her struggle. Mechanical things. Failures. There is one more step but the passion has gone out so why finish.

This is already botched so he doesn't bother to remove the feet. Symbols are worthless when the design is fucked.

Very well. The backup. And building in his brain as solid as a pyramid, the backup plan. Leave the woman her feet. Dead is dead. This one will not run away. Wearily, he empties the gasoline can over the body. In spite of all the planning it is nothing like he thought it would be. Without the head and with the tweed coat black with blood, it looks cold and dead and sad.

He lights the match. Then he hesitates. There is more than one way to redeem this situation. He feels in his pockets for change. None. Something in his belly quickens. This is not as good as orgasm but in the end it may be better. He will go back to the woman's house to make this call.

53

Arch just starts. 'You still into gross killings?'
Fresh clippings for Theo's pile. 'Bitemark?'
'Not sure. But I'm onto it and it's big. Decapitation.'
'Cool.' Envy leaps like a silver fish. *Good story.* 'When?'
'Tonight. Some guy phoned it in.'
'Man or woman?'
'Woman. Like, who else, you know? Offed her and torched her.'
'Where are you?'
Arch doesn't exactly tell him. 'Hands, too. They're still looking for the parts.'
'Are you at the river?'
'It's got this ritual smell to it.' Arch is jubilant. 'Could be the start of something big.'
'So fine. Where is this? At the dump?'
'Chill, read all about it in your morning paper.'
'Where the hell are you, Wills?'
'Look, I just did you a favor. For what you're doing, you don't need to be here. You can catch it on TV.'
Right, that's what Arch really thinks of all his efforts here. Theo shouts, 'OK, asshole. Where?'
Arch makes that crackle you make when you want the other person to think your signal's breaking up. Of course he's calling from his car. 'Gotta go. Stay tuned.'
Yeah they are broadcasting live from the scene. It's one hell of a murder, some poor woman dragged out of her apartment and killed in East Rock Park, two blocks from

307

her home. Mutilated and partially torched by somebody who didn't stay around long enough to make sure the fire took hold. Police had to identify her by a crumpled charge slip in one of her coat pockets because so far they haven't found the head and they're still looking for the hands. The on-camera anchor takes that extra-deep tone TV newswomen affect to convince you that they're serious. For this woman, the timing is just right. Story broke early enough for her to get to the scene to broadcast live and still make it back to the studio in time to anchor the 11 o'clock news. She's trying to sound sober and grieved for the victim, but even from here Theo can see that she's hotwired, buzzing with excitement. This is a big one. Bad as it is for the victim, it's good for her. Her byte on the bizarre killing isn't only going to air in New Haven. Bizarre usually goes big. Her byte may make it onto tomorrow's network wakeup show and if the presentation is glossy enough it just might air again on the nightly news, gazillions of Americans watching with dropped jaws. *Good story.* Terror loose in the world and reporters rushing to the scene with their blood racing and their hair perfect. In case. How do you explain that to your mom?

'Good evening. I'm Tippi Wethers, live from East Rock Park.' Her makeup is slick; her mouth glistens as if she's just wet it. She's lost the topcoat so the people can see her in the fearsome Armani knockoff with the soft lapels. She'd have dragged it off the hanger the minute she got the call. Look her best. In case. 'In the wake of this bizarre killing, New Haven is asking itself why . . .'

Theo's throat tightens. *Good story.* How do you explain your life in the business? Ocelot chewed a baby's face off the summer Theo interned at the St Pete *Times – good story*; two reclusive crones fought to the death, it was weeks before the dead sisters were found. And the question that put the frosting on top and kept the city talking? Which one died first. *Good story.* Sally came in to the *Star* one night leached and exhausted: 'They found the kid. Agh. What's the murderer do after he rapes him and offs him? Stuffs him in a plastic bag and sets it on fire. Destroying the evidence.' Yes she is shaken. You say what you have to say to help her stand back so she can get to work on it. 'Good story.' Leave parts of yourself at home when you go to work today. Tomorrow. For the rest of your life. You can't afford to unpack here: not and do your job. Think too hard about what you have to do and you won't be strong enough to do it. And write your guts out knowing that whatever you say will be in recycling bins tomorrow; that the best you will get is hasty acknowledgement from whoever's in charge: 'Good story.'

The anchor finishes, 'The alleged killer may be identified by secret evidence impounded by the New Haven police.'

Secret evidence. Theo lifts his head. But fucking Arch works in this town; fucking Arch has developed his sources and it's Arch and not Theo who will be heading into the station as soon as they remove the body, winkling the truth out of his new best friend the chief. Phoning in details for *Newsweek.* Unless he's stringing for *Time.* Still Theo's blood is thudding in the old way. He should be out there. He ought to go.

'. . . on the news at eleven. Bulletins as they break.'

East Rock Park is fifteen minutes away. By this time Theo could be in the car. Do interviews. Put this into his book, forty years of serial murders crowned by this one, exclusive to him. No, he should phone Chick. Eyewitness Special to the *Star.* Hell, maybe he should raise somebody at the *New York Times* and see if they need a . . . hell, they already have a person. Shit, their person might turn out to be Arch. Their person is already there and he, Theo Slate, does not know shit about this town. Plus, he's lost his notebook. The one with a few remaining blank pages and his phone log in the back. Wait a minute, his pencils are wrecked. Wait, his last ballpoint exploded all over the back pocket of his jeans. Hey wait, has he eaten? He forgets. Plus he hasn't shaved. He can't go out there looking like this. He goes back to his books.

'I can't do that,' he says to no one. He's not ready to admit he's paralyzed. 'I'm doing this. I'm OK. I'm writing a book.'

Then his hand comes down on a page that changes everything. Some British Jeffrey Dahmer type tries to explain. This is another part of the puzzle.

Add this question to why they have to do it.

Why the compulsion to tell.

Are they doing what they're doing for itself, or for the same reasons this Tippi Wethers put on the fake Armani suit tonight? This killer writes, 'Don't imagine I would have been stopped by the possibility that I could be hanged . . . In these times I was beyond responsibility, beyond regret. There was the terror that followed, remorse as huge as it was suppressed . . . I can't stop thinking about it. I don't feel sorry for myself, I'm just astounded that it could have happened, and to me. I should see something terrible when I look in the mirror, horrible monster with scales or feathers or one big round eye, but when I look in the mirror all I see is me. Same old nice old friendly, pleasant, do-what-you-ask-me-to me.'

It's all I see when I look in the mirror.

Shit!

This drives Theo to his feet. It sends him out of the house. Fuck notebooks, fuck functional pencils, fuck looking like an outsider stumbling onto the scene in a city he doesn't have the first clue about. Right now anything is better than the scene inside his head. When he reaches East Rock Park, everybody's milling under work lights augmented by lights brought in to make the TV anchor's big hair shine. The woman in the fake Armani does a wrapup and the TV van moves out. The top of the news is wrapped up. At least, the cherry on the top. The details belong to the print media, thanks a lot. Rubberneckers and neighbors in coats over bathrobes mill at the barrier while street kids in tough jackets dart in close and feint at the tape until police drive them back. The charred area where the body was found is cordoned by that yellow tape that comes out of factories in rolls thousands of miles long, spooled and ready to ship out all over the country. Nations used to live under flags. Now they travel under this new emblem. Non-biodegradable yellow plastic ribbons surprinted in black: POLICE LINE. DO NOT CROSS.

Arch is busy with a woman Theo takes to be the coroner. He leans in with that insider's confidential slouch and takes notes while she mutters into his ear. Theo wants to get right in there with him but this is not his story, it is Arch's story and so he does what you do. He hangs back. At the same time he is scanning the faces that ring the tape God what is he looking for hears it feels it it is it, '*I should see something terrible when I look in the mirror, horrible monster with scales or feathers or one big round eye, but when I look in the mirror all I see is me. Same old nice old friendly do-what-you-ask-me-to me.*'

OK, so what if Theo forgets and presses too close to the tape. A cop who has no way of knowing he's talking to a reporter straightarms him with the look you give bums. 'You. Stand out of the way.'

You're either one of us or you're one of them. Theo pulls out his press card. 'Reporter. Center City *Star*.'

'OK. Over there.'

Some woman with a big jaw smashes a fist into his shoulder. 'Reporters.'

'We don't make it happen, lady.'

'Goddamned reporters.'

'We just write it down.'

God, Theo thinks. He's stirring like the Mummy in the movie, coming back to life after a thousand years. *I love this stuff*. A car pulls up and two old people spill out, spastic and disorganized, with wild hair and reflected light glinting off eyeglasses put on in such haste that the effect is skewed, leaving Theo to wonder if he's gone blind or they've gone blind.

The mother cries, 'Nadia!'

'Who's that?'

'Fuck, it's the parents.'

'How did they get here?'

'Notified.'

'How did they find out where?'

'Fucking TV.'

'Let me through!'

'Let my husband through!'

'I'm sorry sir, this is a—'

'But she's our daughter.'

'I'm sorry, you can't—'

The two old people are crying and grief is contagious. Some of the rubberneckers and the neighbors are crying too while in the background the kids in tough jackets elbow each other and giggle because that's part of the contagion and this is all they know. The old woman screams, 'Nadia!'

'Nadia!'

Two police move in to hold the old people in place. They don't need to see what's out there. What's left out there. What was out there isn't out there any more. What they are digging for. Will find and bring back. Someone says, 'Sir, the body's gone to—'

'Not a body. Nadia!'

'For God's sake somebody get these people out of here before—'

'I want her back!'

'Chief!'

'Yo.'

'We've found the head.'

a. Initial thinking disorder

b. Crystallization of a plan
c. Extreme tension culminating in crisis
d. Superficial normality
e. Insight and recovery

What does any of that have to do with any of this? With the protective sarcasm of the people who have to work this scene. With rubberneckers jostling distressed neighbors for space in the front ranks behind the yellow tapes and local street gangs jockeying for position and the bereft parents screaming and some of the neighbors sobbing out of sheer nerves could happen to you could happen to me, while the police go about their business spurred by the naked need not to look like bunglers while they're out here in the dark with the press watching them try to do their jobs and waiting for them to make just one slip. This is nothing like the books. This is not the same. But it is the same.

The old man cries, 'Let me see her. You have to let me see her.'

'You don't want to see what's here, Mr.'

'Nadia.'

'We have to see her.'

'Not yet, sir, OK?'

'But she's our daughter.'

Someone says evenly, 'You want to wait until she's looking a little bit more like your daughter.'

Theo should be taking notes.

'She's our daughter!'

'Nadiaaaaa . . .'

Theo wants to rush in there and rescue the poor parents from the next thing. He wants to take them away so they won't have to see what he is detached enough to see: the officer coming out of the bushes with the dirty plastic garbage bag. They need to be spared the way clotted dirt drops as the plastic sags and takes on the shape of the heavy object inside. That would be the head. He should protect them. Throw his coat over their heads and hurry them to his car. Cleverly, he thinks he could close them into his car and take them to some safe place far away from here and help them get better over coffee but at the same time he is thinking, because who he is in some odd way outweighs their grief, *If they start trusting me, I can get their story out of them.*

But the bereft parents' story is not located with them. It is located in the smooth-haired man with the ordinary smile who comes around the corner just as Theo leaves the scene. Who stops short when he sees that it is Theo Slate coming, stops so quickly that his head jerks in recognition, nice-looking guy in his early thirties smooth hair, ordinary-looking, could be you, could be me.

But it is not.

54

– Hello? Stella gropes through massed tranquilizers, through the Thorazine/Haldol/Prozac whatever-it-is fog. He has phoned. He phoned her, and dulled and confused as she is by prison drugs she is excited, standing here in the hall in her ugly jail suit so baggy now it just hangs on her, steel bracelet loose on her wrist, does she forget to eat? She's cuffed to a rail, groggy and unsteady but! On the phone. In a place this big nobody bothers to cross-check records. Does she still have a son after all? They say her son is at the other end but no noise comes out. She shakes the receiver. The meds the prison psychiatrist prescribed to bring her down left her head in jetlag so her body gets places before the rest of her, has he spoken and she didn't hear? – Hello? Oh, please. Hello?

There is a long empty space where his voice should be. Finally the one who cares enough to telephone, the one who may care enough to forgive her for killing him says, – Hello, Mother. It's me.

Oh, son! Stella weeps with relief, tears bubbling into the phone. – Oh Presty, dearest, I'm so glad it's you! Oh son, I'm so sorry, dear. Some fate has undone everything Stella had done to him and where it's been dry ever since they started her on the meds her mouth is wet with gratitude. *Presty. Thank God.*

– No. You know who I am.

– Is it Mr. Mr. You know, from the paper? She is lilting like a girl *thank God now maybe I can warn him.* Can.

315

What. Stop it. Some dreadful progress she has to stop. – I thought you'd never call.

The voice is steely. – Mother, you should know me by now.

– Oh, she says. – It's you. It's him. The new son that is so mean to her. – I thought you were my.

– I am. We all are, remember?

– No. She is thinking oh God yes but oh God no. *All of this evil came out of me?* A part of her goes scrambling after something it can't catch. – I love you, son.

– That's not why I called.

It's him. It's him and he has done awful things. Stella doesn't know who to tell; she can't figure out how to share this. Um. This. The lost nurse in her surfaces and provides the phrase. Burden of concern. So it is not thought out, what Stella says next. She just says it. – What shall I call you, dear?

– Call me right. Listen, Mother. Listen to what I have to tell you and then you tell me you were wrong.

– I was wrong to kill you. She is heaving with remorse. Wrong!

– And about the other thing? Quick. Cruel. – Take it back.

– What? There is something ugly running underneath this conversation. The hint of terrors to come. At the far end of the gleaming corridor a guard sits at a table reading *Allure*. If I screamed would she come? Does she care? – Take what back?

– What you told all the papers. Words hit like stones. *Whap.* – You lied. A terrible lie. Rage shakes more loose. This rolls into her ear like an avalanche: – WHEN YOU STOP THEM THEY ARE GLAD.

This is awful. – My God! The guard gets up from her post and, seeing Stella cuffed to the rail by the pay phone, heads off to the bathroom. They've gotten careless with her since the meds.

316

– Well you can fuck glad and then you can see how this fits. Listen, old lady. Read the papers. Watch TV. See your son in the world and be proud of me! And remember. *I did it for you.*

His joyful passion makes her voice tremble. – I don't understand. Oh please, she says as if she can forestall what he is about to tell her. – Please don't.

That laugh! Jubilant. Cold. – I already have.

Anguish flows out of her. – No!

– And you want to know how it feels? It feels wonderful.

God she is alone in the hall in the prison in the world oh God they are so slack about her now. She is all alone with this; there is nobody to prevent what is coming, nobody to help her, nobody to . . . She groans. – Oh, no.

– Do you want me to tell you what it's like?

– Please don't!

– Yes I will tell you. Yes I will show you glad.

So he does. He goes on and on. About what he did to the woman and how, who she was and what happened at the end the blood the noise, *oh my God that poor woman, did my Presty.* On and on.

– And then I . . . and then. Do you understand?

– Mmmmmm. Stella starts droning, anything to fill her skull so there won't be room. – Mmmmmm oh please anything to keep the words from getting into her head. – *Oh no I don't hear you!* MMMMmmmmmmm.

– You will see it in all the papers. Then you'll know.

– I don't hear you I don't I don't.

– And when I did it, OK? When I did it, Mother. Mother, are you listening?

– No. Stella is flailing now, standing as far from the pay phone as the steel cord will allow and looking for a guard, anybody to tell, she wants them to grab this ugly instrument out of her hand and somehow stop the horror that's spilling out of it.

He just goes on. – When I did it, I was glad.

– Guard!

– Now you be sure and get that into the paper.

She yanks against the cuff and draws blood; straining away she shouts loud enough to bring everybody in the place. – Emergency!

– You get it in the paper or I do another one.

– Guard!

– You be careful what you say about me. And that reporter?

Bludgeoned by grief, slowed by the drugs, Stella is struggling toward awareness. *Responsible. I am. Responsible.* She cries, – It wasn't the reporter! He never said that.

– Mother, I am sending you a present. It's for him.

– But he didn't—

Intent, he overrides her. – And you will see that he gets it. You will give that reporter my present, right?

Parts of Stella are coming back to her. – I did it. *Me!*

– Tell him he gets the truth in all the papers or I do him.

– Oh, God. Noooooo.

This is how he reproaches her. As guards come thudding toward the sound her son says, aggrieved, – I'm going to make you proud.

Now she is entreating him. – *Nooooooooooo!*

But he is beyond her pleas. Stricken, Stella struggles back to her cell and takes her place on the floor by the basin, but not for long. Within seconds, she stands. Her sons. *Maybe they are all my sons.* She presses her hands on the basin. Lets herself down and pushes up. When she is done with this she will begin pacing. In the medical lexicon there are drugs and drugs; pills, you can pretend to take and get rid of later; injections, you can't dodge. But she will do what she can to work them off. She has things to do. There is something she must do. God, help. First she has to get strong.

55

'Yo, Slate. It's me.'
    'Like, who else would start a conversation Yo.'
Arch snorts. 'Hey, asshole, I'm trying to do you a favor here.'
    'Sorry. What you got?'
    'It's about this murder.'
    'Linked with our bitemark guy?'
    'Too soon to tell,' Arch says. 'You better get down here. That is, if you're still into murder.'
    'Hell yes I am.' Theo is in so deep that he may never get out. He's been hauling over his stuff ever since the body was discovered. Oddly, it's getting harder to leave the apartment. It's like being in jail. He's waiting for Arch to say the magic words that will spring him. Behind Arch he hears generic newsroom sounds, mouse clicking – *Are you keyboarding while you talk to me?* – conversation, phones, movement if not action. Arch is surrounded by people with things to do, whereas Theo is alone here waiting for city officials to start returning his calls. 'And you are with . . .' Um. 'You say research on a book?' Back burner. 'I'll tell him you called.' On the rug near him is a half-empty can of beans with a fork stuck in it. *Did I eat that?*
    'Are you on this thing or are you not on this thing?'
    'I'm on it. I'm on it!'
    'You're really writing this book.' Arch's tone brings back the old rivalry – two friends, beady-eyed: *You getting ahead?* He probes. 'So. It's really only a book.'

319

'What the fuck is the matter with a book?'

'I'm asking about time value. Like, you're not going to cash in on my stuff?' That competitive, edgy twang. 'With, like, *Newsweek*?'

'Arch I don't even know what you've got for me.'

'It's big. I just need to hear you say you're not selling anything I give you to the big boys.'

'No,' Theo says wearily. Not that it hasn't crossed his mind, but in the way of these things, he's had his ride. The *Newsweek* connection has vaporized. 'It's really for the book.'

'OK.' Arch drops his voice. 'The police have something they're not telling us.'

'I heard it on TV.' Theo quotes, 'Sealed evidence.'

'Whatever. They're sitting on it, but I got it.'

'You got what?'

'I got a copy of it. One of my sources leaked it, long story. Shitty copy, hard to read, but it does the job. Listen.' Arch takes his face out of the mouthpiece and says in a falsely bluff, stagey voice to someone standing nearby, 'I'll get right on it as soon as I wind this up.' After a pause he goes on in that intimate tone, all spit and confidentiality. It's kind of like getting an obscene phone call. 'There's something in it that you've gotta see.'

'Cool.' It is unclear as to why Arch Wills is doing him this favor. 'Why are you doing me favors? Make up for ditching me in Center City?'

'Truth? Truth is,' Arch says, 'it's in the book.' He clears his throat the way TV doctors do when they're breaking bad news. 'It's kind of pertaining to you.'

'The book? It's in the book?'

'Meet me.' His friend's voice changes. 'You'll see.'

Theo hits Chick's angry bark exactly. 'You're telling me something about this case is pertaining to me?'

'Just get in the car, asshole.'

'What the fuck are you talking about?'

'Just get down here. I can't do this on the phone.'

'I'll be there in five. Hang on. Call on my other line.'

It's Sally. 'I just wanted to see how you were.'

'I love you. Hang on.' He says to Arch, 'Gotta go. I'll be there in ten.'

'Are you all right?'

He's just glad to have her in the room with him. 'Hey, Sal! I'm cool. Why aren't you at work?'

'I am. I just kind of needed to talk to you.'

'But it's four in the afternoon.'

'Give me a break, T. I'm not spying on you. I just. Oh hell, I called because I woke up this morning missing you like hell.'

This jars the truth out of him. 'Me too.'

'Come see me.'

All those gritty nights with the Vent lurking outside their bedrooms repeat on him like bad food. 'I can't.'

Sally's voice is soft. 'Just for the night.'

It's weird. This is about more than the territoriality of love; there is the Vent. 'You come here.'

'Can't, I'm working this weekend.' They both know they're exploring the parameters of the link between them: shipboard romance, or is it durable? Sally presses. 'It's only an hour on the plane.'

'I can't.' As he talks he's gathering his notebook and the Perlcorder, pencils, ballpoints, his keys. 'Something's come up.'

Oh but Sally knows he's been circling the drain. Hurt, she says, 'I don't know what it is with you, you're treating this like some sacred, holy mission.'

Theo says honestly, 'I wish I knew, Sal.' Stella Zax put this in his hands without explaining. 'I don't know what it is.'

'Oh, T.' OK, OK, she lets him know her body misses his body just as much as his misses hers, 'I can't do this much longer, T.'

'Me either. I just have to work this through.' He will not tell her the other thing. He can't do Center City; not with the Vent lurking outside all the bedroom windows of their lives. 'I'm on this story. Ritual murder. May be the bitemark killer, but . . .'

'You mean Arch's story. I saw it on the tube.'

Arch's story. Fuck Arch. 'When I get done, it's going to be *my* story. I get the idea that if I can just get on this while it's happening, if I can only take it apart . . .' He discovers he can't explain. 'Look, I've lined up interviews with the victim's family. A bunch of shrinks. New slant.'

'Like?'

OK, they are down to it. 'Like was there anything about this particular woman that. Ah. Brought it on.'

'You mean, like that she was a woman,' Sally says angrily. 'And probably smaller, like, couldn't fight back. You'd better the hell tell me you don't think this victim was asking for it.'

'No. It's.' Theo is blundering toward understanding. 'Something in her character that drew the guy, like level of vulnerability? Something she is, or does. Like, how do killers target them? Or is it random? Like, is she a born victim? Why her and not you or me?'

After a pause Sally says, 'I think you've found your book.'

So that piece of his life clicks into place. He thinks. 'Thanks. She's not the first. The New Haven cops are trying to link it with these killings in other states.'

'You mean Angola.'

'And Scranton. Albany. Yeah. If I get backstory on all the victims. If I can triangulate and get inside this killer's head . . .' He can hear her getting excited. 'It'll make the Zax murders look as cheap as roadkill. So I've focused.' His head lifts. He has.

'I'm so glad. I've been worried about you, T.'

Bullseye. 'No more than I've worried about you. Fucking

Vent.' He lies; no, it's the truth; no, it's a lie but a necessary lie. 'I was hoping she'd follow me.' He means he was hoping she'd die.

'Oh, the Vent.' In one careless phrase the woman he loves dismisses the woman who hangs like a traveling stormcloud over his life. 'That's nothing.' She rushes on. 'Come overnight.'

'I can't. Not until I've finished this.' He can't tell her that he means: not until we're safe.

'Oh, T. Oh hell, I can come there.'

'Not yet!' Theo is too quick. Without knowing why, he knows it really isn't safe. The red light on his phone is blinking. 'Can I call you back tonight? Call coming in on the other line.' He flicks her off for a minute. 'I'm on my way,' he tells Arch.

When he clicks her back into existence Sally's voice is soft, a little hurt. 'This is about the Vent, isn't it?' Because this is Sally, because they're so close that they know what the other is thinking, she says, 'If that's what's keeping you away, Theo, she's gone.'

It's like swallowing coarse sugar. Sweet grit in his throat. 'That's probably what she wants you to think. I show up and she springs out.' The knife. She may still have the knife.

'She left the Y, T. She took all her stuff. She stopped collecting her meds.'

'She could be watching you.' Grit in his throat and he can't swallow. It won't go down. 'She could be watching you now.'

The next question comes in like a flaming arrow. *Thock.* 'Theo, are you OK?'

Beg the question, Slate. 'I love you. Never better. Look, Arch is waiting. I've really gotta go.' He breaks off. This is terrible and painful. Stricken, he concedes everything that Sally suspects. 'I want to be with you but I have to finish this.'

Then Sally drops this into the air. 'It isn't just me. Some

guy's been asking after you. Says he's a member of the family.'

'Dad and I aren't speaking.'

'Younger. Claims you're related.'

'No cousins. I was an only child.'

'Theo, what are you eating?'

'Oh, sorry.' Theo has been nervously picking cold beans out of the congealed mass in the can and popping them into his mouth. 'Did he leave a name?'

'He said you'd know.'

This chills him. 'What did he look like?'

'Ordinary. Nice-looking guy.'

'What did he want?'

'He didn't say.' Sally pauses. 'Oh. And the Zax woman sent for you. 'S why I called. We got talking and I forgot.'

'I thought you called because you loved me.'

'That too.' There is the sound of Sally sorting through the papers on her desk. 'Chick fobbed her off on me. "You take it, you're a woman." Like he secretly thinks I'm hysterical too. Which is what she was. She wanted you.'

'Too late,' Theo says. Stella has sent for him. It's funny, what this makes him feel. It's like Mother's Day when he's expected to call his mom but forgot to call. He and Stella Zax are linked by some odd common bond of obligation that he has not yet identified. 'Too fucking late.'

'She has something to tell you. That she couldn't tell me. Wanted me to take it verbatim. OK, here it is.' Sally rattles the apposite piece of paper. 'She says, "Tell him I have something for him. Important." I don't know what it means, T., but it's another reason for you to come back.'

'As soon as I finish this.' This means so many things that he can't begin to explain it. 'I love you. Trust me. I've gotta go.' Then before he hangs up he says urgently, 'Be careful, love.'

56

Arch meets Theo in the parking lot outside the *Register*. There's nobody around. Cars whizz by on the Interstate in a blur of white sound. Still Arch says without moving his lips, 'Not here.'

Theo is cool with this. He hates being outside a newspaper where he so doesn't belong that he needs a damn pass to go inside. He only goes places where he belongs. 'Is there a problem?'

'No big mystery,' Arch says.

'You've got something you don't want the desk to know about.'

'Yeah. Like that.'

'Time value?'

'Yeah. No. Yeah.'

'So why me?'

'You OK with two cars?' Arch takes Interstate-95 across the bridge. When they get where they are going, he orders two beers and leads Theo to a back booth.

'So. What.'

Arch pushes a sheaf of photocopies across the sticky Formica. 'Take a look at this.'

Theo barely glances at the pile. He is watching Arch. 'Looks like somebody's high-school chemistry notes.'

'Hardly. Take a look.' Arch lights a cigarette, thinks twice and grinds it out. 'They impounded this stuff last fall. Neighbors reported weirdness in this boarding house on Fountain Street, somebody thumping around in the night, nothing in particular, odd stuff. Room was locked so the cops broke in and they found—'

'Where was the guy?'

'Out the window. And this is only part of what they found.'

'Shit,' Theo says, skimming. 'He wrote it all down ahead of time.'

'You got it. Last week's murder, down to burying the hands. Wrote it ahead of time. The problem is, how far ahead of time?'

'What?' Theo is fingering imperfect copies of some stranger's handwritten notes: careful diagrams and detailed schemes lined up under headings and subheads and set marching across the page like soldiers in an experimental war. The writer has set it all down in a spiky hand that peaks and sinks like the lines on a madman's polygraph. He looks up. 'This guy is crazy.'

'Pretty much,' Arch says. They are in the back booth of a neighborhood deadbeats' bar in East Haven, Arch's choice because nobody in here will care what they are doing here. 'It's for you.'

'Me?'

'You're writing the book. Plus.'

'Plus? What's plus?'

'It's all in there,' Arch says instead of answering.

'Use words.'

'You'll see. This guy, see. Lays it all out for you. What he was going to do. How he was going to do it. He even picked them out. Who.'

'Blueprint for crime.'

'Yeah.'

'This is hot!'

'Not exactly. Like I said, that's the problem.' Arch delivers the kicker. 'The cops have had this thing for months.'

'But he killed her last week.'

'Look at the date.'

It's dated months before. Theo does a slow take. He looks up. 'You're telling me they've had this all this time?'

'Bingo.'

'Why didn't they bust the guy?'

'On what grounds? Public nuisance? Disturbing the peace? Writing stuff that we have a hard time even reading? Until last week there wasn't any crime. Until last week the writer was clean.'

'This.' Theo taps the last page. The part about the head and the hands. 'This isn't clean. Don't tell me this is clean.'

But Arch picks up Theo's buzzword. 'Blueprinted, right down to describing the mark. And the cops didn't do a fucking thing.'

'They could have warned the woman.'

'They couldn't. They never figured out which woman.'

'They could have protected her. Put a man on the writer.'

'Like they have enough squad to guard anything. They wanted to surveill the writer but they lost track of him. Remember, until last week he was only a writer. They quit looking after thirty days. Nothing was happening anyway, the chief pegged the writer for a crank and back burnered the whole thing. Dumped the notebooks in a file drawer and forgot.' Arch has this squint as if he's trying to tell Theo something, but it's not clear what. 'I find it and they sit on my head.'

'There's more than one notebook?'

Arch nods. 'Source says they found something more. Marks all over the walls.'

'They followed up.'

Arch shakes his head. 'No. These guys will look like assholes if it gets out. Liability alone. The victim's family.'

'What a story.'

God Arch sounds tired. 'It's no good to me.'

Theo has a friend, visits a famous artist in an apartment off Lincoln Center. At a certain point the artist says, 'Want to see something special?' He goes to a closet and pulls down two round hatboxes, the old-fashioned kind. He lifts the lids. Inside, two human heads, tanned and cured. Stunned, Theo's friend says the only polite thing he can think of to say. 'Er. Where did you get these?' The artist tells him, 'Guy on 58th Street knows I'm interested.' Theo passes his hands over the secret notebook and asks in his friend's stunned tone, 'Where did you get these?'

'If you want to know the truth I'm fucking a girl in Records. I had to get her a better job at Fairfield before she would even think about leaking this.'

'But you got this bootleg copy. Why not run with it?'

'I can't use the damn thing unless I can figure out how to make the cops admit that they have it.'

'Unidentified leak.'

'They'll claim it's a forgery.'

'You can't authenticate?'

'Not and protect my source.' With an effort, Arch adds, 'Truth is, I'm kind of in love. I wouldn't do that to her.'

'Why me?'

'Bottom line?' The sigh that comes out of Arch is so long that the air around his head starts turning grey. 'Somebody tipped off the chief that the cat was out and I had it. He freaked and warned our publishers. Called the owner of the chain. If I go with the story the city will sue us for blowing the case.'

Theo is assessing. 'So you got this and you can't touch it.'

Arch acknowledges this with a nod. Then he pulls the Perlcorder out of his lap and sets it on the table. 'I hope you're cool with me taping this.'

'OK, Arch, what are you doing with me here?'

'I get even with them in your book. You're what's left, OK?'

Theo nods. It puts him in a novel position. Doing this favor for his friend Arch when they've only ever jockeyed for position at the starting gate. OK, they came up together. Even competition can be a bond. 'I'll give you a whole chapter,' Theo says.

Arch grins. 'Now look at this.' He fans dupes of glossies on the Formica like a full house in a poker game. 'This is his room.' He taps a photo that looks like the death card. 'Get a load of the walls.'

Again the reproduction is bad but the imperfect image makes Theo's scalp crawl. It's like looking into the belly of a rotting corpse. Lines go out of control; they come alive and writhe out of the frame. 'He did all this?'

'The writer. Yards and yards of this stuff all over the room. Walls. Ceiling. Magic Marker crawling onto the floor.'

For a second here Theo is like a kid in the front row at an action picture. No. He's like a kid *in* an action picture. *I have a plan.* 'Then all we have to do is go in there and take the details off the walls. You get your story. It's verified.'

'Forget it.'

'Man, if we're both there . . .'

'I said, forget it.'

'If nothing else we authenticate the book.'

'This is real, OK,' Arch says wearily. 'We both know it's real. That's not the problem.'

'No, man. It's the solution. You've proved your case. Hell, go ahead and write it. Look, your story isn't going to preempt my book.' Yes they are using each other; if Theo takes this copy of the killer's notes, Arch gets to tell his side in Theo's book. But why not more? Why not now? Theo says, 'We could even catch him. What if we check out the walls and the walls lead us to the guy?'

329

'Not a chance.'

'We've broken into places before,' Theo says.

Arch grins. 'But we don't admit it.'

Theo grins back. They are better than average friends. 'We don't admit it but we still can.'

'Too late. By the time the killer does the deed and the cops go back to the rooming house, the landlord's painted over the walls and moved some other sucker in.'

'Shit!' The trouble with Theo is the trouble with any good reporter. He never gives up. 'If they know the room, then they know who the writer is. Why don't they make the bust?'

'They can't find him, Slate.'

'Right.'

'Which is why I got you here. I got you here and you haven't looked at the book. I mean, you've looked at it but you haven't, really.' Arch is no longer smiling. He is at some point beyond serious. It has put ten years on him. He could be an old guy. He could be Theo's father saying, 'Now look at the fucking book.'

OK, maybe he has been backing off this or dancing around it. Maybe it's easier to paw through documents and write about done deals than it is to live with the raw history of murder unfolding, fresh deaths and unwilling victims whose fates are still uncertain. Maybe backstory is less of a personal threat than a killer's life that is still going on. Theo hunches his shoulders and begins to read. Time passes while he reads and Arch smokes. Minutes later, he looks up like a student making a stab at the right answer. The teacher is playing *guess what I'm thinking* and he doesn't know. 'He says if this doesn't go right, he's already lined up the next.'

'Exactly.'

'So. What. We're going to figure out who is the next?'

Arch's face twists into a funny expression. 'It isn't hard.'

'Who?'

'Asshole, it's in the book.'

Theo turns pages until finally Arch snatches the stack away and pulls one page. He shoves it into Theo's hands.

Arch rasps, 'Read it.'

Theo responds angrily, 'Fine. Is this going to be on the quiz?'

'Shut up and read.'

He reads aloud. 'One. Backup plan. *Line up number six*. a. Girl at the train station, new in town, paper sacks, she dropped her instrument case. I picked it up. – Oh, is this yours? – Oh thank you, she says. – What do you play? She has to decide whether to answer. Say, – Looks like a flute. That makes her smile. – It is a flute.' He stops. 'And?'

Arch says, 'See?'

He does but he doesn't. 'Not exactly.'

'Doesn't that sound like someone? Doesn't that sound like somebody you know?'

'I.' Theo wants to say, *don't get it*. He does. Bad feelings rush over him like the moon moving across the face of the sun. He hears his own words falling out, bla bla bla. 'What are you saying to me? What are you trying to tell me here?'

'Look at the goddamn fucking book.' Impatient, Arch grabs the page and reads in a harsh staccato.

'One. advantages

    A. Availability: Smaller than me. Alone. Never be missed.

    B. Looks: Unpeeled face.

    C. Asking for it.

Two. disadvantages

    A. Orange hair. Too conspicuous?'

Arch gives Theo a mean, hard look. 'That nail it for you, Slate? Does that nail it down for you?'

'I don't . . .'

'Flute. Orange hair. Now who does that sound like?'

'No way.' If Theo could back away from this he would back away but he's wedged deep in his corner of the booth.

'Way. Now do you get what we're doing here?'

'I appreciate it, Arch, but it can't be the Vent. The Vent is nowhere near New Haven. The woman is still looking for me in Center City. She's probably on the curb right now, out in front of the *Star*. Unless she got her head together and went back to Columbia.' He realizes as he says this that she could be anywhere.

Arch says patiently, 'So what I'm trying to tell you is what I'm trying to tell you.'

'The Vent.'

Arch nods. 'The Vent.' What he says next has been a long time coming but from the beginning it was inevitable. Like a cannon rolling down a hill it is big and heavy and slow but at a certain point it gathers momentum and comes right at him, smashing him in the midsection and sending him staggering. It threatens to flatten him.

'The Vent . . .' after too long Arch finishes, 'is here.'

'You're sure?'

'I saw her.'

'Where?'

'Outside the train station a couple of weeks ago.' Arch goes on apologetically, 'Man, I didn't want to tell you because I didn't think you needed to know, but now.'

'Now?'

'Look at the goddamn notebook. She's this bastard's next.'

'OK.' Theo is on his feet before he knows it, standing so fast that the table bashes his thighs. Wincing, he slides out of the booth with all his teeth showing; it's as if his face has been burned away to reveal the skull. It rushes out of him like wind in a firestorm. 'OK!'

'Wait a minute, where are you going?'

'Good question.' Abashed, he stands at the end of the booth.

'Whatever,' Arch says. 'If you want to bail on this, go ahead and bail. If you're out of here you're out of here, so fine. But leave me the fucking Xeroxes, OK?'

Theo is by no means running away. He just needs to go somewhere quiet so he can think. He drops the pages on the table. Then he picks them up. 'I'll call you.'

'Before you call me, you can pick up the fucking tab for these beers.'

'Sure.'

As Theo reaches for his wallet Arch says, 'One more thing.'

Theo stops. His hands jerk up in a gesture that would embarrass a white-faced mime. 'What?'

'The other reason you're here?'

'You've warned me, so thanks for warning me.' He turns to go.

Arch overrides his farewell. 'We got a call. Some guy claiming to be the perp.'

Theo stops. 'Confession?'

'Warning.'

'To the cops?'

'To us. Made this statement the *Register* was supposed to print. How he did it and he's glad. He's got some bug up his ass about bad press.'

'You're not going to tell me what the statement is.'

'Last week I wouldn't have told you.' Arch sighs a what-the-fuck sigh. 'But this call, the cops made us sit on it? Don't play to his ego, that crap. I thought you ought to know.'

'You're telling me, but you're not telling me.'

'About the plus. I told you there was a plus.' Arch clears his throat. 'This is the plus.'

'Right. The plus. I thought the Vent in New Haven was the plus.'

'No. It's about the writer. He left this threat.' They are at dead level now. Beyond rivalry and beyond pretense. Arch waits until Theo slides back into the booth and then in a gesture so touching that it surprises both of them he puts his hands on top of Theo's clenched fists and holds them there until the fingers uncurl and the hands flatten out. Then Arch looks at him dead-on with eyes as direct as a little kid's. 'It's this. Run this statement by Friday or he hits the switch and does the backup plan.'

'Shit, what are you going to do?'

'He meant last Friday,' Arch says.

'You mean they sat on the damn thing?'

Arch nods. 'So we don't play his game on this murder, he moves on his threat. He does another one. The next.'

Theo's inner walls are shaking; he can feel his balls shudder and shrink. In another second the quake is going to rend tissue and explode his vital organs and crack all his surfaces and bring the whole structure down. 'The Vent.'

Now that he has brought Theo where he has been leading him, Arch leans back. They are almost finished. 'So this is the plus, that I brought you here to talk about. He's getting fixed to kill her and he's going to do it soon.'

57

They are in none of the usual spots. Arch is a good friend after all. He followed Theo out of the bar and shoveled him into his car and made him ride to the nearest place where he could walk it off. They are going along the coarse, rocky fringe of beach at Lighthouse Point. The sky is no color at all. The Sound looks cold and miserable. The merry-go-round is closed. Theo keeps glancing over his shoulder; whether or not he knows it, his body has dropped into an anxious, defensive slouch.

They both know he is wrestling with a dilemma.

They both know he can't talk about it yet.

'You're sure it was her.'

'The dye job doesn't look so good right now.'

Theo says, 'So you really saw her.'

'I did.'

'And it was really her.'

'What do you think?'

'At the train station? What were you doing at the station?'

'If you want to know the truth I went to the city for an interview.'

This is a measure of Theo's distraction. He doesn't even say *Interview? Where?* 'Was she going in or coming out?'

'What do you think, Slate?'

A rock tips under Theo's foot and he lurches, off-balance. 'I thought she might be leaving town.'

'Why would she be leaving town when she just got to town?'

He hates tripping; angrily, he rights himself. 'What the hell is she doing in New Haven?'

'She came back, I guess.'

'Back?'

Arch gives him a look that passes for incredulous. 'You didn't know? She never made it to New York last September. She got off the bus here.'

'Why would she want to get off the bus here?'

'She said New York was too big for her.'

'How do you know?'

Arch goes on, 'She said she couldn't handle graduate school.'

'What, she sent you a post card?'

'If you want to know the truth, she did.' He says carelessly, 'You weren't her only crush. Just the worst one.'

'And you didn't tell me.'

'I didn't think you needed to know.' Arch adds, 'I figured you didn't want to know she sent you her love.'

Theo is looking for a safe place to regroup. He takes Arch over the jumps. 'So you saw her in the station. Did she see you?'

'Not really. Sort of. She saw me but she didn't recognize me.'

'Does she know I'm here?'

'I'm not sure she knows much of anything.' Arch goes on in a level, break-it-gently tone. 'Truth is, the girl looked kind of zonked. You know the flute?'

'The flute.'

'Yeah, the flute. She was kind of sitting on the curbstone playing that fucking flute.'

'Oh shit.' So they are approaching the point Theo is in no way prepared to reach. His teeth clamp so tight that all the cords in his neck twang. 'Where do you think she is now?'

'Don't ask me.'

Theo snaps, 'You saw the damn woman, you should know.' He would like to think the Vent is socked into the local Y or playing student impostor in the front row of some Yale classroom or that she's come back to New Haven because she's forgotten him. Or to pick up a few things. She could be getting on that train right now. She could be on the train for Manhattan and Columbia where she was, for God's sake, admitted with tuition prepaid. Plus fees. 'I'm sorry. Why should you know where she is?'

'Fuck,' says Arch. 'That's the fuck of it. I do know. She's living in this colony out by the dump.'

Theo sits down. Thud. On his butt in cold sand with stones biting the seat of his jeans. He locks his arms around his knees and looks out at the Sound. What he says when he finds himself able to say something is. Ah. What he says is the obvious. 'So we've got to find her before he does.'

'You got it.'

But his mind is running ahead, looking for other solutions. 'Unless we can catch him.'

Arch squats next to him. 'You mean you, white man.'

'I'm sorry?'

'You.'

Theo whips his head around so they are face to face. 'Wait.'

Arch's irises are shrinking; picture of a friend backing off like a DC7 backing away from the gate. Receding, he says like Marley's ghost, 'One last thing.'

'Wait a minute,' Theo says angrily, 'I thought you got me out here so we could.'

Arch is shaking his head. 'Not we. You. Look, guy. I should have told you and I'm sorry I didn't tell you. The last thing I did before I came out to meet you today was quit.'

'You what?'

'You heard me. The *Register*. They kill my story. I tell

337

them to stuff it. I'm out of here for LA.' Arch checks his watch. 'From Tweed-New Haven in about a half-hour.'

'We came to East Haven because you're going to the fucking airport?'

'Not really.' Arch grins. 'OK. Yeah.'

'And all this with me?'

'Slate, it had to be you. So this, with the Vent? And the notebooks, at least this particular fucking notebook,' Arch says and then he ducks into his canvas shoulder bag as if he's trying to hide his head. He pulls out the blurred photocopy of the notebook and the smeared-looking black and white glossies and tries to foist them on his friend, saying, 'This is all yours.'

'Oh no you don't.' Theo pushes them away.

'Yours,' Arch says.

Theo keeps refusing the packet. 'In hell.'

But Arch won't quit. So they shove the material back and forth in a little wrestling match until pages start getting away. Feeling the tug of the damp spring breeze, Arch releases his hold; if Theo lets go now the whole thing is going to be taken by the wind and so he clamps the mess under his left elbow and makes a lunge for the lost pages, locked into commitment after all. Arch sits back, breathing heavily, and lets him do it.

'OK,' Theo says, exhausted. Accepting it. 'OK.'

58

S he is in an awful place.
   At first he isn't sure it's her.

Then he is.

She is living in a box. Never mind how he got to this point. The geography flew out of control and the stinking rubble kept shifting underfoot as if rotting corpses were struggling to rise. It's phenomenal that he's found her in this warren. He only found her because she was sitting outside. He found her at the end of the first avenue. She was sitting in front of her place. Even though the sky is grey and the air above the encampment is thick with smoke from the incinerator, the Vent is sitting out in front of her arrangement of garbage bags and wardrobe cartons with MAYFLOWER printed across the sides; *We move you coast to coast.* She sits in the cold with her head uncovered and her feet bare. The orange curls are matted now, aggressively colored up to the highwatermark where the dye job quit, probably when Delia Vent got out of the state hospital, which may be where she got the regulation blanket she is wearing like a cloak. The hands showing below the fringe of the blanket look raw from exposure.

Theo's heart hits bottom. She is holding the flute. What he wants collides with what he has to do. He has to force himself to use her name. 'Delia.'

When she does not respond he approaches cautiously, like a demolitions expert circling a live bomb. There are sounds in the heaped debris that surrounds them. He pats his pocket. *Do you really think you can defend yourself with a Swiss Army knife?* But he can't afford to think about what may be happening behind him or what might be sneaking up on them. He has to do this. He is close enough to fan his fingers in front of her face. Still the Vent does not look up. Then she does, and everything inside Theo dies. She's going to latch on to him with that look and it will start all over again.

He says in a low voice, 'Ms Vent.'

She doesn't hear. The Vent looks right at him and does not see. As if she is alone here, she slides the flute to her chapped lips and begins to play. Over the flute-sound Theo hears something moving in the heaped trash and he thinks for a crazed moment that it's all the rats of New Haven coming out to listen. Another part of the forest, he thinks crazily. *The Magic Flute.*

Magic was never here.

They are at the end of a bare space in a makeshift colony that looks like the mother ship in *The Night of the Living Dead*. The little city has accreted in an area where New Haven's discarded junk has escaped the Department of Public Works and slipped out of control. There is no way of telling what's trash and what's somebody's squat. Except for the Vent the colony seems almost deserted, maybe because it's still cold and the regulars have better places to crash. Above the makeshift shelters the city's garbage mountain looms like a 90s Hanging Garden of Babylon. Theo sees massive trucks crawling around the huge plateau on a road that spirals to the top, where bulldozers level each new load of the city's grot and corruption while gulls circle and collect like flies. Everything cast off by the city ends here, compressed and neatly tamped down, unless it's rendered in the nearby processing plant that makes daily transformations under the emblem: SCHIAVONE, ALCHEMISTS. The garbage mountain is a wonder of nature, manmade ziggurat denser than earth. Soon it will be higher than East Rock.

Elements Theo can't see are moving through hidden spaces, as if toward convergence here. Predators? Gangs? He doesn't know. Their situation is urgent. *Get this woman out of here.* 'Hey?' He wiggles his hand in front of her face like a diagnostician asking how many fingers. 'Hello?'

She does not respond. The music doesn't stop. God, Theo thinks. This is so sinister. She could just as easily leap up and jam that thing into my eye. But she doesn't. She just plays on. Listening, he backs off a little and considers the woman as if for the first time. She's been so huge in his head that the reality is pathetic. It was the ugly obsession that made her seem huge. Now she just looks little and harmless and sad. And yeah, Arch is right. Zonked out of her mind. Get close enough to look into her irises and he'll see pinwheels spiraling into nothing.

It was hard to get this far. It's hard doing this. He came for a reason. He has to get her attention. He barks, 'Ms Vent.'

She plays and plays.

Now he is pleading with her. 'What do you want from me?' The Vent. When it got bad he tried to turn her into an object. Anything to make it easier to deal with. An impersonal force. The Vent. But she is a person. A small shabby woman sitting in this blasted landscape making music like a helpless, crazy girl. How is he going to move her? He tries her first name. 'Delia?' Out here in the dump, it creates a bizarre intimacy. Like a whispered offer of love. 'Delia?'

She may not hear. Mozart. She is playing Mozart. Her round, clear eyes aren't focused on him. They are fixed on something beyond him or nothing like him. They are fixed on something he will never see.

He speaks as if to a sane person. 'Look, Delia, we have to get you out of here.'

The tune comes to an end. She draws a little breath. Then she lifts the flute again.

341

'Delia, it's me, Theo. Theo Slate?' Oh shit is he going to have to squat down to get her attention? Is he going to have to take her by the shoulders and shake her awake?

She begins another eighteenth-century tune, tinkling score for those movies about women in long dresses and men wearing satin coats with lace hanging out of the cuffs. So pretty. So at war with here. It is a marvel to observe, how long a string of notes Delia can sustain before she has to draw a breath. How cleverly she breathes without breaking the song. In another context she might seem happy. In this one, there's no way to know. Squatting, Theo tries to catch her eye. It's not his fault he's afraid she'll come to herself and hug him and say, 'I knew you'd come.' And latch on. The flute does not quite drown out the background sound of rats running, of other living things stirring in the debris. At his back larger shadows are moving – the living dead, he supposes, bumping into each other out there, seeing him, OK, seeing him and – look, if somebody hits Slate on the head and takes his money he won't have to do this, so, chill.

'Look, I don't know how to say this, but.'

Madrigal. The new tune could be a madrigal. It sounds like music that conservatory students sing. So pretty. For filthy, zonked-out Delia now, music passes for speech. If she perceives the need to speak. The tune goes on.

Theo goes on. 'Listen. You're in danger, OK? Delia, you're in real danger here.'

Sitting crosslegged in her little cocoon, she just keeps playing. Speechless. Placid, as if her flute is the strongest drug.

'Shit, Delia. You have to get up now. We have to go.'

Nothing.

'You can't stay here.'

What does she care where she stays?

'It isn't safe.'

Safe? What is safe to her?

He trails the offer like bait. 'Just come with me, OK? I'll take you to my house? Get up. Come on.'

But the fires in her head are out. It is as if Theo isn't here.

So he has to touch the woman after all. All the grief she has caused him, she's cost him his life and he has to touch her anyway. He has to get her up and take her home with him. He puts his hand on her arm and then flinches like the demolitions expert who's gotten overconfident. Yes he's afraid this bomb will go off. When she does not respond he takes her by the elbow. His voice is harsher than he intended. 'Come on. Get up. Will you get up for me?'

She pulls away.

God! How is he supposed to explain that the killer's clock is ticking when he can't even get her to stand up? When is he going to kill her? Is he going to kill her soon? He doesn't know. All he knows is that the next victim is here and he has been made responsible and he has to do this. He says what he never expected to say to her. Even though he can't tell if she even knows he's here. Bending close so she will have to hear, he catches a flash of gold at her neck: something on a chain. It is a Phi Beta Kappa key. So he says for the sake of that long-lost student, 'Please?'

She stirs but does not speak.

Theo can't wait for her to not answer. He tries to turn her. He has to catch her under the armpits so he can hoist her to her feet. The blanket falls and he lets go because the smell is intense when did this woman wash last, knew it was bad but never thought it was this bad, the woman who ruined his life is deaf dumb and blind out of mind and her life is his responsibility so he tightens his hold and struggles to get her to her feet strange passive woman in one of her old rayon dresses not warm enough for this and bulky because underneath she has layered other clothes she owns oh God this is so awful her going limp under his hands arms all lopsy the heavy dead weight like a bag of

343

dirt shapeless and leaden as if everything in her is pulling her downward back into the earth. Then she comes partway back into herself and tries to put the flute back in her mouth just as he gets her to her feet. The flute bumps her teeth and she grunts in pain, jolting into awareness.

Theo says reflexively, 'Oh I'm sorry.' He says it for both of them. 'I am so sorry.'

And now for the first time sound comes out of her. 'O.'

'Yes,' he says. 'Delia,' he says. 'OK. We have to go.'

She drops the flute.

He tries to turn her. 'Delia, are you in there?'

A part of her comes to life. 'O.' Then she makes another 'O' and with a savage look, throws her whole weight away from him.

'Don't do that. We have to go.'

A low sound comes out of her. It could be a no.

'Please. You're not safe here.'

'Nnnn.' Yes she is fighting, but the way a stone would fight. Power through inertia.

'Delia, please come on.' She isn't coming. He is desperate. It's like trying to move East Rock. He jerks her hard enough to hurt. 'Come on. I'm trying to save your goddamn life.'

That same wordless sound keeps coming out of her. 'O!'

This is ironic. Theo hears himself saying, 'I'm not going to hurt you, OK?' Wondering as he does so where she hides the knife. She is in an odd state suspended somewhere between here and there. She is greasy with sweat. The skin on his flanks begins to crawl.

'Ooo . . .' The sound is endlessly threatening. 'Ooooooo . . .'

'Don't.' She is outside reason. She is dangerous. He can't be here.

'Ooooo.' What weapon DeliaMarie Vent has or does not have is not the issue here. It's not even a question of what

344

she intends. She intends nothing. What comes out of her now comes from so deep that there is no identifying it. It is the sound of a stone you tortured into speech. It comes out as one long vowel sound, uninflected and loud enough to alert everybody in the colony, loud enough to reach the drivers on the garbage mountain and the workers at Schiavone's incinerators and early birdwatchers on East Rock. She howls to summon the damned. '*Ooooooooooooooooooooooo* . . .'

'Just don't, OK?'

And they come. In the next second Theo is surrounded. The Living Dead come out of wherever they've been hiding. They are shambling forward like zombies to protect and defend one of their own. Nothing is said. Nothing passes between them. Threatened, terrified, Theo lets go of the girl. Like a catatonic, she sinks to the ground and hugs her knees. She is not playing the flute now, she is only rocking on her haunches, howling, '*Ooooooooooooooooooo* . . .'

Around Theo, the living dead lift their shaggy heads and consider him. Nothing is said. No threats are made. He offers no explanation. These look like gentle people but any one of them could be . . . Who? Could be carrying . . . What? He clenches his jaw and with an effort, stays steady even though his belly creeps and all the blood deserts his face. He steps back. He back pedals deliberately, as if backing out of a faceoff with a Rottweiler. Slow step by slow step. He backs around the corner of this particular avenue in junk city, aware at every step that he may be backing into something worse. But when he turns, the way out is clear. Free of the place, he does what you do. He runs.

By the time he comes back with police, she's gone.

The officers look at him and then at the heap of cartons. 'So, your, er. Friend. If she was here, it would appear she isn't here. What did you say you want with her?'

He is not about to tell them what he knows. 'I want to get her out of here.'

The young officer says, 'Sir, if they don't want to be out of here, you can't get them out of here.'

The fat officer says, 'What do you want her out of here for?'

For a minute, Theo considers telling him. But the contraband notebook is locked in his car and his inner sentry warns: *They could put you in jail for that.* 'She owes me some money,' he says.

The young one says, 'You got us out here for that?'

The fat one says, 'You want to file a complaint?'

'She isn't safe.'

'Shit, nobody's safe. You said this was an emergency.'

'It is. Look. The bitemark murder, I—'

The fat one says, 'Nobody said it was a bitemark murder.'

The young one says, 'You got something pertaining to the bitemark murder?'

Theo shakes his head. 'Er. I just heard you had a lead on the case. Like, maybe the killer is hiding out here?'

The fat one squints at him. 'You a reporter?'

'Not any more. I just.'

The fat one says, 'Then what about it?'

'Sir?'

'The bitemark murder. What's this about a bitemark murder?'

'Nothing.' Theo shakes his head. 'OK. This woman I'm looking for. I just thought she might not be safe.'

'What do you mean, safe? You think this is safe?'

'I just meant, with him out there.'

The fat one says, 'How do you know he's out here?'

'I don't.'

The young one says, 'Come on, Bart. He's wasting our time.'

'Give me a minute here.' He turns on Theo. Forty-five degrees out and sweat is rolling into the pockmarks on the fat policeman's face. 'This woman you're looking for out here. How long has she been out here?'

'Off and on since last fall.'

'And you're looking for her now?'

'Something came up.'

'All this time she's been out here and you're not worried about her, and now you're worried about her? What is it with you?'

The young one says, 'Forget it, Bart. Let's go.'

'So. You trying to tell us something we don't know?'

Theo begins. 'No. I'm just trying to find her is all.'

'Maybe you'd like to come in with us for a little talk.'

'I thought your job was to protect—'

'Don't give me that crap.'

'If you mean you,' the young one says, 'we did what we could for you.'

And all the time Theo and the cops are talking there is someone stirring in the litter that stands mounded and tossed and stacked in heaps higher than their heads. Stuff so dense that it will never be separated. If someone is watching him it could be from anywhere. It could be anyone.

'Look, I.' Theo doesn't know how to finish the sentence. These jerks probably haven't been told that the killer has fingered a fresh victim. They probably don't know he's going to kill her soon. 'I'm sorry,' he says, turning to go. 'I'm sorry I bothered you.'

When Theo leaves, the watcher leaves.

The watcher will get to Theo's place ahead of him. He will do what he came to do and he will be stationed outside the apartment building when Theo gets back after stopping at a fast food place and ordering a dinner he does not eat. The watcher will stay in place as Theo parks his car and gets out and goes inside, and if he sees Theo is carrying a brown envelope, it will be nothing to him. He will count the steps as Theo lets himself in and goes upstairs. Standing outside in the approaching night he will see the light go on in Theo's room. And he knows what Theo will see.

It's about his room. Someone has been here. He can see it at once. It is terrifyingly still. Someone has been here but instead of trashing the place, the vandal has done worse violence to his arrangements.

Theo whirls and smacks the wall. 'Bastard. Who are you?'

He has straightened the place up. Whoever it is has destroyed weeks of work. All Theo's books are lined up in neat stacks like grave markers in a cemetery yet to be designed. Someone has pulled out all his place markers and crumpled them up and thrown them into the trash so the edges of the books will be neat. Notes taken on ticket stubs and scrawled on envelopes and scraps of letterhead have been destroyed as trash. All his photos are stacked on the table with the corners squared. Somebody has weighted them with a jelly jar. The tearsheets and Xeroxes have been stuffed into envelopes willy-nilly, anything to get them off the floor and out of sight. The envelopes are sitting next to the photos. The place is terrifyingly neat and still.

And on the door of the pocket refrigerator in Magic Marker, there is a note.

I WARNED YOU ABOUT GLAD. THREE DAYS.

At least it relieves him of decisions. He knows what to do next. He has to see Stella Zax.

59

DeliaMarie Vent

– Oh here, someone says. – Let me help you. You fell.

Fell? Fall? What fall? What kind of fall did she and who is this, warm voice in her ear and where is she? Lying where she, what is it where she fell. Down, she is lying down. She is lying down in another part of the place where whatever happened to her happened yes happened, I saw him, did I? When she wants, she wants so much that sometimes she can see what she wants coming toward her, lover, vision or what? Oh God it was wonderful she thinks he was here or was it all in my mind, no. I heard him yes I think he spoke it was so nearly beautiful him there that voice everything I ever wanted and I was . . . inside I talked my heart out but he didn't hear me trapped inside no noise came out nothing came out of me for too long and then he was gone. It's lost! She is sobbing for the last good thing she had. It is her instrument. She has lost her flute!

Other hands on her but not there or *there* but hands on her that voice she knows he is speaking – Don't be afraid.

But! Rolling so she won't see what she already knows it isn't him – but this one, maybe she should be afraid of him but death wraps her like a warm quilt swaddles her arms and clogs her throat so she won't even say what bubbles in her throat like something bad you ate keep your back to him even though you can't say it he knows what you are thinking – You're not him.

But he is lying next to her in the spot where she fell and she won't struggle no point he rolls her so they are facing.
– Sit up.
  – Oh, it's you.
  – Drink this.
She drinks.
  – Now come with me.

60

Theo is in the only place he can think to go doing the only thing he can think to do. He stands before Stella Zax. 'I'm here.'

'Thank God.'

She has shrunk since he last saw her. She has gone beyond old into some new state that he hopes he will never reach. Whatever she has been through to bring them to this meeting, it has cost her. He reaches out and takes her hands. 'You sent for me.'

'Oh, son. Son!' She smiles that transparent mother's smile.

I am not your. He doesn't even start. He is her son now and it's OK. He gives her a long, steady look. 'If there's something you want me to do, I need to know how to do it.'

'I'm sorry I took so long. I had to get back my strength.'

'You look.' He can't tell her the truth. 'Good.'

'I've been so worried about you.'

'I'm here, I'm fine.'

'I'm so glad.' Stella's once heavy, impassive face is changing before his eyes. The flesh that masked expression has fallen away; her soul is showing through. Her eyes shine with light from a hidden source and she astounds him with a lovely smile. 'I love you.'

He's glad nobody else hears the response this shakes loose – one of those involuntary reactions of the soul. Theo: 'I love you.'

She tightens her fingers on his in a warm grip. 'I didn't know who else to tell.'

They are beyond the need to explain themselves. He says, 'You know where he is.'

'I'm not sure.' Stella Zax has come back to herself in some dimension. Or she has come back as far as the injections will allow. She is stronger now. She made herself strong enough to summon the reporter. Now she needs to be smart enough to talk to him. 'I don't know. I don't even know who he is. He came. He was so harsh! He hurt me and he went away. He kept sending me things. He came again.' She hesitates, considering. 'Then he called.'

Gently, Theo prods. 'Was it about the murder in New Haven?'

'Oh God. Oh, God.' It is hard for her to bring the words up but she manages, in a voice clotted with pain. 'The first time he came, he told me I was his mother. When he came back he told me terrible things. He told me he was going to do it and that I couldn't stop it. I couldn't do anything. My own son and I couldn't even . . .'

Theo says in a low voice, 'You mean Preston?'

'No!' Beneath the surface of Stella's face confusion billows like mud stirred up in still water. 'The new one.'

Alert, Theo prompts. 'New?'

'You know.' She is impatient with the words for not coming; she is impatient with herself for not finding the truth; she is impatient with the message she is carrying, that she can't seem to bring to him. She shakes away tears. 'Oh, son, it'll come back to me. You know!'

'Yes ma'am.'

'Wait, I know. This is important. He told me . . . He told me . . .' It seems to return in increments, bits of knowledge sliding into place like the last squares in a Rubik's cube. Stella says clearly, 'He wants to hurt you.'

'I know.'

'He wants to hurt you and . . .' This has been hard on

her. Her own sad murder committed out of love has been compounded by this fresh one and weighted exponentially by murders done and murders threatened and murders to come. Fresh murders done in her name. 'And he told me . . . I don't remember. Oh God, how could I not remember? This *stuff* they're giving me.' Stella bows her head.

'Don't cry.'

'The meds,' she says hopelessly. 'They're erasing my mind.'

'It's OK.' To Theo's astonishment he puts his arms around her. 'It's OK.'

Outside in the hall the matron becomes aware of movement and looks through the glass square in the door to the room where the little encounter is taking place. She arranged this meeting under orders from the warden. Urgent business, Theo's request. Special favor to the owners of the *Star*. She shrugs and leans against the wall. You never know what transactions you are going to see completed in these places. You never know.

Stella snuffles and straightens her shoulders. She steps away. 'Thank you. So,' she says, as if she's told Theo everything and they are finished here. Dazed, she is blinking rapidly, looking this way, that, as if somebody just sneaked up behind her and yelled into her ear. Disoriented as she is, she remembers the civilities and tries for another smile. 'How are you?'

'Can you tell me anything about him,' Theo says.

'Son?'

'The one who came.'

'Oh no,' she says, shaking her head. 'The meds. Nothing you ever want to take. I couldn't even think when he was here. Hard to remember anything.' She rattles her head, as if trying to get water out of her ears so she can hear him properly. She whispers, 'I've been spitting out my pills. And the shots? I'm fine now,' she says. 'At least I think so. Now that they've changed my meds.'

'Meds?'

'What they give you in these places, when they think you're going – you know.'

'Are you?'

'No. The new doctor changed my meds so I can testify at my trial.'

'I see.'

'This is important.'

'I know.'

Something is shimmering in the air between them. Everything Stella Zax has to tell Theo that she's never been able to say. This strong, sad, diminished woman who has committed murder knows all about murder. Diagnosis and cure. She can tell him what she has done and what the writer of the notebooks has done and she may be able to tell him what's going to happen next. Theo has the idea that this woman holds the answer to everything cupped in her hands and in another second she will hand it over to him. Whole. Everything Stella can't say wells up in her; she inflates slightly and then everything she knows goes out of her in a sigh without words.

'If you can just tell me,' he says in a low voice, 'you never explained what you want from me.'

She tries for a smile and misses. Instead of responding she says in a bright, shaky little voice, 'So I guess that's all.'

'Oh Mrs Zax,' Theo says. 'Oh, Mrs Zax.' Then when it's clear that Stella can't think of one more word to say he touches her arm and reminds her, 'You called me at the paper.' He speaks softly, as if to a terminal patient in the final hour. 'You said you had a present for me.'

'A present?' Pondering, she runs her fingers through what's left of her hair. 'Present . . .'

'Yes ma'am. Unless it was a message.'

'Oh please call me Stella.'

'Stella.'

'Unless you want to call me Mom.'

'I can't.'

'That's all right,' she says. 'That's all right, dear.'

She is drifting. Theo reminds her gently, trying to pull her back. 'You called me, at the paper?'

Loving and anxious to please, Stella repeats, 'I called you at the newspaper.'

'Yes, you did. I would have come sooner but I was in New Haven. Something terrible has—'

She raises one hand. 'Don't. Thursday. Too long ago. I wanted you to come!'

'I'm sorry, I was trying to help someone.'

'It's all right,' she says. Her gaze is dissolving into inattention. 'It didn't come until yesterday.'

'What didn't come?'

'Something. Something he sent me.' Struggling through the clouds that stifle her, Stella says, 'I'm not sure.'

They are nowhere. Theo prods. 'You said you had a present. For me.'

'Did I?'

'Unless it was a message.' At his back the bomb is ticking. Three days. The bastard's note: THREE DAYS. He is down to two. 'And now I'm here.'

'A message.' Stella brightens. She remembers! 'Yes. That was it.' She smiles that intolerably lovely smile. 'Yes. I do. I do have it. It's a present for you. Excuse me a minute.' She turns away. She is fishing in the front of her prison coverall. She pulls an envelope out of her bra. When she hands it to him, it's still warm. 'He sent this. It's for you.'

'You're sure?'

'On the phone he told me he would send it. That's why I called you. It didn't come until yesterday.' She frowns, perplexed. 'I guess he forgot to put in the letter, but here's the envelope.'

'Thank you,' Theo says.

'I'm sorry there isn't more.'

'You did fine.'

'No letter.'

He holds the envelope up to the light to be sure there's nothing inside. There is, of course. There is something but not anything a drugged prisoner in the women's wing of County would think to look for, or note. Working gently, to make sure he doesn't disturb any of the contents, he parts it and looks in. He counts what look like three black pubic hairs. He looks up. 'So this is it.'

Stella is already backing away in apology. 'I'm sorry it isn't more.'

Pubic hairs. He does not want to know whose. 'Oh ma'am, ma'am.'

'Mom.'

Yes, if it will make you happy. 'Mom, if this is all you've got for me I'm still glad you called.' He moves forward as if to give her a hug.

But with a smile like a mother on a birthday delaying the delivery of the big present, Stella Zax shakes her head. 'What's inside is lost.' She brightens. 'But now you have his fingerprints.'

He turns it over. The envelope itself is brittle with age, and stained as if it had been lying abandoned somewhere for longer than Theo's been alive. The postmark is new but hopelessly blurred. Stella Zax is waiting for him to say thanks so he says, 'Thanks.'

'I hope it helps.'

'Yes ma'am.'

'Maybe the FBI.'

The envelope is beyond hope. 'We'll see.' It's too late for the rubber gloves, the Ziploc bag. This thing has been riding next to Stella's wasting flesh for so long that any fingerprints are beyond retrieval. The postmark is illegible. What's important about this gift is not what Stella thinks. He turns it back for a second look at the front. Recognition makes him shudder.

Distressed, she blinks. 'Is something the matter?'

The writer has addressed the envelope by hand, carefully putting down Stella's name and the particulars in that spiky handwriting Theo knows from the notebooks. It's him. Whoever he is. Quickly, he reassures her. 'No, it's fine.'

'I hope it's enough.'

He looks up. 'Everything is fine.' It is. This is a business envelope. The firm's name and return address are on the flap in maroon Engravatone, that raised lettering that passes for engraving among people who don't know. So this is Stella Zax's real gift to him, that she may be too destroyed to know that she is giving him.

THE EDWARD MALLEY COMPANY
Church Street at Frontage Road
New Haven, Conn.

It's the motherfucker's home address. A store. He is living in some big store.

Stella Zax is looking at him with love. 'I wish I had more.'

'Oh ma'am, ma'am.' This woman said what she said to him all those months ago and set him about an unspecified mission; Theo has spent his life since then finding out what; he has survived a stalking and blundered into grisly, scarifying material and walked into places he would never have gone and he has done all this in the understanding that Stella Zax did have a job for him, and in time its parameters would come clear but now, he sees, she is just a huge, sad, loving lady who feels bad about what she did and to his surprise he finds that this doesn't matter. If she has turned him from looking for nothing toward working toward something, then she has done enough. 'This is plenty,' he says.

'I would like to give you more. I'd like to give you everything.'

'Oh, ma'am.' Correcting himself, he hugs her. 'Oh, Mom!'

'Thank you.'

He came here to find out what was expected of him and she couldn't say. It doesn't matter. Theo is changed. Things have changed and now he knows. Directed now, rushed and certain he knows where the killer is, Theo kisses her and goes.

61

Yeah use your plastic on one of the airline slot phones, just need to hear Sally's voice. *Guess where I'm calling from.* 'I love you. It's me.'

'Where are you?'

'Heading into Tweed. I'm on a plane.'

Worry puts an edge on her voice. 'Where *were* you?'

'County.'

'Could you talk a little louder? I said, where were you?'

'I was up at County.'

'You mean *our* County? You were at our county jail and you didn't come down to see me?'

'I couldn't.' He is trying to decide how much to tell her. 'Time pressure.'

Deprived, she cries, 'Oh, T.'

'I know. It's killing me too.'

'You were . . .' She is waiting for him to fill in the rest of the sentence.

This is costing a buck a minute and he can't. 'Stella Zax.'

'I just wish . . .'

'We will.' For the first time since he left New Haven he is able to promise, 'When this is done, we'll have nothing but time.'

'When what's done, T?'

'It's hard to explain. Bear with me?'

'Of course.' He can hear her smile. 'But you haven't told me what you've got.'

'Don't know, exactly. A kind of a message.'

'From?'

He doesn't answer. 'It wasn't much of a message. All she had was an envelope with three pubic hairs.'

'Was there a note?'

'Nothing. Just three pubic hairs.' Cradling the phone, he pulls out the envelope.

'The killing in New Haven.'

'I'm sure it's a match.' Theo's voice comes out of a place he doesn't recognize. 'I think I know where he is.'

'Oh God,' Sally says. 'Whatever you're thinking, don't.'

'It's no big deal, I don't think.' He reads her the address on the flap. 'Some downtown department store.'

'Don't go alone.'

'I have to.' He doesn't know whether this is Theo Slate reporter talking or another Theo that he is just now getting to know.

'Call the police.'

'I can't. I'm on a plane.'

So she catches him. 'And you are . . .'

Talking on the phone. 'Right. OK, then. I won't, OK? It's kind of about Arch.' It's about Arch but he knows there's more to it; it may be that he is honoring Stella's charge to him. 'I'll be fine, I just have to do this. I love you and I'll get back to you.'

'This isn't a movie, Theo. Call the police.'

'It's a store, Sal. It's perfectly safe.'

'Don't do anything until I get there.'

'You're not coming,' he says.

'You're not going alone.'

'I don't . . .'

How quick Sally is, good friend as well as lover, teasing. 'You don't want me to get the story before you do?'

'*I love you!*' Anxiety makes him shout. 'I don't want you to be anywhere that he is.'

'Anyplace that *who* is?'

'I don't know,' Theo says.

The flight attendant's voice is a tinny intrusion. 'All electronic equipment must be turned off.'

In a weird way, he does know. *He knows me. I am going to know him.* Brisk and urgent, Sally is beginning another question he can't answer; the plane has begun its descent. 'Now stay put. Gotta go.'

Sally's signal is breaking up. He thinks she says, 'I'll see you soon.'

Theo shouts, 'For God's sake, stay put.' The flight attendant is heading his way. Around him, people shift uneasily and stare.

'. . . your tray tables to an upright position.'

'I just hung up,' he tells the uniformed woman who is bearing down on him with the glare of an outraged nurse. 'Sorry if I interfered with your landing. I . . .'

As it turns out, they don't land. Freak storm, air traffic confusion, plane rerouted to Hartford where it sits on the ground for an hour. Theo could run from Hartford to Tweed in the time it takes to get back to his car. By the time he takes I-95 to Frontage Road all his synapses are jangling, popping and misfiring; everything in him strains forward. He is like a runner stalled at the post, crazy to begin and at the same time terrified.

I WILL SHOW YOU GLAD.

The department store sits on the corner of Church Street and Frontage Road. It can't be that dangerous. Big store, customers, clerks around. If this is where the killer wants to meet him, fine. What does he, want to give himself up in front of an audience? Yes Theo is writing the lead in his head. Adrenaline will keep him going even after he sees the place. He imagined his problem was locating the killer – a geek in the office or behind a counter or selling women tight shoes that they don't want, run your finger along her arch and mark her for death. All he has to do is go in, he thinks. The problem then will be reading the crowd.

Glancing in the rearview mirror, he speaks aloud. 'Does it show in your face?'

Big store, people around. But the Edward Malley Company is closed. Stained cement slides down its face like scales off a sick dragon. The show windows are boarded up; the doors are locked. The parking garage is stupendously empty. The place has been closed for decades. Driving around the block, Theo sees signs – littered cigarette butts and beer cans and mashed styrofoam cups. People do come here. God, he thinks. Maybe this is where they hole up in the winter, when the dump is too cold. Good thing or bad thing, other people around? He can still double back on the police station and . . . No. It's getting late. He has to do this.

'OK,' he says to no one. Louder. 'OK.'

He parks on the side street and pulls his flashlight out of the glove compartment. What am I, going to defeat him with this? He'd do better with the Perlcorder in his coat pocket. He pats it like a cop tapping his piece. *OK, man. You just talk in here.* He opens the trunk and grabs the handle to the flimsy jack. Feeling like a bit player in a B movie, he sticks it in the back of his belt under his jacket. He makes a second circuit of the building, trying doors. Nothing yields. Then he takes the ramp into the garage. A string of work lights washes it in pink. It's clear from the rubble and the stink that people come here. In time he finds an opening. Window with the boards pried loose. When he pushes, the boards yield and he slips inside where he stands, blinking, waiting for his eyes to accommodate. Some part of himself that he does not recognize has slipped out of real time. *Theo, this isn't a movie.* I dunno, Sal. If it isn't a movie, I could be in deep shit here.

Black is black no matter how often he blinks. It's like velvet in here, moist and rank, thick with shapes he can't identify. He is in a place without light. He thinks to use his flash and then he thinks he'd better not. Whoever's here, he won't alert them. If someone is waiting for him, he needs to see that person first. Otherwise this enemy he does not know is going to find him and smoke him. Impeded by rags that catch his toes and cartons and bottles and things he can't identify, he feels his way along the walls until he hits the door. He is afraid to open it. He waits until darkness piles up on him and staying inside in this tight little room is worse than whatever waits outside.

For no reason at all he mutters, 'OK, asshole. It's me.'

He opens the door. The space he looks into is vast and lighted in patches by single bulbs burning in hidden places. The floor of the abandoned department store is on the open plan, divided now by partitions and hastily erected stalls left over from some misbegotten attempt to turn it into a mini-mall. The stench in the place is not surprising. It's not even overpowering, it's just part of the fabric of abandoned pasts and outworn needs and the detritus scattered by life's discards, who have found their way inside and holed up here in the defunct store. There is a rustle of breath as if of one tremendous communal sigh. Somebody coughs. Oh yes he is afraid. He is afraid and for the moment disoriented, as if the darkened storeroom has left him dumb and blind. Then he screams. 'Uh!'

Someone has just spoken his name.

It makes him wild. 'Who!'

'You came.' A hand clamps his bicep. *Hold still.* The notebook-writer has stopped writing for good. He is the speaker now.

Theo does not pull away. He understands that he can't. 'You.'

'You. Reporter. You got my message.'

This is so weird. At the moment, Theo is not afraid. All this seems to be somehow fated. This guy will tell his story. Theo will write it down. It will come out OK. 'She said it was for me.'

'For you. The envelope, to bring you here. Your present.'

They are moving now, on a path Theo does not know but the speaker knows by heart. 'They're not what you think.'

'The hairs? I know what they are.'

'The question is, whose.'

'I thought they came from the—'

'From number five? No.' The voice is even, almost bland. 'That's not where they came from.'

'The girl with the flute. If you've hurt her . . .'

'You mean poor little number six?' The speaker propels Theo down the last avenue to an open space and pushes him onto the frozen escalator. 'Orange hair?'

'Yes. Delia.' *For God's sake I have come here to save Delia. I don't even like her but I have to save her life.*

'Delia. That isn't a name. She doesn't have a name. Climb.'

Wait. Something he needs to verify. Theo stops climbing. 'The hair in the envelope. Delia's, right?'

'No. Now, climb.'

Theo stiffens. *No!* The speaker does not have to tell Theo whose hair it is. His teeth lock like the gates to hell. Hatred boils inside.

Something sharp cuts through his coat and nicks the flesh that covers his ribcage. 'I said, climb.'

At the top of the escalator Theo turns. He says irrationally, 'If you got me here to kill me, just fucking try.'

The bland, smooth voice goes hard. 'I brought you here to take my story, reporter. Get it right and get it down.' Gripping Theo's arm, the speaker pushes him into a sharp U-turn. 'Over there. Now look at that. That's glad. I told you I would show you glad.'

Glad waits at the far end of the floor.

The speaker has arranged it. He has made a tableau. Dazed and looking drenched, DeliaMarie Vent is sitting crosslegged on the floor in the center of a shattered three-way mirror out of one of the store's ruined fitting rooms. She sits like an icon with her face lifted, glazed and empty as a dish. Decades of dust diffuse the glare from the circle of flashlights the killer has set on the floor around her. They are all pointing up, so that shadows strike the woman's face like Halloween makeup and make it impossible to read. At this distance, she looks like the figure in a shrine.

'Delia!' Relief turns his muscles to water; against all reason, he half-expected to find Sally here.

'Don't bother. She can't hear you.'

'You haven't . . .'

'Not yet.' He does not laugh. He just says in that mild, even, bank-teller tone, 'I haven't done anything to this one yet. Now do you understand why I have brought you here?'

'Wait,' Theo says. If this was a movie he would be stalling for time; he doesn't know what he's doing. Trying to reach the damn woman, his hated personal stalker who is in danger now, he supposes, if this was a movie he would be shuffling like a prisoner, but drawing his captor along. He reaches for his pocket. 'My recorder. I need to turn it on.'

But the speaker jabs his ribs. 'Don't bother.'

'If I'm supposed to tell your story.'

'You don't need that.' He does not exactly laugh. 'Don't worry. You'll remember this.'

'But you.'

'My name is Haik. Spell it right. And remember this.'

Theo tries, 'Delia?' Now they are close enough to the figure in the triptych for Theo to see that the girl's OK but she is not OK. She is awake but not. She sits in lotus position like Krishna with palms pressed together in prayer or meditation, but the hands are taped together. Her mouth is taped. 'Delia, it's me!'

'Don't bother,' Haik repeats. 'She can't hear you.'

'Delia, get up!' The man is right. She is so nearly catatonic that nothing registers. She won't get up because she can't get up.

'And even if she does . . .'

'What are you going to . . .'

'That's what I brought you here to tell you,' the speaker says. 'Along with a couple of other things.'

God the reporter in him never dies. 'Your story.'

'Not exactly. *Glad*. I brought you here to show you glad. You see that arrangement? Everything perfect. You want to know why? Because I made a plan and followed the plan and sooner or later . . .'

'You're going to carry out the plan.'

'Exactly. And I do *not* want you to stop me and I won't have the mother stop me, not the mother not Father and not the police, nobody stops me because I don't want to be stopped. *When you fail you are killing your mother*. Instead . . .'

Theo strains against him. The grip tightens. 'Instead.'

'Listen, she's the beginning but she is only the beginning.' The voice is still controlled but there is a change in it; the speaker could be suppressing a laugh. 'Give me your flashlight.'

'How did you . . .' Theo is surprised by rage. He gnaws the inside of his mouth and hands it over.

The killer lights his own face. 'This is me. I told you I would show you glad. Look at me. Get ready. Now you will see glad.'

So Theo sees his enemy clearly. Handsome. Ordinary. *Could be you. Could be me.* The man only a little older than he is, is cleanshaven. Hair freshly cut. He looks so unexceptional, he is so nearly smiling. Bland. Holding the light on his smooth face with one hand while in the other he grips the taped end of a bayonet blade, military regulation, army surplus, available in any store my God it is so fucking banal and the tone this man uses is banality itself, almost pleasant, concerned! 'You don't look very glad to see me.'

'You don't know what I am,' Theo says shakily. 'You don't know me any more than I know you.'

'You,' Haik says with contempt. 'You don't know anything. The next, for instance. The next is not who you think.'

'Look, the woman is fucking catatonic, you can't—'

'Oh, her. She's nothing.'

Hatred overwhelms Theo. 'What are you telling me?'

'She was only my backup.' My God the man is smiling. 'The next. That isn't the next.'

Theo's head boils. 'The hell! You can't.'

'I can. I'll do the next . . .' He pushes something into Theo's face, so close that Theo's vision blurs and he can't take it in.

Then he does. Sally's silk nightshirt. 'In hell! Sally is—'

The voice is sharper than the weapon Haik carries and it cuts deeper. 'You don't know where Sally is. That present I sent you. The one in the envelope. Where do you think that comes from?'

Grunting, Theo wheels on him. The noise that comes out of him is beyond speech. 'Agh!'

And the sound that comes out of the killer is close to laughter. 'Haaaaaaaa!'

'Bastard. You!' Outraged, Theo hurtles forward and the flashlight flies as he charges into his enemy, who meets him with that odd cry of hilarity that escapes some lovers during sex. They collide, grappling until pain sears Theo's arm and blood goes; he lunges again and the killer pushes him so hard he falls *you will fucking have to kill me* floundering Theo who tries to get up but is caught ass-first in a heap of empty cartons inchoate and gasping with rage and trapped and nearly powerless; by the time he rights himself Haik has vaulted the rail to the escalator and is clattering down the metal treads; fury pulls Theo to his feet and sends him pounding after him like a broken field runner clearing obstacles in the littered first floor; he follows Haik through the storeroom door while it is still swinging – he is that close – and in the dark Theo charges for the place where he thinks the window is and shoulders the boards away and snakes his way out without even thinking that his quarry could be waiting right here and that he has the power to end this quickly with his jagged bayonet.

Heedless, Theo hits the cement with an animal cry he's never made before. He can hear the footsteps of his quarry ahead he sees him running as the killer rounds a cement stanchion and strikes out for the far end of this tier and then stops midway and dashes up a ramp to the second tier. Screaming, Theo pursues; he is beyond knowing where his voice is coming from or what keeps him going or how he can run so fast when something hurts but what the fuck is hurt can't know there's no time to deal there's just no fucking time to deal, Theo Slate sprinting across the second floor of the long garage to the point where the garage itself bridges the street between this defunct store and the next dead enterprise, running behind the row of cars clumped at the far end where the killer has already opened the door to the little glass bridge that leads across the next street and into the Chapel Square mall waiting just long enough for Theo to see and follow so that as Theo thuds across the bridge and out into the sparsely populated mall he hears somebody roaring and perceives that somewhere along the way he has pulled out the tire iron and is waving it and the sound is coming out of him, that to the bystanders here Theo Slate looks more dangerous than the silent man running ahead with the bayonet.

Again Haik plunges down an escalator, running past

shoppers who cling to the rails and when he reaches the bottom he pauses, as if he is waiting for Theo to catch up. When Theo hits the top step his quarry darts for the exit and again the man hesitates as if to signal Theo *this way, I am running this way* and Theo hears himself screaming, 'What do you want? What the fuck do you want?'

Poised at the fence that separates the sidewalk from the New Haven Green, the killer waits until Theo emerges. Then with a cry Theo cannot hear he raises the bayonet blade in salute. And in the second before he vaults the fence to the Green, he tears off his shirt and throws it under the wheels of a car. Then, when he is certain Theo sees which path he's taking, Haik turns and runs.

So that there is some design to what is happening here, as if Theo is acting out an intricate scheme that the writer of the notebooks laid out on a page that nobody else can read. By the time Theo reaches the Green he hears sirens but he keeps on running and his quarry keeps on running yes but slower now what does he – what he wants what does he Theo doesn't know but if he catches him he will by God bash his fucking head in spill the brains and see the blood and then he'll . . . running faster and faster crossing the next street heading for the – looks like a courthouse – killer running Theo running up the steps and reaching – yes, at last – reaching the top Theo open-throated now producing pure sound and his enemy

Stops

And turns

And speaks

'I will show you glad.'

So that when the police spotlights go on, transfixing the pursued and his pursuer in the glare they will pick out:

The writer/speaker. No. The killer. Haik. The lights will pick out Haik pinned against a stone column bare-chested and panting with the bayonet blade raised against Theo, Haik ordinary by day but pumped and enormous now and in this light stony and transformed, a good match for the stone Roman soldiers guarding the place, perfect for what he is. And they will pick up Theo Slate caught in mid-step, lunging with the tire iron raised – the bleeding, disheveled Theo Slate who in a standoff just might be taken for the perp and not the injured party here, the two of them face to face now and into eternity with Haik looking fulfilled and joyful as more squad cars pull up like predators circling to feed on a corpse and Theo is transfixed in terror and rage with blood in his eyes and his belly trembling until in the crowd massing far below somebody grabs the speaker and he hears a woman's voice, pulling him back into his life. *'Theo.'*

'That's Sally!' He wheels on Haik. 'Bastard! Why did you tell me—'

'Why else?' Haik laughs. 'To get you here! So, are you going to do it? Don't you want to do it now?'

Pushed beyond the limit, torn, savage and furious, Theo is beyond speech. He is reduced to a guttural snarl.

'Go ahead!' Laughing, Haik lowers the bayonet blade and with his arms spread and his head back, waits. 'Now, Slate. Go ahead!'

Trembling with rage, Theo raises the iron higher.

Sally's voice cuts through everything. 'Theo!'

He whirls.

'What's the matter with you, Slate. Come on!'

Then as clearly as if he has said it, Theo hears what he knows: *We don't do this, Stella. Others should.* He falls back.

Haik's voice rises in agony. 'What's the matter with you? Come *on*!'

'Theo, it's me.'

And it is. 'I'm coming!' Theo drops the iron. Turns, and then with everything drained out of him begins flowing backward down the worn granite steps to a place at the bottom where, mesmerized, he backs into the crowd and becomes one with them and from this consolidated position, waits. He and Sally will stand among the other insiders while armed police form a circle and move slowly up the steps *just give us a reason to shoot you. Give me just one reason.* And what Theo hears coming out of his gut now surprises him, Theo Slate – still want that story? – Theo Slate crying, 'Don't . . .'

62

1. Analyze.
2. Organize.
3. Plan.

There is no more writing it down.

63

. . . while on the top step of the courthouse the killer waits
for what must happen and in an astonishingly graceful
gesture, pulls the end of the drawstring around his waist
freeing the loose ends and faster than Theo can tell what
he is doing, steps out of his pants.

He is naked in the lights. As if he is alone here, Haik
looks over the heads of the crowd on the Green as if he
can see through the glare into the night beyond and then
he looks down at the police fixed in place just below him
on the steps.

He speaks to them. No. Theo's irises snap tight and then
open wide in shock. Haik speaks to him. Only Theo will
know what the killer is saying, and the dilemma of whether
to report it and how – will be the material of the rest of his
life. Poised on the top step with his arms spread and the
bayonet blade gleaming, the murderer is speaking directly
to Theo Slate, who knows this as surely as he knows that he
is here and what brought him here. Who is the only one who
knows what the transfixed killer is saying and understands
what happens next.

With his pale skin gleaming in the floodlight glare, Haik
raises the bayonet. 'Glad?' he says in a tone that will not
carry beyond the shell of concentration that encloses them.
'You think you know glad? I will show you glad.'

Then in a gesture so swift that Theo does not even
comprehend what the killer is doing until it is accomplished,
he smashes the bayonet point deep into the vulnerable flesh

at the point where his ribcage stops and with tremendous strength fueled by madness drives the blade in and drags the cutting edge down his belly to the point where it hits the pubic bone and stops. As if he has done nothing, he pulls it out.

For a second, nothing happens.

With his back arched, Haik looks to heaven. Then he begins to scream.

'Glad,' he screams. The word comes out of him again in one long shout that goes on as if it will never end. 'Glaaaaaaaad.' Then it stops.

Everything has stopped.

The killer's breath stops. As if he has vowed not to breathe and will never breathe again. The world is in stasis. Police. Theo. Sally, gripping him hard. Then with a strangling sound the figure on the step takes air into himself in deep sobs. Gasps in shock at the pain. Coughs! The deep gash Haik has made in his own body pops wide. And glistening in the merged spotlight beams, essential parts of the dying killer – stomach – intestines – my God, what else? – everything Haik used to be spills out in a pulsing, glossy tangle on the courthouse steps.

In the moment when everyone freezes in horror, Theo disengages rapt Sally's fingers and slips away. He loves her but this is something he has to do. It's nothing he can leave to the police. He needs to do it and he needs to do it alone. He ducks under the bannered yellow plastic tape the police have strung – show your colors, right, the emblem of another of our national spectacles, pick up the details, TV 8 live from downtown New Haven bulletins as they break – and because the officers at the barriers are fixed on keeping people *out* nobody notices that one of the central figures from the drama inside is slipping away. Shivering, Theo skirts the mall and enters the parking garage. He finds the opening to the dead department store on the first pass and slips inside and walks through the littered storeroom as easily as if he's carrying a light.

He goes up the frozen escalator two treads at a time.

DeliaMarie Vent is sitting exactly where he left her, swaying inside the obscene triptych with her hands locked in her lap and her eyes fixed on something he will never see. Whatever threat she used to be is locked inside her. She is catatonic now.

He speaks even though she can't respond. 'Delia, it's me.'

Gently, he undoes her hands. He tries to lift her. 'It's me,' he says again. 'I came to help you. Come on,' he says, finding a way to grab her under the armpits in spite of the smell and raise her in spite of inertia and pull her along in spite of the dead weight. This time he actually has her on her feet. He will get her moving. He will get her to the hospital. God knows who she will be when she comes back to herself but right now she is his to take care of and he keeps his voice even and kind. 'Come on, OK? It's time for you and me to quit this. This is a terrible place, Delia, you don't belong here.' He turns her as if she is going to walk and takes the weight as her knees buckle and she sags against him. He will have to carry her. OK. 'Let's go.'

Strait

Kit Craig

When urbane, attractive Will Strait comes to teach at Evard College, the close-knit community of the isolated university campus welcomes him with open arms. But Clair Sailor, whose husband Nick was responsible for employing Strait, senses something wrong. As her friends desert her, as her children are ostracized and a series of increasingly frightening accidents begins to plague her family, Clair is convinced Strait is to blame.

The more she learns of Strait, and the secret he hides behind his all-too-perfect facade of family and career, the more Clair is sure that the man her husband invited into their lives is intent on destroying them. But can Clair convince anyone else of what is happening? Before it's too late?

0 7472 4937 7

Watch Me

A. J. Holt

FBI agent Jay Fletcher's life is her work, and she knows her work, using her computer genius to bring to justice some of America's most brutal murderers, can save lives. Her special project, C-BIX, a pro-gramme that can flush potential serial killers out of innocent databases, is about to reap rich rewards for her agency, yet somehow Jay isn't the heroine she should be. For C-BIX is swift, effective and, at the moment, illegal . . .

Sidelined to a fire-investigation unit in Santa Fe, Jay cannot bear to walk away from C-BIX. And when she gets wind of a local serial killer, she can't resist trying to track him down. It is then that Jay stumbles on the haul of her career – an Internet network of serial killers hidden behind a computer role-playing game. One by one, Jay begins to hunt down the network's members, dispensing her own brand of swift justice, whilst the monstrous leader of the group, the Iceman, remains a single step ahead of her.

Eventually, pursued by her own desperate demons from the past, Jay Fletcher must come face to face with a terrible truth: you set a thief to catch a thief, and to catch a serial killer she's become the very thing she abhors . . .

0 7472 4933 4

A selection of bestsellers from Headline

All Headline books are available at your local bookshop or newsagent, or can be ordered direct from the publisher. Just tick the titles you want and fill in the form below. Prices and availability subject to change without notice.

Headline Book Publishing, Cash Sales Department, Bookpoint, 39 Milton Park, Abingdon, OXON, OX14 4TD, UK. If you have a credit card you may order by telephone – 01235 400400.

Please enclose a cheque or postal order made payable to Bookpoint Ltd to the value of the cover price and allow the following for postage and packing:

UK & BFPO: £1.00 for the first book, 50p for the second book and 30p for each additional book ordered up to a maximum charge of £3.00.
OVERSEAS & EIRE: £2.00 for the first book, £1.00 for the second book and 50p for each additional book.

Name ....

Address ....

....

....

If you would prefer to pay by credit card, please complete:
Please debit my Visa/Access/Diner's Card/American Express (delete as applicable) card no:

Signature .... Expiry Date ....